FLINTLOCKS

AND

FLAMES

by
Lucille Graf

PublishAmerica
Baltimore

ISBN: 1-4241-2292-9
PUBLISHED BY PUBLISHAMERICA, LLLP
www.publishamerica.com
Baltimore

Printed in the United States of America

DEDICATION

For Ray because you believed in me

THANKS

This book could not have been written without the help of others. There are many, but I would like to mention a few who made the work a little easier:

Colonel James F Morrison, Third Battalion of Tryon County Militia, who sent me tons of information about the people on both sides who fought for what they believed in.

Roberta Schaal, my sister, who read the manuscript with an unbiased and critical eye, and offered helpful suggestions.

The staff of the Dunham Public Library, Whitesboro, New York, and the Mid-York Library System, Utica, New York, who never failed to get me the research material I needed.

All the people who were gracious enough to let me tape their talks about the war, everyday life, the forts that protected the folks in the Mohawk Valley, and so much more.

Bonnie Pulis from Johnson Hall New York Historic Site, Johnstown, New York, who shared her knowledge of Sir William Johnson, Molly Brant and other family members and friends.

Everyone and anyone who encouraged me along the way.

Last but not least:

Ray, my husband, who was patient (all of the time), supportive (definitely), loving (without question), and who worked harder than I did to make this book possible.

Thank you from the bottom of my heart.

PROLOGUE

Albany—Colony of New York—1765

For the past hour, Laurice Howell had been watching and waiting for a man she did not know. She closed the sturdy wooden shutters on the inside of the bedroom window and muffled the noises coming from the muddy street below.

She turned away from the window, sat down on the narrow bed and cuddled against the woman who had been a mother to her for the last three weeks.

"Maybe he won't come," Lauri said.

Catherine Wilkins wrapped her arms around the frail shoulder of the nine year old girl she had come to love.

"He'll come," she said.

A man named Elder Baxter had sent a note to William and Catherine Wilkins to tell them that he was in Albany to take Lauri to the Mohawk Valley, and would be at the their house at ten of the clock.

Catherine drew Lauri close, and in her mind's eye Catherine saw Will sobbing as he told her of the Howell's death and burial at sea.

"They came down with a fever," Will had said. "No rash, cough, shakes. In two days they were dead."

"No one else got sick?" Catherine asked.

"No one, not even the girl."

"Strange," Catherine said.

"We sewed the bodies in canvas and Captain prayed over them. We had locked Lauri in Captain's cabin, but she got out somehow. She came up on deck just as her mother and father slid into the sea."

Catherine had reached for Will's trembling hand, "How awful for the child."

"I had all I could do to hold her. I think she would have gone over the side after them. I can still hear her screaming, 'Mama can't swim. Mama can't swim. She'll drown.'"

Catherine felt someone shaking her.

Lauri was staring at her, "Did you hear what I said?"

"What?"

"I said—If Captain Spencer hadn't sent that letter to Mr. Baxter…"

"Captain's an honorable man," Catherine said. "Your father wanted Mr. Baxter to be your guardian and Captain respected his wishes."

"Can't you and Will be my guardian? I could stay with you when Will goes back to sea with Captain Spencer. Don't you miss Will when he's gone?"

"Of course," Catherine said.

"Then why can't I live with you until Mama and Papa come for me?"

"Your mother and father are in heaven with God."

"Why?"

"God needed them."

Lauri sobbed. "I need them more."

CHAPTER 1

Mohawk Valley—York Colony—April 1765

Elder Baxter had the team hitched before sunrise, and was well on his way to Albany by the time the first rays touched the valley.

The letter from Captain Aaron Spencer informing him of the death of James and Alva Howell had arrived yesterday. James had been Elder's best friend and Alva the only woman Elder had ever loved.

Stunned by the news, Elder had paced the parlor floor in the house he had built shortly after his marriage to Belle Dingle.

Elder was aware that Belle, was watching him.

Belle laid the unfinished sewing in her lap, and drew her shawl around her thin shoulders to ward off the chill that still lay over the valley. Another time she would have demanded that her husband lay up more logs, but it was the letter that interested her now. Warmth would have to wait.

Her faded blue eyes studied his finely chiseled features. A slight smile creased her pale lips. Did his hands really tremble? Was that a quiver of his lower lip?

"It's from Pennsylvania, isn't it?" Belle demanded, "From that woman."

Belle made no effort to hide her jealousy. She knew how beautiful was the face on the miniature painting inside the cover of the pocket watch her husband carried. Belle was thirty five, acutely aware no one had ever considered her attractive.

She felt the muscles squeezing in her chest. Her breathing was disordered. She clutched the front of her muslin kerchief.

"Well, Mr. Baxter?" Not once in their fifteen years of married life had she called him by his given name.

Elder choked back a sob. "The Howells are dead."

"Those no-account friends of yours you were going to sell my land to? Good riddance, I say."

"Hold your tongue woman," Elder glanced at the paper in his shaking hands. "The letter says their little girl is alive. I'll be leaving for Albany at sunup to fetch her."

Belle watched Elder grope for the door latch and stumble out into the April chill.

She felt another stab of pain in her chest. She picked up her mending and began to sew. She did not feel the needle prick her finger, nor notice the blood drop on her best white table cover.

"I'll not have that orphan living in my home," she whispered. "That child will be sorry she ever saw the likes of you or me."

Much of the King's Highway had turned to mud where the snow had melted. Elder was too distressed to notice the lurching and rocking of the wagon when the wheels hit the ruts. He had decided to take the wagon though he would have made better time astride a horse.

The Howells must have brought some household goods. Not many, he supposed. If things were as bad as James' letter had painted them, most of their belongings had probably gone on the auction block with the rest of the farm

James had been duped by his brother. He had entered into a risky business venture. He had lost all that he and Alva had worked so hard for.

When Elder had learned of the Howell's troubles, he had encouraged James to leave Pennsylvania, and journey to the Mohawk Valley. He had told James that he had plenty of land that he would sell to him. James could pay him back when things improved.

The last letter Elder had received from James said they would be leaving

Philadelphia by boat and would sail to New York. They would come up the Hudson to Albany as soon as the river was free of ice. Elder had heard nothing more.

Elder took his watch from his pocket and opened the case. Tears fell on the portrait of the only woman he had ever loved. He would never see Alva again. James Howell, his closest friend, had taken her away from him years ago. Now, death had taken her away forever.

A strange turn of events, Elder thought, remembering the day he had asked Alva to marry him. Even now, he felt her gentle touch as she laid her hand on his arm.

"You'd soon tire of me," she had said, her voice soft and tender.

"How could I ever tire of you?"

"Oh, Elder, Can't you see? I'm like James, quiet, tedious, too reserved. You're full of life. You'd find me dull. I couldn't tie you to a humdrum marriage." She had stood on her tiptoes and kissed him. "You'll always be my dearest friend."

He could not deny that he had been foolhardy and rash in his youth. He had left Pennsylvania when Alva rejected him, and had taken his disappointment with him. He struck out for York colony with no thought of what he would do when he reached it.

Fortune had smiled on him. Or was it misfortune?

He had met Eustis Dingle, a wealthy landowner. Dingle was more than happy to rid himself of his eldest daughter, with her homely face and sour temperament. The Dingle family had breathed a collective sigh of relief when Elder took his bride west to the Mohawk Valley, away from her Albany home. The dowry had been substantial, but Elder often regretted that his common sense had not overridden his desire for wealth.

Elder was nearing his mid thirties, a handsome man, with a cleft chin, slightly graying hair that still held a wave, and a body many a younger man would envy. What did he have to show for his years? Wealth, a wife and three children who did not think he was worth a fig.

Elder spent a restless night at an inn a few miles west of Albany. His sleep had been filled with dreams of Alva. He reached for her, but she disappeared before he could touch her.

He slowed the horses as he topped the hill overlooking the city the Dutch had called Fort Orange. He rested the team.

Over a hundred years had passed since the Dutch had surrendered it to the English. The city had grown since his last trip. He could see newer houses in the Georgian style, although the Dutch influence was still strong. There were plenty of gabled houses, the end of the buildings facing toward the street.

Old stone Fort Frederick, overlooking Duke Street, still stood guard over the city. The hospital, a place, to his way of thinking, where people went to die, was north of the fort.

Gray clouds hung low over the Hudson River. He could just about make out the old ferry headed toward the eastern bank, and the road that led to New England. The ferry was a small rectangle amid the larger ships, some anchored mid river waiting for a berth. Other ships, sails unfurled, were moving south down the river, possibly carrying his furs.

The English had eagerly jumped into the thriving fur trade which the Dutch had built with the neighboring Indians. By 1700 Albany had become the chief fur trading center in the American colonies. Elder's own dealings with the Indian and white trappers had made him a wealthy man.

He had not been to Albany in over a year, conducting all his business by post. He disliked the hustle, bustle, the jostling on the city streets.

He urged the team on. He wanted to find a place within walking distance of the Wilkins. He would seek out his factor and make arrangements to pay the Wilkins for their care of the Howell child.

It took him almost an hour before he found THE OX HEAD, an inn near the river. It looked to be a fairly respectable tavern. The food, he had been told, was tolerable and the bedding clean. The landlord, he had been cautioned, ran the place with an iron fist, running roughshod over everybody who worked for him.

Elder stood in the doorway, watching.

A burly man with dirty blond hair and bushy eyebrows ran a fingernail over the pine table, scraping off some dried food the scullery maid had missed. He grabbed the thin girl as she put her back into her work. She winced in pain as the man's stubby fingers dug into her shoulder.

"This ain't fit for a dog to eat off of," he snarled. "See them boards is scrubbed clean."

Elder wanted to throttle the man, but he was not a brawler and the man's bulk alone would have made short work of him. He was not a fool, either.

He stepped up behind the bully. "I've need of a boy to deliver a message."

The innkeeper turned around, his scowl replaced by a broad grin.

Hypocrite. Elder tried to keep his voice civil. "Can you find me a trustworthy lad?"

The landlord answered with a bellow and a scrawny boy came running from the back room.

"This here's my son, Tom," the barkeep said. "Ain't no boy trust worthier than him."

The lad never looked at his father.

Elder saw Tom tremble. "Come with me, lad." He pointed to a table.

The boy followed without question, his father close on his heels.

"I want him to deliver a private message," Elder said.

The innkeeper glowered, thought better of it, and moved away, keeping his eye on his son.

Elder gave the boy the Wilkins's address. "Deliver this card and wait for an answer. Do you know where the street is?"

Tom nodded.

"Good. Tell them I'll call at the time they say." Elder reached into his pocket and handed the lad some coins.

Before Tom could put them in his pocket, a large hairy fist scooped them out of his hand.

"He ain't respectful of money," the landlord said. "Ain't no need for him to be. I see to his keep," The big hand shoved the coins deep into his pocket. "Get back to your chores, boy."

"I've need of your son's services," Elder said. "Surely you can spare him a few minutes."

Grumbling, the innkeeper went back to the bar.

"Come to my room when you return with an answer, Tom," Elder said. "The next coins will be yours to keep. I'll not be a noodle around your father again."

CHAPTER 2

The sun was just rising when Elder woke to the sound of jingling bells, and the voices of boys herding the cows to the pastures outside the city. The river smells hung heavily on the spring air.

He dressed carefully for the meeting with the Wilkins, making sure his buff colored breeches were clean and his waist coat brushed. His unpowdered hair was tied at the nape of his neck with a dark green ribbon.

A nagging voice asked, as it had a hundred times before, *Why did you come to Albany? Is it to take the child back to the Mohawk Valley because James had been your best friend and Alva the only women who had won your heart? Or is it to pique Belle?* He pushed the annoying question to the back of his mind.

At precisely ten of the clock, he climbed the stoop of the Wilkins' handsome brick house. Down the street, a Dutch woman, wearing strangely styled wooden shoes dipped her broom into the soapy water in a wooden bucket and washed the steps of her house. She waved and called a cheery, "Good morgen."

Elder nodded and tipped his best beaver hat. "Good morning to you, my good woman."

He raised the heavy brass knocker on the Wilkins' door and rapped three times.

A smiling woman of about thirty, with dark blue eyes and coal black hair opened the door.

Elder handed her his card. "Good day, Madam."

She read it quickly. "Good day Mr. Baxter. I'm Catherine Wilkins. Please, do come in."

He followed her to a small room just off the entrance hall. Books on seamanship crowded open shelves. A large globe of the world, supported by a stand, stood in the corner. There were several navigational charts on the desk.

A tanned, muscular man of about fifty, shook Elder's hand, "Captain Aaron Spencer, at your service, sir."

He gestured toward the man who had been seated in a high backed chair near the fireplace, a fellow in his mid thirties, with curly blond hair and piercing black eyes.

Captain Spencer said, "This is my First Mate, Will Wilkins."

Elder acknowledged the introductions with a smile and a nod, "Captain, what happened to James and Alva?"

Spencer settled himself on the edge of the desk before he answered, "Fever, Strange, Very strange. They were the only ones stricken. We buried them at sea."

Shocked, Elder reached for the desk to steady himself.

Spencer and Wilkins guided him into a chair.

"Unmanly of me," Elder said. "Most unmanly."

"My apologies," Spencer said. "I can be thoughtless, I'm afraid."

Catherine offered Elder a glass of wine.

He waved her hand away. "And the child?…"

Catherine set the glass on the table. "She's here—with us."

"I'd like to meet Alva's daughter," Elder said.

Catherine and Will exchanged glances. She moved to Will's side, grasped his hand.

"There's something we'd like to discuss with you, Mr. Baxter." Will squeezed Catherine's hand. "We've grown fond of the child. We'd like her to stay with us."

"What about your own children? Won't that be a burden for you?" Elder asked.

"We have no children, Mr. Baxter," Catherine said.

"James was my best friend," Elder's words came slowly. "Of course I want to do right by the child. I'll give your request serious thought. Now, may I see her?"

Catherine left the room, and returned shortly, holding a young girl by the hand.

"Lauri," Catherine said, "this is Elder Baxter. He is…was…a friend of your mother and father."

Elder fought the urge to embrace the girl. She was the image of Alva. Wavy brown hair fell to her waist. Her large gray-green eyes gave no indication of her thoughts, just as Alva's never had.

Here was a child he could love. He took her small hand in his, blinking back the tears that filled his eyes. "Your mother and father were the best friends I ever had. I'd like to be your friend, too."

"Thank you, sir." Lauri offered a slight curtsy, but she did not look at him.

During the next week, Elder visited Lauri every day.

He, Will and Catherine, had agreed that it would be best to let Lauri learn to know him a step at a time. Elder and Lauri played children's games, and he let her win most of the time, but bested her once in a while. Life was not a game, and she would have to cope in the real world.

They explored the old parts of Albany. He told her stories of the Dutch settlements, the takeover by the English.

He filled her head with tales of life in the Mohawk Valley, of his home and children.

He told her about the things he, and her mama and papa, did when they were children. How they would sneak off into the woods and smoke corn silk; the time her papa tipped over the necessary just for the deviltry of it—and with a man in it, too.

Little by little he won her over.

One day when they were walking down by the river, Lauri said, "Mama and Papa are angels. They have wings and they're going to fly down and take me back with them." Lauri tugged on his sleeve. "Will they find me if I go with you?"

"They'll find you wherever you are."

Each time Elder came to see Lauri, Catherine and Will's apprehension increased. Catherine was close to tears. "Isn't there something we can do to keep Lauri?"

"He has the law on his side," Will said. "Her father's letter is clear. Mr. Howell named Baxter as her guardian."

Will began to pace. "If Baxter cared anything about the child, he'd let her stay here. I've done some checking. This isn't about the child. It's about him. He was in love with her mother. He couldn't have her mother, but now he can have her daughter."

The color drained from Catherine's face. "Will, you aren't suggesting…"

"Of course not. I'm just saying Lauri is the closest he'll ever come to having Mrs. Howell."

The more time Elder spent with Lauri, the more he knew he must not lose Alva again.

Two days later, Elder sat on the wagon seat, waiting to start the trip to the Mohawk Valley.

Captain Spencer tried to hand Elder a small bag. "The Howells told me they sold everything to pay their passage here. They had no money. After they died, my crew collected what they could for the child."

Elder shook his head, refused to take it. "I can provide for her."

"Then keep it for her dowry. At least she won't come to the marriage a pauper." Spencer set the bag on the wagon seat and stepped away. "I wish you would change your mind. Catherine and Will have come to love her very much."

"I understand, Captain, but I feel I must honor James's wishes."

Up stairs, in Lauri's bedroom, Catherine wiped away the tears that slipped from under her long, black lashes. "My, but I do believe you'll be the prettiest traveler on the road today."

Lauri was dressed in a long fur trimmed cloak and hood. Her muff had been tossed on the bed. Much as she hated to leave the Wilkins, she wished Catherine would take her outside. She was perspiring under the warm clothes.

Catherine took a package from the chest of drawers near the window. It was a doll dressed just like Lauri; fur trimmed cape and hood, dress, even to the tiny shoes on the doll's feet.

Catherine handed her the doll. She wrapped her arms around Lauri, and held her close. "Love her as I love you."

Will came to the bedroom door. "It's time."

Catherine picked up the muff from the bed, and handed it to Lauri.

The Wilkins finally appeared on the stoop. Catherine's tears had dried on her alabaster skin, but Will's eyes were moist.

Lauri clung to Catherine. "I want to stay with you."

Will whispered in Lauri's ear. She kissed him, and let him lift her onto the wagon seat.

Elder slapped the reins across the horses' rumps and the wagon moved down the rutted street.

Lauri turned for one last look, raised her hand to her lips, and blew a kiss. Catherine was leaning into Will's protective arms, sobbing. Lauri watched until Elder turned the corner, then settled herself beside him. She clutched Catherine's doll to her heart.

Her few weeks with the Wilkins had been pleasant, but they had no children and she was lonely. Besides, they were old, at least thirty.

She stole a glance at the man beside her. He was even older, as old as her mother and father, but he had children, someone she could play with.

Elder let the horses set the pace as they strained up the hill, taking them away from Albany, away from the Wilkins.

A few miles beyond Albany, on the King's Highway, headed toward Schenectady, he halted the team. He jumped from the wagon with surprising nimbleness. The sun was higher in the sky and a chill April wind was picking up. He came back with two fur robes which he passed up to Lauri. He used one to pad the hard wooden seat, the other, the larger one, would serve as a lap robe. Even bundled up in his warm great coat, he minded the cold. He would buy coals for the foot warmers when he found a reputable looking inn where they could stop for their noon meal.

Lauri snuggled closer to him for warmth. "Is the knight's castle near your castle? I saw a picture in Catherine's book. She said it was a knight. He lived in a castle."

She prattled on, "He was dressed funny." Her forehead wrinkled into a frown. She paused, trying to remember the word.

"Armor?"

"Yes. Armor. Even his horse was wearing it."

"I don't have a castle, Lauri, and there haven't been any knights like that for hundreds of years."

"Catherine said Sir Wilford or something, lives by you. Ain't he a knight?"

"Sir William Johnson? He doesn't wear armor and his horses don't either."

Lauri was disappointed. In her day dreams, and just as often in her night dreams, a knight in the shiniest armor anyone had ever seen, riding a magnificent white stallion, rescued her from the devouring dragon. He was completely covered by his suit of armor and she never saw his face until he had her safely behind the walls of his majestic castle. Once there, he removed his helmet. He was the most handsome man in the world. He was her father.

The afternoon shadows lengthened. Time, Elder decided, to start looking for a place to spend the night. He found a small inn, close to the King's Highway, run by a jolly Englishman and his wife. There were few other travelers. Elder was pleased. He had no wish to expose Lauri to some of the ruffians that often stopped for a night's rest.

The early arrivals also pleased the innkeeper. It was plain to see that the traveler was a man of means, who could pay for a night's lodging. He might even offer a little something extra toward their meal.

The landlord showed them a small room on the second floor. It was bare except for the bed in the corner.

"It will do," Elder said. "Bring a pallet for the girl and a screen for privacy."

CHAPTER 3

The Meadows—Tryon County—1765

A soft morning breeze from the south promised warmer weather. Elder hid Lauri's small bag containing her money in the wagon's false bottom, then he folded the lap robe and put it in the back of the wagon next to Lauri's two small trunks.

As the day improved, Elder and Lauri loosened their warm outer clothing, and let the sun shine fully on their heads and necks.

They turned off the King's Highway, climbed a hill, and took a road leading west. The horses picked up the pace, eager to be in their own stalls, noses buried in a bucket of oats. He had difficulty holding them back. He was in no hurry. He and Belle were sure to have a set-to.

The Meadows came in sight. He saw that the other horses he had purchased from Sir William Johnson for breeding stock had been let out to pasture. They lifted their heads, trotting to the fence when the team came down the lane.

"There's your new home, Lauri," Elder said.

Lauri's spirits sank. There was no castle, just a shuttered, brown stained, clapboarded house with a center door, and a large chimney on each end. The house did not look friendly.

There was a barn and some outbuildings beyond the house. Smoke was rising from the chimney of a small cabin.

The meadow in front of the house stretched to a forest of evergreens and bare limbed hardwoods. A road broke through the forest and a ridge of hills rose in the distance.

"Why are there dark patches on the hills?" Lauri asked. "Look. They're moving."

"They're shadows on the hills," Elder explained. "See how the clouds hide the sun? The shadows move because the wind is blowing the clouds away."

Elder halted the team in front of the barn door. From the corner of his eye he saw two neighbor boys, Walter Butler and Jason Dayemon, ride into the yard. Walter sat straight and tall on one of his father's fine steeds, Jason was astride an old mule. Walter was having trouble pacing his sleek mount to the mule's slower gait. His horse had been bred to race; above all—to win—a trait his rider shared.

The boys were a strange contrast. Walter was the son of one of the richest men in the Mohawk valley. Jason's father, one of John Butler's tenants, was a man who scraped to keep body and soul together, to put food on the table for his wife and four sons. He farmed a small plot of land. Elder would not have been surprised to learn that George Dayemon did not have enough money to pay his debts.

The two boys slid from their mounts. Walter tied the reins of his sleek horse to the ring on the front of the barn. The rope Jason used to control his dumb beast was simply draped around the animal's neck.

"Either of you boys seen Effsie?" Elder said.

"No sir."

"You lookin' for me, sir?" A thin, bent old negro hobbled out of the barn. He was nearly bald, except for the few white hairs that stood straight up like a cockscomb.

"See to the horses, Effsie. Make sure they're fed and rubbed down," Elder said.

Effsie patted the horses as they nuzzled against him, "Good to have you home, sir," he said.

Elder grinned. "You old faker. It's not me you're glad to see. It's these two old nags."

"No sir. No sir. It's you, sir."

"At least someone's glad to see me. How's Old Olga?"

"She be fine, sir. She be glad to see you. Now she have a man to feed who'll 'preciate her cookin'."

Once, when Lauri was supposed to be sleeping, she heard Mama and Papa talking about going to live at Elder Baxter's place.

"I know I won't be able to abide the old biddy," Alva said. "I'll never understand why Elder married that witch."

Lauri spotted a corn broom leaning against the side of the barn, the kind a witch would ride in the dead of night. It must have been the broom that reminded her of that night in the Pennsylvania farm house.

She half expected to see the witch, dressed in a long black dress, flowing black cape and long pointed hat, sneak around the side of the barn, hop on the broom and fly away. Common sense told her such a thing was not about to happen. Witches only rode their brooms in the dark of night.

Before Elder had a chance to lift Lauri from the wagon, the homeliest woman she had ever seen, dressed in a somber, dark blue dress, came out of the house. She had no curves at all. She had a sharp pointed nose, thin lips, graying hair and long bony hands. A crone, for sure, just as her mother had said. The woman really was a witch.

"That's my wife, Belle," Elder squeezed Lauri's hand. "Don't ever let her know you're afraid."

Belle walked toward the wagon with long, deliberate steps.

"You—girl—get down here." She saw Lauri shiver, slide closer to Elder, and slip her small hand into his.

Elder climbed over the wheel, dropped lightly to the ground, and lifted Lauri off the wagon seat.

Three jabbering children, two girls and a boy, ran from around the side of the house, crowding between Lauri and Belle.

"Geoff, take Lauri's trunks into the house," Elder said.

Geoff scowled. "Jason, you do it."

Jason started to move toward the back of Elder's wagon. His body seemed to go in all directions at once when he walked. His arms dangled from his too short sleeves and his legs were bare where his stockings failed to meet his breeches.

Lauri covered her mouth to keep from laughing. He reminded her of a puppet a traveling peddler had once shown her when he stopped at the Pennsylvania farm. It was controlled by strings and moved in all directions at once when she tried to work it.

Walter looked to be a year or two older than the scrawny puppet, better dressed, but his shirt and breeches were just as grubby. He brushed his dark hair away from his eyes. He was good looking, if you liked boys.

"I'll do it," Walter said.

"You a toady, Butler?" Geoff said.

"You want me to wash out your mouth?" Walter clenched his fist and lunged toward Geoff.

"There'll be no fighting here," Elder said. "Geoff hold your tongue. Butler hold your temper."

Walter hoisted the heavier trunk onto his shoulder.

Jason struggled to lift the other one.

They started toward the house.

"Walter Butler," Belle's piercing shriek stopped Walter in his tracks.

Jason bumped into him, and went sprawling.

"Take her things to Old Olga's cabin," Belle looked down her pointed nose at Lauri. "She's not family. Leave her with Olga in the kitchen. You—girl—go with the boys." Belle hitched up her petticoats and walked away.

Jason scrambled to his feet.

Lauri clutched the doll tightly to her chest.

"Such a pretty doll," Patience said. "Look, Felicity, it's dressed just like she is."

"She won't have no time to play with dolls," Felicity told her sister.

"Why not?"

Geoff said, "She's an orphan."

"What's an orphan?"

"She don't have a mama or papa." Felicity made a face. She had to tell her stupid sister everything.

"Why not?"

"They're dead, noddy," Geoff said.

"That's enough," Elder said. "I'm ashamed of the three of you. Go with the boys, Lauri. I'll work things out with Belle."

The boys started walking again. Lauri hurried to catch up.

"Come on," Walter said. "We'd better do what Belle wants."

The door on the back of the house was ajar. They could smell the stew cooking in the large cast iron kettle hanging on the fireplace crane. They went inside.

"Why you in my kitchen? Out." Broad of hip, full breasted, Old Olga's dark eyes challenged anyone who dared invade her kitchen. Strong black hands reached for the broom standing in the corner

When she spotted Lauri dressed in her fur trimmed cloak and hood, Old Olga's face softened. Her lips parted in a smile to show even white teeth.

"My, ain't you pretty. You best be getting' to the other part of the house, missy. The likes of you don' belong in no kitchen."

"That's exactly where she belongs." The witch was standing in the doorway.

Lauri moved closer to the boys. Jason took her hand and squeezed it.

"I told you boys to take her things up to Olga's," Belle snarled. "You—girl—change your clothes and get to work. You do know how to work, don't you?"

Behind Belle's back Geoff, Felicity and Patience took it all in.

Belle disappeared into the hall. The children followed behind, but not before Patience stole one more look at the doll.

"Doan' know why Mistress wants a fine, young lady like you workin' in my kitchen, but we best get to it," Olga said. "She can be in mighty mean spirits when she gets her back up. You best change them pretty things. She brung down some of Patience old clothes."

Lauri took the faded dress from Old Olga. Someone had mended it many times. The fine stitching brought back a painful memory. Her mother's delicate handwork had lengthened the life of many a dress.

Old Olga said, "You boys best be on your way 'fore Mistress come back."

They high tailed it out of the door.

"You best hide that doll, gal," Old Olga whispered, "Miss Patience got her eye on it for sure." She went to a drawer and took out a piece of old muslin and reached for the doll.

Lauri handed it to her without question.

Old Olga rolled it in the soft cotton cloth, made sure it was well protected, then wrapped some paper around it and tied it securely with a string. She took a stone from a cool place in the chimney and slid the package in.

"They eats 'xactly at six," Old Olga said, "and Mistress gets mighty upset if the supper ain't done proper and served straight on."

CHAPTER 4

The Meadows—June 1765

April was swallowed by May. June pushed May aside. June's warmth brought the trees to life. They leafed out, and it was harder to see the shadows on the hills.

"You're the talk of Johnstown," Elder shouted at Belle during one of their daily quarrels, "Let the child be a child. What harm can it to do if Lauri goes with Walter Butler and Jason Dayemon once in a while?"

Belle glared at him. "You think I care what anyone in that town thinks? I don't want her here. She's just another mouth to feed. As long as she stays, she'll live by my rules."

She left Elder gaping after her and marched into the kitchen where Olga and Lauri were making pies.

"You—girl," Belle pointed a bony finger. "You are to attend services every Sunday. You will ride with us to the church, but you are to sit in the back with the slaves and indentured.

"You can have the rest of the day to yourself. I know those two boys have been here asking for you. Why Walter Butler would bother with that Dayemon trash and you is beyond me.

"You are to conduct yourself as a good Christian girl should. I'll not abide you behaving like a heathen."

With a swish of her petticoats, Belle left the room.

"Hallelujah," Olga clapped her hands and did a little dance. "I'll send Effsie to tell young Butler. He and young Mister Jason come lookin' for you most every day."

Lauri made a sour face. "They're boys."

The following Sunday, Lauri and Jason were fishing while Walter was stretched out under a tree with a book in his lap.

Lauri walked over to peer down at Walter "You got pictures in that book? I like to look at pictures. I make up stories and pretend."

"Mr. Baxter should send you to school in Johnstown. It's free. Won't cost him."

"Belle says I can't go. I can cipher some, write my name, but I can't read."

"What do you say, Jason?" Walter said. "Should we teach her?"

"Nah. She'll be as smart as us."

"Why do you have so many books?" Lauri asked.

"I'm going to be a lawyer."

Jason snickered. "You ain't fourteen yet. You going to be the youngest lawyer in York colony?"

"Not the youngest. Just the best."

It was another Sunday, but Lauri had not been allowed to go to church or fishing with Walter and Jason. Lauri knew it was a special day. She just did not know why it was so special.

"Olga, why are you making such a fancy dinner?"

"The baronet's comin'." Olga said.

"Sir William Johnson's coming here? Will I have to curtsy, and call him Sir William?"

"That's his name, ain't it?"

"How'd he get to be a baronet anyway?"

"All's I know," Olga answered, "is that he got so chummy with them Indians the king seen fit to make him some kind of a boss over them, and he sees they's taken care of. They's supposed to fight just like white folks if there's trouble."

"You mean, like a war?"

Olga hummed as she basted the meat. Her dark eyes sparkled and a smile played on her round face. "Ain't seen Mistress Baxter so nervous since he come last time."

She motioned Lauri to come closer. "Miss Molly comin' to dinner with Sir William. Mistress Baxter ain't gonna like it when Miss Molly show up. She doan favor her."

"Why not?"

"She and Sir William ain't married, leastwise not by white folks rules."

"They have children don't they?"

Olga nodded.

"Then they must be married," Lauri said.

"Child, you sure is a caution."

"Will I get to see her?"

"Maybe. Maybe not."

"Is it true," Lauri wanted to know, "what Walter and Jason told me? That she caught Sir William's eye when she jumped on the back of a horse an English officer was racing around the track. Did she really ride round and round with him?"

"Maybe. Maybe not," Olga said, "Might just be a story them Indians made up. They likes to fun the white folks. True or ain't, Miss Molly sure caught his heart.

"Sir William sent her and her brother, Joseph, to white folks school. Ain't that somethin'? An Indian who can read and write. Some white folks can't do that."

"Walter's teaching me to read and write," Lauri said. "He stashes books and a slate in his saddlebags, and he shows me how to make the letters and the words."

The sparkle left Olga's eyes and the smile disappeared. "You better not let Mistress Baxter find out. She skin your hide."

The rest of the day passed slowly until Felicity called from her post at the parlor window. "Pa, Sir William is here."

Elder followed Belle from the other room, took his watch from his coat pocket, checked the time, and smiled. One thing about Sir William; he was punctual.

Belle rested her hand on Elder's arm and together they stepped outside to greet their guest.

When Sir William handed Molly Brant down from the coach, just like she was a real lady, Belle could hardly hide her displeasure. She had invited the baronet, not that Mohawk woman who lives with him in sin.

Belle had looked the other way when she learned he had married Catherine Weissenberg on her death bed to legitimize their three children but his liaison with Molly Brant nettled her.

Johnson had not married Molly Brant according to church or civil rite, and being a good Christian woman, Belle could not overlook the fact that an Indian ceremony was an insult. Just because he was so chummy with the Iroquois they had made a covenant with the crown, and the king had seen fit to appoint him Superintendent of Indian Affairs in North America and had made him a baronet, he could not be excused from doing what was right and proper.

Molly lifted the sweeping skirt of her green silk gown as she stepped from the coach. A satin slipper peeked beneath the folds of the skirt. The bodice clung to her provocatively, and the low cut neckline accentuated the fullness of her breasts.

Belle's brow drew into a frown of disapproval. How dare that Indian display herself like that before fourteen year old Geoff? Belle's lips drew into a tight line when she caught him perusing Sir William's Mohawk woman. What she failed to notice was Elder's approving smile.

Elder presented his two daughters, who gave a polite curtsy. He introduced Geoff, already a strapping youth. Molly greeted each in turn, speaking in Mohawk. Her words to Geoff—a remark about his manly prowess—brought a rebuff from Sir William. She merely laughed in her deep throaty way.

"And where would the young one be?" Sir William said.

"We have no other children, Sir William," Belle said.

"It's the little colleen I'm wanting to see. Lauri, isn't it?"

"Why in the world would you be interested in her?"

"'Tis a bright little tyke I hear she is, Belle, and she'll be after taking my heart, what little Molly's left me."

"Why, Sir William, Laurice Howell is nothing but an orphan staying under our roof through the goodness of our hearts."

"Come now, Belle," Sir William said. "Where are you hiding the lass?"

"I'm not hiding her." Belle's voice rose sharply. "Lauri. Laurice Howell. Where are you?"

Lauri slipped from the side of the house where she had been hiding, her bare feet dragged in the dirt. She curtsied awkwardly before the baronet, but she only saw the beautiful Indian woman standing before her.

"So you are little Lauri," Molly said in English. "Sir William is right. You are a very pretty little girl. You will be a beautiful woman one day."

Belle hurried her guests inside. She made sure Lauri was not seen again.

CHAPTER 5

The Meadows—July 1765

Lauri sat on a large flat rock, her legs pulled up to her chest, her chin resting on her knees, her doll safely hidden in the folds of her skirt.

She was in the small cave she and Jason had stumbled upon one day when she had sneaked away from her chores.

It looked like nothing more than an outcropping of rock. The hole, carved out by wind, sleet, snow, rain and hard driven winter storms, was well hidden by a piece of broken rock.

Jason said it was an old bear's den.

They called it *OUR CAVE*.

Lauri was hiding. She had caught Patience stealing the doll from the hiding place in Olga's kitchen. There had been a tussle. Lauri had grabbed a clump of Patience's soft black hair, yanked hard, and snatched the package.

"I was going to put it back," Patience wailed.

Lauri tugged harder. "Liar."

Lauri heard Belle rushing from the other end of the house, and dashed out the kitchen. She sprinted down the road toward the protection of the woods.

Patience was still crying when Belle reached the kitchen. Elder was close on her heels. Felicity and Geoff were not far behind.

Patience ran to her mother. "I only wanted to play with the doll. Lauri took it away from me."

"My poor little darling." Belle stroked Patience's hair, and held her close.

Elder said, "Patience, you had no right to take Lauri's doll."

"Mr. Baxter, you dare scold her?" Belle snarled. "It's that orphan you should be punishing. Bring her here. I'll teach her who rules this house."

"You'll do no such thing. What Patience did was wrong, but Lauri had no right to hurt her. I'll speak to her."

"Yes, Mr. Baxter, coddle that horrible child."

Screened behind the saw toothed boulder, Lauri settled herself so she could see anyone coming along the trail. She had taken care not to disturb any of the plants and bushes; just as Jason and Walter had taught her. She felt safe in her hiding place.

The July sun could not make its way through the narrow opening and there was little warmth inside. Dampness from the dirt floor seeped through Lauri's petticoats, and she went to get one of the blankets she and Jason had hidden. She wrapped one around her, and returned to her spot near the entrance.

Tears streamed down her cheeks. Why did Ma and Pa have die? Why didn't they live, so things could be as they used to be?

Everyone had abandoned her.

Ma and Pa were dead. Catherine and Will were far away in a city she would never see again. They said they loved her, but they sent her away with a man she didn't even know; just because he said he was a friend of Ma and Pa.

"Love her as I love you," Catherine had said when she had given her the doll; yet Catherine had sent her to live with a spiteful old shrew.

Belle Baxter was a witch—a hag who had cast a spell, dooming Lauri to a life of drudgery and heartache, and Elder was afraid to stand up for her.

What was she going to do? No one cared.

In her heart she knew that wasn't true. Olga and Effsie cared, but they were slaves. What could they do to help her?

Jason and Walter cared.

She knew what she would do. She would spend a couple of days safe inside the cave, then she would go to Walter's mother. Mrs. Butler liked her and would let her share a room with Deborah, Walter's sister. Word could be sent to Will and Catherine. Lauri would get Mr. Butler to take her to Albany to live with them.

It would all work out. She knew it would. She would be rid of them all—Belle who had hoarfrost in her veins and a lump of ice for a heart.

She would no longer be afraid of Geoff with his arrogant ways, his sly eyes and sneering smile. She hated him for the way he bullied Jason.

She would get away from sneaky Patience, who spied on everyone, and had tried to steal the doll.

She would be free from Felicity's rages and ceaseless taunting. Oh, she knew where Felicity had learned to be so hurtful—she had mastered the art of wounding at her mother's knee.

More than once Belle had said, "That orphan belongs with Olga and Effsie. She's a jackstraw—a—nobody—just like they are."

And Felicity had parroted the words—jackstraw—nobody—ORPHAN!

Old Olga had been taken a-back when Lauri told her about Felicity's scornful taunts.

"Why child, she be green eyed with jealousy. You's gots so many people loves you, poor Miss Felicity just 'bout sick over it. We loves you, Effsie and me—and young Mister Jason—why child, he just 'bout worships the ground you walks on. And even young Mister Butler—ain't he 'bout the best friend you got?"

Thinking back over Olga's words, Lauri knew she could never leave. How could she do that to Jason? He was the one who took care of her, comforted her when she was sad.

She closed her eyes and let the tears slide down her cheeks.

"I knew you'd be here." Jason had slipped so quietly into the cave, he startled her. "What'd you run for?"

"Patience stole my doll. I took it away from her." She spread her skirt to show him. "I ain't going back."

"You can't stay here."

"I can't go back. Belle will whip me, for sure."

"Mr. Baxter won't let her."

"She'll just wait for the right time and take a switch to me. She done it before."

Jason stared at her. "Does Mr. Baxter know?"

"He's afraid of her. She's a witch."

"Ain't no such thing."

"Yes. My mother said so. Belle's a witch, but I ain't afraid of her."

Jason went to the back of the cave, found a blanket and wrapped himself in it. When he came back, he found a log, rolled it up to Lauri, and motioned for her to sit beside him. He drew her close, and pulled their blankets up around their heads.

Mosquitoes buzzed around their ears, under the blankets and inside their clothing. Even worse were the black flies. Hot weather usually meant an end to them but there were enough stagnant pools of water near the cave for them to breed.

Lauri's eye was nearly swollen shut and Jason was covered with welts. She laid her head on his shoulder. She was tired, overcome with loneliness, always pushing away the feeling of being unwanted, unloved.

It was different when she was with Jason. She felt safe.

Jason got up to look around the cave. He had grown so much in the last three months he was forced to stoop. He had lost his wooden puppet look. He was no longer Walter's shadow. He was his own person.

He picked up a stout stick, and poked the pine boughs they had laid up for a bed the last time they visited the den. He hoped to high heaven he would not hear the sound of a timber rattler, coiled and ready to strike. He was afraid of snakes and the thought of finding one in the bed terrified him. There was no snake.

He checked the jugs they had stashed there, tasted one, and spit out the stale water. "I better fill these before they come looking for you."

"You didn't tell where I was."

"No, you dolt, but you've been gone so long they're sure to start looking for you. Ain't no need to fret. I'll stay. If I get caught I won't give you away. I'll think of something."

He slipped from the cave, and filled the jugs at the creek. He came back to the cave.

"We're going to need something to eat." He set the jugs on the dirt floor, and left. He came back carrying berries in the front of his shirt.

"We'll have to be careful. They ain't going to last long." He looked down at his stained shirt. "Ma's going to cuff me a good one when she sees this."

The afternoon shadows lengthened. Calling voices got their attention. They watched the men pass by, and they heard the voices fade in the distance.

Darkness was beginning to cover the valley and soon the cave would be plunged into blackness. They went out to relieve themselves before bedding down for the night, each keeping a sharp eye out for any movement that might mean they had been found. They ate the berries, climbed under the blankets, and snuggled close for warmth. The day's tension was finally eased by sleep.

Daylight was slow finding its way into the cave, bringing with it little warmth.

Jason woke early. Dreams of his mother had troubled his sleep. She must be wild with worry, imagining all sorts of terrible things had happened to him. He had been gone for almost a day, and he didn't want to spend another night in this damp confining place.

"You sure toss a lot in your sleep," Jason said when Lauri stirred.

She rubbed the sleep from her good eye. The other was still swollen shut, and her face was puffy from the black fly and mosquito bites.

"I guess we can't stay here."

"We got to get you somewhere before you get a fever. You sure ain't no pretty sight."

"I can't leave my doll here," Lauri said, "I'll break it or throw it away before I let Patience have it."

"Give it to me." He bloused his shirt and slipped the doll into it. "I know just what to do with it."

They finished the rest of the berries, made sure no food was left for preying animals to find, re-stacked the blankets and left the cave.

They moved silently down the road leading to The Meadows. They stopped when they saw the crowd milling about. Woodsmen, farmers, trappers—John Butler and even Sir William Johnson—were gathering for the day's search.

Among the group was a man Lauri had never seen before. He was wearing a cloth shirt and jacket, clout, buckskin leggings, and moccasins.

"That's Joe Brant,—Thayendanegea—Miss Molly's brother," Jason whispered. "He's even brought his Mohawks. They're better than bloodhounds. They'd have found us for sure."

Lauri shivered. She would have died of fright if one of Joseph Brant's Indians had come upon them.

Brant didn't look like a fierce warrior, but Walter had told her that Thayendanegea had gone with William Johnson when the boy was only thirteen, and had killed a French officer at the battle of Lake George. Brant had eaten the officer's heart because he believed the man's bravery would pass on to him if he ate the heart of a courageous man.

The very thought of it had made Lauri sick.

"Look there—with Thayendanegea—that's John Johnson, Sir William's son," Jason said. "I never thought he'd be out looking for us, too."

Young Johnson was almost as tall as his father, lacking an inch or two. He was fair complected, like his mother, Catherine Weissenberg.

John and Joseph looked to be about the same age but there was something more commanding about Brant.

Lauri pulled on Jason's arm. "What are you looking for?"

"Walter. I thought he'd be here."

"Over there." Lauri pointed to where young Butler sat alone, apart from the crowd, his head buried in his hands.

"Stay here." Jason slipped away through the trees.

He crept as close to Walter as he dared. "Don't turn around and don't speak," Jason said, "I'm going to give you something."

Jason pressed a small, knobby object into Walter's hand. "Take this and put it in your saddle bag and don't let Patience see you."

As quietly as he had come, Jason was gone.

Walter slipped the package into his shirt, rose and walked slowly toward the barn.

"Where'd you go?" Lauri asked when Jason returned. "I don't like being alone. I'm afraid."

Coloring up to his hairline, Jason planted a kiss on her cheek. "I love you, Lauri." He squeezed her small hand, and they moved out onto the road.

The crowd came running toward them.

Jason's father was the first to reach them. "I ought to whup you good, boy." He hugged his son so hard Jason thought his ribs would surely break. Tears tumbled down George Dayemon's weathered cheeks.

"And you, girl," George said, "we'd all but given you up for dead."

Jason said, "I found her, Pa, wandering around in the woods. She was lost."

Elder Baxter pushed his way through the crowd, took Lauri in his arms. A huge grin creased his cheeks and tears glistened in his eyes.

Six people stood apart, on the edge of the crowd.

Old Olga and Effsie clung to each other. Their child had returned. They had come to think of Lauri as their own; to treasure and protect, as they would have treasured and protected the girl that death had taken from them ten years earlier.

On the fringe, Belle, Patience, Felicity and Geoff regarded the scene with differing emotions.

A pain stabbed Belle's chest, and she clutched the front of her dress. Too bad the twit hadn't remained lost. Mr. Baxter was making a fool of himself with his sentimental display. All he had done since Lauri had run away was fret about her welfare; ignoring the fact that his own daughter had been abused.

Patience's heart sank. Lauri did not have the doll. Either she had lost it or thrown it away.

Felicity smiled. Lauri had bested Patience. The doll was gone.

Geoff scowled. That oaf, Jason, was getting more than his share of attention.

Geoff let his gaze wander to the girl. So, she and Jason had spent the night alone in the woods. If she were a few years older, he would have enjoyed doing the same thing. If his appraisal was correct, she would have possibilities. She was much too skinny and young now, but her dreamy grey-green eyes, full rose colored lips made the future something to think about.

Let Jason and Walter spend their time hunting and fishing. He was reaching manhood. He was interested in a sport of another kind.

CHAPTER 6

The Meadows

Sir William touched Lauri's swollen face. "Ah, me little colleen, 'tis easy to see you fed the black flies."

He laid a hand on Jason's shoulder. "And you, me lad, found our girl. I applaud you for a job well done."

He turned to Elder Baxter and George Dayemon. "I would like to have Doctor Daly look at the children. With your permission, of course."

"Most kind of you, Sir William," Elder replied.

"'Tis a fine thing for you to do, Sir," George Dayemon said.

"The least I can do, George. You helped bring me back from Lake George when I took that blasted ball in my leg."

"'Twas a small thing I did, Sir William."

"It was much more to me."

"If you'll allow me the time," Elder said, "I'll have Old Olga get clean clothes for Lauri."

Johnson nodded and Baxter went off to talk to Olga.

Sir William smiled down on Martha Dayemon, standing quietly at her husband's side. "Would you care to accompany your son in my coach, Mrs. Dayemon?"

She looked to George for an answer.

"Go girl," George said, "I'll bring something clean for Jason as soon as I can."

Elder returned, Olga at his heels carrying a bundle of clothes. Effsie followed at a respectful pace behind them.

Lauri ran toward Olga, arms outstretched.

"Lawsy, child, you sure gived us a fright," Olga said. "Doan' never do that again. Doan' never."

"I won't, Olga. I promise." She felt a gentle touch on her shoulder.

"Time to go, little colleen," Sir William said.

Lauri climbed aboard the baronet's coach. She had never seen anything so grand. She perched herself on the edge of the seat. Mrs. Dayemon sat between her, and Jason. Elder, and Sir William settled themselves across from them.

"We were so worried about you both." Martha Dayemon's friendly smile put Lauri at ease.

A twinge of guilt pricked Lauri's conscience. In her hurry to escape Belle, the idea that anyone would be concerned never crossed her mind.

"Jason found me. He was very brave." Lauri stole a look at the boy beside his mother, and grinned at the way the color came to his face.

It was easy to see where Jason got his good looks. Martha Dayemon was neither plain nor beautiful, not like Lauri's mother. Like Jason, she had clear, dark eyes that saw into a person's soul. Her hair was a tad lighter than her son's, and her shoulders drooped slightly from years of hard work, her hands were rough and calloused, but she had a woman's softness about her.

Two riders drew rein beside the coach; John Johnson and Joseph Brant.

Lauri shrank back against the leather cushions. Her heart beat wildly. She prayed she wouldn't be seen by Brant.

"It's good your friend found you," Thayendanegea said, "but my Mohawks would have brought you back unharmed."

A smile creased Sir William's Irish face. "Joseph, ride to The Hall with us. I have things to discuss with you. John come along, stay for supper. It's been too long since we've had a meal together."

"I would like that very much, sir," young Johnson said, "but I have business to take care of. There's still much to do before I leave for London." He looked at the children and gave them a friendly smile. "I wanted to see that they were all right."

"When do you receive your title, John?" Elder said.

"October or November. At the convenience of the king, of course."

"Then we must remember to address you as Sir John."

"I hope being a baronet won't set me apart from my friends."

"Johnny Johnson or Sir John, you'll still be one of us," Elder said.

Young Johnson waved, wheeled his horse and trotted down the road toward Fort Johnson.

Elder changed sides, lifted Lauri to his lap.

Joseph Brant tied his horse to the back of the coach. When he returned, he climbed into the coach, and settled himself next to Sir William.

The voices of the men, deep but subdued as they discussed business and valley affairs, lulled Lauri into a restful sleep.

She was still dozing when the carriage rolled up the drive to Johnson Hall. Elder nudged her awake. She rubbed her eyes, then opened her good one at the sight of Sir William's baronial home. She never imagined there would be such a beautiful house in the wilderness.

Unlike the dark grey stone of Fort Johnson, Sir William's former home near the Mohawk River, Johnson Hall was a white wooden building, scored to resemble blocks. It was larger than Fort Johnson and had a more welcoming appearance.

Two grey stone block houses protected the manor on either side. Red coated soldiers were drilling on the parade field where Sir William held his councils with the Indians.

Molly Brant was waiting on the steps as the coachman reined to a stop.

"Is Daly here?" Sir William asked.

"He's in his cabin," Molly said.

"Good. I'll take the children there."

He turned to the others waiting in the coach. "If Doctor Daly thinks it necessary for the children to remain, I'd like you to spend the night here. At any rate, stay and sup with us. George should be here shortly. Mrs. Dayemon, please extend my invitation to your husband.

"Joseph, wait for me in my office. That bloody business with Chief Pontiac is becoming more troublesome every day."

Brant followed his sister into The Hall.

Sir William and the others headed for Doctor Daly's office.

Daly's examination of the children was efficient and thorough.

"No fever. That's good," Daly said. "Clean them up. I'll put some salve on them. It will help with the itching. They'll want to scratch. Make sure they don't. See that they don't develop a fever. Bring them back tomorrow. I'd like to see them in the morning."

George was waiting when they returned to The Hall. He agreed to stay the night only because he had seen the anxious look on Martha's face.

Jason could hardly contain himself as he told his father about Doctor Daly, of the medical books, the bottles of medicines and the surgical instruments. George tried several times to shush his son.

"Let the boy talk, George," Sir William said. "It's been an exciting two days, eh boy?"

"I meant no offense, Sir William," Jason said.

"None taken, lad."

Martha had never seen such a grand house. The center hall was big enough to hold a ball. She could picture the ladies dressed in brocade and satin, their hair styled in the latest fashion, powder and rouge on their faces. The men would be wearing bright colored waist coats, satin breeches, a powdered wig atop their own natural hair. The crown's officers would be dressed in their red regimental uniforms.

If she had known the truth, she would have seen that the center hall was more often filled with Indians from the many tribes the crown had commissioned Johnson to oversee. It was his responsibility to pacify and mediate difficulties between the tribes themselves, as well as resolve the problems that were arising with greater frequency between the Indians and the white settlers who were pushing onto Indian lands; either stealing it or buying it with cheap whiskey.

Molly appeared in the doorway of a room at the far end of the hallway. She moved toward the group with quiet grace.

"The children are well, I'm told."

"Ah, me Molly-0," Sir William said, "your sources keep you well informed. King George's officers should be so fortunate. We'll be having guests for dinner and overnight."

"I'll see to it."

The evening meal, served in the smaller family dining room, was simple but nourishing. The baronet kept up an easy conversation with the men, while Molly and Martha listened quietly. Jason and Lauri had been included with the adults although the Johnson children had eaten earlier.

Before withdrawing to his office to enjoy a pipe with the men, Sir William drew Jason aside. "You seemed greatly interested in what Doctor Daly did."

"Oh yes, Sir William. Doctor Daly must know lots of things. How to treat bites and broken bones and wounds and sick people."

"Would you like to be a doctor?"

Jason was thoughtful for a long moment. "I'd like to help people, but it must cost a pretty sum to become a doctor."

"That it does and hard work, too."

"I'm not afraid of work, Sir William."

"No, lad, I don't believe you are."

The seed of an idea was taking root in Sir William's head. Daly was getting older. Johnstown and the valley were growing. There was a need for a younger doctor. If Jason Dayemon were interested, something might be worked out.

The baronet limped toward Daly's office. He would speak to the doctor about an apprenticeship for Jason when the lad was old enough.

Sir William waited three years before he asked Jason if he still wanted to be a doctor.

"I thought you didn't think I was smart enough," Jason said.

"No, lad," Sir William said, "You were too young. Doctor Daly says if you're ready, you can start your apprenticeship now."

CHAPTER 7

Johnstown—June 1773

The road out of Johnstown was hard packed, but the moisture beneath the surface crept slowly through Lauri's thin shoes and coarse woolen stockings. It was warm for early June and it felt good. Perspiration dampened her forehead and little droplets of water slid down her back.

Winter in the Mohawk Valley had been long and confining and she meant to savor every bit of warmth she could. The sun felt good on her pale face, but it would take more than this to bring color and fullness to her hollow cheeks and erase the purple shadows beneath her eyes.

She was thinking of Jason. She hoped he would soon come home from King's College in New York where Sir William had sent him to further his study of medicine.

Doctor Daly had approved the idea. "He has a quick mind," he told the baronet, "and we've a sore need for men like him."

Sir William agreed. He had watched Jason's progress, and Johnson had not reached his position in life by letting a golden opportunity pass.

While Jason was gone, Lauri lived on memories…the days she, Jason and Walter explored the woods, the boys helping her with her ciphering and reading.

The day Jason came to say goodbye was the most painful memory of all. She had been in back of the Baxter house churning butter, and Belle was giving her a tongue lashing. She had learned to turn a deaf ear to Belle's ranting.

As he walked toward her, she had seen the flash of anger in Jason's eyes when he heard Belle shouting like a fish monger's wife. Lauri had stopped her work, and had run to meet him.

Jason caught her in his arms. "Be careful, Lauri. You know how mean Belle can be."

"I don't care." She took his hand and led him toward the cabin.

Jason closed the door and latched it, shutting out the torrent of threats Belle hurled against it.

Lauri took a package from a chest near her bed and shyly handed it to him. "I hope you like it."

He unwrapped it and held the shirt against him, noticing the fine stitches. She must have spent hours making it.

"It ain't good enough for New York," Lauri said, "but you can wear it when you get back. I made it big enough."

"I'm full grown and you're near to it." He took her hand in his, caressing the calluses. He gently kissed each finger. "I'll be a long time in New York. Will you wait for me?"

She kissed him lightly on the cheek, then laid her head against his broad chest so he couldn't see her tears.

He tipped her chin up, then slowly lowered his head until his lips touched hers.

This was nothing like the quick peck he usually gave her, and Lauri felt a stirring deep inside. She gave herself up to this new feeling, hardly daring to breathe.

When he released her at last, they stood for a long time without speaking, their eyes saying everything that was in their hearts.

She was seventeen now, a woman grown, old beyond her years. So many things had happened since Jason left. Olga had been taken ill and for all of Doctor Daly's skill, had died, leaving Effsie and Lauri to mourn her. Overcome with grief, Effsie lost interest in life, even his horses. The Baxters were forced to buy two more slaves. Belle was so annoyed she wanted to sell Effsie. Elder refused.

Even with the new slaves, life at The Meadows had become increasingly difficult. Both were terrified of Belle. The girl, not much older than Lauri, could not gather her wits about her, and could not learn her duties. More and more, the burdens fell upon Lauri.

Belle and the children became more demanding, working Lauri until she thought she would drop.

As she developed, Geoff began to pester her, making suggestive remarks, trying to touch her whenever he found her alone. Once he had cornered her in his bedroom when she was cleaning and had almost succeeded in disrobing her.

The sounds of Belle's footsteps on the stairs stopped him. "If you tell anyone, I'll kill you!"

Lauri never doubted his word.

She avoided him after that; until the day he found her alone in the barn. He had wrestled her to the floor and was about to force himself on her when Elder chanced upon them. He had taken his riding crop to his son. Bleeding, but not cowed, Geoff staggered to the house.

Tears streamed down Lauri's cheeks. She struggled to adjust her clothes.

Elder reached his trembling hands out to her. "I told you I'd take care of you and all these years I've failed. I'll make it up to you."

"And still you coddle her, Mr. Baxter." Belle's scrawny frame cast a thin shadow on the dirt floor. "The little slut has driven my son mad with lust and you…I want her sent away."

Elder did take Lauri away—to Catherine Butler.

Catherine was furious when Elder told her what had happened.

"Of course Lauri's welcome." She murmured soothing words, comforting the trembling girl in her arms.

When Walter heard, he went into a rage, storming about Butlersbury's front room, struggling to control the urge to smash anything he could lay his hands on. He cursed Geoff with such vile words his father had to remind him of Catherine's presence. Walter apologized, but his anger would not be quelled and he began to curse again with such viciousness Catherine left the room

"For heaven's sake, son, control yourself,." Catherine said before she stepped through the doorway. "Consider Lauri."

Walter sank into a chair. "Is she all right? Was she raped?"

"Not as far as I know," John Butler said.

"I could kill Geoff."

"And hang for it."

"Will she press charges?"

"What good would it do? It's her word against his, and Geoff has money and influence en his side," John said.

"Elder saw. He could testify."

"Lauri would never place Elder in such a position."

Walter rose and started for the stairs.

"Let her rest, son. It will be hard enough for her to face you when she's calmed down."

Walter left the house. His wrath surfaced again. He found the old ax beside the barn; the one he used to work off his anger. The blade smashed into the log

Watching from the window, John shook his head; worried that Walter would not vent his rage. He turned away and went to calm his wife.

The shadows on the hills were lengthening when Walter felt a gentle touch on his shoulder. He looked up to see Lauri, her face drained of all emotion. He took her in his arms and held her. She—was dearer to him than he cared to admit.

"Jason ain't to know," Lauri whispered. "Promise me, Walter. He ain't to know."

"He's sure to hear…"

"No. I couldn't bear it." She clung to him, resting her head against his chest. She could hear the beating of his heart. "I'm so ashamed."

"It wasn't your fault. *It wasn't your fault.*"

Sobs racked her body and he held her close until there were no tears left.

She stayed with the Butlers until Elder rented a house for her in Johnstown. She found work at Gil Tice's tavern, adding to her earnings by taking in sewing and mending.

Christina, Gil's wife, took a liking to her.

They were working together in the kitchen. "I know I ain't no good at fancy talk like you, Mrs. Tice," Lauri said. "I ain't never learned how. Belle Baxter wouldn't let me have no schooling, even if it was free."

"You can read and write, can't you?"

"Walter and Jason learned me. My ma started learning me a little before she died."

"That's more than some folks can do," Christina smiled. "First thing you must remember is not to say ain't."

Lauri giggled. "Walter used to tell me there ain't no such word as ain't."

"He's right," Christina said.

"I thought he was funning me."

"No, my dear, he was telling you the truth."

Lauri's mind was still in a whirl when she saw Johnson Hall. If only Jason would return. Would he remember she had promised to wait for him? Would he still want her? He had not been back, not once, though he wrote often.

She knew Jason was working for a cabinet maker, Marinus Willett, to help pay some of his own expenses.

"It's that Dayemon pride." Walter had told her. "Jason feels he's accepted too much from Sir William."

Whenever she saw Walter, she asked about Jason. Walter was studying law in Albany, and his trips to the valley were irregular. Walter was home now. He had already tried several cases where he defended debtors, often for no fee.

"After all," he said, "if they don't pay other people they aren't going to pay me. Sometimes I don't even offer a defense. They're guilty anyway." He smiled that funny little smile she liked so much. "I have my share of good cases. Then I charge."

Lauri forced herself to stop her day dreaming. She paused briefly to listen to the sound of a creek's rushing waters. When she reached the stream's bank she stopped to watch the water splashing over the rocks, then turned and walked to a small pool, well hidden from the road. Today the water dashed against the earth. She saw only the swirling foam—as disturbed as her emotions.

She went back to the road, unaware of the approaching horse until the rider spoke.

"Where are you going, Lauri? You're a long way from town." Elder sat his horse well, still straight of back. There were streaks of grey through his wavy hair.

"Johnson Hall,." Lauri said.

"That's a long walk for you. Ride with me. I'll take you there."

He lifted her to the horse's back, placed her in front of him, slipped his arms around her small waist. The clean scent of her frail body filled his nostrils and he felt an inner stirring that troubled him.

He eased his horse down the road, slowed the pace, reluctant to release her. He should have shifted his position. He knew Lauri was quite unaware of the effect she was having on him.

It had been a long time since he had experienced these feelings. In all his married life, he had never felt this way toward Belle. His relations with her had only been a physical release, and it was no surprise when, following Patience's birth, Belle told him she would no longer share his bed. She had given him three children, had done her wifely duty and would no longer subject herself to such a degrading act.

When they reached Johnson Hall, Elder reluctantly handed Lauri down and sat smiling at her.

"Please give my apologizes to Sir William," he said. "I must head for home, though I much prefer his company to any at The Meadows."

He touched his crop to his temple and turned his horse down the lane toward Johnstown.

Lauri walked to the back of the house. Slaves worked the fields, clerks were in the storehouse counting pelts.

She had often seen Sir William tending the fruit trees he had obtained from New England. All this busyness seemed a part of the man, an extension of his vibrant personality.

She remembered the first time she had seen the two stone block houses the baronet had ordered built when the Indian Chief, Pontiac, threatened to ravage the Mohawk Valley, to run the river red with blood.

Lauri never liked the gloomy grey stone guardians, though they probably would have saved Sir William's household if Pontiac had not agreed to the peace treaty at the council at Oswego. Still, Lauri wished they weren't there. They reminded her of war, and war meant death.

She entered the quiet kitchen in the outbuilding. A negro cook was bending over the kettle which was suspended on the fireplace crane, ladling soup and making cooing sounds. She looked up without interest, and nodded to the little girl seated near the hearth. The child scurried out of the room, returned in a few minutes, and motioned Lauri to follow her.

Molly Brant, the Brown Lady Johnson some valley folks called her, was seated near the window in the baronet's office-bedroom. Shafts of sunlight streaked through the irregular panes of glass, picking out the highlights of the long braids, the blackness accentuated by the white doeskin tunic she wore. A piece of unfinished needlepoint lay in her lap.

One year old Susanna and the two year old toddler, Mary, played at Molly's feet.

Molly picked up her needlepoint. "Didn't I see you ride up the lane with Elder Baxter?"

"What's that? Elder's here?" Sir William was sitting at his desk, reading a letter. He smiled when he saw Lauri in the doorway.

Lauri offered a polite curtsy. "He begs your pardon, Sir William. He did bring me, but he had to go back to The Meadows. He wishes you and Miss Molly well and hopes you will understand."

"Too bad. It's been a long time since Elder and I have talked over a glass."

At the sound of their father's voice, Mary tottered over to him on unsteady feet, and Susanna crawled crab like almost as fast. Sir William bent, scooped them up and planted a kiss on each head.

"Jason's coming home." Sir William held up the letter in his hand. "I've made him my personal physician along with Doctor Daly. Maybe if Jason were here now he could fix me up good enough to go to John's wedding in New York."

Sir William looked tired and ill. The ball he had received at the battle of Lake George was still in his leg, and he suffered from recurring dysentery. The years of keeping the covenant chain strong between the Iroquois and the crown were taking their toll.

"Lauri," Molly said, "Jason would make you a good husband."

Sir William chuckled, "Playing match maker again, me Molly-0? Best be careful, colleen. She's matched more than one couple in the valley." He turned serious. "You'd do well to heed Molly's advice. You're young and healthy. You should marry and raise a family."

"I'm only seventeen."

"Nigh past marrying age." Sir William humphed. "It's not good for a lass as pretty as you to be alone. There's many a rake in the valley that's not to be trusted. I've not told Jason you're living in Johnstown. Time enough for him to find out when he gets here. I hope it's soon."

CHAPTER 8

New York City—June 1773

Jason's schooling at King's College was at an end, and in a few days, he would leave New York, and return to the valley to take up his duties at Johnson Hall. The invitation to join Walter and Sir John for dinner had come as a complete surprise. He had not seen either of them in two years.

Walter had come to the city to attend Sir John's and Polly Watts' wedding; not as a personal friend of young Johnson, but to represent the Butler family and out of respect for Sir William.

Jason had overspent on clothes and was in debt to Marinus Willet, the cabinet maker who had hired him for wages. The money Jason had earned had bought a work horse for his father. It replaced the old mule George Dayemon had used for so long. George had been told the horse was a gift from Sir William, in payment for what George had done for Johnson after the battle at Lake George.

Jason dressed carefully. He felt like a dandy as he checked his fawn colored breeches, light blue waistcoat and dark blue coat with the turned back cuffs and lining to match the breeches. The tailor had tried hard to convince him lace shirt cuffs and stock were the height of fashion. Ruffles were even more than he wanted. He and the tailor had reluctantly agreed to settle for that. He had drawn the line at silk stockings, settling for good cotton, grudgingly agreeing to a design on the calf. He told himself it would make a good wedding outfit when he married Lauri.

Walter sat on the edge of Jason's bed. He shifted his weight every now and then, trying to find a comfortable spot. He finally gave up and began to pace.

"If you have finished. preening," Walter said, "let's be on our way. I've hired a carriage, and it's costing me a goodly sum."

The coachman had charged Walter an outrageous fee to take them to the Battery. "Worth your life to go there at night."

Jason slid Walter's last letter into his pocket. Butler had written in glowing terms about being a lawyer, going into detail about the cases he'd tried, some successful, others not. There had been word about the Butler family, and Sir William's failing health. There was a brief mention of Lauri. She was well, was concerned that Jason was working too hard, was waiting for him to come home.

The few letters he had received from Lauri spoke only of the weather, the state of her well being and some gossip about the valley. She was not schooled, but that did not account for the lack of personal details.

They left the cramped room Jason rented from the Widow Carmichael, and walked down the refuse strewn alley to the corner where the apprehensive coachman waited.

"It's too far, and too dangerous," Jason had said when Walter suggested walking to the tip of the island. "The press gangs and toughs will be out."

"Is that why you carry a pistol in your waist band?"

"You'd do well to have yours," Jason said.

Walter drew his coat aside to show he was armed.

The carriage rattled down Greenwich Street, past King's College and headed for the Battery, or the Mall, as some people called that part of Broadway. It was a place Jason rarely visited. He was too busy with lectures, diseases, cures, courses on anatomy, dissections—when a body could be bought or stolen—surgical procedures, and some direction on midwifery.

Walter paid the driver and the coachman hurried back up town.

"Highway robber," Walter grumbled.

They were early for their meeting with Sir John. They strolled along the herringboned patterned brick walk, always alert to what was going on around them, their pistols within easy reach.

"What will happen to Clarissa Putnam and the children?" Jason asked.

"Sir John has set her up in a house across the river from Fort Johnson," Walter said.

"Shouldn't think Polly Watts would take kindly to having her husband's mistress living so near. What about the children? Margaret and William, isn't it? How old are they now?"

"Six and four. Something like that."

"I always thought Sir John would make Clarissa his wife. Sir William seemed fond of her."

Walter shrugged. "Clarissa doesn't come from the right family. Seems to be a case of do as I say; not as I do." He stopped, looked around in all directions. "I thought I heard something." They began walking again. "I'd think Polly would come with a very substantial dowry."

"The Johnson's are well fixed themselves."

"It's the political connections, too. John Watts has represented the city of New York in the Assembly for several years. They're also related to the De Lancys, Schuylers. Who knows who else. I don't imagine the Watts object to having a Baronet in the family."

Walter stopped, sniffed. The stench from the harbor was stomach turning; an open sewer, a place where slop jars were emptied each day. Rotting garbage floated on the water. The tide thumped the bloated carcass of a dead cow against the piling.

In the harbor a British naval vessel lifted and dipped with the ebb and flow of the sea.

A patrol of Red Coats from Fort George eyeballed them closely and moved on.

Jason and Walter walked into a poorly lit section of the Mall.

"Be ready," Jason said. "The patrol has probably told the press men about us."

Walter's fingers closed around the grip of his pistol.

As if on cue, they were accosted by a gang of ruffians.

"Tell your black hearted masters they've picked the wrong men." Jason had his pistol in his hand. "We're loyal English subjects on our way to see the Baronet, Sir John Johnson."

"And I'm havin' tea with His Majesty." A scruffy bully stood apart from the others. He slapped a heavy cudgel against his gloved palm. "Take 'em, boys."

"First one to try, gets a ball through his heart." Walter pointed his gun at the bully. "You want to be the first to die?"

The ruffian blanched. "Take 'em, you cowards."

"Do it yerself. I ain't takin' a ball for nobody." The others turned tail and disappeared down a rubbish cluttered alley.

"Two to one, now," Walter said. "Odds in our favor. Make your move."

"Another time, dandy. Just you and me." As fast as he had come, the thug was gone.

"Let's get out of here before they come back," Jason said. "There'll be more next time."

Their hearts were still pounding when they found themselves at Number One Broadway where Sir John was staying with his future in-laws, Captain Archibald and Anne Watts Kennedy, Polly's sister.

They presented themselves, and were taken directly to the room where Sir John, Polly Watts and the Kennedys awaited them.

Jason could easily understand why Sir John had been charmed by his soon-to-be bride. Polly Watts was attractive, though not as pretty as Lauri. She had an enjoyable wit and a finely developed social grace that put him at ease.

After the required courtesies the trio excused themselves.

The evening began on a pleasant note, with an enjoyable dinner. There was much catching up on news of the valley. Jason was disappointed that neither Walter nor Sir John mentioned Lauri, nor the Baxters. His questions were ignored and the conversation shifted to another topic when he tried to ask about them.

Sir John pushed himself away from the table. "Thank you, gentlemen. I have enjoyed the evening. Walk with me to the Kennedy's and we'll hail a carriage for your return up town."

They had not gone far when, from a side street, Geoff Baxter swaggered toward them offering pleasantries to Sir John and Walter. He ignored Jason. He fell in step beside Sir John, elbowing Walter out of the way.

Walter placed a hand on Jason's arm, slowing their steps and dropping back a few paces. "I don't think it was an accident Geoff happened on us. Watch yourself."

"What's he doing here in New York? Sir John's wedding?"

Walter shook his head. "Not likely. Running away from his gambling debts probably. He's been in trouble before for not paying up. He'll be found sooner or later. He knows what to expect."

"Is that what happened to his face?" Jason said.

A deep scar ran down the left side of Geoff's face pulling his lips into a mocking smirk. Whoever had done this to him had just missed his left eye. A might closer and he would have lost his sight. Geoff, who had once been almost as handsome as Walter, now had a face that would turn any woman away.

Before Walter answered, Geoff suggested they stop for a drink of rum. "The King's Arms. What do you say, Jason?"

"That rebel place?" Walter said.

"To let the rabble see what good king's men look like." Geoff raised his hand in a mock toast. "To Sir John's health and happiness."

Sir John started to protest, but Geoff, already well into his cups, was weaving his way toward the King's Arms.

He slowed his steps and the others caught up with him. "You know the place, Dayemon. It's where The Sons of Liberty hatch their plots."

"I don't know anything about hatching plots."

Walter moved close enough to Jason to whisper, "Don't let Geoff roil you."

They made their way to the inn where they were taken to a table near an open window. A gentle breeze cooled the crowded room.

At a nearby table, three men were engaged in an earnest discussion. Jason recognized them: Isaac Sears, John Lamb and Marinus Willett, members of The Sons of Liberty.

When they were seated, Jason scrutinized Geoff's face with a physician's eye.

Geoff glared at Jason with contempt. "Not pretty, is it Doctor? Someday when you're man enough to hear the story, I'll tell you how I came by it."

Walter and Sir John stiffened and exchanged anxious glances.

The hum of voices at the next table stilled. Jason turned and saw Marinus regarding him over the beak that the cabinet maker called a nose.

"There's some of the radicals, Sir John," Geoff said, nodding toward the three men.

"They're treasonous fools, with nothing better to do than stir up trouble," Walter said.

"Radicals who'd abolish the crown if they could." Geoff's words carried over the drone of conversation.

"They won't take up arms against the king," Walter said. "They know they're no match for the British."

"What do you say, Doctor?" Geoff taunted. "Speak up, or are you afraid to admit you're one of them?"

"I've no quarrel with the king," Jason said.

"No loyalty, either." Geoff glanced at the next table. "You'll bring their rebellious slop back with you, and give the Palatines just enough to warm their bellies until they think they're as good as us."

"You can't hold them down forever," Jason said.

"The Palatines have been driven from one land to another because of their stubborn religious beliefs," Sir John said. "Who but the English have treated them so well? Queen Anne took in thousands of them."

"Taxed the honest, hardworking Englishmen, to boot," Geoff added. "All the while the Palatines were stealing their jobs. Then the dogs came to the colonies and we've been plagued by them ever since."

"They still blame the British regulars for not protecting them from the French," Jason countered.

"They had the militia," Sir John said. "They had Nicholas Herkimer."

"As far as they're concerned," Jason argued, "they did it on their own, no thanks to the English troops."

Geoff took a swig of rum. "Men like Sir William and John Butler drove the French out of the valley—not the Palatines. They're living in peace, ungrateful whelps, and now they don't want to help pay for the war."

"Don't forget, Jason, they prospered like the rest of us," Walter said. "Their wheat, and pearl ash brought the same high prices at Albany and New York as ours did."

"Agreed," Jason said, "but look at the price they're paying because of the laws pressed on them. It was their boycott of the Stamp Act and the Sugar Act that helped to force Parliament to repeal them."

Nearly all talk in the room had ceased. Ears strained to hear the exchange going on between the four seated by the window.

"They resented those laws," Jason went on. "They aren't English subjects. They have no say in the laws that affect them, not even local laws."

"They receive honest counsel. I've represented a few myself," Walter said.

"And did a good job, I'm sure," Jason agreed, "but they want to speak for themselves."

Sir John interrupted. "Most of them only speak German. They know nothing of English law."

"Their sons are bright enough to learn, given the chance," Jason said.

Geoff's face was scarlet. "You think just because a nobody like you can boot lick your way up, anyone can. Stay on the farm where you belong. We know how to rule people like you."

Jason lunged, his arms reaching for Geoff.

Geoff pushed against the table, knocking Jason off balance. Geoff's chair tipped over with a crash. He was on his feet, unsteady. He reached for the knife in his boot.

Sir John grabbed Baxter's arm.

Jason stumbled toward the door; Walter at his heels.

"He'll have the law on me," Jason said.

"Not likely. Sir John would have to testify and Geoff can't chance that. He's up to his bloody neck in debt to Johnson with his gambling. He's not safe in Albany. That's probably why he's in New York or else to try and get more money out of Sir John. Johnson's fed up."

Walter stopped walking. He searched Jason's face. "Just what are your political leanings?"

Jason put a hand on Walter's shoulder. "Put your mind at ease. I've no stomach for politicking or soldiering. That's your game. I just don't like…"

"What?"

"Injustice."

"You call repaying a just debt an injustice? I've defended too many malingerers to be swayed by such talk."

They began to walk again.

"That man, Willett, did you see how he stared at me?" Walter's hand went to his throat, "I've a strange tightness here. I've a feeling we'll meet again."

Jason was in a foul mood the next morning when he opened the door to Marinus Willett's cabinet shop. He had let Geoff goad him again.

And there was Lauri. How many sleepless nights had he spent worrying about her? Was she ill? Was there someone else, some stranger, a newcomer to the valley? A man who was not a buffoon like him? Maybe she was married. The idea stabbed him to the quick.

He should have told her how important she was to him. He had loved her for so long. That would never change. He should have made that clearer before he had left for New York. Two years was a long time for a woman to wait for a fool who had not made his deep feelings known.

He slammed the door.

Willett looked up from the chair he was working on. He sat back on his haunches.

"A close call last night, lad."

Jason nodded.

"The man, what did you call him? Baxter?"

"He's bullied me for years," Jason said. "I've been too much of a coward to fight back."

"Not from what I saw last night."

"I wanted to kill him." Jason struggled to control his shaking hands. "If he thinks I'm not loyal to the king, so be it. You and the others have nothing to do with it."

"Your political feelings are none of my affair. You've never betrayed me or The Sons of Liberty. I'm grateful for that." Willett went back to his work. "You'll be leaving soon?"

"Next week," Jason said.

Willett stood up, grasped Jason's hands with both of his, wrapped his calloused fingers around Jason's.

"We've hard times ahead," Willett said. "I hope when we meet again we won't be facing each other over the barrel of a gun," Marinus picked up a draw shave. "What about your friend…Butler, isn't it?"

"Loyal to the king."

"I thought as much."

CHAPTER 9

The Mohawk River—June 1773

Jason stretched his long legs against the pine planking of the batteau. His shirt was open to the bright summer sun that warmed the black hairs on his chest.

The going was tediously slow. The sluggish current shifted the bars of sand, and the batteau ran aground. The batteau men, heaved on the long sturdy poles, struggled to push the boat free. Others jumped into the river, grabbed the ropes and pulled. Jason slid over the side to help drag the batteau into deeper water.

They were a grimy, hard working lot. Their backs bent with the oars now that they were in a deeper channel. Despite their efforts, they made little headway. Debris piled up against sunken logs and often the batteau had to be beached until the crew could chop away a tree whose roots had been undermined by the river.

The willows at the water's edge swayed in the soft summer breeze, maples cast irregular patterns along the lazy river. Out of the endless stretches of forest, brooks and small creeks flowed over jagged rocks. The Mohawk twisted and turned back upon itself, winding its way through the broad, fertile bottom land.

Jason sized up the stone buildings set back from the river, the grain fields edged by irregular stone fences, safe on high ground. When the Mohawk River overflowed its banks, as it had for centuries, the farmlands were enriched by the fertile silt from beyond Fort Stanwix.

They slipped silently past Guy Park Manor where Guy Johnson's fishing skiff was beached. Now that Sir William's son-in-law was taking over more of the baronet's duties, Guy was finding less time to use the boat.

Workmen were busy rebuilding Guy's house. It had been struck twice by lightning during a severe thunderstorm. The only thing that had been saved, Walter had said, was a bed. Furnishings, as well as other valuables had been destroyed. Guy's sketches, drawings and manuscripts were gone.

The batteau slipped past, and Fort Johnson, Sir William's former home, appeared in the distance.

Jason had risen early to wash the bear grease from his body. He hated the smell, but it was a necessary protection from the gnats, mosquitoes, deer and black flies that infested the lowlands bordering the river.

At Jelles Fonda's trading station he got a horse. He left his trunks and books there, promised to return in a few days with Jelles' mare, and headed over trail toward Johnstown. He let the horse climb steep Switzer Hill slowly, saving her for the long ride to Johnson Hall.

At the top of the hill, Butlersbury, with its' beaded, foot wide clapboards, bordered by the lilac bushes that had lost their fragrance weeks ago, stood stark and silent. None of the children were about, and he supposed Catherine Butler was busy at the hearth. Thin columns of smoke drifted lazily from the chimney of the beehive oven.

He often wondered if Mrs. Butler yearned for a big house like Johnson Hall. If she did, she kept her counsel to herself. John Butler would probably be against such an idea, what with taxes so high and all.

A little beyond Butlersbury a road branched off to the west. He considered taking it. It led to his family's cabin. He'd been away a long time and he was anxious to see them, but he had an obligation to Sir William. After he saw Sir William, and before he took up his duties at The Hall, he'd spend time with his folks.

The road dipped into the forest. On either side, a sea of straight trunk giants; hemlocks, spruce and sharp needled pines, bottoms gaunt and bare, competed with each other for the sunlight. In the low places, where a brook gushed and leaped over the rocks, white birch and willows offered relief from the green.

Jason let the horse set the pace. He settled into the saddle to enjoy the smell of the woods.

It was not long before he found himself thinking of Lauri. Why had Walter avoided his questions? Was she ill? If she was, he would nurse her back to health.

What else could it be? Had the Wilkins found her after all these years and taken her back to Albany with them? Belle Baxter would be loathe to let her go, but she had no legal claim to her. For that matter, neither did he.

The thin sunlight sifting through the trees shortened and the sun began to dip into the western Indian country. The lights of Johnstown were a cheery, welcome sight. New houses nestled side by side on what had been timberland when he had gone away. He moved down the quiet street. The yellow school house he had attended stood empty. He passed by the wagon maker, William Phillips, and the miller, Peter Young. He rode by the place where he had once bought a hat from James Davis. At Peter Yost's tannery, the smell made him wrinkle his nose.

The courthouse, gaol and stocks loomed ahead, dark and uninviting. The horse picked its way carefully and then the sound of laughter drifted from Gilbert Tice's tavern.

Jason turned up the familiar road leading to the white house on the hill. In the twilight, he could see the soft glow of candles through The Hall's windows.

He dismounted at the steps, sprinted to the door and raised the heavy knocker. The door was opened by Billy, Sir William's butler, and his black face beamed when he saw Jason standing there.

"Lawd Amighty, Sir William sure been waitin' on you ever since he heard you was comin' home. Two Mohawks brought word you. was comin' up river."

Billy darted into one of the rooms, to reappear close on Sir William's heels.

A warm smile creased the baronet's face as he grasped Jason's hand and drew him into a fond embrace.

"Welcome home…Doctor," he said.

He looked older than his fifty eight years, his face lined and drawn from fatigue. The pain from his leg wound, and chronic dysentery still plagued him.

The hall clock struck six.

"Come lad. You must be famished. The Mohawks said you came straight from Jelles Fonda without so much as a bite to eat. Billy tell Molly that Jason's here and have the cook send up a meal."

Jason smiled. "By your leave, Sir William, I'd like to wash up."

"Indeed. It's a long dusty ride from Fonda's."

Shadows cast by the candles in the silver candelabrum on the sideboard played tag, darting here and there about the painted ceiling and papered walls. The persistent song of the male katydids in the trees outside the window disturbed the quiet night.

Sir William motioned to Billy standing near the fireplace, violin in hand. "Pour us some wine, then play us a happy tune on that fiddle of yours. This is cause for celebration. A glass, eh Jason?"

Billy brought the wine and a pipe for each of them, then began to play an Irish tune.

"You bring joy to my heart, Billy," Sir William took a drag on his pipe. "So, Jason, you put those surgeon's hands to work making cabinets while you were away."

"I can't go on accepting your generosity forever, Sir William."

"I wish there were more like you. My purse is nearly drained by others who do nothing for themselves."

"Marinus Willett would agree with you, Sir William. He could ill afford to pay me," Jason ate slowly, enjoying the first good food he had in days, savoring the delicate wine. His pipe, unlit, lay on the table beside him.

"I seem to recall someone named Willett," Johnson said.

"He was at Frontenac with Colonel Bradstreet and Ticonderoga with General Abercombie." Jason sipped his wine and relaxed.

"Willett. Yes, of course, with Oliver De Lancy's battalion. He and an Irishman, a young lieutenant, by the name of Muncy, if I recollect correctly, rallied the men after Lord Howe was killed. Did you know that?"

Jason shook his head.

"That fool Abercombie marched his men straight into the French line of fire. For five hours the British stormed the breastwork with fixed bayonets and the French shot them down. 2,000 men killed, wounded or captured because Abercombie wanted to fight on an open field."

Sir William placed his hand on his forehead.

Jason anxiously studied Sir William. "Are you feeling ill?"

"No, lad, just a tired old man. Too old to go to my own son's wedding."

"Sir John understands."

Sir William knocked the ashes from his pipe and drained his glass. "Your friend, Willett, I trust he's still a king's man?"

"His feelings for the king have changed, I'm afraid."

Sir William scowled. "Did he change yours?"

"I guess I never thought about it one way or the other."

"There's trouble brewing. I hope you don't have to make a choice."

"Willett's father is true to the crown. He's disowned his son."

"Tragic," the baronet said. "It would break my heart if John and I were to have a falling out." He rubbed his eyes and yawned. "Stay the night, Jason."

"I appreciate that, Sir William. I'd like to get an early start for The Meadows. I'm anxious to see Lauri."

"She's not there."

"Where is she?"

"In Johnstown. You didn't know?"

"Walter never mentioned it." Jason ran his hand over his eyes. He had been too blind to see. It wasn't a stranger who had stolen Lauri's heart. It was Walter. "How long has she been there?"

"A year, I believe." Sir William said.

"No one told me."

"I'm sure all will be cleared up when you talk to her tomorrow."

Jason didn't answer. He'd have to sleep on it.

CHAPTER 10

Jason spent a fretful night, but with dawn's breaking, he knew what he would do. Walter was his best friend, Lauri the woman he loved. He would wish them well and go on with his life.

Lauri had told him that her mother had chosen James Howell, Elder Baxter's best friend.

Elder had left Pennsylvania, traveled to the Mohawk Valley, married Belle.

There were, Jason decided, a couple of things he would not do. He would not leave, and he would not marry a woman like Belle. When, and if he married, it would be to a loving and caring woman who would give him loving and caring children.

He found Sir William, looking worn and haggard, already at work in his office. Molly was with him.

Jason greeted them with false cheerfulness. "By your leave, Sir William, I'd like to take some time to spend with my family and I've need to pay a courtesy call on the Butlers."

The baronet and Molly exchanged glances; no mention of Lauri.

"Agreed," Sir William said. "Daly will understand."

"I'll see him shortly. I'm anxious to get to work."

"There'll be plenty of that, me lad. I've brought four hundred Highlanders here to settle my land. I've told Daly I want them all inoculated. I don't want smallpox wiping out all I've worked for these many years."

As Jason neared his family's cabin he saw his father and his younger brothers working a small strip of land east of the house.

Jason's father spotted him, waited for his eldest son. "Your Ma's a might put out, you just getting' to see her after bein' here nigh on to a day."

"I had to pay my respects to Sir William, Pa. It was late when I got there. I spent the night."

"Best get to the house, boy. Your Ma's probably spied you from way back."

Martha Dayemon had seen her son—her doctor son—long before her husband. She stood in the doorway, fighting back tears.

Jason slid from the saddle. His long legs carried him to the door.

"Ma," Jason said, "I'm sorry I didn't come here first. I felt I owed it to Sir William after all he's done for me."

Martha let the tears flow. "You done right. We'll have more time to talk now."

It was almost noon before George and the boys came in. It did not bother George if some people thought he was an uncaring man. It was enough that Martha knew he was giving mother and son some private moments together.

After the noon meal blessing, George nodded, and the boys began to ply Jason with questions. *What was New York like? Were there many soldiers in the city? Did he see Sir John? What of the wedding, Martha wanted to know. Was Polly Watts as pretty as everyone said?*

George settled into the Windsor chair, a treasured piece of furniture Martha had brought to the marriage, a family heirloom, a wedding gift from Martha's mother.

When Jason left the next morning not a word had been said about Lauri.

A courtesy call on the Butlers, then he would go to see her. He owed her that much.

Later that day Jason sat in the saddle staring at Lauri. She was weeding the herb garden in front of a white frame house, a small place, in need of painting.

He couldn't believe that in the two years he had been away, she had grown even more beautiful. She had become a woman. When he left she had been a mere slip of a girl with a hint of what she was to become. Now she was high breasted, slim waisted and narrow hipped. He could see why Walter had fallen in love with her.

The mare whinnied. Jason dismounted and looped the reins over the fence.

Lauri rose, ran toward him, reaching for him. He didn't embrace her and Lauri lowered her arms, puzzled.

"Let's go inside," she said.

There were only two rooms divided by a double faced fireplace. The walls had been recently white washed and the pine floors daily sanded.

There was a straight backed bench, a couple of single chairs, and a narrow chest. Her bed was close to the fireplace, a warmer place to sleep in the frigid Mohawk Valley winters. There was no sign of a man in the house; no breeches, shirt, coat, hose, pipe or gun. There was only one bed pillow.

The other room, the kitchen, had a pine table with a bench on either side. A stone sink had a bucket half filled with water. Lauri poured a dipper of water into a basin and washed the dirt from her hands.

"Why are you living here?" he demanded. He had a right to know. She couldn't go sneaking behind his back with Walter and expect him not to be hurt. He placed his hand on her chin and forced her to face him.

"Belle didn't want me there any more."

"She never wanted you." It rankled him because she was sidestepping his question.

Was it easier for her to see Walter away from prying eyes? He cursed himself. Who were the bigger sinners? Walter and Lauri for what they might be doing? Or he for accusing them without proof?

"Why didn't you tell me?" he demanded. "Why didn't Walter tell me? Are you both too ashamed?"

"Yes, I'm ashamed," she said. "I made Walter promise not to tell you. There's nothing you can do about it."

He pulled her to him, crushing her against his body.

"You're not Walter's wife yet." His lips pressed hard against her mouth.

She pushed him away, raised her hand to strike him.

He caught her wrist before the blow landed.

She tried to pull away. "You're no better than Geoff. He tried to force himself on me. Elder heard my screams. He beat Geoff with his riding crop."

Now it made sense to Jason—Geoff's scarred face—his taunting words—

'Someday when you're man enough to hear the story, I'll tell you how I came by this face.'

"Sir William knows, doesn't he?" Jason said.

Lauri nodded.

"And Walter?"

She avoided his eyes. "Mrs. Butler took me in."

"Walter never told me."

"I didn't want you to know what happened. I made him promise not to tell you."

"You were almost raped and I'm not to know?"

"I want to forget what happened."

He wrapped his arms around her. She needed his comfort, not his censure. His voice was muffled in her hair. "Then you don't love Walter?"

She stepped out of his embrace, her lips curling at the corners. "Are you a complete dolt? It's you I love. It's always been you."

"What about this house?"

"Elder found it for me."

Jason felt the anger welling up inside. Elder was still providing for her, and he could not offer marriage.

"I'm happy here," Lauri said. "I'm working at Tice's."

"A bar maid?"

"Heavens, no. Mrs. Tice wouldn't let me do that. I help in the kitchen. She even taught me not to say ain't. Didn't you notice?"

"You speak as properly as any New York belle I ever met."

"And how many of those did you meet?"

"A gentleman never kisses and tells."

"And how many New York belles have you kissed?" She began to pout.

He smiled; that smug know it all smile that annoyed her so much. He kissed her again. Slowly, tenderly.

The shadows on the hills had lengthened by the time he took his leave. His broad shoulders filled the open doorway and he beckoned to her so he could kiss her once more.

"Shut the door," Lauri had seen a slight movement across the street. "Mrs. Wemple is watching."

He closed it and took her in his arms again. Maybe he'd wear those fancy clothes at a wedding after all.

CHAPTER 11

Jason was in no hurry to get back to Johnson Hall. He relaxed in the saddle, and tried to sort things out in his mind. It would be a long time before he could ask Lauri to be his wife. There were debts to be paid, work to be done with Doctor Daly at The Hall. Sir William's Highlanders would take much of his time, not to mention the servants and slaves, as well as the tenant farmers. There would be few precious moments to spend with a new bride and he meant to savor every one of them when they married.

Daly was just returning from a circuit when Jason drew rein before the doctor's cabin. The older man greeted him heartily.

"Come in. Come in." Daly unlatched the door and motioned Jason to follow.

Daly looked tired. "Join me in a toddy. I've need of it. I swear Sir William means to inoculate the whole valley—the whole world—if he could."

Jason laughed. "He owns a good share of it."

"That he does, from Lake George to the salt lake of the Onondagas."

Daly set the kettle to steaming over the coals he had stirred. "Glad to see the fire has been kept for me. My girl knows how much I'm in need of refreshment when I return from one of these circuits."

"I hope Sir William isn't planning on sending us west into the Indian country," Jason said.

"Don't suggest it. I'm sore enough now. Been on the old nag for days "Sir William wants all the Highlanders inoculated. I've been out trying to get them to agree to it. They're mule headed. They want no part of it."

Daly settled into a chair near the fireplace and began mixing the sugar, spices, brandy and hot water. He poured the toddy into the tankards on the table beside him, gesturing to Jason to take one.

Touching his mug to Jason's, he smiled. "Good to have you home again, Doctor."

"Not many people have called me that."

"You ever inoculate anyone?" Daly asked.

Jason shook his head. "I've seen it done. Had it done myself."

Daly looked surprised. "Sir William wants you to take a class of Highlanders—that's what you call the people you inoculate, isn't it? He wants you to take them up to the Sacandaga."

"There's hundreds of them. It'll take me weeks." Jason began to pace.

"First we have to win them over. They say it's against the laws of God and nature. Scared they'll get the pox, if you ask me." Daly took a long swig of toddy, wiped his mouth with the back of his hand. "Sir William's called them in. Two days hence. Giving them a choice. Be inoculated or it's back to the old sod."

"That's strong arming."

"That it is lad, that it is. You've got to talk them into it. They've not listened to me and most don't have the means to get back."

"I haven't seen Lauri in two years, and now I'm being sent to the Sacandaga for God knows how long."

"Consider it your first payment to the baronet," Daly said. "Sir William always collects his debts."

The grove, where Superintendent of Indian Affairs, William Johnson, held his Indian councils, was filled with Highlanders; the men dressed in their kilts, their broadswords at their side. Worry lines creased the women's faces. The children, clinging to their mothers were quiet, sensing the fear and hostility. The men, jaws set, eyes hard fast on Jason, gauged his every word and movement.

Jason stood on The Hall's steps, reading the sullen faces. He saw Sir William watching from his office window. He knew it was a test, and he was not going to fail. At Jason's right, two scarlet coated corporals and a sergeant sat at a long pine table, sheaves of papers before them. A bee flitted from bush to bush, then winged off.

"Doctor Daly," Jason began, "has told you Sir William wants you to be inoculated. He wants to protect you from smallpox."

A deep growling murmur swept like a wave over the crowd.

Jason pressed on. "No one I know of has died of smallpox after they were inoculated."

Distrust was plain on their faces, but no one challenged him.

"You'll be a little sick for a few days, but you'll get better and you never need worry about getting the pox."

"How's it done, mister?"

Jason searched the crowd, but could not find the questioner. It sounded like a woman or maybe a young boy.

"We make a couple of scratches on your arm," Jason said. "Deep enough to put some pox pus under the skin."

The grumbling crowd pressed forward. He held his ground, put up his hand for silence, and when they had settled down, he went on.

"Just enough to make you a little sick. Sick enough to put you to bed."

"'Taint natural to put a sickness in a body." A thin, wrinkled woman with a crooked body pushed through the crowd, shaking her fist.

"On the contrary, madam," Jason said, "we've known for fifty years that it works."

"You ain't fifty," the old woman said. Her mouth was twisted into a toothless grin.

"You're quite right, madam. I'm not fifty, but other physicians have done it. So you see, we know it really works."

"Can't be." someone said.

"Surely you're not calling Doctor Dayemon a liar, sir."

"And who might you be?" the deep male voice said.

"Walter Butler." He moved through the Highlanders to stand beside Jason. "Doctor Dayemon speaks the truth."

"You a doctor?" the man wanted to know.

"Legal advisor."

"How do we know we can trust you?"

Walter presented his most disarming smile. "We all know lawyers don't lie."

The crowd erupted in a loud guffaw.

When the laughter had trickled to a giggle or two, Walter continued. "Both Doctor Dayemon and I have been inoculated. We're living proof."

The old woman persisted. "How long's the sickness take?"

"Three weeks," Jason said. "You'll feel poorly for a few days, run a fever, get a few sores, some pox. When you're better, you'll wash in rum or vinegar, dress in fresh clothes and you'll be allowed to leave."

They began to grumble again. "My family needs me…. Three week's too long…."

Jason stood his ground. "That's how long it takes."

"Who'll care for my crops, my stock?" a deep voice asked.

"Your neighbor, and you'll take care of his when he goes to get inoculated," Jason said.

The old woman twisted her arthritic body around to face the crowd. "I seen the smallpox. It ain't pretty. These men says they been fixed. They look hearty enough to me, be it true. Even bein' sick for three week's better'n dying with the pox."

Jason let them mull over what he had said, speaking once more when the grumbling died down.

"Sign up at the table. If you can't write, put your X on the paper. The sergeant and corporals will write your name after it."

He felt a tug on his sleeve. A boy he judged to be about eight was regarding him with large anxious eyes. "We gonna have to swim, mister?"

Jason and Walter exchanged puzzled glances.

"If we don't get scratched with the pox," the boy said, "we gotta go back. We don't have the means."

"Your father's a good man, son." Jason tousled the boy's carroty hair. "He'll do what's right."

The youth disappeared into the crowd.

Jason turned to Walter. "Wait for me at Tice's. I'll meet you after I speak with Sir William."

Walter, waited alone at a table in the corner of the dining room, watched Jason cross the floor in easy strides. He leaned back, rested his elbows on the arms of his chair and made a steeple with his fingers, his rum untouched.

Jason settled into the chair across from Walter. "I'm to leave for Sacandaga as soon as possible." He flexed his shoulders to ease the tension. "Sir William 's agreed to let Lauri be inoculated."

Here and there, the tables were beginning to fill, and the buzz of male voices filled the room. Three couples sat in quiet conversation apart from one another, waiting.

The heat of the day had found its way into the dining room and Walter loosened his shirt at the neck. He slid his untouched rum across the table to Jason.

"What did the boy mean, 'Are we gonna have to swim?'" Walter said.

"A ploy. Sir William knows they can't go back. He's crafty. It worked. They're lining up like cows to be milked."

"He's used you, too," Walter said.

"I suppose."

"How are you to get it all done? Fall's only a few months away."

"A doctor from Albany—he's done it before—and two from Schenectady are coming up. The Albany man's there now, seeing to the building. We're to do a hundred at a time."

"Women and children, too?"

"Even infants."

Walter shook his head. A dark lock fell over his forehead.

"When did you get back?" Jason asked. "I was up to Butlersbury a few days ago. They weren't expecting you."

"Last night. Had enough of New York. I high tailed it over here when I heard what was going on. Figured you'd need my help."

"You'll watch over Lauri? I don't trust Geoff."

Walter sat up straight, his eyes fixed on Jason's face. "She told you?"

Jason nodded. "Why do you have to be so loyal?" His jaw tightened. "Do you know the hell the two of you put me through? I even accused you of stealing her from me."

"It would make me a happy man if she'd have me."

"She won't. I'll see to it."

They eyed each other for a long time, neither saying more, silently admitting what they knew to be true. They both loved the same girl.

They walked out together, the rum untouched.

CHAPTER 12

Sacandaga—June 1773

Lauri had never been so sick; thrashing about on her straw pallet, the same dream repeating—again and again and again—disturbing her sleep until she was exhausted.

In her dream she was standing in a clearing, two large cabins before her. The smell of freshly cut cedar logs mingled with the odor of rum, vinegar and limewater.

The sound of the Sacandaga's flowing water was muffled by the forest. The green of the trees, merged with the blue cloudless sky, like a painting on canvas.

Everything seemed to be crushing her; the stifling muggy heat, the stillness of the forest, the sullenness of the Highland men, the submissiveness of the women and the obedient compliance of the children; like lambs being led to slaughter.

Jason introduced the three other doctors—faceless faces—nameless names. Only she and Jason had faces, only she and Jason had names.

"Time to go in." Jason would say, draping his arm across her shoulder.

They entered the cabin, the other women trailing behind.

"Where are the men?" Lauri said.

"They've gone to the other cabin," he told her. "We have to keep you separate so you women can have privacy during your illness."

She did not understand, but she did not question him. She was not ill, and had agreed to be inoculated only because Jason had asked Sir William to allow her to be included with the Highlanders.

The women were told to remove everything but their chemise. Their clothing, as well as the children's, was taken away, cleaned, tagged and placed on a shelf until the day they would leave.

Each person was given a straw filled pallet on a sleeping space off the floor, slop jars underneath.

The women were lined up while Jason and the other doctors made a small incision in their skin, placed a piece of lint soaked in pus on the cut and laid a square of clean linen over the gash and bound the wound with dried thread. The children wailed but quieted at their mother's command.

Lauri would wake up, glance around with lifeless eyes and fall back to sleep, only to have the same dream. Had she been able to raise her voice louder than a whisper she would have told Jason what she thought of him and his inoculation. Her choice of words would not be those a lady should use.

When at last she was lucid, she found Jason standing at her bedside. How many days had she been lying there? She had lost track of time.

The worry lines seemed to fade from his face when she opened her eyes. She thought he wanted to kiss her, but would not; not if front of the others. Maybe he would do that later when he could kiss her the way a man in love should.

Jason placed a cool cloth on her forehead. "The worst is over," he said. "You'll be able to go home soon."

Someone brought her milk from which the butter fat had been removed, and also some soup; vegetable, since no animal food was allowed.

As her mind cleared, she began to remember.

Jason had scratched her arm, put the dreaded disease into it, purged her with calomel which left her bowels so empty there was nothing left to pass, given her what he said was tartar emetic that made her vomit until there was nothing inside to heave.

Lauri remembered Jason telling her that the inoculation would take effect after the third day. Three or four days later she was feverish and had chills. Pain, such as she had never known, shot through her back, loins and shoulders. She thought her head would burst like an over ripe melon smashed along a roadside.

These were the symptoms of smallpox, he said, as if that should mollify her. He hovered around her like a mother hen, vexing her.

"Go away!" She wanted to scream. "Let me die!"

On the ninth day, the pustules appeared. Jason kept a steady watch, all the while attending to his other patients, worrying the other doctors who were anxious about his well being.

He became testy, churlish.

"I can carry my own load!" he snapped when they offered to relieve him so he could get some much needed rest.

Pus formed, became encrusted, and by the fifteenth day Lauri's head was so swollen, Jason prayed she would not go blind.

Three days later the encrustation was complete, the scabs began to fall off. By the third week she was free from contagion and ready to report to the supervising cleanser of the shifting room where she washed in rum and was fumigated.

She dressed in fresh clothes and waited for Jason to take her to the place where Walter sat outside the limits set by the doctors for the safety of the populace, although there was no populace for miles around.

Soldiers from Johnson Hall, who had smallpox the natural way or had been inoculated, patrolled the periphery against trespassers, especially curious Indians.

"The tribes are touchy enough without bringing an epidemic down on their heads," Sir William said.

Lauri would have collapsed if Jason's strong arm had not supported her. The heat threatened to press her into the ground, bearing down on her like a giant granite slab. She could hardly move her feet.

She watched the Highlander families climb into their wagons, the horses snorting and stomping their feet, impatient to be away from the biting horse flies.

Jason handed Lauri up to Walter, miserable at the thought of sending her off with another man who loved her.

"Take good care of her," Jason said. "She's had a bad time." He was irritable. He had never been so tired, and it would be weeks before he would see her again, weeks she would be spending with Walter.

"I'll take her to Butlersbury. Mother will tend to her. Lauri's all right, isn't she?"

"We wouldn't let her go if she wasn't well."

Walter settled Lauri on the seat beside him, tucking a light robe around her knees. She leaned her head against his shoulder and closed her eyes.

The Highlanders began to move down the narrow trail toward Johnstown. Walter took his place at the end of the line, and waited until the last wagon was out of sight, holding back until the dust settled. He reached down and touched Jason's shoulder.

"I didn't mean for it to happen," he said. "Lauri doesn't know."

Jason forced a smile and clasped Walter's hand. "You won't have her, you know. I'll see to it."

Walter clucked and the horse started. Lauri lost her balance. He wrapped a protective arm around her shoulder, and drew her close. It wasn't long before she fell asleep.

He lagged behind. He could still hear the creaking of the wagons, the shouts of the men cursing the horses.

He needed time to sort things out. He slapped the reins across the horse's rump and it picked up the pace. He had to reach Butlersbury in all possible haste. Her nearness was disturbing.

Catherine Butler treated Lauri as her own, fattening her with delicious meals and tasty drinks, seeing that she rested several times a day. Deborah was thrilled to have her adopted sister, as she called her, with them. Walter's three brothers accepted Lauri with indifference. John Butler took it all in with an indulgent smile.

Shortly after she was taken to her room, Lauri heard Walter and his father talking in the yard outside her window. She could not hear what was said, but they seemed to be having some sort of disagreement. Walter mounted his horse, and raced down the road. John Butler shook his head, turned on his heels and walked back into the house.

When Catherine spoke to John about it, he chuckled. "My dear, are you blind? The lad's in love with her."

Lauri had not seen Walter since the day she arrived. She could not fathom what she had done to nettle him. He came back a day before she left Butlersbury, but did not explain his absence of nearly a fortnight.

She had nearly finished packing her few belongings when she heard Walter and his father arguing in the yard. She went to the window, and watched Walter stomp toward the barn. She saw his brothers shake their heads and Walter began hitching the team.

Catherine and Deborah gave Lauri an affectionate squeeze when she came out into the yard. The boys waved, then returned to their chores in the barn. John hugged her, and lifted her up. She had a brief flash of memory; of a day long ago, of a young girl dressed in a fur trimmed cloak, clutching a doll, also dressed in a fur trimmed cloak. The girl was lifted onto a wagon seat beside a stranger, leaving behind love and security.

Walter sat stiffly on the seat. He gave the reins a smart snap, and they moved down the road. The clop of hooves and the creaking of the cart were the only sounds as they left Butlersbury behind.

Lauri was glad to see her house was as she had left it, although the herb garden was nearly overgrown with weeds. She unlocked the door and stepped inside, but not before she saw a face at the window across the street.

Walter followed her into the house.

"Whatever would I do without you?" she said, standing on tiptoes to kiss his cheek.

His lips found hers and he kissed her. He could not be this near to her and not take her in his arms. For a sensible man he was as confused as a schoolboy in love for the first time.

The passion in his kiss unnerved her, but she responded to his caresses, slipped her arms around his neck, and gave herself up to the thrill that surged through her.

His hand slid down her back, and he pressed her hard against him. The sharp intake of her breath brought him to his senses. He turned on his heel and walked out without a word.

CHAPTER 13

Sir John, and Stephen Watts, Lady Mary's younger brother, were on their way to Johnson Hall to see John's ailing father. Stephen spotted the young woman as she walked along the dusty road ahead of them.

"Who is she, John?"

"Laurice Howell," Sir John said. "I would have expected her to be betrothed to Jason Dayemon by now."

"She isn't?"

"Not that I've heard."

"Hurry, John, I want to get a look at her."

Stephen walked his horse until he was beside Lauri.

She was a might too thin, Stephen thought, but she might offer a diversion while he visited his sister and brother-in-law. He was nearing nineteen, out from under his mother's constraints, and life at Fort Johnson was becoming somewhat tedious.

Sir John joined them. "Good morning, Lauri."

She looked up and smiled when she saw the young baronet.

"Good morning, Sir John," She dipped a curtsy. "I wish you and Lady Johnson every happiness." She continued to smile at him. "It's good to have you back."

"My Lady and I thank you," He nodded toward the young man beside him. "May I present my brother-in-law, Stephen Watts."

"Mistress Howell," Stephen leaned down and took her hand, brushing it with his lips. "I was not expecting to find such beauty so far from New York." His eyes captured hers and held her hypnotized.

Sir John turned away, afraid he would laugh at such twaddle.

"I hope Sir William is feeling better," Lauri's words were directed to Sir John, but her eyes were on the handsome young man who gazed at her so intimately.

"No, he's bedridden much of the time. I was hoping Jason might bring something new that would help him. Stephen and I are on our way to see him."

Young Watts heard nothing of the conversation. He was aware only of the beautiful young woman whose hand he still held.

Sir John's mount danced sideways and snorted his impatience. John stroked the horse to calm him. "Stephen, we must be on our way."

Stephen shifted in his saddle, casting a questioning glance at Sir John. "Yes, yes," he said. He released Lauri's hand and tipped his tricorn. "I hope we meet again soon, Mistress Howell."

They rode off down the road leaving Lauri to stare after them. No man had paid her that kind of attention, not even Jason. Geoff only wanted her body. Walter wanted her, too. She had felt his need. Yet, it had not been lust. If she didn't know better, she would say it was love.

This was something new; a man who paid her compliments with his eyes and touch.

She watched them turn onto the road to The Hall

I hope you do see me again, Mr. Watts.

What harm would it do to see someone else? Jason had not declared his intentions, except to say he loved her. Loved her? Like a friend? He had said that when he was twelve years old.

His kisses now were not brotherly. Maybe he had learned to kiss that way when he was in New York.

He had always been her rock, and she loved him, but was she in love with him? She was inexperienced in the ways of the heart. Maybe she should not rush into any kind of union just yet.

Sir John and Stephen rode for nearly a quarter of a mile in silence before Stephen spoke. "You say Mistress Howell is not betrothed?"

"I would have expected Dayemon to have asked for her hand long ago."

"The man must be a fool to let that tempting morsel slip away."

Johnson laughed. "Best not let Polly hear you talk like that. She'll pack you off to New York."

"I want to see more of her, John."

Sir John reined in his horse. "Don't trifle with her, Stephen. Life has not been kind to her."

Stephen raised a questioning eyebrow.

Sir John nudged his horse, and as they rode, he told Stephen about Lauri's life—her arrival at The Meadows following her parent's death, her friendship with Jason Dayemon and Walter Butler, Belle's treatment of her.

"Belle's a mean spirited shrew," Sir John said, "nasty as all hell. Mulish, too, when she wants to be. Elder did nothing to help the child until Geoff tried to rape her."

"Geoff?"

"Baxter's son. Elder set Lauri up in a house in Johnstown, and Gil Tice gave her a job at the tavern."

"I do want to see her again. How can I arrange it?"

"I understand she plies a fine needle. You need another shirt, don't you?"

"You'll not tell Polly."

Sir John smiled. He liked young Watts, who was slowly crossing the line from youth into manhood. "Man to man, it shall be our secret."

Three days later, Stephen stood on Lauri's doorstep, fidgeting with the stock around his neck. He had a creepy feeling he was being watched. He thought he saw someone at the window of the house across the street. He turned for a better look. Nothing. Was it his imagination?

He raised the knocker.

Lauri opened the door, her look of surprise changing to one of pleasure.

"Mistress Howell," Stephen said, "Sir John told me that you're a fine seamstress. I've need of a new shirt. Would you...?"

"Please come in." She stepped aside so he could enter.

"I dare say a pair of eyes are watching us," Stephen said.

"Oh, you're quite right, Mr. Watts," Lauri's eyes twinkled, as though she considered the idea amusing. "Mrs. Wemple keeps watch over me."

Stephen held out a parcel for her inspection. "The merchant said it was his finest linen."

Lauri opened the package. It was as the storekeeper had presented it; the finest linen. Stephen must have paid a dear price. The shopkeeper might have sized Watts up as a fop, but it would not take him long to realize that the handsome stranger was Sir John's brother-in-law. No, Stephen would have bought it for a fair sum.

Stephen felt like a dismissed child when she told him when to return for the shirt. He could think of no excuse for lingering. He started for the door.

"Mr. Watts," Lauri hastened to say. "forgive my lack of manners. Would you like some cider?"

"Yes. That would be refreshing. It's a long ride to Fort Johnson."

She came back from the kitchen carrying two pewter mugs.

He seated himself on the bench, stretched his long legs, crossed his polished boots at the ankles. "Sir John tells me you have been inoculated against smallpox. That's a very brave thing to do."

"Jason—Doctor Dayemon—tells me it is perfectly safe."

"I'm sure he gave you sound counsel."

He found himself watching her every movement; the way she brushed a stray curl from the side of her cheek, the delicate way she used her hands to describe something—especially the way her eyes shone when she spoke of Jason Dayemon. Why should he feel a prick of jealousy when she mentioned the young doctor?

He rose, reluctant to leave, but he had already stayed longer than was proper. He bade her goodbye and kissed her hand, holding it longer than he should, pleased to see she made no effort to withdraw it.

He strode down the walk, humming softly to himself. He glanced across the street. Beyond a shadow of a doubt, he saw someone step back from the window. He touched his forehead in a salute to Mrs. Wemple, and mounted his horse.

CHAPTER 14

Stephen had tossed on his bed most of the night. Sir John's words troubled him—'Don't trifle with Lauri, Stephen. Life has not been kind to her'.

Stephen had thought that having a fling with Lauri would be nothing more than a lark. She was, after all, only an orphan raised by a wealthy family. His friends had told him such a person was to be used and tossed aside. They were wrong.

He was glad he had come to the Mohawk Valley with his sister and brother-in-law. He had not expected this turn of events when they left New York the Monday following the wedding.

He had wanted to see the frontier wilderness and find Indians. Instead, he had lost his heart.

Stephen stopped Sir John's carriage in front of Lauri's house, tied the reins to the picket fence, and walked up the path to her door.

Once again he found himself raising the knocker, and once again he saw the curtains move at the window of the house across the street.

"Come with me and show me the countryside," Stephen said when Lauri opened the door. "You have the day free, don't you?"

"Let me grab my shawl."

He helped her into the carriage, and they rode out of town.

She took him past Butlersbury, and the cabin where Jason's family lived.

When they turned on to the road to The Meadows, he asked her to take him there.

"I've never been back," she said. "There are too many bad memories."

"Then we won't go."

He turned the carriage around, and almost collided with a horseman racing down the road; a man in his mid twenties, his hair carelessly tied at the nape of his neck. His straggly beard, disheveled clothes, and watery blue eyes stamped him as one who was well into his cups despite the early hour.

Stephen had never seen a man so badly scarred, nor such viciousness in anyone's eyes.

He felt Lauri tremble, and he touched a reassuring hand to hers. She swayed against him. He pulled her into his arms, and she clung to him, quivering.

Geoff Baxter had once been handsome enough to attract any girl he wanted, going as far as entertaining the idea of marrying the daughter of a well to do Albany merchant. She would have brought a substantial dowry; enough to let him enjoy his gambling. Her father would cover his losses. Scandal was one thing the old man wanted to avoid at all cost.

She was a pretty girl, no raving beauty, but would satisfy him until he tired of her. There would be no such thing as a divorce; her father would insist on that, and if the old fool offered him a bribe to avoid any hint of gossip, so much the better. He would be well paid for his discretion, but most certainly would not give up his carousing and gambling.

Geoff never looked at Watts. Without a word he rode on.

Shaded by the maples, he watched the carriage roll down the road. The macaroni had not looked back to see if he was being followed.

No matter; he had no quarrel with young Watts, and there was no use getting Sir John's dander up. Johnson had made it plain enough he wanted Geoff to settle his gambling debts.

Stephen Watts was of no consequence to him. There were three others whose scores needed settling:

That chit Lauri, most of all; riding around in Sir John's carriage, acting the lady. She was the reason people shuddered and turned away when they saw his face. She would pay and pay dearly.

Jason, Sir William's pet, who had been trained to be a doctor, had been sent to King's College, and was now part of the baronet's household.

His father—the man who never loved him or his sisters,—who showered his affection on that orphan. Worst of all; had marked him, making it impossible to form any kind of relationship with a respectable girl, forcing him to take to bed the dregs of the foulest taverns.

They would all pay. He had time. He would wait. They would all pay.

Fort Johnson

That evening, after Polly had retired for the night, Stephen told Sir John about the encounter.

"That was Geoff Baxter," Sir John said. "It's a good thing you were there. Heaven only knows what he might have done. He's never forgotten the beating he took from his father. He's like his mother. There's no forgiveness in their hearts. They've lost control of Lauri, and it rankles them."

John Watts, Polly's and Stephen's father, on his way to Montreal and Quebec, had stopped at Fort Johnson to spend some time with his new son-in-law. "You're sure Stephen's no trouble?"

"None at all, sir," Sir John said.

"He's gone much of the time," Polly said, "though I don't know what he finds to interest him."

Sir John smiled. "He's a young man, my dear. There's much for him to see."

"Well, I've not seen much of him," John Watts grumbled. "His mother will be greatly disappointed to hear he's not seen fit to visit with me."

Polly glanced at John. *Father's being petulant*, her look warned. "He's but a mere lad, father. He means no disrespect."

"I suppose you're right. Young people today have no tolerance for the old."

Shamed by Polly's gentle scolding, Stephen spent the next few days and evenings with his father, uncomfortable in his company, unable to shake off the feeling John Watts suspected something. Had a look, a gesture, given him away? Watts never questioned him, and Stephen was relieved when his father left to continue his journey to Canada.

Fall was in the air.

Polly and Stephen were just finishing a late breakfast when they heard Sir John in the entrance hall.

He was smiling when he strode into the dining room. Dust covered his riding clothes. He loosened the stock at his neck, and tossed his riding crop on the sideboard.

"Good news. Father is feeling a little better. He's planning a sport day." Sir John picked up a slice of fried ham from the chafing dish and began to nibble.

"He says he wants the whole valley to meet his daughter-in-law...the most beautiful daughter-in-law a man can have." John brushed Polly's white palm with his lips.

Polly laughed. "John, I vow your father brought the old blarney with him from Ireland."

"A sport day, John? What is it?" Stephen asked.

"Games and contests. Horse racing, boxing. And food. You've never seen so much food. The whole valley pours out for sport day. And he's planned a grand ball, just for you, my love."

"Is he well enough?" Polly said.

"It's what he wants to do. He may not have much more time, Polly. If it makes him happy, so be it."

"When will it be?" Stephen asked.

"In a couple of weeks."

Stephen laid his fork on his plate.

"Polly," Stephen said, "there's something I must tell you. I'm courting a girl. She's Elder Baxter's charge."

Polly clasped her hands in her lap. "The Howell girl? John's told me about her."

"I want to escort her to the sport day."

"I must meet her first. Then we'll discuss it."

Stephen kissed Polly on the cheek and hurried from the room.

"So that's what's wrong with the lad," Polly shook her head. "No wonder he's been acting in such a strange way."

"He fashions himself in love," Sir John said.

"Don't be foolish, John. What would he know about love at his age?"

"Ah, my sweet, weren't you the same age when you fell in love with me?"

"It's different with a girl," Polly said. "Men take longer to decide such things."

Sir John laughed heartily and kissed her.

"John, the servants may be watching."

He kissed her again and led her by the hand up the stairs to their room.

CHAPTER 15

Tice's Tavern

Stephen's mind was abuzz with plans and problems. He had to tell Lauri about the ball. What if she was stubborn, and refused to attend. What if Polly proved difficult?

John would help. He had said Lauri had been unkindly treated by life. Yes, John would stand by him.

It was nearing noon, and mid-day meal preparations at Tice's were underway. Stephen found a table in the corner of the taproom, away from the steady hum of voices, the clatter of dishes. He held a tankard of grog between his slender hands; hands that had never done a hard days work. He would have to make the watered rum last a long time. He was not used to hard drink. John even refused him anything stronger than wine.

"Ready for another?" Gil Tice towered over him, waiting to refill Stephen's mug.

"No," Stephen said, "I still have plenty."

"If you're not going to drink, maybe you'd like to eat," Gil said.

Stephen pulled his gold watch from, his coat pocket. It was well into meal time. He could not sit here nursing a mug of grog. A plate of Christina Tice's delicious food would give him time to consider what he would say to Lauri.

The Road to Fort Johnson

The carriage rolled down the dusty road toward Fort Johnson. Stephen had overcome Lauri's arguments about attending Sir William's big doings. He had even talked her into meeting Polly.

They came over the crest of the hill and started down.

The Mohawk River sparkled in the sun. It flowed east, in no particular hurry to reach the Hudson River; taking its own sweet time as it divided and drifted past a large island and several smaller ones.

Outbuildings were clustered around the grey stone, three storied house that faced the King's Highway.

A big barn and stable were downwind of the house. As they neared the buildings a man led a black horse toward the paddock.

"That's Polly's," Stephen told Lauri. "Isn't she a beauty?"

Stephen pointed out the cooper's house, bake house, the pigeon house, and the aqueduct which ran from the mill dam to the mill.

As they neared the main house, a small, white, clapboarded building straddling Kayderosseras Creek attracted Lauri's attention.

"Clever idea, isn't it?" Stephen said. "It's the necessary house. The stream washes away the…."

Lauri blushed.

"Polly would be shocked," Stephen chuckled "Not a topic for polite conversation, she'd say."

Stephen stopped the carriage in front of the house, hustled to Lauri's side, and lifted her out.

"Did you notice there is no door on the back of the house? John says because the house sets so close to the hill in back, it would have been easy for the French to take the house if they ever attacked. Sir William had the blockhouses built for protection during the war, too."

Lauri trembled as she walked slowly toward the front door. Why had she ever agreed to come here? Stephen's firm grip on her arm was the only thing that kept her from running away.

"You'll love, Polly," Stephen said. "She's kind and caring."

"But she's Lady Johnson."

"She's Polly, for all her fancy title. Besides, Sir John is on our side."

Unlike Johnson Hall, the receiving room was not painted and papered in bright colors. The windows were deeply set and there were shutters inside and out, as useful for protection from the French and Indians as for warmth.

A large fireplace used up much of the end wall. A one hand clock, taller than Sir John, stood in one corner and a harpsichord sat in the other. Stephen had told her Sir John had learned to play it when he was in England.

Lady Mary was seated on a straight backed chair. Sir John stood beside her. Lauri offered a proper curtsy when Sir John welcomed her and presented her to Lady Mary.

The afternoon passed. Sir John entertained them with a few selections on the harpsichord. Lauri sat enraptured. She had never heard anything as beautiful as the quills plucked the strings while Sir John's fingers deftly traveled the keys.

The meeting went well, in spite of Lauri's fears, and when it was over, Polly had agreed to the loan of a gown and had even offered, with Stephen's and Sir John's help, to teach Lauri the cotillion, quadrille and minuet.

Lauri laid her head against Stephen's shoulder as he drove Sir John's carriage toward Johnstown. "You were right. Lady Mary is kind."

A few miles from Fort Johnson, Stephen stopped, and took Lauri in his arms, and kissed her. She did not resist.

The weeks before the sport days were busy ones for Lauri—trips to Fort Johnson for fittings, dinner with Sir John, Lady Johnson and Stephen, and their other guests who seemed to come and go like the flow of the Hudson River tide at Albany. She felt shy and ill at ease among the gentry at first, but they took such delight in teaching her the dances that she finally relaxed.

Lauri found the figures were not too different from the country dances she already knew, only more sedate and precise.

"To give you time to flirt with the handsome unmarried men," Polly said.

Lauri blushed. "What would Stephen think of me?"

Evening—Fort Johnson

Candles were burning in the long narrow back room Sir John used for an office. Now and then the flames flickered and the papers on the desk rustled.

Stephen quietly paced in the reception room. He needed to talk to John. The questions he needed to ask would affect not only his own life, but Lauri's as well.

John's relationship with Clarissa Putnam was a difficult matter for Stephen to discuss, but he had to know how John had handled the matter when he asked Clarissa to come live at Fort Johnson. How had he resolved the problem of Sir William's refusal to approve a marriage between the two, forcing John to put her out of his life and bed?

"Stephen, stop that incessant pacing," Sir John stood framed in the doorway. He had removed his stock, and his shirt was open at the neck. Little drops of perspiration stood out on his broad forehead, his hair was damp at the temples.

"I'm sorry, John, I didn't mean to disturb you. I have a problem."

"That's plain to see. Come in here if you want to talk about it."

Sir John closed the door into the hall and the one connected to the reception room.

"I want to take Lauri to New York," Stephen said.

Sir John's brow wrinkled. "Just how do you plan to do that?"

"I was hoping you might help."

"Me?"

"I've no money."

"Nor is it likely you'll get any if you try such a foolish thing."

"I was hoping you might give me an advance. I'll repay you when I reach my majority. I have money coming."

Sir John stroked his chin. "You're young, Stephen."

Watts started to protest.

Sir John raised a hand to silence him. "To help you would place me in a most difficult position. There's Polly and your family. I'd hardly be starting off on the right foot." He placed a brotherly hand on Watts' shoulder.

"Turning Clarissa, and the children out was the hardest thing I've ever had to do. I love Polly, but I feel less of a man for what I've done to my first family."

"I love her, John."

"Don't ask that of her, Stephen. It will break her heart and yours if you must give her up someday."

CHAPTER 16

Jason rounded the corner on to Lauri's street. He saw Sir John's carriage draw up in front of her house. He stopped and waited.

The driver, a young man about his own age, jumped down, looped the reins over the picket fence, and went around to the other side. He had a jaunty, carefree air, and when he lifted Lauri from the carriage he held her too long and too close. He kissed her gently.

Jason sat his horse watching, tired after the long weeks at Sacandaga, cursing himself for counting the days until he could be with her. It was plain to see she was not biding her time. How many others beside Walter, and this macaroni did she have on the string?

He had been a fool to come directly to Lauri. He should have gone to Johnson Hall.

He fought the urge to charge down the street and claim what was his. Weary as he was, he could not hope to best the handsome young fop. Despite the easy way the fellow moved, he looked like he could give as good as he could take.

Jason rode away.

Doctor Daly's Cabin

"You look tired to the bone," Daly said when he answered Jason's knock. "Have a bite to eat and then sleep as long as need be."

Jason slept the clock around and then some. It was late when Jason, still groggy, stumbled into the outer room.

Daly was busy at his desk. He looked up from his work, scowling at Jason's gaunt face and scrawny body. "We've got to fatten you up, lad."

"There wasn't much time for feasting," Jason said.

"I dare say there wasn't from the looks of you," Daly leaned back in his chair. "I'll tell Sir William you're back. He wants a full report when you feel up to it."

"I'll go over to see him this afternoon."

Daly smiled. "You're just in time for the sport days Sir William's planning."

"All for my benefit, I suppose," Jason said.

"Should be," Daly agreed, "but it's to show off his new daughter-in-law. The Irish take great stock in such things, you know. I heard she brought her brother with her. Likeable young lad, so I've been told.

"I'll have my girl draw you a bath. Take a good soak. You'll need it. You'll be darn near as busy here as you were at Sacandaga. Damned if I know how the women around here get themselves knocked up the way they do. One nipper after another, with a girl child thrown out for good measure."

Jason threw himself into his work with Daly. This was why he had trained, but the long hours in the saddle, tending Sir William's tenants drained him of what little energy he had.

Night found him sinking into a restless sleep, disturbed by dreams of Lauri, and the day he had left Sacandaga. The last of the Highlanders had gone home. Everything but the medical supplies had been destroyed.

"You did a fine job, doctor," the Albany doctor had said. "Get along to your girl. I'll finish here."

The dreams, and Walter's nagging had brought him back to Lauri's doorstep, his hand ready to grasp the knocker.

"She ain't there. Ain't been there much to speak of since young Watts started comin' round."

Jason whirled around to see Agatha Wemple step through the open gate and hobble down the path on aching feet.

She pointed a bony finger toward the herb garden. "Ain't tended to that, neither."

She squinted at Jason. "Ain't you Doctor Dayemon?"

"I am."

"Well, you're wasting you're time, young man. Young Butler ain't been around neither. Young miss ain't gonna have nothin' but heartache with the likes of Lady Johnson's brother."

Jason stormed past her. She was like a broadside, hawking everyone's business. How she could see so much with her fuzzy vision was beyond him.

In the time he had been away, Lauri had seen fit to take up with someone else, and he had worried it was Walter who had stolen her heart. Instead, she had set her sights higher.

Well, let young Watts have her. If Watts broke her heart, so be it. She had done a good job of breaking his.

They saw each other only once before Sport Days. It was a brief meeting that ended in a confrontation; each accusing the other of indifference.

He and Walter continued meeting at Tice's in the evening. Sometimes they both made it. Just as often as not only one showed up.

It had been an especially hard day, and Jason was glad to see Walter waiting for him. He plopped into a chair and Walter pushed the mug of rum across the table to him. Jason took a long swig and felt the tension easing from his tired body.

It didn't take Walter long to say what was on his mind.

"Have you seen Lauri?"

"She has no time for me."

"Good heavens, man, she's waited two years for you. How much longer do you expect her to wait?"

"Watts seems to be doing a good job of keeping her busy."

"It's nothing but an infatuation. Watts will be going back to New York soon. What then?"

"That's up to her," Jason took another swallow of rum.

"Easy," Walter warned, "that stuff will do you in. I don't fancy lugging you back to your cabin."

CHAPTER 17

Johnson Hall—Early Fall, 1773

Steamy August with its stifling humidity, haze that veiled the hills with a gray shroud, and made the mist and fog rise above the river and streams slipped into September.

The day of the festivities, and the introduction of Sir John's bride, arrived on a soft warm breeze with just a hint of fall in the air.

Tice's tavern was filled to overflowing. Men came from Schenectady and Albany, as far away as New York and New England, to buy Sir William's blooded horses.

Lauri was ready when Stephen arrived to take her to Johnson Hall. She had even remembered to chew some fresh parsley to freshen her breath.

Stephen helped her into the carriage, and as they passed townspeople, she could tell from their glances that her friendship with Stephen was common gossip.

Farmer's wagons, vendor's tents and Indian bark shelters clustered along the road like little villages. Smoke from cook fires drifted toward the sky, carrying with it the mingled aroma of roasting game, baking bread and stewing vegetables.

The Palatine farmers were tending the animals they hoped would win the most skilled breeder award. Men trudged toward the tents where they had left their older sons to keep watch over the crops they had entered for judging. They were mindful of the fact that there were those who were not above damaging another man's product.

Others had come to learn about the sheep Sir William had introduced to the valley. They were considering raising them as a hedge against the time when there might be a blight or a lowering of the price of wheat.

Vendors checked their wares.

Here and there groups of men were already gambling. Lauri spotted Geoff. He did not in even notice her.

Stephen's chatter helped to lessen her jitters, but when she spotted Jason talking to Doctor Daly and Walter, the butterflies in her stomach began to flutter.

Stephen drew the carriage to a stop, handed the reins to a servant, and bounded nimbly to the ground.

Doctor Daly smiled a greeting and Walter walked over to meet them.

"You're as pretty as ever," Walter said. Lauri leaned toward him. His hands encircled her small waist, and he lifted her out of the carriage.

Jason stood stiff and unbending. He was wearing the shirt she had made for him, loose fitting now because of the weight he had lost at Sacandaga.

Daly nudged him, his lips mouthing words Lauri couldn't hear. Jason gave the doctor a scorching look and stepped toward them.

"I'm Doctor Dayemon," Jason reached to shake Stephen's hand.

"My pleasure, Doctor. Stephen Watts.".

"You'll be returning to New York soon, Mr. Watts?"

"I have some unfinished business to attend to—" he shrugged, "then who knows."

Doctor Daly introduced himself, and moved on.

"Save a dance for me, Lauri," Walter said before he faded into the growing crowd.

"You're looking well, Lauri," Jason said.

"You took good care of me."

"No more than I'd do for any of my patients," He wished them a good day and walked away.

"How much longer are you going to act like an ass?" Walter demanded when Jason stepped up beside him. "That was uncalled for."

"I thought I was quite civil."

"You haven't been civil to anyone since you came back. You'll lose her if you don't use your head."

"She's made her choice."

The area where Sir William held his councils with the Indians was already filling with people. Noise and merriment were the order of the day. Children raced everywhere, flashes of red, white and black, stopping now and then to gaze in wonder at the caged animal that looked like a human.

One father told the small child at his side, "It's a monkey."

There were pits of roasting oxen, pigs and other delicious smelling meat at the far end of the field. Servants were setting out platters of fruits and vegetables, the like of which Lauri had never seen.

Sir William came out of The Hall, looking pale and tired, leaning heavily on the arms of Elder Baxter and John Butler.

"Ah, me little colleen," the baronet said when he saw Lauri standing there, "you get prettier every time I see you

Lauri flushed as she made her curtsy.

"John and Polly are waiting for you Stephen." Sir William moved slowly down the steps and into the milling throng. Butler and Baxter walked him to a chair set up for the reception line, chuckling as they left him grumbling about being treated like an invalid.

A spontaneous cheer went up from the crowd when Sir John and Lady Mary stepped out on to The Hall porch. They were followed by Sir John's brothers-in-law and sisters—Guy and Polly Johnson, Daniel and Nancy Claus, and Lady Mary's brother, Stephen Watts.

The young couple waved and, with the others, moved out into the grove to be presented. They joined Sir William in the receiving line.

Lauri stood alone at the edge of the crowd. People began to queue up to offer their good wishes to the newlyweds, and to get a close up look at the bride in order to judge for themselves what kind of an asset Polly Watts would be to the Johnsons.

Lauri saw Walter join his family near the head of the line. Jason and Doctor Daly stepped into place with the other members of Sir William's household.

Elder was on his way to join Belle and the girls when he spotted Lauri, and came over to her. "Look at Sir William, Lauri, sitting in his chair like the lord of the manor."

Why hadn't it occurred to him before? All these years Sir William had been building an Irish plantation system; gathering family and friends bound to him by lineage and fidelity to the King.

Those who waited in line had been arranged according to the baronet's patriarchal social system. Family members were first, followed by old friends; the Butlers being foremost.

British officers, wealthy Indian Department contractors, mostly Irish, English and Scotch came next.

Colonel Nicholas Herkimer had come down from his big, red brick house in the wilderness near the little falls, but he, like other Dutch, German and Palatine families, was standing toward the rear.

What would happen, Elder wondered, to Sir William's little world when he died? Sir John was content to live the life of a country gentleman, and while he would inherit the bulk of the estate, he did not have his father's drive or desire for leadership.

The political reins would most likely be handed over to Guy. Happy and jolly, Guy also had an arrogant streak and a haughtiness that kept him from mixing with the common people.

Dan Claus was probably the most astute and capable of the three men, but he was neither blood kin, nor an Englishman

Over the years Sir William had manipulated control over the valley. He had even managed to wrest a county away from Albany. He had named it Tryon in honor of the Governor, a slick political maneuver. He had drawn up the county's boundaries, succeeded in having Johnstown named the county seat, appointed the local officials, controlled the militia, selected the craftsman, tradesman and tenants, who through their industry, added to his coffers.

What bothered Elder was Sir William's exclusion of the Dutch, German and Palatines for the higher offices. They lacked Johnson's leadership, but because of envy and spite, they were waiting for the opportunity to destroy and devour everything Sir William had worked a lifetime to build.

Elder caught a glimpse of Belle glaring at him from her place in line. He gave Lauri a hug, and went to join his family.

As soon as he could sneak away, Stephen joined Lauri and they disappeared into the milling crowd. There was so much to see—a greased pig chase, foot races, a slippery pole climb, not to mention all the food that was waiting to be tasted. It was hard to decide what to do first. They laughed until their sides ached at the wryest face making contest, covered their ears when the worst songs were sung.

Stephen credited himself during the country dances and dared her to do as well at the upcoming evening ball.

Sir John joined them as they walked back toward The Hall.

"Come along you two. Brant and William of Canajoharie are going to wrestle," He chuckled. "They've been doing this since they were boys and Joseph always loses. William's bigger, stronger and younger."

"Where's Polly?" Stephen said.

"She begged off. She said she was tired."

Stephen gave Lauri a questioning look.

"Go along," she said.

As they walked away, she heard Stephen ask, "Joseph's a little old for this sort of thing, isn't he?"

They were too far away for her to hear, but she could see Sir John's animated gestures, and wondered if he was explaining William of Canajohari's relationship to the Johnsons.

She had heard Elder Baxter and John Butler speak of him many times. Following Caty Weissenberg's death, Sir William had taken the niece of the Mohawk chief, King Hendrick, for a wife according to Indian custom. She had borne him three children—William of Canajoharie and two daughters.

Lauri wandered away to stroll The Hall grounds. She was so deep in thought she did not realize anyone was walking beside her until she heard Deborah Butler muttering peevishly under her breath.

"Deborah, what's the matter?" Lauri asked.

"It's Walter, always lecturing me. 'Nice girls don't chase boys,' he says. 'Act like a lady, Remember you're a Butler.' The old prig."

Deborah raced on, her words almost tripping over one another.

"I was talking to Peter Johnson. Oh, Lauri, he's so handsome. I've waited ages for him to notice me," She looked at Lauri, her eyes dreamy. "Then Walter came along and dragged me away."

"He actually hauled you away?"

"Of course not, but he might as well have. It was so embarrassing. I'm sure Peter was going to ask me to dance with him tonight. Now he thinks I'm just a child. He'll probably never speak to me again."

"Of course he will. He's too much like Sir William. I don't think Walter really frightens him."

Lauri guided Deborah to a bench.

Deborah continued to complain about her brother. She finally paused long enough to take a deep breath, and turned to Lauri with a wistful sigh. "I envy you so much."

"Whatever for?"

"To have three handsome men in love with you."

Lauri's reaction made Deborah giggle.

"And who might they be?" Lauri asked.

"Jason, of course, though he hardly matters—he's been in love with you since you were children—Stephen Watts and Walter."

"Walter?"

"Like a moon sick calf," Deborah said, relishing her chance to tell the secret she had harbored so long. "Do you remember when you came to Butlersbury to stay after your smallpox inoculation?"

Lauri nodded.

"And Walter was gone for almost two weeks?"

"Yes."

"He couldn't bear having you so near. It was tearing him apart, knowing you love Jason. I heard him telling my father." She made a face. "Noble, true, loyal Walter. Instead of fighting for you, he did the honorable thing. He left."

She squeezed Lauri's hand. "Marry him, Lauri, then you'll truly be my sister. He'll be so busy making love to you he won't have time to preach at me. I can chase Peter all I want and I won't have to act like a lady."

Lauri watched Deborah flounce away. Her mind raced back to the country dance earlier in the afternoon. Walter had been there, gracious but reserved, ever so gentlemanly when he danced with her.

Three handsome men, Deborah had said.

Stephen Watts? Not likely. It was surprising their paths had ever crossed.

If Walter was in love with her, why didn't he come to spend time with her like he used to. She had never forgotten the feeling of his lips on hers the day he brought her back from Butlersbury. She knew then, as she knew now, that it was not lust he felt for her.

"Jason, of course," Deborah had said, "though he hardly matters."

Jason mattered a great deal, but it was plain to see he didn't care for her. Not the way she cared for him.

He was too busy to give her a thought.

CHAPTER 18

"Joseph lost, just as Sir John said he would," Stephen settled on the bench beside Lauri. "The horse races are next. Would you like to go?"

A good sized crowd had already gathered to watch the race. Lauri and Stephen found a spot near a tree on a slight mound where they could see. Lauri looked up to see a young boy inching out toward the end of a branch.

The starting gun fired and the horses were off.

The horses were rounding the second turn when Lauri and Stephen were startled by the sound of a breaking limb. The boy fell to the ground at Lauri's feet.

Stephen reached to help him.

"Don't touch him, Watts. Let me have a look at him," Jason pushed his way through the people clustering around and knelt beside the half conscious lad. "His arm's broken."

The boy, moaning at Jason's touch, began to stir and thrash around.

"Help me hold him down, Watts. Careful now," The lad struggled all the more.

"I need something to cut with," Jason said.

A fashionably dressed woman elbowed her way through the crowd. She took a scissors from the etui at her waist and gave it to Jason.

"Get your hands off my boy," A stumpy farmer, built like an ox, broad of shoulder and body, short and thickset, seared Jason with his soot black eyes.

"I have to cut his sleeve," Jason said. "He broke his arm. Lauri come here."

Before she realized what he was doing, Jason had raised her skirt and cut a long strip from her petticoat.

Male hoots of approval rippled through the crowd. There was the sharp intake of female breath and a few, *"Well, I never...indecent...did you see that? He bared her ankles."*

As if out of nowhere, Walter appeared and handed Jason several small straight clean cut branches to use for a splint.

Lauri, Jason and Walter chuckled. It was yesterday, when they were children, helping one another.

Jason picked up the boy and motioned the father, Lauri and Walter to follow. Before Butler could join them, the lawyer, Christopher Yates, hailed him.

"Walter. Wait," Yates said, "I've a case I'd like to discuss with you."

The room where Doctor Daly had attended Jason and Lauri was still the same. The mortar and pestle, scarred from hard use, sat on the counter. On the shelves were the bottles and mixtures Dr. Daly, and now Jason, used when caring for the sick. Their instruments were neatly arranged inside the cabinets.

Jason laid the boy on the table. "Hold him down," Jason told the father, "I don't want him to fall."

He went to a drawer, took a key from his pocket, unlocked the drawer and removed another key. He unlocked a wall cabinet, took out a bottle of yellow liquid and mixed it with saffron and canary wine. He locked the cabinet again and dropped both keys into his pocket.

"Lift his head. Easy now. He's in pain and I don't want him thrashing around," He raised a glass of the liquid to the boy's lips, "Drink this."

A beefy hand grasped Jason's wrist.

"What are you giving my boy?"

"Laudanum—opium—just enough to ease the pain."

The man's grip tightened.

"There's no need to worry," Jason said. "I won't give him too much. He won't become attached to it. He'll just drop off to sleep, then I'll set his arm."

The man released his hold and Jason could feel the blood flowing back into his arm. He walked over to the wall and took down some wooden arm splints. "It doesn't look like the bone has broken through. That's good."

The boy drifted into a slight stupor, moaning slightly when Jason removed the makeshift splints and unwrapped the strip of cloth cut from Lauri's petticoat.

Jason set the arm, wrapped it with an eighteen tailed bandage lapped in a diagonal crisscross pattern, made sure it was laid smooth to give tightness and support, and placed the arm in the hollow wooden splints. He attached the longer of the two pieces, the one with a palm support, to the outer one. Brass studs held the leather straps in place, keeping the two pieces together.

He looked up when he heard a faint tapping. A tilt of his head sent Lauri to open the door.

A frail scrawny girl, scarcely younger than Lauri, obviously pregnant, and carrying an infant on her hip, stepped cautiously into the room. Her skirt, blouse and chemise were as faded as her blue eyes, her face as colorless as the hair she had tied with a narrow strip of eel skin. Large anxious eyes settled on the young boy.

"Ain't no need to fret, Jossie," the farmer said. "Ain't nothin but a broken arm."

He scowled when he saw she was alone except for the child she held against her. His coal black eyes hardened and a muscle worked in his short neck.

"Where's the rest of the youngens? Ain't I told you to keep them with you?"

"I asked your sister to watch them."

"Ain't her place, and Adam ain't no concern of yours. Ain't I told you that?"

She withdrew into the protection of her narrow drooping shoulders.

"This here's my wife, Jossie," the farmer said. "Adam's ma died some six months ago and left me with a passel of brats. Jossie's pa's got too many faces to feed so me and Jossie got married. Been good for both of us, ain't it Jossie?"

She didn't answer.

The boy, still groggy from the laudanum, began to stir.

Jason helped him sit up and slipped a sling around the lad's arm, tying it at his neck. "You won't be much use behind a plow for awhile but your Pa will find other chores for you to do."

"You can wager on it," the farmer said.

"Bring him back in two weeks. That splint's not to come off until I see him."

"I've set broken bones myself," the farmer said, "I'll see to it. It's a long ride up here."

"Where're you from?"

"Up along Caroga Creek."

"Is there a doctor up there?"

"No."

"Then bring him back. That's a nasty fracture. Take the splint off too soon and his arm could become useless. He's a husky lad. Good around the place, isn't he?"

"Works like an ox."

"Then the ride back here will be worth it. An ox is hard to come by. You've got one ready made. Two weeks."

Jason helped the boy off the table, steadying him until he got his balance.

"Come along, boy," The father started for the door.

"You'd better give him a hand," Jason said.

The older man kept walking. "Jossie, you're so all fired worried about Adam, help the cripple."

After they left, Lauri asked, "Will he bring him back?"

"Not likely."

"But you said Adam might not be able to use his arm if that old buzzard takes the splint off too soon."

"And his father will curse him for it and me, too, most likely."

"He never offered to pay you."

"I didn't expect he would. I'm sorry about the petticoat.

"What about Jossie? What will happen to her?"

"Probably wear out like his first wife," Jason closed the door and leaned against it.

Lauri reached for the latch.

"Don't go."

"You expect me to stay just because you tell me to? How long have you been back from Sacandaga? Three days? Five days? More than a week? You've never been to see me."

"Oh, I've been to see you," he said. "I went to your house first, before I even told Sir William I was back, but you were too busy riding around in Sir John's carriage with that New York jackanapes, Watts, to even notice me. You enjoyed letting him hold you, didn't you?"

"You were spying on me."

"No, I'll leave that to Mrs. Wemple. I asked you to wait for me. Remember?"

"I waited. I waited for two years. How much longer am I supposed to wait?"

"I nearly killed myself taking care of you at Sacandaga and as soon as you got back to Johnstown you took up with Watts."

"You've no claim on me."

"What about Watts? Does he have a claim on you?"

She refused to answer.

"Don't be a fool," Jason said. "Watts will be going back to New York."

He opened the door and watched her walk away.

The day cooled and the activities wound down.

Sir William presented snuff and a few pounds of tobacco to the winners of the greased pig chase, the boxing and wrestling matches, the greased pole climb and other contests.

The first rider to cross the finish line in the horse race went home with a bearskin jacket.

There hadn't been any brawls and Sheriff White had not made any arrests. It had not been necessary to hold a Court of Py Poudre to settle disputes between traveling vendors and local tradesmen.

By wagon, in carriages and on foot, people streamed from The Hall. Weary mothers, many carrying a sleepy tyke in their arms, trudged toward Johnstown, prodding tired children ahead of them.

The guests who had been invited to the ball drifted toward the house to rest and ready themselves for the evening's festivities.

CHAPTER 19

Johnson Hall

Lauri paused on the staircase landing. She turned her attention to the other guests who had already gathered in the first floor hall. The room was a kaleidoscope of colors as they moved about greeting one another, stopping to speak to a friend, then drifting off to join another group.

She scanned the crowd to find a friendly face. Jason and Walter stood near the doorway of the blue parlor. She could see Walter's lips moving, but Jason did not seem to be listening. He was staring at her as if he were seeing her for the first time.

In a sense, she supposed he was. Certainly he had never seen her brown curls piled high on her head, two coils trailing down behind her left ear and resting on her bare shoulder. He had never seen her dressed in an emerald green silk brocade gown, looped up at the sides and back to reveal the pale yellow silk petticoat embroidered with white daisies.

She raised her hand to her throat. The bodice was cut lower than she liked, and she wished the trim around the neck was as wide as the lace that flared at her elbows.

Her pulse quickened. Jason was the most handsome man in the hall; even if his dark blue coat, his waistcoat of lighter blue and his fawn colored breeches were a trifle loose on his lean frame.

She saw Walter stop in mid sentence and look her way.

Walter would make a wonderful husband and they would have a good life together, but she couldn't marry him unless she could give her heart completely. There was a part of her that would always belong to Jason.

She returned Walter's smile and went the rest of the way to the bottom of the stairs.

Stephen watched and waited on the opposite side of the foyer. He smiled broadly as she walked toward him. He patted her hand lightly when she rested it on his arm. Together, they went to pay their respects to Sir William.

"Be a good lad, Stephen, and bring me some rum.," Sir William dismissed him with a nod of his head. He crooked a finger, and Lauri bent to hear his whispered words.

"When are you going to get that dolt, Jason, to marry you? I don't have many years left and I want to see my namesake."

Stephen returned, and Sir William took the drink. "Ah, that's a good lad," He took a small swallow. "Now, get upstairs, you two. I hear the music."

Lauri hesitated. Sir William flashed her an Irish smile and raised his cup.

When she and Stephen reached the head of the stairs, Lauri saw John and Catherine Butler engaged in a lively conversation with Elder Baxter.

Belle stood next to Patience and Felicity, who were seated at the far end of the room. She had never made any effort to hide her dislike for the Butlers. She called them *Dogs of the Johnsons* and had once confided to her sister, 'I've heard that Catherine enjoys—well, you know—what men and women do in bed.'

Christina and Gil Tice joined Stephen and Lauri. "How lovely you look, Lauri," Christina said.

"Prettiest girl here." Catherine Butler had left the men when she saw Lauri come upstairs. Catherine laid a kiss on Lauri's cheek.

"If you ladies will excuse me," Stephen said, "I'll say hello to Mr. Butler and Mr. Baxter. Will you join me, Mr. Tice?"

Gil made an exaggerated bow. "Charming ladies, I'll take my leave if you will be so gracious as to allow me."

"Tah," Christina chided him, "off with you and your fancy talk."

The dance was beginning, sending the men scurrying to find their partners. The floor began to fill as couples took their places. Stephen returned, gave Lauri's hand a squeeze, and they went to join the other dancers.

Patience and Felicity sat alone, stiff as statues.

"I've only had two glasses of Madeira," Jason said, "but I must be drunk to let you talk me into dancing with the Baxter girls. Come on. Let's get it over with."

Walter grinned. "Which one shall it be?"

"What difference does it make?"

Jason and Felicity joined Stephen and Lauri.

She thought him gallant and considerate. He smiled and was attentive to Felicity.

The music began. Lauri was surprised to see he was a very accomplished dancer. He moved through the figures with ease. It was quite clear he had not spent all his time studying.

She looked at him and saw that he was smiling at her; that silly smile that annoyed her so much.

Lauri recognized the music for the next dance. It was a reel—spirited and lively. Someone, she had no idea who, whisked her away from Stephen. They joined three other couples in the contra line. Before she could get her wits about her, she was following the prompter's cues:

NUMBER ONE COUPLE GO DOWN THE CENTER

She stole a quick look at her partner before they reached the foot of the line. He was a beefy man with hands as big as a bear's paw. He towered over her. He was taller than anyone she had ever seen.

BACK TO THE TOP

In spite of his size and rough appearance, he was not clumsy or awkward. He led her though the figures easily, and when the prompter called:

NUMBER ONE COUPLE PEEL THE SET

His right hand locked onto her right arm, squeezing so tightly she winced. He gave her a vigorous turn and spun her on to the next man who reeled her by the left back to him. The movement became more forceful each time he sent her on to the next man in line.

"Sorry, little lady," he whispered as he turned her for the last time, "I don't mean you no harm, but I got paid good coin for this."

He sent her spinning toward the stairwell.

He sprinted down the stairs, taking them two at a time, raced out the door toward the tavern where Geoff Baxter waited. Baxter had promised a goodly sum, which the bruiser intended to collect after he assured Baxter the dastardly deed had been done.

Jason caught Lauri before she tumbled down to the landing.

Stephen elbowed him aside, and led her to a chair.

Sir John and Lady Mary hovered over her, angry and worried.

"I'll have the scoundrel found and flogged," Sir John said, but the culprit had disappeared.

"John's right," Stephen said, "Whoever did this needs a good comeuppance."

"Stephen," Lauri said, "please take me outside. I need to be alone, to get myself together."

She stood on the porch letting her eyes adjust to the darkness of the starless sky. The air was clean and crisp, refreshing after the oppressive smell of heavy perfume, spirits and stale tobacco smoke inside The Hall.

She began to tremble, not from the cold, but the realization that someone disliked her enough to actually pay to have her hurt.

If she had ever needed comforting she needed it now.

She saw Jason standing alone in the shadows of the blockhouse wall. She moved toward him.

"You shouldn't be outside alone," he said.

She stepped into the flickering light of the pitch torch. "Hold me, Jason. Just hold me."

He wrapped her in his arms, stroked her back, kneaded the tight knots on the back of her neck until he felt her relaxing against him.

He released her and began to pace, running his fingers through his dark wavy hair. "I can't even protect you from some ruffian."

He came back to her, took her in his arms again, and drew her close.

"I want you, Lauri. I want you for my wife, but I can't ask that of you when I have nothing to offer. I don't know how long it will be before I'll have enough money to marry you. I won't hold you bound."

He searched her face, reading the hunger in her eyes and lowered his lips to hers. He kissed her long and deeply

He pushed her away, held her at arms length.

She tried to move toward him.

He shook his head, slipped his arm around her waist, and together they walked toward the house.

Early Morning—Johnson Hall

The sky was still black velvet. The sun had not made an appearance when Stephen was summoned to Sir John's and Polly's room. He dressed quickly, shrugged into a robe, and ignored the grumblings of the other men with whom he shared the room.

The house was quiet. The servants had removed all traces of the ball of the night before. He made his way across the empty hall, and knocked on the bedroom door.

Polly and John were bundled in their warm robes, seated at a small table close to the fireplace, sipping a steaming brew. Their faces were somber, their eyes troubled.

Bright orange fingers of flame wrapped themselves around the big logs, but did little to take the chill from the room.

"This came by express yesterday," Polly said. She slipped a letter into Stephen's hand.

There was no mistaking John Watts handwriting. Stephen broke the seal.

WE HAVE BEEN APPRISED BY A PERSON WHOSE NAME WE CANNOT REVEAL BUT WHO NEVERTHELESS WE BELIEVE TO BE OF HONEST CHARACTER THAT YOU

HAVE BECOME ENAMORED WITH A YOUNG WOMAN OF QUESTIONABLE VIRTUE. RETURN HOME WITH ALL POSSIBLE HASTE.

Stephen handed the letter to Polly, slumped into a chair, leaned his elbows on his knees and lowered his head to his cupped hands.

"How can he believe the lies of a person who is too much of a coward to come forth and be named?"

Polly read the letter and passed it to Sir John. She took Stephen's hand in hers, sympathetic and compassionate, more mother than sister, although she was only fourteen months older.

"What will you do?"

"What choice have I?"

Sir John placed a brotherly hand on Stephen's shoulder. "Polly received a letter from your father, too. He took her to task for not telling him."

"I'll take Lauri back to Johnstown," Stephen said. "I'll make arrangements to leave for New York as soon as I can."

Polly's soft voice stopped him as he opened the door. "What will you tell Lauri?"

"Nothing. Only that I'm needed at home." He turned to face them. "I don't want to leave her."

Polly went to him. "It's for the best."

"Who would write such lies?" Stephen quietly closed the door and went to his room.

It was pushing mid morning when Stephen stopped the carriage in front of Lauri's house.

"May I come in?" It was the first time he had spoken since they left Johnson Hall.

"Of course."

He followed her to the door, snatched the key from her hand when she fumbled with the lock.

It was cool inside. The banked fire gave off little warmth. He paced behind her while she stirred the ashes.

He nudged her out of the way. "Let me do that."

The bellows breathed life into the embers. They began to glow. He added some kindling, and it burst into flame. He placed some larger pieces of wood on top. They caught and a little heat began to creep into the room.

"What's wrong, Stephen?"

"I'm going back to New York."

"When?"

"In a few days."

"I was afraid I'd done something to hurt you," Lauri said.

His lips found hers, and he hugged her fiercely, not wanting to let her go. "No. No. You would never hurt me. I'm needed at home."

He kissed her once more and walked to the door. As he reached for the latch he saw the linen he brought her lying on the table; her scissors, and thread neatly arranged on top.

He stepped out into the crisp September day. He would only have memories to remind him of her. She had never made his shirt.

CHAPTER 20

Johnson Hall—Summer, 1774

The flood tide of white settlers had begun as a ripple, lapping at the mountain forests of Virginia, growing to a wave washing the shores of the Ohio until it threatened to flood the glens and glades of the Mississippi.

From their longhouses and bark shelters, the eyes of the Delaware, Mingo and Iroquois watched the whites pouring onto the lands which the king across the wide water had promised would forever belong to the Indians. They and the king's man, William Johnson, called Warraghiyagey by the Mohawks, had put their marks on the paper at Fort Stanwix.

Were these men foolish enough to turn their backs on their chief across the wide salt lake? Surely they would be punished for breaking the treaty. Everyone knew, red and white alike, that the king had set a boundary which would prevent the Indians from being pushed farther from their ancestral hunting grounds.

How many times had they turned their backs on their dead forefathers, picked up their blankets and kettles, and moved their women, babies strapped to cradle boards, while the land hungry whites stripped the forest, driving out the deer and other game?

The Indians sat around their council fires and waited. While they waited,

Captain Michael Cresap stirred the embers into a flame by killing three peaceful Indians near the Ohio.

Emboldened by Cresap's act, some traders killed the Shawnee Chief, Silver Heels. An aged Delaware Chief, Bald Eagle, was shot while he paddled in his canoe. His canoe and his scalped body were later found drifting down the river.

The death wailing in the primeval thickets found its way to the Longhouses of the Iroquois. The brother and sister of the Cayuga Chief, Logan, were murdered after first being made so drunk they were unable to defend themselves.

While the Delaware, Shawnee and Mingo fell upon the Virginia settlements, Logan appealed to the Onondaga council for support in his revenge. Their eyes turned toward the east.

Warraghiyagey, blood brother of the Mohawks, would avenge these murders.

Sir William had been talking with the tribal leaders since June 19th when a large party of Onondagas arrived to tell him that the chiefs of all the Six Nations were on their way to hold a conference with him regarding the critical state of Indian affairs.

600 Indians poured onto Sir William's land around Johnson Hall. Bark shelters sprang up everywhere. The odor of Indian cooking hung on the muggy summer air. Dogs and children raced wherever they wanted. Sir William's own purebreds had been sent to Fort Johnson to prevent them from mating with the Indian dogs or from being stolen or eaten.

On July 8th the Indians held a meeting with him. They earnestly requested the release of a young prisoner who was being held in the Johnstown gaol. They feared, they said, that the young man, who had been imprisoned for the robbery and murder of four Frenchmen on Lake Ontario, might die since he was not used to being shut in. His friend, who had been confined with him, had already ridden the pale horse.

Sir William listened carefully, agreeing to their request, since restitution had been made. The Indians had brought in bear, raccoon skins. These, as well as other skins, amounted to the loss suffered by the Canadians; a loss Johnson thought to be much exaggerated.

It was his hope, he told the Senecas, that they would remain faithful to his majesty's compassion and that it would be the last of the irregularities on their part.

The Chiefs of the Six Nations held another council with Sir William on July 9th. This meeting, like the one the day before, was also attended by his sons-in-law, Daniel Claus, Deputy Agent of Canada, and Deputy Guy Johnson acting as Secretary.

The three of them sat at a long, intricately carved mahogany table. Several quill pens, ink stands and stacks of papers, weighted down with a tomahawk, were in front of Guy. The men from the Indian Department, who would interpret in the attending nations' language, were scattered among the assembled Indians.

Jason stood on the sidelines, anxious about Sir William's health. Before Sir John's marriage, the baronet had been forced to take to his bed. Now Sir William was spending more and more time there, rising only to take care of the most pressing business. Many of the Indian affairs had been turned over to Guy, but the gravity of the death of Logan's relatives demanded Sir William's personal attention.

The Oneida Chief, Conaghquayeson, opened the meeting with the Ceremony of Condolence on the death of the young Indian prisoner.

Walter translated the Oneida words into English, his strong clear voice carrying over the crowd. He spoke slowly, distinctly so Guy could record every word.

Each interpreter in turn spoke in the language of the Mohawk, Onondaga, Cayuga and Seneca nation.

Jason found a shady place to sit, away from the packed bodies, close enough to keep an eye on Sir William. It was going to be a long, long day.

Serihowane, a Seneca Chief, rose and began to scold Sir William.
Brother Warraghiyagey

He asked Sir William not to believe all the bad reports about the Senecas. He reminded the baronet that the English had not kept their word, and wished the English were as sincere as the Senecas.

What about the Fort Stanwix Treaty? It was supposed to act as a barrier between the Indians and Whites. Time and again the treaty had been broken.

The Indians, he said, had been told by the settlers that the whites would live wherever they pleased.

The tribes hoped the whites would be restrained. If they were not, the squatters would have to answer to a higher authority.

The Seneca Chief was a showman.

As proof of the Seneca's sincerity, he produced the Chain Belt of Alliance, the beaded belt that had been delivered to them at Niagara in 1764.

He turned slowly so all could see, then solemnly showed it to Sir William.

He saw the change in Sir William's expression. His words were having the desired effect.

He waited for John Butler to translate, for the other interpreters to speak, for Guy to record his words.

Serihowane asked Sir William to intercede with the king and the governors on their behalf. On their part, the Indians would try to keep their young men quiet.

To show their sincerity, he presented Sir William with a beaded belt.

A Cayuga War Chief rose and addressed Sir William, saying how disagreeable it was to their nation to have traders continually among them who sold rum, and thereby occasioned much mischief and trouble. He asked they might be stopped and that the traders would bring their goods to the markets on the Mohawk River and not dispose of anything to their people, and at their towns.

When the chiefs had concluded their business, Guy helped Sir William to stand. Warraghiyagey waited, making sure all eyes were on him. Like a trained thespian, his voice reached out to those seated before him. He would, he said, give his answer on Monday.

Sir William, his face an unhealthy grey, his eyes dull, his breathing labored, leaned heavily against Jason, as they climbed the steps into the house.

"They'll not be easily mollified this time. It's bloody rotten, this thing Cresap's done, starting a border war. You're too young to know much about the French trouble but your father remembers. He was with, me, God bless him."

"He's told me many times."

"But you have to live through it, lad, to know the real hell of it."

"They'll listen to you, Sir William. They always have."

Sir William shook his head. "We're in for bad times. Cresap in the west and those arrogant cowards in New England, dressing up and calling themselves Mohawks and dumping the tea. They brought it down on their own heads. The crown's right in closing Boston port."

Long shafts of sunlight streamed through the multi paned windows laying a golden carpet on the highly polished bedroom floor.

Jason eased the baronet onto the edge of the canopied bed and Johnson folded into the feather pillows, motioning to his manservant, Billy, to remove his dust covered boots.

"You'll not be doing this much longer, Billy," Sir William said. There was resignation in his voice.

"I ain't goin' nowhere, Sir William. I'll always be here to help you," He had one boot almost off. "You ain't goin' to sell me, is you Sir William?"

"Who could replace you, Billy?" Sir William closed his eyes. "Where's Molly?"

"Tending to the children, sir," Billy said.

"Tell her I need her. And Guy and Dan, too. We have to go over…"

Jason interrupted, "You need to rest, Sir William."

"Time enough for that when this nasty business is over and done with. Daly's here if I need him. You're worse than a mother hen, Jason, always clucking at me to take care of myself.

"Hie yourself off to my sweet little colleen. Off with you now," He shooed Jason away with a wave of his hand.

"Billy," Sir William said, "get Joseph, too."

As he rode into Johnstown, Jason remembered a bitter March night in Tice's Tavern. The wind that rattled the windows, sent up swirls of snow to stick to the frosted panes.

"You are, without question, the biggest fool I know," Walter said. They sat hugging the fireplace for warmth, talking over their flip. "If Lauri loved me as much as she loves you, I'd marry her if I was a pauper."

"You'll never take a wife," Jason set his mug on the scarred table, "You're married to the king's law."

Walter had been right. He had neglected Lauri, thrown himself into his work, caring for the Johnson family. Lady Mary had become pregnant in October, and he had attended her until she and Sir John left for New York to spend the winter.

During the snowy nights, when sleep was slow in coming, he tossed on his cord bed, concerned about Sir William's and John Butler's tenants.

When daylight finally arrived and a sleigh could not carry him to the isolated cabins, he had put on snowshoes and trudged, more dead than alive, to sit for hours at the bedside of someone beyond his help.

It had been a busy winter. Summer proved to be more so.

Lauri's front door was ajar, the windows thrown wide open. Jason dismounted and looped the reins over the fence. As usual, Mrs Wemple was watching. A grin pulled up the corners of his mouth. He waved and he heard a distinct "hmph" as she moved away from the window. He trudged up the path.

"You look tired," Lauri said when she answered his knock.

"I am. It's been a long day."

"I've never seen so many people in town. Did you know Governor Franklin is here from New Jersey?"

"I saw him at the Hall." No use repeating the gossip that the reason for Franklin's visit to Johnson, just at the time of the council meetings, was to learn how the problems on the frontier would affect the land speculation in which he, and as some intimated, Sir William, were involved.

"Is there going to be an Indian war?" Lauri asked. "I heard Gil talking to some travelers and they said the Indians are all riled up about settlers taking land on the Ohio."

"It's the Pennsylvanians and Virginians. They're the troublemakers," Jason said. "When a man's hungry for land he doesn't care who he steals it from. Besides, that's hundreds of miles from us. There won't be any Indian attacks in the Mohawk Valley."

CHAPTER 21

July 11, 1774

Sir William could see Joseph, Guy and Daniel through the window in front of his desk

Beads of perspiration stood out on Sir William's broad Irish forehead and trickled down the sides of his face. It was stifling in the room, but it wasn't only the heat that made the baronet sweat.

Both Doctor Daly and Jason had urged him, in the strongest terms, to let Guy handle the council affair, warning Sir William that the strain could possibly kill him,

Sir William refused. "Damnit, you know the tribes are waiting to hear what Warraghiyagey has to say," He slumped in his chair. "There's no one but me to do it, and this time I may not be able to help them."

It had been useless for the doctors to argue. While Daly anxiously waited outside, Jason had stayed in the house with Sir William.

"I hate to put on this damned coat," Sir William reached for the scarlet jacket he had draped across the back of his chair, and stepped out into the hall.

Jason followed.

Johnson smiled when he saw Molly, and spoke softly in Mohawk, urging her to support the nations in their time of trouble.

Molly, barely able to veil her concern, touched his hand for a brief moment and her lips lightly brushed his.

Sir William walked out into the brilliant sunlight where the tribes waited.

The baronet was no longer a young vigorous man who could take the stifling July heat. His strength was being sapped, while he listened to each long, tedious oration.

The council fire burned. The chiefs and ranking members of the Six Nations took their places, wondering who would answer their grievances, Brother Warraghiyagey or the king's representative, Sir William Johnson, Superintendent of Indian Affairs in North America.

Sir William was an imposing figure in his gold trimmed scarlet coat, white breeches and shiny black boots. Despite his age, he stood tall, taking in everything happening around him.

Perspiration dampened his uniform but he forced himself to concentrate on the business at hand.

He willed his voice to remain strong. He could not—must not—falter now. Too much hung in the balance. The cord that bound the Six Nations to the crown was fraying, and could become nothing more than a thread which could break at any time.

He began his address:

Brothers

He told them he was glad to hear they persevered in the Remembrance of the Engagements, and he hoped they would abide by them. He spoke of the release of the young Indian as proof of the English Government's tenderness toward them. He assured them he did not incline his ear to evil reports, nor were they in any way suspected.

He was pleased to hear they had preserved the Great Belt. He reminded them that they should keep the contents of it, and the other belts he had given them, in Remembrance. If they did this, they would be able to keep their people in good order, and prevent those who lived a distance from them from following evil Councils, which would reflect on their Confederacy.

As for the culprits who had committed such despicable acts, he assured them, they would be sought after and punished, but it was not easy to find them in so extensive a country, and it was up to the Indians to also seek out and punish those, who by their mischief, afforded encouragement to others.

Then, like a father reprimanding a child, he reminded them that many chiefs to the southward were the real authors of the mischief done by the Indians.

He would, however, lay their complaints before His Majesty and the Governors concerned, that everything that could be done would be done to restore peace and afford them the satisfaction they deserved.

Next he turned his attention to the Cayuga's complaint, telling them he would do everything in his power to prevent further trouble with the traders.

When he had finished, Deckarihoga, Chief of the Canajoharie Mohawks, addressed Sir William:

Brothers

He reminded Sir William that they had never obtained any satisfaction against *that old Rogue, the old Disturber of our Village, George Klock, his artifices and evil conduct*, and because they doubted the English would afford it to them, they found it necessary to mention it before the presence of the whole confederacy so they might espouse their cause, as it was their duty to do.

He did not dwell on the times Klock had cheated them out of their land, instead he went to the heart of the matter:

Klock had seduced one of their young fellows to go with him to England where he displayed the young man at a show and cheated him out of his money.

Sir William answered that they had no need to bring it before their Confederacy, that he would again lay the matter before the Government and use all his power to gain satisfaction for them, and they should refrain from any act of violence. He was authorized, he said, to tell them *Klock's conduct was disagreeable to the king.*

The chiefs listened, impassive as bronze statues.

Warraghiyagey's words did not ring true. The Mohawks, Keepers of the Eastern Door, lulled by his honeyed Irish tongue, had opened the door for him, and he had left it ajar, allowing scoundrels to enter and steal their land.

Disagreeable to the king? Would that get back the lands cheated from the Canajoharies? If Sir William sat in his great house and did nothing while Klock robbed his Indian neighbors, what help could the western tribes expect? Events on the Ohio proved the colonial government could not, or would not, control their people.

Jason left Molly in the house, and went outside to mix in with the crowd listening to the council business. He paused in his wandering long enough to study Joseph Brant sitting by himself, a pace away from the council, like an island separated from the banks of a turbulent stream.

Joseph was a solitary figure, not wholly a part of either the white or red man's world. Even his clothing revealed his confusion about where he belonged; a breech clout over his leggings, moccasins on his feet, but his barrel chest was covered by a white, full sleeved shirt.

Jason moved closer to the baronet, troubled by the slowness of Sir William's faltering words when he ordered pipes and tobacco for the chiefs and adjourned the meeting.

"Whatever may happen," Sir William told the council, "you must not be shaken from your shoes."

He swayed on his feet, and gripped the edge of the table for support.

Guy and Daniel grabbed him and, despite Dan's painful gout, struggled to carry him into The Hall. Jason sprinted toward them, but Joseph was already there. Joseph pushed Dan aside and carried Johnson to his room.

Joseph sat him in a chair. Molly knelt by his side, her tears washing his hands.

Sir William's head lolled to one side, his mouth was slack with flecks of foam at the corners. He rallied slightly when Jason spoke to him.

Jason and Doctor Daly tended to him, using all their skill and knowledge. Sir William revived long enough to ask for Brant.

Joseph, his dark eyes filled with tears, stooped to hear Johnson's words.

"Joseph, control your people. Control your people. I am going away."

Word of Sir William's death spread quickly. An Indian messenger was sent to inform the judges of the Circuit Court, which was in session. The continual tolling of the church bell alerted those who had not heard.

In hushed tones, people talked of Sir John's mad dash from Fort Johnson, how he pushed his horse to the limit until the steed dropped dead, and he was forced to buy another along the way.

He arrived too late to see his father alive.

Only the sounds of the muffled drums and an occasional sob from someone lining the route disturbed the silence as the funeral procession slowly made its way from The Hall to the Anglican Church in Johnstown where Sir William would be laid to rest.

The pall bearers, Governor William Franklin of New Jersey (Benjamin's son) and the Justices of the Supreme Court, wearing crapes and white scarves, as specified in the baronet's will, led the mournful procession. Their white gloved hands rested on Sir William's casket in solemn tribute.

Sir John, stoic in his grief, was followed by Guy Johnson and Dan Claus. 15 year old Peter Warren Johnson, the oldest of Molly's sons. Joseph Brant, William of Canajoharie, as well as Young Brant, whom the baronet acknowledged as his, came next.

Jason and Daly took their place behind the Butlers. Other Johnson friends were behind. The sachems of the two Mohawk villages, each wearing a black stroud blanket, crape and gloves, according to Sir William's wishes, took their place in line.

"We did all we could, lad," Doctor Daly said. He reached out a comforting hand to touch Jason's shoulder. Nothing he said, nothing he did, eased Jason's pain. Poor boy.

In less than a week Jason had brought a new life into the world, and watched another slip away. He had delivered Lady Mary's first child, and watched helplessly while Sir William had passed away.

Jason had not yet learned the heart wrenching lesson that a doctor, no matter how skilled, no matter how hard he tried, was helpless when the Higher Power called.

Before they entered the church, Jason spotted Lauri standing among the other village mourners, tears streaming down her face.

When the service was over, and he had paid his last respects to the man who had done so much for him, Jason left the church. Lauri was gone.

He found himself on her doorstep, but before he had a chance to reach for the knocker, she opened the door and held out her arms to him. A great sob, deep within, racked his body, and he wept bitterly for the first time since childhood.

CHAPTER 22

Adam Loucke's Tavern—Stone Arabia—
August 27, 1774

Seven weeks after Sir William's death, Christopher Yates came up from Schenectady to Adam Loucke's tavern in Stone Arabia. He dismounted, tied his horse to the hitching post in front of the long, low, rambling inn, crossed the wide open stoop, and entered the traveler's room. He strode past the bar with its array of bottles, glasses, decanters and pewter mugs. The fireplace was flanked. by glass doors that clearly displayed the delft blue and white punch bowls, and the plates with the pictures of the Prince and Princess of Orange in flaring and vivid yellow.

Over the fireplace mantel, with its curious elaborate patterns, moldings and sunburst, hung two very long Queen Anne muskets, a cartridge box, and a very old, smooth and yellowed powder horn:

MADE AT LAKE GEORGE, SEPTEMBER 17, 1755
I, POWDER, WITH MY BROTHER BALL, A HERO
LIKE, DO CONKER ALL

On the wall hung prints of Martin Luther, Frederick the Great, King George III and the French king, Louis XIV, who had warred against the Rhine provinces. His picture dangled upside down. Beneath were words written in German:

THIS IS THE MAN WE ALL SHOULD HATE:
WHO DROVE US FROM OUR HOME;
WHO BURNED THE OLD PALATINATE;
AND SENT US FORTH TO ROAM

In the room at the end of the bar, several men were engaged in an animated conversation. There was no mistaking the voice of Isaac Paris, with his inborn French distrust of the English, store keeper and wealthy land owner, and who served as a Supervisor of the Palatine District. Yates also picked out the voices of Palatines Andrew Finck, another important land owner, as well as Adam Loucke, and John Frey, a Major in the Militia and a Justice of the Peace.

Yates took another look at the pictures of the two kings. What he and the four men in the other room were going to do could very well be considered treason. He took a deep breath, shrugged and stepped through the doorway.

"How the hell did you keep the rest of the riff-raff out?" Yates said. "There's not a man in the bar room."

"Told them I was only serving Tory liquor," Loucke said.

Yates clapped him on the shoulder. "Tory or not, I could use something to wet my whistle. None of that cheap Indian stuff though, Adam."

It was a hot August night. Some Schiedeam schnapps or Mohawk hard cider would taste good.

The men crowded around him, shaking his hand, demanding news of Schenectady, Albany and Boston.

"Damn glad you're here, Yates," Loucke said. "We're right serious about forming a Committee of Safety. God knows we'll need it the way things is going with Boston blocked up." His red face became even ruddier as he spoke. "Ain't nobody but us is going to look out for us. We ain't got no say one way or 'tother. The Johnsons and Butlers seen to that."

The other men muttered and nodded in agreement. It was the longest speech they had ever heard Loucke make.

"Adam's right, Chris," John Frey said. "This thing's got to be drawn up legal. That's why we wanted you here. What we got to say has got to be done right."

"I've minded my own business and never meddled in nobody's affairs up to now," Loucke said, "but I ain't going to be walked on no more."

"Who's going to protect us if things go bad?" Andrew Finck said. "Sure'n hell it won't be Albany. They'll only be looking out for their own hides."

Isaac Paris agreed. "Ain't nothing west but a few scraggly settlers and Indians. You can bet your boots Guy Johnson will keep them red devils under his thumb."

"Reverend Kirkland will keep the Oneida neutral, Isaac, maybe even bring them over to our side," Finck said.

"Ain't the Oneida I'm worried about. It's the Mohawk and Seneca that scare me."

John Frey sat smoking a clay pipe, listening. "Joe Brant's got a passel of nieces and nephews with Johnson blood. How many at last count?"

"Eight," somebody said.

"Blood's thicker than water," Frey continued. "Brant's not going to turn his back on his in-laws."

Paris snorted. "Guy's already acting like he-'s in charge of Indian affairs."

Loucke came back from the bar room with quills and ink. He gave them to Yates and Frey.

"More than likely the crown will approve Guy's appointment," Yates said, "but Brant's not going to let Guy run the whole show. He doesn't trust him."

Yates and Frey sat down at a long table and began to make notes. They had to take a stand, to say what was on their minds.

Ideas were rejected, selected and finally accepted. When the meeting broke up they had decided to draft a document that presented their views, aired their determination to help support and defend their rights and liberties.

Both men stood up, stretched and flexed their fingers.

"Sure glad you came," Loucke said, shaking Chris's hand. "Ain't a better lawyer this side of Schenectady."

"Walter Butler's damn good," Yates said.

Paris stroked the stubble on his chin. "He's never won a debtors case that I heard of. Wasn't he Elizabeth Maginnis's lawyer when she sued George Herkimer for 500 Pounds?"

"After she'd warmed his bed for six years and he'd married Phil Schuyler's cousin, Alida,." Finck added.

"Yes, but George refused to enter a plea and the case was dropped," Yates said.

"What do you suppose Molly Brant will do?" Paris said, "Sure'n hell Sir John ain't going to let her stay at The Hall."

"Probably move up near Joe Brant," Loucke said.

"That's a bad thing," Paris said, "having her so close to Nicholas Herkimer. The Indians do enough spying without having a nest of 'em on his door step."

Yates made ready to leave.

"Where're you stayin'?" Frey said.

"Tice's Tory Tavern. Where else?" Yates could still hear them laughing as he rode off toward Johnstown.

"Here it is," Yates said when they met again. He showed them several sheets of paper, each written in his own flowing script. "It's pretty long," he went on, "so I'll give you a quick sketch of what it says and then you can look at it yourself."

He paused. "There are nine resolutions. They're pretty long. I'll just tell you the gist of them. You can read them and mull it over later:

"We acknowledge George III as our king, will give our true and faithful allegiance, and will support and maintain him on the throne."

"I'm no Englishman," Paris grumbled, "Why should I do that?"

"Hush up, Isaac. Let Chris finish. We can fight about it later," John Frey said.

"I laid out our feelings for the state of affairs caused by the blocking up of the Port of Boston. The acts of Parliament for raising revenue on the backs of the American colonies, abridging our liberties and privileges.

"We will gladly submit to the laws of Great Britain—

Paris scowled.

—as long as they are consistent with the security of the constitutional rights and liberties of English subjects. We consider these rights to be so sacred we cannot permit them to be violated."

"I cited the taxes laid on us by Parliament. We can only be taxed by the consent of the colonies," Yates told them.

The others laughed when they saw Paris grin his approval.

"We oppose the blockade of Boston and will support the people of that city."

"Because of the gravity of events, we think it necessary to send delegates to a general Congress and will select five gentlemen to go. We also agree to abide by the regulations made by the Congress."

Yates continued, *"We will appoint a standing committee of the county to correspond with the committees of New York and Albany."*

"There's more," Yates said, "You can read them yourselves." He laid the papers on the table and sat back in his chair.

The others crowded around him to get a better look. It was one thing to listen to him tell what the resolutions were. Seeing them in legal terms on paper sobered them.

Were they placing their necks in a noose?

Isaac Paris stepped back from the others, a smile turning up the corners of his mouth.

Now the Johnsons and the Butlers would realize it took more than a whack with a king's sword to make a man important.

CHAPTER 23

Johnstown—Late Winter, 1774

Jason was tired.

Tired to the bone.

He was tired of rising before the sun in the dead of winter, strapping on snowshoes because the snow was too deep for a horse and sleigh, to trudge to some isolated Highlander's place.

Tired of the sullen way they treated him, their resentment because they had been bullied into leaving their crops and animals when Sir William ordered they should be inoculated against smallpox.

He was tired of Walter's carping. Ever since the Tryon County Committee of Safety had been formed, Walter had ranted and railed, calling them traitors, and worse.

Most of all, Jason was tired of not being able to marry Lauri.

He was tired of being tired.

So much had happened since he had come back to the valley and had taken up his duties at The Hall. He had almost lost Lauri to Stephen Watts. Sir William was dead. Molly had taken her brood, first to Fort Johnson, then to her brother, Joseph Brant, at the Canajoharie Castle.

Jason decided he would finish Sir John's reports in the morning. He set the papers aside, made sure the shutters were secure, added more logs to the fire and readied himself for bed. He was unaware of the man making his way toward Sir John's office in the stone blockhouse that was set apart from The Hall.

Sir John conducted his business from the fireproofed, stone office that had once been his fathers, so that, as Polly pointed out in no uncertain terms, the family routine would not be disrupted. She insisted the house was only for family use. Young Anne was demanding, and Lady Johnson was testy.

When the young Johnsons had moved into The Hall, Lady Mary had immediately put the servants to work scrubbing and cleaning the house from top to bottom. She was particularly offended by the smell of the unwashed bodies of the Indians, trappers, merchants, hangers-on and freeloaders who had filled the house during Sir William's time.

She ordered the floors be scoured with sand and lye, beds to be stripped and washed with camphor or turpentine to kill bed bugs. Everything washable—table and bed linens, clothing, curtains, towels—were boiled in water leached through wood ashes, scrubbed with soft soap, and placed to dry wherever possible.

Walls were washed and plaster whitewashed.

Brass, pewter and silver were polished and windows cleaned.

Although it was months since her brother-in-law, Guy, had taken over the Superintendency and the Indians now sprawled in the large hallway at Guy Park, she still complained that the smell of their unwashed bodies lingered in The Hall.

"At least we can walk from room to room without fear of stepping on someone," she said.

Geoff Baxter hunched his shoulders against the bitter wind, and fought his way toward Sir John's office.

He had found a way to get even with Jason.

He was on his way to set things in motion; using Sir John as a dupe. He would have to be careful. Sir John was no fool, but if things went as Geoff planned, Doctor Jason Dayemon would be ruined.

Geoff was in a foul mood. He had spent the early part of the evening gambling at Tice's, losing more than usual. His father was becoming increasingly difficult, refusing to increase his allowance or advance him any more money. Not only that, but Elder was preoccupied, acting strangely, neglecting his business.

Belle had withdrawn into her shell and now that he and his sisters were grown, paid little or no attention to them.

Patience and Felicity did nothing but whine and complain. There was no hope of them ever landing a husband, and he had made up his mind he would not be responsible for them after his father's death.

Geoff swayed on his feet and clutched the edge of Sir John's desk to steady himself. The drinks he had guzzled earlier made him dizzy. The warmth of Sir John's office made him fuzzy.

Sir John, Guy Johnson, and Dan Claus had retired there after dinner to talk about the disruption the Tryon Committee of Safety was causing in the valley. Geoff had insisted he had an urgent matter that must be addressed.

"Jason's a threat," Geoff told Sir John, "You can't trust him. He'll turn traitor the first chance he gets. He's too dangerous to have around."

Sir John rolled the stem of his partially filled wine glass between his fingers. "He's the Hall physician."

"Jason will side with the Whigs. Mark my words."

Sir John downed the wine in a gulp, rose to prowl about the room, as he often did when deep in thought. "I have no reason to question his loyalty. He's made no secret he wants no part of politics."

"Have you forgotten New York?" Geoff said, "When he nearly killed me?"

"As I remember it, you provoked the whole thing."

"Did you know he keeps in touch with that rabble rouser, Marinus Willett? Isn't that his name? Calls himself a Son of Liberty. Always stirring up trouble."

"What proof do you have?"

"Proof? What proof do you need?"

Sir John was being more difficult than he had counted on. He wanted this business to be over with. His blood was running hot. There was a barmaid waiting for him, and if Gil Tice got wind of it, she'd be out on her ear before he'd had his fun.

"It's your duty to get rid of him," Geoff snarled.

"Duty!" Sir John thundered, "You come here with your petty jealousy and talk to me about duty? I know my duty. I may be drunk, but I know why you want Jason out of the way."

"You're wearing blinders," Geoff saw Johnson stiffen, "Begging your pardon, Sir John. I meant no offense, but Jason should be watched."

He bowed to Sir John, nodded to Guy and Dan. "By your leave gentlemen, I'll bid you goodnight."

The seed that Geoff planted took root. Sir John wrote to his father-in-law, John Watts, asking about Marinus Willett's activates.

The news from Watts was not encouraging. Willett was still active in the Sons of Liberty. The Committees of Correspondence in the colony, Watts added, were in constant communication with one another.

Sir John's mood was as gloomy as the sky outside his office. Here, in the valley, the Tryon County Committee of Safety was beginning to flex its muscles.

Sir John picked up the rest of the unopened mail. There was a letter addressed to Jason Dayemon, Physician. The other name on the envelope was one he did not wish to see—Marinus Willett.

Geoff was right. Jason might be a threat.

Walter and John Butler were closeted in Butlersbury's front room with Jason. Catherine Butler had shooed the children upstairs when Jason appeared at the front door, visibly upset.

"Sir John discharged you? Why?" Walter frowned.

Jason was not making sense. He had always been loyal to the Johnsons, accepting every task without complaint.

"Sir John found a letter Marinus Willet sent me," Jason said. "He thinks I'm feeding him information."

"Willett? The fellow you worked for in New York?" Walter asked. "Why would Sir John think that?"

"We've kept in touch," Jason told him, "Sir John wrote his father-in-law asking questions about Marinus. Watts says he's giving the crown's people hell. It was the first I'd heard of it. Marinus knows I'm not interested in that sort of thing.

"I'm at loose ends. I need a place to live. I suppose I could go to the cabin Sir William left me near Nicholas Herkimer, but I don't want to leave Lauri."

John Butler said, "I've been to that cabin. Solid place, but then what else would suit Sir William. The Mohawks have a town not far from there, you know. Probably why he picked the place. Good land, too. You ought to grow anything you need or want."

"That's the trouble, sir. I don't know much about that sort of thing, been too busy to learn. I'd rather stay in town, where I can treat patients. That's if anybody will take me on as a doctor when they hear Sir John has let me go."

"My tenants like you," John said, "It won't make any difference to them as long as they know we believe you. I'll put in a word." A smile creased his Irish face and the corners of his eyes crinkled. "I've a house—close to Lauri."

"The rent?" Jason asked.

"For you, lad, twice what I'd charge anybody else."

John Butler was true to his word. He did have a house close to Lauri and when Jason protested the amount of rent, Butler smiled and walked away. It was far less than he would have accepted from anyone else.

The house smelled of dust and mildew, but with Lauri's help, it had been set to rights. It was small, but in good repair, and had three rooms, one that was large enough for him to use to treat patients—if he was ever lucky enough to have any.

Lauri busied herself sprinkling Tansy to discourage ants, and she hung clusters of the button like yellow flowers near the windows and doors.

Jason's open medical chest sat on a table in the middle of the room. He checked it carefully, making note of how many tapes, thread, pill boxes, glass and clay medicine bottles, single, double rolled and foliated bandages, were in it. He had remembered to put his tortoise shell tweezers in the box.

Lauri watched with interest as he methodically examined his surgical instruments: the large amputation saw, so like a carpenter's saw it could easily be mistaken for one; the curved and straight amputation knives, a scalpel.

"Do you use all these?" she asked.

Jason smiled. "I have."

Satisfied that he had all the instruments he needed: surgical scissors, probes for locating musket balls in a wound, the retractor for drawing aside the lips of a wound, and the forceps for removing bullets, he closed the medicine chest and put the surgical instruments away.

He placed the cobalt blue bottle of Laudanum next to his small supply of opium on the shelf of the wall cabinet, locked the door, checked to make sure it was secured and slipped the key into his pocket. He set the mortar and pestle, pewter bowl and lancet he used for blood letting on the counter below, looked around to be sure he had not missed anything, happy to be settled at last.

A cozy warmth filled the room The fireplace had a good draft, and John Butler had assured him that it would do a fine job of keeping him comfortable, even on the coldest winter day.

Lauri settled into a high backed chair next to the fireplace. "I'm worried about Elder."

"Is he sick? Maybe I should have a look at him."

"No. Oh no, Jason. Don't do that. I don't want him thinking I'm talking behind his back."

"What seems to be the problem?"

"He…. he acts strange."

"How so?"

"He comes to see me everyday."

Jason smiled. "I would, if I could."

Her fingers twisted and untwisted the corner of her apron. "I'm afraid of him. He calls me by my mother's name, as if she was still alive."

Jason's house, around the corner on the side street, was separated from Lauri's by a small cemetery. From his window he had a clear view of her house beyond the weathered grave stones. He started when he saw Elder's horse tethered to the fence.

He grabbed his coat from the peg by the back door, shrugging it on as he hurried cross lots thru the cemetery.

He knocked twice before Lauri opened the door, plainly relieved to see him. It was obvious that Elder was not.

Jason had not seen Elder for several months and he was surprised to see the change in his appearance. Elder's clothes were disheveled, his hair unkempt, but most worrisome were his wild eyes.

Jason had seen eyes like that often enough in the New York alms houses where he had spent what little free time he had doing what he could for the wretches chained like a rabid animal to the wall in the dank basement with its overpowering smell of human waste and rotting garbage.

"You look peaked, Elder," Jason said, "Let me fix you some St. John's Wort. It will perk you up"

"I know what St. John's Wort is used for," Elder snarled, "There's nothing wrong with my sensibilities."

There was no question in Jason's mind; Elder had lost reason. Lauri had cause to worry.

CHAPTER 24

Late January, 1775

Elder sat alone in the shadowy corner of a tavern on the road half way between Johnstown and Fort Johnson, so deep in thought he did not hear the bawdy jokes or raucous laughter of the rowdy men seated at the table at the far end of the room. Years ago he had been in a tavern in Albany, much like this one. He had considered bringing Belle there. He never did.

Because of Jason, he had been forced to cut back his daily visits to Lauri to one or two a week. Disgusted, Elder stopped completely. Without fail, Jason would arrive and would make no effort to leave.

It would be easy to brood, but Elder refused to be upended by the young whippersnapper. Instead, he found a man, who, for the price of a cheap drink, agreed to nose around and report back to him. The fellow told Elder that a man, probably someone with a grudge, had paid a visit to Sir John shortly before Johnson discharged Jason.

An untouched mug of flip sat on the table. Elder had stopped drinking half an hour earlier. He needed a clear head. What he would do depended on what fresh information the man would bring.

The news was good. Jason had gone to attend one of John Butler's tenants and would not return until late.

Elder hurried outside, pulled his greatcoat tighter to keep out the cold, and headed for Johnstown.

As she went about her work, Lauri hummed an old tune her mother had taught her long ago. Strange, she had not thought of that song in ever so long. She heard a horse whinny and went to peer out of the window. A sleigh had stopped in front of the house. The impatient horse pawed the snow.

Curious as to who it might be, she answered the knock at her door.

Elder stumbled into the house. He reeked of spirits.

"Hurry, Alva, put this on." He draped a heavy woolen cloak around Lauri's shoulders and pulled the fur edged hood over her head. Somewhere, in the deep recesses of his mind, he remembered a little girl wearing a cloak much like this one. She had carried a doll; a doll that was dressed just like the little girl. Who was she?

"Alva, we've no time to lose," he said. "It'll be dark soon and we have to go as far as we can tonight." He grasped her arm. His grip tightened until she whimpered.

His fingers relaxed, "We'll go anywhere you want. Charleston. Savannah. London. Paris," He drew her toward the door, "I can give you all the things you've ever wanted. I have money. What has James ever given you?"

Lauri managed to pull away from him. Her heart beat wildly.

Think. Think of something. "My daughter," she said, "I can't go without Lauri."

He let go of her and glanced around the room. "Where is she?"

"Outside playing." She had to get him out of the house. She moved out of his reach.

"We don't have time."

"I can't leave. Not without her."

He caught her again, pinning her arms at her sides. His lips found hers.

His foul breath churned her stomach. She managed to push him away.

"I'll have to get some things together." She reached for the back of a chair to steady herself, "I want you to be proud of me. I can't go looking like a beggar."

"There isn't time. James will…"

"…never know." Lauri interrupted Elder. "I can't leave without my child."

"I'll help you find her."

"No. You're a stranger to her. She'll be afraid. Come back later. Give me a chance to tell her we're leaving."

He brushed his hand across her temple. "I could never refuse you." He kissed her again.

She bolted the door behind him as soon as he left, and watched to be sure he had driven away, hurried to make sure the back door was also latched. All the windows were secure, but she checked to be certain.

Jason's house was dark. He had not returned.

The realization that she was on her own set her to trembling. What if Elder returned. He was almost certain to do that. He could be like a dog worrying a bone. He would not give up. Would he break down the door and take her by force?

She made herself look out of the window again. She could see Mrs. Wemple moving about in her house across the street. Maybe she should go to her. No. Elder could be waiting. It would be easy for him to grab her. She was no match for his strength. It was safer to stay where she was.

She crawled into the corner of the bed, made herself as small as possible, prayed for darkness, stared at the door. Her ears strained for the sound of his horse and sleigh.

He came back in less than an hour. This time he didn't bother to knock, and when he found the door barred, he beat on it, demanding to be let in. She had never heard such vile language, never been called such filthy names. Not even Belle had abused her so.

She huddled in the farthest reaches of the bed, unable to control her shaking. When she heard him walk around to the back of the house, she slipped between the wall and the side of the bed. He rattled the door but the lock held. She heard him try the windows. Thank heavens he did not break a pane. Cursing, he stomped away.

Day settled into evening. Dusk was replaced by the darkness of night. She lay cramped and shivering on the cold floor. The embers in the fireplace were turning to ash, and she did not dare move from the protection of her hiding place. He might be lurking outside.

She woke from a deep sleep. Her body ached from the confinement of the tight space in which she had hidden. There was the stillness of death in the room, the darkness pressed down on her until she thought she would suffocate if she did not climb out of there.

She crawled across the bed, set her feet on the chilly floor and gripped the bedpost to steady herself. She took a few steps toward the window. She hesitated in the middle of the room, sensed the presence of another person.

A hand covered her mouth and she felt the sharp blade of a knife.

"One sound and I'll slit your pretty little throat."

The voice belonged to a face disfigured by a riding crop.

There was no one to save her now.

CHAPTER 25

Agatha Wemple was cross grained, and the silver-grey pewter sky did nothing to improve her disposition.

She had spent much of yesterday afternoon peering out her front window, and when Elder Baxter had stopped his sleigh in front of Lauri's house, staggering toward the front door, her interest was piqued, indeed. Whatever was young miss thinking—letting that drunken lout into the house?

When he left, Agatha had sighed with relief, but he had returned, and in a fit of anger had stormed around outside, hurling obscenities and demanding to be let in.

Agatha had been sorely tried not to march herself over to Sheriff Alexander White and demand that Baxter be hauled off to gaol where he belonged. Second thoughts had gotten the better of her. Drunken men could be more than just plain troublesome.

It promised to be another dreary day, and there was a decided chill in the house. Cold always worsened the aching in her bones, and she had slept in her woolen dress rather than burn what little wood she had left. She wrapped a heavy shawl around her frail frame and limped to the window.

The snowy road was empty, but there was a stirring of life here and there in some of the houses along the street. Smoke drifted from the chimneys as women busied themselves making breakfast for their families. The thought of cooked porridge made her stomach growl. If she waited a few more hours to eat she could stretch her meager portions enough to last till tomorrow. No one must ever know of her dire straits. She would not go to an almshouse.

Young miss should be up and about, getting ready to head out to Tice's tavern.

Something was wrong.

Agatha stood staring at Lauri's house, mulling over the situation. She knew everyone said she was a busybody; this was no time to prove them wrong.

She pulled her shawl tighter around her shoulders, stepped out into the cold, crossed the road, and limped through the snow to Lauri's house. She was filled with foreboding, and when she eased Lauri's door open, her hands flew to her mouth stifling a scream. Lauri lay sprawled across the bed, a blanket thrown over her. Her bloody clothes were strewn around the room.

From where she stood on the threshold, Agatha could see the bruises on Lauri's face, and arm.

Persistent pounding, and anguished cries woke Jason from a sound sleep. Some midwife unable to cope with a difficult birth? Thank heaven she had sense enough to come for help, and not let the parturient woman labor so long that neither the mother, nor the child could be saved.

He struggled into his breeches, sliding his foot into the one handy shoe he was able to find.

He was surprised to see Mrs. Wemple on his threshold.

"It's young miss." She choked back a sob. "She's bad hurt."

"Where is she?"

"Her place."

He bolted past her, kicked off his shoe, his shirttail flapped as he sprinted through the graveyard.

The inside of Lauri's house was in shambles; the table and chairs overturned. The settle had been toppled. The few precious possessions that had once belonged to Lauri's mother and father, the things she so lovingly stored under the seat, had been scattered or smashed.

He stepped inside, every muscle in his body tense. He scanned the room to make sure no one was lurking about and cursed himself for not bringing a weapon. No time to worry about that now.

The room was cold. Cold as a tomb Lauri's tomb? Don't be a fool. Think. Think like a doctor.

Lauri lay on her side. A blanket covered her bare back and buttocks.

He bent over her for a closer look. She was a mass of bruises. Blood had dried on her mouth and other parts of her body where the skin had been punctured. Teeth marks…What kind of an animal was this brute?

She didn't appear to be breathing.

She's dead. *Oh, dear God. She's dead.*

He eased her over onto her back, and listened for a heart beat. It was faint but steady. Her chest rose and fell in a long slow motion.

The coverlet, the one Lauri especially prized because her mother had made it, lay in a heap beside the bed. Tenderly, and with deliberate gentleness, he pulled the blanket around her battered body, and wrapped her in her mother's coverlet.

He was more than half way back through the cemetery, cradling her in his arms like a new born, when he spotted Mrs. Wemple hobbling toward him.

"Is she…?"

"Alive," he said, and hurried on. Tears streamed down his cheeks.

She turned and followed him back to his house, no longer aware of her aching joints.

"Build up the fire. I want it warm in here," he said when he heard Mrs. Wemples's labored breathing. He looked around to see her leaning against the door frame, watching him with worried eyes as he slipped Lauri into his bed.

"Set some water to heating," he said, "You'll find stones outside the back door. Put them in the kettle and when they're warm wrap them in a shirt or any kind of cloth you can find and bring them to me. Find all the blankets you can. There must be more in the house somewhere."

He stripped off his shirt and breeches and slid into bed beside Lauri, drawing her close to him. He began to shiver as she drew his body heat from him. He turned abruptly when he heard Mrs. Wemple gasp.

He was in no mood for a lecture on decency. "We both know what happened over there. She's going to die if we don't get her warm. Now get to work and help me."

He heard Mrs. Wemple adding more logs to the fire, the sound of the outer door opening and closing, then the plunk of stones being dropped into the kettle.

It was a slow, demanding process and he marveled at the fortitude of the old woman.

Jason felt Lauri's body warming. He felt her stir and she rolled over toward him. Her eyes met his, and before he could protect himself, he felt the force of her knee between his legs. With a howl of pain, he tumbled onto the floor.

Mrs. Wemple came hobbling to the door, warm blankets in her arms.

"Don't stand there gawking at me, woman. Give me something to cover myself."

She tossed a blanket to him, and he wrapped it around his waist. He struggled to his knees, grabbed the side of the bed.

Lauri stared at him, and cowered when he reached to touch her. The muscles in her throat worked to force a scream. Nothing.

"She's damaged in the head," Mrs. Wemple whispered. She sat down on the side of the bed, took Lauri in her arms and held her against her bony chest. She rocked her as a mother would a child.

"Poor, poor lamb," Mrs. Wemple looked up at Jason with tear filled eyes, "You'd best leave. The sight of you makes her worse."

Mrs. Wemple was right.

He knew little about treating impaired sensibilities, despite his work in the New York pest houses. He had seen what happened to people who suffered impairment of the mind, even those who were kept at home. Lauri would live, but would she ever be the same? Would she ever be his wife? Could she ever be a wife?

He got to his feet, clutched the blanket around him, picked up his clothes, and went into the other room. He put on his shirt, woolen stockings, and breeches. They warmed his cold legs, and his taut muscles began to relax.

He unlocked the medicine cabinet, took out the bottle of laudanum, poured a measured dose into a molded horn cup and called Mrs. Wemple.

"Give her this," he said when she came to the door, "It will ease the pain."

He handed her the cup. "Tell me when she falls asleep. I've got to know how badly she's hurt. It's important we prevent corruption where she's been torn. I'll need you to help me make flaxseed poultices."

There was also the possibility that Lauri would develop lung fever. He considered bleeding her, but decided against it.

There were more immediate problems that needed his attention. He had not noticed any places where a bone had pierced her arms or legs, but he needed to take a closer look to be sure.

Amputation was the course for a compound fracture to prevent mortification. The wound could become turgid and filled with malignant pus resulting in gangrene. He knew he could never perform the operation himself, and he was not sure, that at his age, Doctor Daly was up to it. Lauri was too young and beautiful to be maimed but if it meant her life....

"Drink this, Lamb," he heard Mrs. Wemple say, "it will make you feel better."

The laudanum worked its magic. Before long, Lauri was sleeping.

A careful examination reassured him. With Mrs. Wemple's help he checked for signs of redness around the lacerations on Lauri's body. Finished, they went into the other room to make the poultices. When they had used all the flaxseed they made them from bread and milk.

The day did not brighten, not even as the hours dragged on.

The sound of Gil Tice calling him brought Jason up short.

"Lauri's disappeared," Tice said when Jason let him into the house, "Her house has been trashed."

"She's here. She's been through an ordeal."

"I'll get the sheriff," He turned to go.

"No," Jason grabbed Gil's arm, "White will only bully her. Lauri's been through enough. Besides it won't do any good. She can't speak."

Jason gestured toward the closed bedroom door. "She's in the other room. Mrs. Wemple found her and came for me. That's all I know."

"That old busy body—That gossip knows?"

"Keep your voice down," Jason took a key from a drawer, and gave it to Gil. "Lock up Lauri's house. No need to have anyone snooping about or stealing her things. Lord knows, she has little enough as it is."

"I'll see to it." Gil reached for the latch. "I'll have to tell Christina. She's sick with worry."

Mrs. Wemple came and went throughout the day, shaking her head in answer to Jason's unspoken question.

The longest time she spent away from Lauri was to fix some broth, ordering Jason to eat with her. She looked exhausted, but she scolded him severely when he suggested she get some rest.

She squinted at him over the top of her spoon. "Now I ain't sayin' he done it, but there's something you should know. Long's you ain't going to let that high and mighty sheriff near my poor little lamb, I might's well tell you."

"Get on with it."

"Yesterday, Elder Baxter was at my poor lamb's house. I don't know what happened, but he left, and when he come back he was down right mean tempered. Young miss wouldn't let him in, and he beat on the door somethin' fierce—called her all sorts of filthy names.

"It's my fault. Mr. Baxter kept pounding on the door, yelling, 'I'll be back. I'll be back.' I should have gone for Sheriff White like I thought of."

Jason patted the old woman's bony hand.

She snuffled, "I'll get back to her now. I just thought you should know. I'll be staying here until I know she's better."

She wagged a crooked finger in his face. "I'll brook no nonsense. There'll be no more sliding into bed naked next to my sweet little lamb. A doctor you may well be, but you're still a man."

Jason was in a foul mood. For several days, he had turned patients away, pleading indisposition.

Voices outside, and the persistent pounding on the door brought him to the window. A man, his head wrapped in bloody rags, sagged in the arms of two companions. Jason went to the door to let them in.

The injured man was one of the biggest persons Jason had ever seen. There was something familiar about him. Of course! He was the man who had nearly killed Lauri the night of the ball at Johnson Hall.

How many kinds of fool did they take him for?

He sat the fellow on a chair and removed the filthy bandage. The cloth was soaked with animal gore. There was no extravasated blood.

He made a great pretense of examining the man's head. When he was finished, he went to his surgical cabinet, took out the T shaped trephine with its circular saw like edges and held it so the three men could get a good look at it.

"What's that?" The injured man gaped at what looked to him to be a core drill.

"A trephine," Jason said.

"What's it for?"

147

"You might have a fractured skull. I need to cut down to the bone so I can relieve the pressure and allow the discharge of inflammation from the durra matter."

"Durra matter? What's that?"

"Brain lining. I have to find the best place to make a hole in your head, then I have to take off enough scalp and pericranium to apply the trephine and make a circular cut on either side of the fracture." He eyed the other two men. "Of course, I'll need help. Come back tomorrow and bring these husky fellows with you to hold you down."

The color drained from the man's face, and he bolted for the door, his two friends close on his heels. They nearly collided with young Butler who stood, grim faced, in the doorway.

"What was that about?" Walter closed the door behind him.

"Scum—snooping around."

"Snooping? Why?"

"Lauri's been raped."

"Good God. Who?"

"Elder Baxter. She's stupefied, hasn't said a word since I brought her here. She nearly froze to death before Mrs. Wemple found her. Baxter probably sent those three rotters to find out how badly she was hurt."

Walter shook his head, "Baxter's dead. That's what I came to tell you."

"What?"

"Shot himself in the head—bloody mess." Walter reached in his pocket and pulled out a gold watch, opened it, and handed the timepiece to Jason.

A beautiful young woman, not yet twenty, smiled at Jason from the miniature painted inside the case. Jason's hand began to tremble. "Lauri."

"Her mother more likely. Look at the clothes," Walter said.

"Where did you get this?"

"From a young Mohawk. He said he'd found the watch on a dead man and took me back to the body," Walter slumped into a chair. He wiped his sweating palms on his thighs, "I need something strong. It was a shock, I'll tell you, when I saw it was Elder."

Jason took a bottle from the top shelf of his medicine cabinet. "Drink this."

Walter took a long swallow, and nearly choked, "What is this?"

"Pa's special."

Walter drank again, and choked again, "I gave the Mohawk some coins for the watch and when I opened the back I saw the picture. I thought I ought to tell you before I went to the sheriff."

"Don't tell White about the watch or what I told you about Elder. It's not likely those brutes will say anything. They're probably half way to Albany by now. They don't want White clamping them in gaol for something they didn't do."

"I'll have to inform him of Elder's death."

"Agreed, but that's all."

"I can't withhold knowledge of a crime."

"What crime? A man killed himself. That's all you know."

"White stays at Tice's tavern. He's sure to find out about Lauri."

"I'll take care of that. I'm Lauri's physician. I can refuse to let him see her."

Walter ran his long fingers through his dark wavy hair, "It's hard to believe. Elder loved Lauri."

"And attacked her worse than an animal would," Jason walked over to the hearth and heaped more logs on the fire. They caught, crackled, tossed sparks up the chimney. The red—orange tongues of flame lapped at the logs until they blazed.

"White's like a bulldog," Walter said, "He won't let go until he's got what he's after."

"If it's Lauri he's after, he won't get her. I'll go to Sir John if I have to."

CHAPTER 26

Jason removed the flannel and poultice and examined the lacerations on Lauri's body.

When he saw the yellow-white matter, he grinned broadly. "Ah, laudable pus."

"And, pray tell, what is that?" Mrs. Wemple stood with him at Lauri's bedside.

"A good sign, Mrs. Wemple. A very good sign."

The flaxseed, milk and bread poultices had worked. There was no sign of mortification or corruption.

Lauri was healing.

He reached for her hand, and she did not shrink from his touch. "You're getting better. You'll be up and about in no time." He turned on his heel, left the room, walked to the hearth and pounded his fists on the mantle. He felt a soft touch on his shoulder.

Mrs. Wemple had followed him. "You're a good man, Doctor Dayemon."

Jason continued to stare into the blazing fire that filled the house with warmth but did nothing to chase away the chill in his heart.

"She hears, you know," Mrs. Wemple said. "I told her to nod once if she knew what I was saying and she did. I told her all you done for her. She ain't afeared of you no more."

Sheriff White demanded to see her. He blustered, threatened, accused Jason of blocking his investigation of Elder Baxter's death.

"Felo-de-se," Jason said. "The man was disordered in his senses. He killed himself and you know it."

"And the Howell woman—how much does she know of Baxter's death?"

"Nothing. She's ill. Too ill to be told."

"Withholding knowledge of a crime is a serious offense."

"Careful what you're accusing me of, Sheriff—so's slander."

Lauri was suffering from melancholia and he was beside himself. He gave her daily doses of the reddish brew of St. John's Wort until his meager supply dwindled. When that was gone, he made a tea of lemon balm or from the rosemary leaves Lauri had grown in her herb garden.

No use trying to get St. John's Wort from Schenectady or Albany. The Committee of Safety had made it plain to him that they considered him a dog of the Johnsons and they would seize any medicine sent to him. He was not, in their opinion, a friend of liberty.

There had been no discussion or spoken agreement, but Jason and Mrs. Wemple settled into a compatible routine.

Mrs. Wemple took charge of the running of the house. She took care of Lauri's personal needs, fussing over her, brushing and fixing her hair, dressing her in the clothes that Christina Tice sent.

Jason returned to his practice, visiting patients in Johnstown, but he refused to see anyone at his house.

"Jason." The voice was weak.

He glanced at Mrs. Wemple. She had heard it too.

"Jason."

This time he was sure. He reached the bedroom door in two bounds. He found Lauri sitting unsteadily on the edge of the bed, clutching at the bedclothes.

He heard Mrs. Wemple crying softly behind him. "Fetch my banyan, Mrs. Wemple. We want to keep her warm. We have a guest for supper."

He wrapped the oversized garment around Lauri and she seemed to disappear, like a lost waif, in the folds of his dressing gown.

When Franz Berg, one of John Butler's tenant farmers, sent word that his son was sick, Jason was reluctant to go. He was sure he was being watched and as soon as he was far enough away, Sheriff White would pounce on Mrs. Wemple, demanding to question Lauri.

"Pooh, Doctor. I know what people say about me…I'm a gossip, I know everybody's business. Well, they're right, and I know some things about that old blowhard sheriff he don't want told. He won't get by me."

As he rode away early the next morning, Jason thought about the things Mrs. Wemple had said. He believed her when she had added: "No need to worry, Doctor. What went on here between you, me, and my sweet lamb, will stay right here."

Berg's boy was suffering from sore throat distemper. Most doctors put great stock in bleeding but Jason felt uneasy doing it to someone so young, but he had no leeches. He bled the wailing, frightened boy. He poured the blood from his pewter bleeding bowl into a pot for Mrs. Berg to empty, wiped the basin and the double sided blades of his lancet and put them into his medicine chest.

"Give him thyme sweetened with honey," he told the worried mother. "If he isn't better in a few days, send for me."

It was late afternoon when he neared Tice's. The day was getting colder, and he blew on his hands to warm them.

Gil's stable boy hailed him. "Hold up, Doctor Dayemon, sir. I'm to tell you Mr. Tice needs to see you." He took hold of the bridle and Jason slid from the saddle.

"Is someone ill?"

"Oh no, sir. Nothing like that. All I know, sir, is that I was to tell you to come to the tavern. I'll tend to your horse, sir."

The barkeep looked up when Jason entered the taproom, nodded toward Gil's office, and bent his head to continue the conversation he was having with a townsman.

Jason hustled down the hall. He paid no attention to the serving maid's inviting smile. She pouted and turned her attention to the traveler sitting alone in the corner.

Through Gil's open office door, Jason could see Gil, Christina and Walter waiting, grim faced.

Gil looked up from the stack of papers on his desk and motioned to Jason to join them. Christina sat in a straight backed chair beside her husband's desk, her hands clasped tightly in her lap. Walter stood by the closed window.

Gil closed the door to assure privacy. It was warm and crowded in the small room.

"Jason, there have been threats against you," Walter said, "Those three men—especially the one you bullied with the trephine—have been stirring up the riffraff in town. They're threatening to sack your house and take Lauri by force."

"We thought it would be good if we brought her here," Gil said.

"Where Sheriff White could get at her? She would be in a fine fettle, wouldn't she? Hasn't she suffered enough?"

Jason stormed out of the room and out to the stable to see to his horse. The boy had already rubbed it down and given it feed.

By the time he reached his house, he had made up his mind what he would do. As he came up the walk he saw Lauri and Mrs. Wemple seated near the fireplace.

He threw his coat over a chair and put away his medical supplies. "Mrs. Wemple, would you be so good as to give Lauri and me some private time?"

She took her heavy shawl from the peg by the front door and drew it around her frail shoulders. "I'll check on my house and be back in time to get the meal on the table."

Jason's and Lauri's gaze met and held. Neither heard the click of the latch as Mrs. Wemple closed the door behind her.

Jason sat down on the settle and took Lauri's hand in his. "There's been an accident. Elder's been shot."

"Is he—?"

He pulled her close. "I'm sorry."

"Did Geoff kill him?" Her voice was muffled against his chest.

"Elder shot himself. Geoff's disappeared. There's no sign of him."

"I should have gone with him."

"With Geoff?"

"Elder. He wanted me to go away with him. He thought I was my mother. His mind was playing tricks on him."

"You refused."

"I fooled him. I told him I couldn't leave without my child; I had to find her. I told him to come back later."

"He did, didn't he? He came back and raped you."

She leaned away from him and stared into the fire. The flames were a blur of yellow and orange. "No. It was Geoff. I locked everything after Elder left. Windows, doors, everything. I don't know how Geoff got in."

The steady beat of the clock ticked off the minutes.

"I'm thinking of going to the cabin Sir William left me," Jason said. "Will you go with me? As my wife?"

"You don't know what you're asking."

"I'm asking you to be my wife."

"You feel sorry for me."

"I love you." He made her face him. "I've loved you ever since that first day I saw you."

"I was a child then."

"And you looked so alone, so afraid. I wanted to take care of you then. I want to take care of you now."

"How can you want me? Knowing that I…"

"I love you."

In a voice as soft as eiderdown, she whispered, "I've loved you for so long. I've dreamed of being your wife, being with you all the rest of our lives, giving you strong sons and beautiful daughters. Why did you have to wait so long?" The tears that blurred her eyes spilled down her cheeks. "You deserve a woman who can be a real wife to you; who's not afraid to give you sons."

CHAPTER 27

Jason held the lap desk on his knees, staring at the pages of his account book, not seeing the words and numbers made by the broad strokes of his precise handwriting.

He had made a royal mess of everything. Sir John had let him go. The king's people did not trust him, and neither did the members of the Committee of Safety. They were making it next to impossible for him to get the medicines he needed. He had told them he had no quarrel with their political views, but they still refused to deal with him.

Mrs. Wemple returned sputtering, brimming with indignation.

"Scum. Dirty rotten scum." She dropped her shawl over the back of the settle.

"What is it, Mrs. Wemple? What's wrong?"

"I was set upon. Scoundrels, every one of them. Demanded to know what happened to Lauri. I gave them what for. Devil take me if I didn't." She made an indelicate noise. "Called you a woman stealer. Accused me of helping you, threatened to tar and feather both of us." She looked around the room. "Where is my sweet lamb?"

Jason leaned back in his chair and nodded toward the bedroom. "You might as well know, Mrs. Wemple. I asked her to marry me."

"It's about time. Well? What did she say?"

He slammed the account book shut, shoved the stopper into the top of the ink pot, threw the quill pen into the lap desk. "I'm going to be a bachelor for a long time."

He stood, straightened to his full height, and yanked his coat off the chair where he'd thrown it. "Don't wait supper."

He stepped out into the cold evening, banged the door shut behind him, wondering if the scalawags that had waylaid Mrs. Wemple were still prowling about.

He needed to talk to someone. If Walter was still at Tice's maybe he would lend a sympathetic ear.

Walter sat alone at the table. He steepled his hands, rested his chin on his finger tips, and closed his eyes, looking for all the world like he was praying.

He was not.

He was vaguely aware of the buzz of male voices, of the talk about the dispute between the colonies and Britain. Now and then a man would try to defend the action of the New Englanders.

Gil's tavern was a Loyalist stronghold. Only a stranger or a fool would express support for the radicals.

If these sentiments were allowed to smolder they could become a blazing inferno. Father would turn against son, brother against brother.

Friend against friend.

The scraping sound of something heavy being dragged across the wooden floor brought Walter upright. He opened his eyes to find Jason slumped in a chair across the table from him.

"Are you still in love with Lauri?" Jason asked without preamble.

"What if I am?"

"I told you once you'd never have her. I'd see to it. I was wrong. You can't make someone love you, anymore than you can stop loving someone. I give up my claim."

Walter bristled. "She's not chattel, you pompous fool."

"I asked Lauri to marry me. She turned me down. I'm going to live in the cabin Sir William left me. Take care of her." Jason got up, turned, and walked away.

The next day Walter Butler, Gil and Christina Tice showed up on Jason's doorstep. There were kisses and hugs for Lauri, and though not one of them mentioned her thinness and pallor, they were painfully aware that she would be a long time getting over her ordeal.

Jason had not returned since leaving the night before, and Mrs. Wemple was worried.

"Looking after a sick child." Gil suggested.

"Or helping a midwife." Christina offered.

Nursing a big head, more like it, Walter reasoned, but kept his counsel to himself. Jason was not a drinker and he had seen Jason drunk very few times in all the years of their friendship. It did not take much to lay him low, and Walter had never seen a more pitiful soul.

The next three days, Gil, Christina and Walter, came together to see Lauri.

On the fourth day, Walter was not with them. It was late afternoon when he finally arrived at Jason's house.

Mrs. Wemple, beside herself with worry, answered his knock.

"No need to fret," Walter assured her. "Jason's been tending to a very sick man. He's sorry he hasn't let you know, but he can't leave until he's sure the man's all right."

Walter had found Jason, upstairs in a dingy, cluttered tavern room on the road to Fort Johnson. He was reeking of rum, moaning and thrashing about in the rumpled, dirty bed. Jason was not capable of sending word of his whereabouts; he was tending to a very sick man.

"How long has he been like this?" Walter asked the tavern owner.

"Nigh on to three days. Get him out of here, Mr. Butler. When he ain't groaning, he's singing. A bull moose sounds better'n him."

"Keep him here. Two, three days at the longest. Don't let him have anymore to drink."

The barkeep ran his hand over the stubble on his chin. "Don't know as I can keep him any longer. My customers are complaining.about his loud bellowing."

Walter thrust a fistful of coins into the man's oversized hand. "See to it."

"Thank ye, thank ye, Mr. Butler. I'll do my best, my very best."

Walter was annoyed with himself. He was a fairly successful lawyer, had defended clients against some of the most difficult opponents in the valley, always to the best of his ability. He had squired some of the most beautiful and eligible women in Schenectady and Albany, and knew that more than one of them would have been flattered if he had courted them. The thought of being rejected by the mere slip of a girl walking beside him had him tongue tied.

If he was to tell her of his feelings for her it had to be now. Today he had to return to the tavern where he'd left Jason in the landlord's care.

Walter had been aware of Lauri's somber mood long before she asked him to take her to the church where Sir William was buried.

"Sir William and Miss Molly used to tell me I should marry Jason," Lauri said as they left the church. "It isn't like him to be gone so long without a word. Do you think he's gone up river to his place near Colonel Herkimer?"

"No, he's not there."

"You know where he is, don't you?"

Walter stopped, turned Lauri to face him, and nodded. "He told me he asked you to marry him and you turned him down. I'd like your permission to court you."

"Walter, I…"

"I'm not asking for a commitment now. You need to think about it. Maybe in time you'll learn to love me, and find it in your heart to become my wife."

Lauri took his hands in hers. "You are the most loving, kindhearted person I know, but I can't marry you. I can't marry anyone."

Walter started to speak.

Lauri put her finger on his lips to shush him.

"I'm damaged goods."

CHAPTER 28

Johnstown—April 1775

It was three months since Geoff's attack; a week since Jason had asked Lauri to become his wife, and Mrs. Wemple and Lauri were bickering.

"I can't marry him. I don't want his pity."

"You've been through something awful, I'll allow you that." The old aches had come back. Mrs Wemple was feeling mean spirited. "It ain't nothing no married woman ain't put up with one time or 'tother, excepting the beating, that is, and no woman should have to put up with that, even if she is wedded lawful."

She folded her clean chemise and laid it on the bed with the rest of the clothing she was taking back to her house. "Biggest fools I ever seen. You out walking with young Butler, and him supposed to be Doctor's best friend. Courting you behind Doctor's back. You going to marry young Butler?"

"He's not courting me. Walter's a friend."

"I suppose I ain't? Who was it nursed you? Sat with you? Washed you? Fed you?" She made an unrefined noise through her nose. "Emptied your slop jar."

"I'm sorry," Lauri said. "Please don't leave."

"Save your sorries, Missy. You been right hurtful to Doctor, and him the most protectiveness man I ever seen." She wagged a crooked finger in Lauri's face. "Might be he's found hisself a girl who has a hankering for him. Can't say as I rightly blame him."

Mrs. Wemple picked up her bundle, walked to the door, reached for the latch. "Go back to Tice's. I ain't going to stay and see you break that nice young man's heart."

Lauri watched Mrs. Wemple trudge across the street.

She had told the old woman a half truth. Three months had passed, and her courses had not come. She was carrying Geoff's child. As much as she despised the father, she would love the baby. It was her child.

She grasped the window sill for support and fought to control the panic that threatened to overwhelm her. Geoff could be lurking outside. He must know Jason was seldom there. If he had seen Mrs. Wemple leave, he would know there was no one else in the house. She pried her fingers loose, forced herself to bar the door and latch the windows.

Where did Jason keep his guns? No matter. She did not know how to use one, and she was shaking so much she would probably shoot off her own toes. The picture of shooting herself in the foot brought on a fit of hysterical giggles.

She stopped with a hiccough when she heard someone pulling on the latch. She glanced around the room for a place to hide. The bedroom. No. Never there. She would not make it easy for Geoff. She would fight him every inch of the way, with every breath. She hurried to the kitchen and grabbed the butcher knife.

"Lauri." A light tapping. "It's Jason. Open up."

She was still trembling as she unbarred the door. She collapsed into his arms, still holding her weapon.

"Easy." Jason took the knife from her hand, slipped his arm around her waist and eased her onto the settle. He went to his medicine cabinet, took out some Chamomile to brew a tea.

"Drink this," he said. "It will make you feel better." He sat down beside her and took her hand in his. "What were you going to do with that knife? You could have killed me."

"I thought it might be Geoff."

Jason looked around the room. "Where's Mrs. Wemple.?"

"Gone."

"Where?"

"Back to her house." The tea was making her groggy.

He helped her to her feet.

She swayed against him.

"Lie down," he said. "You'll feel better."

It was dark when Lauri opened her eyes. She slipped quietly from her bed, crept into the outer room and into the wing chair near the fireplace.

She must have dozed. She sat up with a start. Someone else was in the room. She reached for the butcher knife. It was gone.

A candle flickered to life. Jason stood in front of her. He had washed, shaved, and was wearing clean clothes.

"Feeling better?" Jason asked.

She looked small and frail in the big chair, her feet tucked under her.

"I'm going back to Gil and Christina," Lauri said.

"That isn't necessary."

"We can't live here, together, alone."

"Marry me."

"I'm carrying another man's child."

"Marry me."

"I'm afraid."

"We've been all through that. I've told you I'll be patient. What does it take to make you believe me? I love you. You love me. What else matters?"

"Something terrible has happened to everyone I've cared about. We were supposed to come here; my mother and father and me. Everything would be better. We were going to be happy, but they died.

"Elder was good to me. Then something happened, and he killed himself."

"Happenstance," Jason interrupted. "Your mother and father were taken ill with fever. Elder was insensible in his head. It had nothing to do with you."

She flinched when Jason's lips first touched hers, but as his mouth caressed hers, she responded with such passion she felt him struggling to restrain himself.

Lauri felt his arms tighten around her. Jason's kiss destroyed Geoff's ghost. She was safe, protected; safe enough to marry Jason.

The next day, Jason sat his horse, gazing at his family's cabin. A white plume of smoke slowly rose from the cobblestone chimney into the dove colored sky. He had ridden aimlessly for over an hour until he found himself at his father's doorstep. Maybe guilt had brought him here. It had been weeks since he had seen his family. It would be even longer before he saw them again.

"Been some time since you come by." His father scowled and stepped aside as Jason walked through the doorway.

Jason's brothers slapped him on the back.

His mother greeted him with a kiss.

He slipped her arms from around his neck and covered both her hands with his. "I'm going to marry Lauri. We'll be leaving Johnstown."

George went to the fireplace, took his pipe from the mantle, filled the bowl with the tobacco he had grown, sat down before the fire, and stretched his long legs toward the hearth. "This got something to do with what happened to Lauri?"

"You've heard?"

"Ain't nobody who ain't," George said.

Martha motioned to the younger boys to leave.

"Let them be," George grumbled. "They ain't innocent babes. You've heard too, ain't you?"

The boys glanced at one another and nodded.

"Pa's right," Jason said. "I'd rather they get the truth from me. Let them stay."

"You know who done it?" George asked.

"Geoff Baxter."

"Ain't surprised," George said. "Too bad about Elder. Ain't natural for a man to take his own life."

"Elder was a sick man." No need for anyone to know more.

"Poor Belle. What do you suppose she'll do?" Martha said.

George snorted. "Snag herself another husband."

"And those two girls?" Martha worried.

The boys snickered, poked one another. "Ain't nobody gonna marry them beauties."

"That ain't Christian." Martha chided.

"But true." The boys burst out laughing.

"Going to that place Sir William left you?" George asked.

"Yes sir." Jason said.

"Ain't many people up there is there? Less you count them Canajoharie

Indians and they ain't going to need you when they got their medicine men hopping around, blowing smoke all over the place, and shaking rattles and feathers at them sick people. How you figuring on making a living?"

"Trapping maybe. Do a little farming."

"You ain't never farmed in your life." George groused. "Hardly know which end of a seed to stick in the ground, I 'spect. You going to leave Lauri alone while you go traipsing around in the woods looking for beaver? Like's not, you'll get caught in your own trap."

"Don't be so hard on the boy, George." Martha said.

"Just trying to talk some sense into him."

"I can't pay taxes on the place up river and rent to John Butler, and I've got to get Lauri away from here." Jason ran his hand through his hair. "There's not much chance for me to make it as a doctor here anymore."

"Never did understand why Sir John let you go," George said.

"He thinks I'm against the crown."

"Are you?"

"I'm not against anybody. I just want to be left alone to go about my business."

"We might all be choosing sides," George said.

"Did you know the Committee refused me medicines?"

"You need those," Martha said.

"That's no never mind to them. I refused to pledge allegiance to their cause and I won't agree not to buy British goods. I'll take medicines any place I can get them."

"Is it true Sir John has swivel guns around Johnson Hall?" George said.

"His Highlanders are armed," Jason told him. "Guy has part of his regiment under arms and drilling. That's why the Committee doesn't want powder or ammunition sent up this way without their say so."

"So it's come to that." George ran his calloused hands over his chin and shook his head. He took his pipe from his mouth and pointed the long stem at his son. "It ain't going to be easy. A man's needs is different. A woman don't always take to wifehood like a man does to husbanding. A bed ain't a favorite place for some women."

"George!"

"If I wound your puritan sensibilities, Martha, take yourself off somewhere. I dare say, Jason being a doctor, he's seen more of a woman than most married men."

"The boys…" Martha protested.

"Nigh on to manhood. Let them stay." He got up from his chair and stood looking down at Jason. "You always was one for takin' care of some hurt thing. Guess there ain't nobody hurtin' worse than Lauri. Martha, get that bottle of sack we been savin'. And six glasses."

The younger boys snickered.

George swung around to glare at them. "Don't go thinkin' I'll allow you drinkin' anytime you want," he turned back, smiling at Jason, "but this is special." He reached out and embraced his oldest son.

CHAPTER 29

Tice's Tavern

A wedding. Christina Tice's eyes sparkled. Oh, how she loved a wedding, and who deserved the kind of happiness that came with a good marriage more than Lauri and Jason.

Gil grasped Jason's hand. "I hope you will be as happy as Christina and I."

"I'm so happy for both of you," Christina said, wrapping Lauri in her arms. "You, my dear, will stay with us until the wedding."

"What about Sheriff White?" Jason protested. "How are you going to keep him from bothering Lauri?"

Gil grinned. "I'm sure Sir John can be persuaded to send the sheriff on a wild goose chase; at least long enough for you two to be long gone."

Wedding Day

Christina stepped back for a final inspection before Lauri went to join Jason and take their vows."I'm so glad you're wearing my wedding dress."

With a nip here and a tuck there, she and Mrs. Wemple had fitted it to Lauri's thin frame.

During one of the fittings, Christina had eyed Lauri's backside. "What do you think, Mrs. Wemple? Should she wear a rump or a hen basket?"

"Rump."

"Oh, yes." Christina agreed. "She has no shape there at all." She went to the trunk in which the gown had been stored, pulled out a pad stuffed with cork and tied it around Lauri's waist.

It was not an elaborate gown, but it was pretty, a pale peach bodice and sleeves lined with linen. The skirt, made of the same material, was looped up in back over a green petticoat, box plaited at the bottom, the whole of which was spattered with delicate yellow, pink, blue and dark green flowers. The neck and sleeves of the bodice were trimmed with the same green silk. Ruffles, the color of the bodice, were pinned to the sleeves.

They had fussed and fluttered over her, fixing her hair first one way, then another, arguing about whether she should paint her face and wear a patch on her cheek, finally deciding she was pretty enough without anything artificial.

It was time.

Mrs. Wemple wiped a tear. "I'll miss you, my sweet little lamb."

Lauri kissed the old woman.

Mrs. Wemple opened the door to the hall where Gil waited to escort the bride to her waiting groom, and hustled down the hall, and slipped quietly into her seat.

Christina kissed Lauri. "For luck," she said, "and may you and Jason be as happy as Gil and I are."

Lauri and Gil paused before they entered the room he had provided for the ceremony. Through the open door, she could see Walter standing, stone faced, at Jason's side.

Jason's family, Catherine Butler, and the boys waited for the bride. Deborah Butler was already weeping.

The soft buzzing of voices quieted when Christina took her place as Lauri's witness.

Gil patted Lauri's trembling hand. "Jason loves you very much."

Gil gave Lauri a quick peck on the cheek, handed her to Jason, and went to sit with the others.

Lauri and Jason joined hands and faced Justice Magistrate, John Butler. He had read only a few words when he stopped, his eyes focused on the back of the room. The metallic click of the latch made everyone turn to see who it was. There was a slight murmur, a shuffling of feet as the wedding guests rose as one. The ladies curtsied and the men bowed. Sir John and Lady Johnson had slipped into the room.

Sir John nodded and John Butler continued.

Lauri barely heard his words.

"With this ring I thee wed," Jason said, and as proof of his love, slipped his grandmother's gold wedding band on her finger.

Lauri's eyes misted.

The last words were read, and in a quiet voice, John Butler said, "You can kiss the bride."

Jason brushed his lips over Lauri's cheek and took her with him to the back of the room to speak to Sir John.

"We'd be honored if you'd join us," Jason said.

"This is a time to be shared with family…" Sir John grasped Jason's hand.

"And friends," Jason added.

"Thank you for that. May I kiss the bride?"

Lauri offered her hand and Sir John lightly kissed it.

"May I have the pleasure of escorting you, Mrs. Dayemon?" Sir John crooked his arm and Lauri pinked. She laid her fingers lightly on his sleeve, and allowed herself to be taken into the next room where a feast was waiting for the wedding party.

Lady Mary's lighthearted laugh, delightful as the tinkling of a tiny silver bell, followed them. She placed a small soft hand on Jason's arm. "I was so hoping you would attend me when my time came. John says Doctor Daly is too far along in years. He's engaged a doctor from Albany."

"You'll be well taken care of," Jason reassured her. "Sir John wants nothing but the best for you."

Gil had set a plentiful table but the conversation was subdued despite Lady Mary's best efforts to engage those around her. Sir John, she noticed, was doing no better. She had not expected Jason's family, Mrs. Wemple or even Christina Tice to feel comfortable.

Walter Butler, who was usually a delightful dinner companion, was quiet. Only Gil Tice, Catherine and John Butler seemed to be at ease.

Jason was rather somber for a bridegroom. Lauri, pale and thin, only toyed with her food.

Was Lauri pining for Stephen and how would she feel if she knew he asked after her in every letter? It was, Polly supposed, her duty to tell her brother that Lauri was married. It would not do to mention these things to John. He would only be annoyed.

"Polly," he would say, in that stern voice he used when he was irritated with her, "you're letting your imagination run away with you. Turn your thoughts to something more useful."

She was roused from her musing. Walter Butler was standing, a glass of wine in his hand.

"Jason," Walter said, "you've been my best friend for more years than I care to admit to. We've had our fair share of scraps and scrapes, some that have changed the color of our mother's hair, I'm afraid."

There were chuckles around the table.

"Lauri," Walter continued, "you've kept us from maiming one another, forced us to bury the hatchet, been the bond that kept us together, but you've come between us more than once, in ways you may never know."

He paused, swallowed hard and there was a huskiness in his voice when he spoke again.

"You'll always have a special place in my heart."

Catherine Butler and Martha Dayemon dabbed the corners of their eyes. Deborah sobbed. The Butler and Dayemon boys were quiet and subdued. John Butler and George Dayemon looked solemn.

"A toast," Walter said.

"Hear. Hear," the male voices chorused.

The guests stood, even Sir John and Lady Johnson. They turned toward the newlyweds, and lifted their glasses.

"Jason. Lauri. May you have a long life and all the happiness you both deserve."

CHAPTER 30

Gil led Jason and Lauri down a long hall, past the living quarters, to a small room tucked away in the corner opposite a flight of stairs that went to the kitchen.

He opened the door, and with a theatrical bow and a wave of his hand, he said, "Best room in the house. Far enough away from the other guests so they won't disturb you and far enough away so you won't disturb them." He was still chuckling as he went down the stairs.

The room was clean but plain, sparsely furnished; a double bed, a chest on chest and a wing chair.

Jason went to the chest and began searching through it.

"What are you looking for?" Lauri said.

"Blankets and a pillow."

"You can't sleep in a chair."

"Then I'll sleep on the floor."

She pressed down on the mattress. It was certainly softer and more comfortable than the floor or chair. "We can't spend the rest of our lives in separate beds."

"I told you I'd make no demands on you."

"It's big enough for two." Her voce quivered. "Turn around."

A knot in one of the burning logs exploded

A startled "Oh," made Jason whirl around. Lauri's gown lay puddled at her feet."

Clothed only in her chemise, she made a desperate effort to pick it up.

"Get into bed," Jason said. "It's chilly in here. I'll put more logs on the fire."

The rope creaked as she crawled across to the far side of the bed. She scrunched herself into a ball and lay facing the wall, pulling the covers up to her chin. She could hear him removing his clothes, placing them, and her petticoats and dress on the chair.

The room was plunged into darkness when Jason blew out the candle.

She felt the bed shift under his weight as he slid in beside her. She held her breath, trembling, waiting, but he turned his back to her and fell asleep.

She relaxed, fell into a deep sleep and had a dream; one she often had in childhood. A knight on a white charger rescued her from a devouring dragon, carried her to the safety of a majestic castle. When they were inside, he left her alone in a cavernous room where fireplaces, with openings higher than a giant is tall, burned logs as big as trees.

He returned and they were no longer in a castle. It was the bedroom in Gil Tice's tavern. The fireplace was narrow and the burning wood was fast becoming embers.

He had removed his armor and was dressed in fawn colored breeches, light blue waistcoat, dark blue coat with turned back cuffs, and lining to match the breeches. They were the clothes he had worn at the wedding.

He was the most handsome man she had ever seen.

He was Jason.

The rays of the sun did not quite reach the wing chair where Jason sat, fully dressed, his long legs stretched out toward the logs blazing in the fireplace.

Jason heard Lauri stirring under the covers. "Get dressed," he said. "Gil and Cristina have breakfast ready."

He stood up, stretched to his full height and moved toward the door. "I'll wait for you downstairs. Don't dally, We've a long way to go today. I want to pay my respects to the Butlers and say Goodbye to Walter."

He stepped into the hall and quietly closed the door behind him.

It was a tearful farewell for Lauri, Christina and Mrs. Wemple, who was living at the tavern now that she had taken over Lauri's job. Mrs. Wemple had proved she was not the busybody and gossip that people said she was. She had taken care of Lauri and never spread a word of what had happened.

The leave-taking went quickly. Gil had seen to that; reminding the women of the long trip ahead and that there was work to be done at the tavern.

One more hug, one more kiss from Christina.

Mrs. Wemple kissed Jason on the cheek. "You're a good man, Doctor Dayemon. Take care of my sweet little lamb."

Gil's stable boy, was waiting in front of the tavern.

Jason led Lauri down the steps toward the sleek riding horse tethered to the hitching post, and the large work horse that dwarfed the boy. "How do you like them, Lauri?" Jason asked.

"They're yours?"

"Ours," Jason said, "Wedding gifts. The big one's Goliath. Mr. Butler says I'll need it to clear the land. Wasn't much clearing done when Sir William owned the cabin."

"He's big enough to do that. Maybe you can hire out. He looks strong enough for any kind of work." Lauri reached up and stroked the horse's nose.

"This is Lightning," Jason patted the steed's withers. "Say hello to the pretty lady, Lightning."

The animal bobbed his head and nickered.

"Walter taught him to do that. He said the Schenectady girls thought it was sweet, the Albany girls thought Lightning was adorable."

"And Walter was wonderful." Lauri added.

"Remember how Walter used to like to race on the King's Highway? This is the horse. Know what Walter said to me? See if you can control him any better than you did me."

He untied the horse and motioned the boy to follow.

When they reached his house, the wagon was there, just as the smithy had promised. The canvas top Jason had insisted upon flapped in the gentle breeze.

The boy tied Lightning to the back, and hitched Goliath to the wagon. He checked the harness once more and stepped back, satisfied everything was secure.

"You don't recollect who I am, do you, sir?"

Jason studied him closely. "Guess I don't."

"Remember two years ago? At Sir William's field days a boy fell out of a tree and almost landed on Miss Lauri?"

"Adam?"

"My pa was supposed to bring me back in two weeks, and you told him not to take that wooden thing off."

"Your arm looks fine. Must be he didn't."

"He tried, but I fit him off and he whipped me but good, till I couldn't stand it no more. Jossie tried to stop him and he hit her. Knocked her down…would have kicked her, too."

"She was expectant," Jason said.

"Don't know what come over me. Just couldn't take it no more; her so sweet and kind to us young ones, nicer than our own ma." Adam swallowed hard but his voice was steady. "I picked up a pitch fork…stuck it as hard as I could in pa's belly. I thought I killed him."

"You aren't sure?"

Adam looked down at his feet. "Jossie told me to get as far away from there as I could, she'd take care of everythin', but I had to stay as close as was safe." He took a deep breath. "I send money to her when my brother comes to see me. He told me pa was dead."

"Does Gil know?" Jason asked.

"I told Mr. Tice my pa got killed by a bear, same thing me and Jossie told the young ones."

He straightened his shoulders and looked Jason in the eye, daring him to argue. "I got to take Jossie away. I'm gonna ask her to marry me. She needs a man who loves her, to take care of her. Somethin' happened to Jossie when pa hit her and she fell. The baby ain't right. She's had it hard takin' care of what ain't even hers and now her pa wants to marry her off to somebody worse than my pa."

"She's hardly more than a child herself." Jason rubbed his hand over his chin. "Let's see, Adam, you must be all of fourteen now."

"Sixteen."

Jason grinned.

"Nigh onto fifteen." Adam admitted.

"Where will you go?"

"My ma's got kin in New Jersey. Her brother come up once, wanted to take her back when he saw what pa had done to her. Pa said nobody was gonna take his whippersnappers or his wife, neither. They was his property and nobody was gonna take what belonged to him. Near killed my uncle, beat him so bad."

Jason placed his hand on the boy's shoulders. "Good luck Adam and be careful." He shook Adam's hand and the boy turned and walked down the street, his back a little straighter, his shoulders squarer.

Jason went into the house. Lauri followed. She took one last look around the room. Nothing remained to remind her of the days she had spent healing under Mrs. Wemple's and Jason's tender care.

"We'll be ready as soon as I put my medicines in the wagon." Jason picked up his medical supplies and went outside.

The street was empty, except for their wagon. The snorting and stomping of the big horse was the only thing disturbing the quiet morning.

Lauri let Jason help her up onto the wagon seat, watched him lock the door, and drop the key in his pocket. He walked around to the other side of the wagon and climbed up beside her. He snapped the reins and they slowly drove out of Johnstown.

The smoke from Butlersbury's chimney drifted toward the east. Catherine and Deborah waited next to Catherine's garden. In a few weeks it would start to sprout and she would give it tender care. How many times had Walter and Jason stolen carrots from the garden when they were boys and then blamed it on the rabbits when she confronted them?

Catherine took the key that Jason gave her. "Walter will be disappointed he missed you."

Catherine did not need to be told that Jason was not the only one Walter would miss. Ever since he had learned that his best friend and the girl he loved were to be married, he had crawled into a shell; so unlike him. When he had the chance to go with his father to Guy Park, he readily agreed.

"Guy Johnson's called a council," Catherine said. "The Albany people, and some of them up here, are worried about which side the Indians will take if the Boston trouble spills over here."

"Whose side do you think they will take, Mrs. Butler?" Jason asked.

She shrugged her shoulders. "Heaven only knows. Whoever gives them the most presents, I suppose. I'm not sure Guy can control the tribes like Sir William did; or Joseph Brant can for that matter. John's been in the Indian

Department for a long time and I worry every time he has to go out...Now Walter is in it, too. I hope and pray the Indians stay out of it."

She walked around to Lauri's side of the wagon and helped her down. Catherine's eyes misted and she held Lauri close to her. "God bless you and keep you, my dear."

"I'll miss you, Mrs. Butler. You've been like a mother to me."

Jason reached for Lauri's hand as Catherine helped her climb back onto the wagon seat.

Catherine walked around to the other side and Jason leaned down so she could kiss him goodbye.

It was a far piece to his cabin between Joseph Brant's house at Canajoharie, the Upper Mohawk Castle, and Nicholas Herkimer's place near the little falls.

At Caughnawaga they turned on to the King's Highway, the road that led westward from Schenectady, past Guy Park, Fort Johnson, the five year old grey stone Palatine Evangelical Lutheran Church at Fox's Mills that most people just called the Palatine Church.

A little farther on were the Klock, and Nellis lands, and on the south side of the river Nicholas Herkimer had built his fine brick house.

A settlement, called Stone Ridge by the 200 or so people living there, had grown up on the northwest side of West Canada Creek at the German Flatts. Beyond that, the road had been allowed to deteriorate. It continued to Cosby's Manor, turned south at Deerfield, crossed the Mohawk River at the abandoned Fort Schuyler. It went on to the Indian village of Oriska, then on to Fort Stanwix.

At noon they stopped to eat the lunch Christina had prepared for them. Jason watered the horses and found a place for them to graze. It was a quiet spot beside the river and they tossed crumbs to the ducks that waddled ashore and to those drifting on the flowing Mohawk.

As they rode on Lauri became drowsy. She snuggled up to Jason and rested her head against him arm.

He slapped the reins over the horse's rump and Goliath picked up the pace, but Jason was forced to slow down again. The frost had been out of the ground for weeks but it had left potholes that caused the wagon to sway and lurch each time a wheel dropped into one.

It was getting toward late afternoon and as they drove on. Jason began looking for an inn where they could spend the night. There always was the threat of robbers, should they be forced to spend the night beside the road, but the danger of a foraging bear or even wolves was more of a concern to him.

He spied a single story building on the north side of the road and as they got closer, he could read the sign: NELLIS TAVERN. There was a house and a block house on the flatlands near the river. The land had been cleared long ago. A man was working the fields.

Jason pulled into the open spot next to the tavern, wrapped the reins around the rail. "Wait here. I'll see about spending the night."

"Ja, a room I have." The proprietor gave his name as Christian Nellis.

"My wife and I would like privacy." Jason told him

"Ja. Ja. Upstairs, I have such a room. You have a horse?"

"Two. And a wagon."

"The barn you can use. I will do nothing if someone steals your horses or wagon."

Nellis was still alone when Jason brought Lauri into the tavern. "Mein wife will soon have the room ready."

A buxom Palatine woman—Christian Nellis introduced as his wife—served a wholesome supper: meat pie, apple butter, johnnycake, and Indian pudding. Jason and Lauri washed the meal down with cider.

Two men, wearing muddied boots and a strong barn smell, clomped into the tavern. They ordered beer and seated themselves at a table near the bar.

The older man spat into the fireplace.

"A broom you'll get over the head," Mrs. Nellis said.

"Frau Nellis you're like all Palatine women," the older man snorted, "beset with purgation."

"Fancy words. Foul man."

He ignored her. "Seen any Indians, Nellis?"

"Nein."

"Maybe they ain't going down to Johnson's. Maybe they're going to mind their own business." The younger man suggested.

"And maybe they'll lift your scalp." The older man puckered up, saw the broom in Mrs. Nellis's hand, swallowed his cud of tobacco and gulped his beer.

He doffed his dirty wool hat when he spotted Lauri. "Didn't mean to affright you about the Indians, Mam."

Mrs. Nellis humphed.

CHAPTER 31

Lauri became violently ill during the night, vomiting until she retched. Jason brewed a tea of Chamomile, but she could not keep it down. He held her in his arms until she fell into an exhausted sleep.

The next morning he helped her dress for the trip. He had given her a small dose of Laudanum, and she was unsteady on her feet.

Mrs. Nellis's suggestion, "We should send for Doctor Petry, Ja?" brought a smile to Lauri's pallid face.

"No thank you, Mrs. Nellis," Jason said. "I'll take good care of her."

He fixed a place for Lauri to lie down in the back of the wagon. It would be slow going today. The road was getting worse, and he did not want to jar her anymore than he could help.

Her groan startled him. He turned to see that she had kicked off the covers, wrapped her arms over her stomach, writhing in pain. Another moan brought him scrambling over his seat to her side. Then he saw the blood.

The touch of a calloused hand on her forehead roused Lauri.

"Mein name is Gerda Heinrich." Clear bright eyes looked down at her and the frown on the woman's face disappeared. "It is good. You have open your eyes. Some hearty broth I will bring you. You will eat and soon you will feel better, Ja?" She patted Lauri's hand, and walked out of the room.

Lauri tried to raise herself up in the bed, but a sudden pain, low down, forced her back against the pillow. She tried to block out the memory of the sudden cramping, the almost unbearable pain, the blood. Then she remembered the blessed blackness.

The woman returned. She set the bread and bowl of broth on the table next to the bed, and helped Lauri sit up.

"Liebchen," she said, "slow you eat." She fed Lauri small sips of broth and stayed with her until she heard the click of the door latch.

Jason slipped into the room and Gerda quietly left.

He took Lauri in his arms, and held her close.

She clung to him, her wet cheek pressed against his. "I lost the baby, didn't I?"

"Hush, Sweetheart. Don't think of that now."

"Stay with me."

Lauri drifted off to sleep and when she woke the house was quiet. Jason was stretched out beside her. For a long time she watched the even rise and fall of his chest. She reached to brush the hair that had fallen over his forehead, then pulled her hand away. He must be worn out. She let him sleep.

"Two more weeks she must rest," Gerda protested the first time she found Jason helping Lauri out of bed. "It is like childbirth, Ja? Three weeks I lay abed when my sohn is born."

"She needs to get her strength back," Jason said.

Gerda walked away, muttering in German.

The next day he walked Lauri to the bedchamber door and back to the bed.

She felt weak and dizzy and wanted to lie down but he would not let her. She continued to get better, and when she was able to go into the kitchen he sat with her by the fire.

"You and Karl have been so kind to us." Lauri was helping in the kitchen while Gerda prepared a special meal for their last evening together.

Gerda smiled at Lauri. The sleeves of Gerda's chemise were pinned up and, for the first time, Lauri noticed that the hair on Gerda's arms had been burned off, like so many other women who singed their arms when they put them in the fireplace oven to test the baking temperature.

"So goot your Jason is to you," Gerda said. "Day and night he stay by your side. Sleep, I say to him. I will watch. Nein. Not till he is sure you are better does he leave you."

There was a long silence before Gerda spoke again. "I was afraid of him at first—pounding on the door—you all blood—I think maybe he kill you. Maybe he kill us, too."

"Why did you let him in?"

"Karl finally know what he say." She folded her arms and made a rocking motion.

"Baby." Lauri said.

"Ja." She saw Lauri's chin quiver. "Karl open door, little. Your man push his way in. He is crying. Bed, he say, he must put you in bed. He ask for ice. When you in bed, he put ice inside you. Ice will stop flow, he say." Gerda searched Lauri's face. "How he know this?"

Lauri did not answer.

It was a bittersweet evening; the last time the four of them would be together. The women sat apart from the men, talking quietly.

The men were in deep conversation, their voices low.

Karl leaned toward Jason. "Nicholas Herkimer will be a goot neighbor. Not all men are so goot. Some will not trust you. They do not like the Johnsons and you are from Johnstown."

A log tumbled onto the hearth. Jason pushed it back with the toe of his boot. "And because I come from there, they will be sure I am a friend of the Johnsons? And Herkimer? Will he trust me?"

"He will wait. He will see."

Lauri and Jason were back on the King's Highway at first light.

Although warm weather had come to the valley, snow still clung to the Spruce, Balsam and Hemlocks in the Adirondacks. Patches of ice still covered parts of the frigid, swift flowing streams rushing toward the valley grist mills.

The Mohawk River opened, and farmers like Karl Heinrick waited for the sun to dry their fields so they could plant their barley, corn and wheat.

If the wet weather in England continued, wheat prices would increase beyond last year's eight percent. It had already forced England to open its ports, and it would no longer by necessary for the ship *SIR WILLIAM*

JOHNSON to smuggle American wheat into the British ports; a joke the Palatine farmers thoroughly enjoyed.

Jason did his best to keep the wagon from lurching but the road worsened the farther they traveled.

Lauri gripped the side of her seat to keep from falling off. "Why didn't you tell the Heinricks you're a doctor?"

"What kind of a doctor am I? I couldn't save Sir William. I couldn't save the baby, and I might have lost you."

Gerda's words came back to her. "So goot your Jason is to you. Not until he is sure you are better does he leave you."

In one night Geoff had almost done what Belle had never been able to do…break her spirit. Jason loved her, married her, would have raised her child. She wouldn't let Geoff ruin her marriage.

"I love you," she said. "Just be patient."

He kissed her then, an almost shy kiss at first. Her arms came around his neck and she returned his kiss with no shyness at all.

As they moved farther away from the Heindricks' farm, the trees grew closer to the road. Not many were in full leaf, but later they would form a shady canopy. At every break in the undergrowth, Jason eyed the river.

"I want to find a shallow place to cross." he said.

It was early afternoon before he found a place he thought was safe. Both horses shied when they stepped into the cold water but he coaxed them across.

They came to a clearing and there, on a hill side, was the church that Sir William had ordered built for the Mohawks. It was as John Butler had described it; a plain wooden structure, with a bell tower and steeple, unlike the limestone Queen Anne's Chapel, built fifty eight years earlier for the Mohawks at Fort Hunter on the lower Mohawk River.

Indian women were working the soil on the flat land below the church. One looked toward the couple on the wagon, said something to the young girl with her, then went back to her work.

"That must be Joseph Brant's place." Jason pointed out a frame, clapboarded building with glass windows, fireplace, a stone cellar. There was a stout Dutch barn, and smaller out buildings that stood a short distance from the house.

There were other houses nearby, and a cluster of Indian dwellings.

"I wonder if Miss Molly is living here," Lauri said. "I hope so. I'd like to go see her, once we get settled. It'll be nice having someone we know being so near."

Jason clicked his tongue and the big horse began to move. "We will, but we'll have to be careful."

"Why?"

"Folks up here that don't like the Johnsons, or the Butlers."

"How could any one not like John or Catherine or Walter?"

"It's what they stand for."

"The king?"

Jason nodded. "They'd like nothing better than to see the Johnsons and the Butlers knocked down a peg or two, and maybe us with them, if they found out I was Sir William's physician."

"They don't even know us. That's not right. If we leave them alone, will they leave us alone?"

"I hope so."

The horse was slowing, and Jason snapped the reins to speed him up. The village fell behind them.

They came to a bend in the road. There was a cedar roofed house a short distance ahead of them. A Dutch barn with high doors, front and back, had been built close to the house to protect it from the cold winter winds. There was a stone foundation a few feet away from the house, all that was left, apparently, of the original cabin.

The older fields around the house were treeless. Three stumps remained on a small rise where a man and a young boy were straining to pry out the roots of a big tree. With one great heave, the two broke the roots free.

Jason considered stopping to water the horses at the well sweep between the two buildings, but decided against it. He had an anxious feeling about the place. Someone here could cause trouble.

A young woman stood alone inside the wattle fence beside the road. "Hello mister," she called when they came within hailing distance.

"This road take me to Nicholas Herkimer's place?" Jason asked.

"If you keep to it."

"And I suppose I'll pass by Sir William Johnson's cabin."

"Have to take a right farther down from here." She stayed inside the fence and began keeping pace with the wagon. She looked at him with a boldness that made him uneasy. "Ain't nobody there."

She pulled out some of the twigs and branches from the fence, tossed them carelessly aside, hoisted her skirt above her ankles and stepped through.

"The old caretaker run off 'bout a month after the baronet died. Said he weren't going to keep it up for nobody but Johnson. Place has all gone to weeds. What's your name, mister?"

"Dayemon. Jason Dayemon. This is my wife, Lauri."

"I'm Susannah Freye. At your service…Jason Dayemon."

They came to a thicket. The girl stopped and they moved on. Jason did not look back.

CHAPTER 32

Jason's Cabin

Jason's place was neglected, as Susannah had said. The kitchen garden—if it could be called that—had not felt the blade of a hoe or spade in years. The weeds were choking what few vegetables still struggled to push their way through the ground.

He pulled the wagon to a stop, pressed the foot brake, hopped to the ground and went around to the other side, and lifted Lauri out.

Before Jason and Lauri left Johnstown, Sir John had summoned Jason to his office.

"My father had the cabin built because he wanted a place to rest on his way to and from Indian councils at Oswego and Niagara. He used poor judgment, I'm afraid. It's too close to the Mohawk village and Joseph Brant. It would have been an affront to refuse the hospitality of Brant and his family, and the village elders. He never used it.

"He let trappers use the cabin on their way down the valley with their pelts. My father was shrewd, you know. They brought him the best furs.

"He wanted you to have the cabin in appreciation for all the care you gave him and for your loyalty.

"It was not in his will, you understand. By rights it belongs to me. I won't go against my father's wishes. I've had Walter Butler draw up the legal documents. The cabin and the land are yours."

Sir John stood up, gave the papers to Jason, shook his hand, wished him well, and left the room.

The latch string on the cabin door was out; the way the caretaker must have left it when he abandoned the place. Jason pushed. The door swung open, and sagged on rusted hinges. He stepped inside.

The fireplace had a good draft, judging from the ash on the hearth. Charred pieces of tables and chairs were scattered around the room. The cupboard shelves were cluttered with bits of broken mugs and dishes. Filthy blankets, little more than rags, lay where they had been tossed on the beds.

The walls were tightly sealed. None of the glass windows had been broken, but light streamed through a hole that had been chopped in the roof.

Raccoons had chewed the legs of chairs and beds. Mice droppings were everywhere. The place reeked with the odor of urine and feces.

"We can fix it," Lauri said.

He whirled around, grabbed her wrist, dragged her outside, and pulled her toward the wagon.

"Where are we going?" Lauri demanded.

"Back to Johnstown," Jason answered. "I won't let you live in a place like this."

"Don't I have a say about it?"

"No."

"I don't want to go back to Johnstown," Lauri said. "There's nothing for me there. Sir William wanted you to have this place. He meant it for us.

"I'm not afraid of soap and water. I can pull weeds and you can burn them." She slipped her arms around his neck. "I want to live here with you."

They went back inside. He made a circuit of the room.

He stopped in front of her. A smile tugged at the corners of his mouth. "Are you going to stand there or are you going to get to work?"

Her eyes were bright with excitement. "It's got a real wood floor." She pushed aside the smashed dishes with the toe of her shoe. "I can make a rug to put beside the bed. I can make a quilt. We'll be snug and warm all winter."

He muffled her with a kiss. Tomorrow he would climb up and see what was needed to fix the hole in the roof.

Lauri set about putting the cabin to rights.

Jason busied himself patching the hole in the roof. He built a temporary shelter for the horses. It was not much more than a lean-to made of branches and bark, but it gave them cover.

He put together a makeshift table and bench, a cobbled up affair that would have made Marinus Willett groan.

He used planks and the caretaker's bed to build a Jack bed; the head and one side supported by the cabin walls and only needing one post at the outer corner.

When all the inside work was done, they turned their attention to planting the seeds Jason's father had given them. Corn, beans and squash were put into each mound. The corn would grow out of the top of the piled dirt, the beans would use the stalks for a pole, and the squash would cover the ground to keep out the weeds. They fertilized the soil with some of the fish that Jason caught. A good crop would keep them through the next winter.

The Freyes

Jason inched his way across the cabin roof and searched for the top rung of the ladder with the toe of his boot. He did not see the four people gawking at him as he slowly made his way down. His right foot was still on the ladder when a hand clamped on to his shoulder, nearly shoving him off balance, and in one swift movement, spun him around.

"Your name's Dayemon, ain't it?"

"Yes."

The man pinning him against the wall was taller by half a head. Muscles bulged beneath a sweat stained shirt.

"Freye. Josef Freye." He let go of Jason's shoulder and a hairy hand grasped Jason's palm. Freye stepped aside and Jason saw three people standing a few paces away.

Freye beckoned to the older woman. "This here's my wife, Hannah."

Mrs. Freye, a frail looking woman who barely came up to Josef's chest, offered an awkward curtsy.

Josef pointed to a good looking boy on the threshold of manhood. He favored his mother, slightly built, with the same shy expression.

"That's Dolf," Josef said. "You already met Susannah."

There was nothing shy in her manner. She stepped up and stood so close she brushed Jason's arm.

Freye looked up at the roof. "Think that roof patch's gonna hold?" He didn't wait for an answer. "First rain'll tell. Ain't right what them heathens done."

"You know who trashed the place?" Jason asked.

"Some worthless Indians passing through, more'n likely. None of Brant's done it. They're Christian, so they say. They got too much good feeling for old Johnson to do it. Your wife here?"

Freye started walking toward the front of the cabin. "Sure would like Hannah to meet her. She gets lonesome for a woman's company. She ain't got nobody but Susannah. Ain't many other women nearby 'cept them Indians. We ain't partial to Molly Brant."

The cabin door was ajar.

Josef stopped, and looked in. A woman was putting things that looked like apothecary jars on the shelf. Bottles of all sizes and shapes, neatly labeled, were lined up in a neat row.

Surgical instruments were laid out on the table. He had been a boy during the French trouble but he had seen limbs cut off and he knew a scalpel, an amputation saw, a straight and curved amputation knife, when he saw them.

"Lauri," Jason called, "our neighbors came to pay a visit."

Lauri spotted the burly man. She hustled outside and closed the door.

Jason reached for her hand and pulled her close. "Lauri this is Hannah Freye."

"Mrs. Freye." Lauri acknowledged.

Hannah answered, "Mam."

"Dolf," Jason nodded toward the young man standing next to Hannah.

Lauri gave him a friendly smile.

Color rushed to Dolf's face, and taking a cue from his mother, managed a strangled, "Mam."

"You remember Susannah." Jason continued.

Neither greeted the other.

Josef stepped forward. "Josef Freye." He took Lauri's hand in his, holding it longer than was necessary.

Lauri managed to slide her hand from his and wiped it on her apron. "Sorry, I can't ask you in. We're not settled. The place is a terrible mess. I don't have it cleaned up." She was prattling but she couldn't stop her tongue.

Josef's smile turned into a scowl. "Don't you fret little lady. We just come by to be neighborly. You go back to what you was doin'."

He motioned to his family and the four of them trudged down the road. Susannah looked back over her shoulder. Her smile was meant only for Jason.

The Freye's had finished their evening meal and, as usual, Josef had groused at Hannah about the plainness of the food. "Ain't you never gonna cook somethin' fit to be et?"

Hannah didn't answer. She had learned long ago not to set him off when he was in that mood.

She picked up her mending, took a seat next to the fireplace, trying her best to see by the flickering light. She had asked about buying a candle, but Josef had said that the price was too dear. If she couldn't see to mend in the evening she should do it in the daytime and, she could do it, too, if she wasn't so lazy and pokey she couldn't get her chores done before dark.

Dolf came in from feeding the supper scraps to the pigs, saw his father and sister with their heads together, so wrapped up in some kind of gossip, they paid him no heed. He took a seat near his mother. She was having trouble threading the needle.

"Ma," he said, "let me do that."

He heard Josef snort and Susannah snicker. He felt the old anger welling up inside him. He and his mother meant nothing. Susannah was the only one, other than himself, that Josef cared about.

His hand clenched into a fist. One day he would stand up to his father, but not tonight. It would only go harder on his mother.

He heard Josef say, "Dayemon's a doctor."

There was no mistaking the excitement in Susannah's voice when she asked, "You sure, Pa?"

Josef's head bobbed a yes. "I seen all them saws. I know what they're used for. I seen arms and legs cut off. That pretty little wife of his had them saws laid out on the table."

Susannah put on a long face. "She ain't pretty."

Josef patted her hand. "Ain't nobody pretty as my little gal."

"You want me to find out, Pa?"

"You be careful, missy. He's a married man, new married at that. Don't you go makin' no trouble."

Let Pa caution her about Jason being a new married man. She had seen his scrawny wife. He'd tire of her soon enough. She'd see to it. "You want to know or not?"

Josef shrugged. "Ain't no harm in tryin', I suppose."

Hannah Freye moved quietly through the woods. She had slipped away unnoticed. Not that it made any difference. Josef had gone to see Nicholas Herkimer; most likely to stir up trouble for that nice young man who had moved into Sir William's place. As if the new neighbor did not have enough on his mind; what with repairing the damage to the cabin, clearing the weeds, and planting a crop. She hoped he would get enough to tide him and his wife over the winter. If not, she would see that they got some of theirs. She would not let them go hungry.

Josef would be angry, but over the years she had become good at putting things over on him. She would risk it.

Susannah had gone down the road to wait for the doctor to come along on that spirited horse of his. Did Susannah really think her mother did not know she was setting her cap for Jason Dayemon?

Just like Josef's head was turned by a pretty face, and a well shaped ankle, Susannah was taken by a good looking man, especially if he had prospects.

Dolf was working the far field. He was the only good thing to come out of her marriage to Josef Freye.

Hannah kept to the path in the woods. She was not taking any chances on meeting Josef on the road or being seen by Susannah.

Hannah was going to set things right with the Dayemons. She had thought hard and long on it. Josef had made an ass of himself, and Susannah had acted like a trollop the day the family had visited the new couple. Hannah wanted them to know that not all the Freyes were like that.

She came out of the woods a short distance from the Dayemon's cabin. The riding horse was gone. As she walked up to the front of the cabin she could see that the latch string was in. She could hear someone moving inside. She tapped lightly. It became suddenly quiet. She rapped a little harder.

"It's Hannah Freye."

The bar lifted and the door opened slowly.

Hannah blanched. Lauri Dayemon stood facing her, a pistol pointed directly at her.

Lauri lowered the gun to her side and motioned Hannah in.

"Land," Hannah said. "You put a fright into me."

"I'm sorry, Mrs. Freye. Jason worries about me being alone. He insists I keep the gun handy"

"I got Dolf to teach me how to use a gun. I ain't so scared of Brant's Indians, but we do get a stranger come through here now and again. Oh my, I'm forgetting what I come for. I ain't here to cause trouble. I come to beg pardon."

"Whatever for?"

"Josef weren't well mannered when we was here before. He can be thorny sometimes."

Hanna glanced toward the row of neatly labeled bottles on the shelf, the herbs on the counter top, the mortar and pestle. "I know what some of them things is."

Lauri stiffened.

"Don't get your back up, Mrs. Dayemon. Ain't nobody's business but yours. Land, we've need of another doctor. It's a far piece to Doctor Petry. Josef's just pestered 'cause nobody told him.

"I'd like us to be friends, you and me. A woman can get an empty feelin', livin' away from her family, and nobody to talk to. I'd like to come and see you now and again."

"That would be nice," Lauri said. "Maybe I could visit you sometime."

"Don't do that. Josef ain't no kind of a man a pretty mite like you should be around. Susannah, she tends to the moody side. I could send Dolf for you, though, if Josef and Susannah go away. They do sometime."

CHAPTER 33

Colonel Nicholas Herkimer's Place

"We got to watch, Dayemon."

For the past half hour, Josef Freye had been sitting in the small building Nicholas Herkimer used for a store, trying to make his friend and neighbor listen to him. He had come because Herkimer was a member of the Committee of Safety, representing the Canajoharie District.

Josef lived in the Canajoharie District. He knew his duty. It was up to good men, like him, to report anything suspicious, and Jason Dayemon was, in his eyes, suspect.

He considered most doctors who had crossed his path to be braggarts, puffed up with their own self importance. The fact that Jason Dayemon had made no effort to present himself as a physician gnawed at him.

"So uneasy a man you are." Nicholas Herkimer studied the paper in his hand, more preoccupied with the shipment of goods he had just received than Josef's problem. He tallied the kegs on the floor in front of the counter: six ankers of brandy, eight ankers of rum, ten ankers of molasses.

Josef reached out and grabbed Herkimer's sleeve.

The store keeper turned, annoyed. "You talk too much, Josef. First, I finish." He went on checking the boxes of strouds, axes, steel traps, fish hooks and lines.

Herkimer spoke in German to Sam, the black slave he had bought in New York twenty-three years earlier. Sam's quick mind had impressed Herkimer, and he had taught Sam, not only how to speak German, but to do some ciphering and enough writing to keep simple records.

Sam put the dry goods on the shelves as Herkimer checked off the list: eight yards of black serge, seven yards of shalloon, one yard of buckram, four skeins of silk and two sticks of silk twist.

Herkimer tossed a half dozen sheath headed buttons on the counter and turned his attention to Josef for the first time. "Now, we talk."

Josef forced himself to remain calm. "Dayemon could be a danger to us."

"Ja," Herkimer chortled, "he could cut off your arm when you are shot in the leg."

Herkimer's unconcerned attitude about a matter Josef considered important was troubling, and he was beginning to wonder if some of Herkimer's enemies weren't right about him. It was well known that some of Herkimer's family had Tory leanings, and some people in the valley thought Herkimer needed watching.

Josef pressed on. "Dayemon lives in Sir William's old place. How do we know that Johnson ain't sent him to find out what's going on up here."

"He's just a doctor." Herkimer assured him.

"Maybe he ain't just a doctor." Josef dogged the idea. "You ever seen him before?"

"Ja."

"Where?"

"Johnson Hall. When the baronet showed off young John's new wife." Herkimer wiped his hands on a dirty cloth laying on the counter top.

"That the only time?"

"Nein."

"When?"

"Sir William's funeral."

"Don't mean nothin'." Josef conceded. "I'd gone myself if I had the means."

"Dayemon was Sir William's physician."

Josef ran his hairy hand across his mouth. "A Johnson dog on one side and Joseph Brant for a neighbor on the other."

"Nein. He's no dog of the Johnsons." Herkimer folded the paper in his hand and gave it to Sam. "Dayemon wouldn't sign the oath."

Herkimer could see the question in Josef's eyes. For a man who liked to think of himself as smart, Josef could be thick sometimes.

"To the king." Herkimer said. "Dayemon's still a friend of Marinus Willett."

Josef swatted at a fly flitting around his head. "Ain't never heard of him."

"You have big ears, Josef. You will. You will."

Josef left Herkimer to his tallying, and for a long time stood outside staring at Herkimer's house. He had never been inside, and he knew it was not likely he ever would. Herkimer was a farmer like he was, but Herkimer was a wealthy farmer and an influential man.

Some day, Josef told himself, he would be a wealthy farmer, and an influential man. Pandering to the right people wasn't beneath him

Jason was tending the patch that he and Lauri had planted. He leaned on the hoe handle, resting his chin on his folded hands, watching the black man racing toward him on a horse, leading another mount.

The negro stopped. His horse danced, and the man patted his horse's neck to quiet him. "One of our girls is birthin'. Mrs. Herkimer say, 'Go get Doctor Dayemon.' The midwife, she do nothin'. Doctor, don't let my girl die."

"I'll get my case." Jason disappeared into the cabin. When he returned, the negro handed him the reins, and before Jason could mount, the man was already tearing down the road.

Jason heard the wail of the parturient woman, and he drew a deep breath. He had never been able to close his ears to the sounds of a woman's pain when she was giving birth.

Old women, and very small children were gathered in the road that led to the cabin where the young girl was birthing. A baby crawled in the dirt, and a woman snatched him out of harms way as Sam and Jason raced down the street.

A barefoot boy in a frayed shirt, and ragged britches, a hole worn through at the knee, squatted alone beneath an old oak tree, almost hidden by the undergrowth. He never stopped watching the cabin, and each time the girl screamed with a birth pain, he hunkered lower on his haunches.

Sam's feet touched the ground almost before the horse stopped. He turned a rage filled face toward the boy, then dashed inside the cabin. Jason followed close on Sam's heels.

A girl, fifteen at the most, lay on a straw mattress on a narrow cot. She still had a child's bones and Jason wondered if she was developed enough to get the baby out.

A contraction, and the girl wailed.

Jason shoved aside the women crowding around the girl. "Who's the girl's mother?"

An anxious woman answered.

"You understand English?" Jason demanded.

She nodded.

"Hold her hand. She's going to need you. The rest of you—get out."

Sam reached past the woman, and clasped the child's hand.

"Let the mother do that," Jason said. "Wait outside."

Sam protested, but a soft feminine voice urged him to do as he was told.

Jason pushed the girl's bloody shift above her waist and crouched at the foot of the cot.

He felt for the baby. The head was down but the arms and legs were to the front. The umbilical cord, wrapped around the infant's neck, could strangle it.

Another doctor would have performed a craniotomy but he was repulsed by the crushing of a baby's skull, simply to make the removal of a fetus easier.

His legs began to cramp. "Get me a stool."

He felt something pushed under him and he carefully eased himself on to it.

It was going to be a difficult delivery.

He was aware of a ruckus outside, but he kept his mind on the problem at hand.

Women's voices, angry: "Stop, Cassius, you kill old, Sam.

The voices were raised in increasing volume until an authoritative male commanded, "All of you, clear out. Sam, get back to work."

Sam began to argue.

"When the overlooker tells you to get to work, Sam, you get. Cassius ain't nothin' but a boy, for all he fathered your girl's tadpole, but he's a strong buck, and I'll not have him ruin you. Colonel Herkimer's put a lot of time and money into you. Remember that. Now, get to work. You'll know soon enough when it's born.

The overlooker watched Sam shuffle toward the store. When the old negro was out of sight, he began searching for Cassius. The boy was gone.

Jason did his best to save the child, and the mother. He laid the squalling boy on the girl's stomach. She took a quick look at the child, managed a weary smile, and fell into an exhausted sleep.

"Get a wet nurse. He's a hungry one." Jason shrugged his shoulders to relieve the tension.

Black hands took the squalling baby away.

For the first time, Jason was aware of the woman who had been at his side during the delivery. She was young—Jason reckoned her to be in her twenties—her voice soft, German.

There was blood on her clothes.

"I'm Maria Herkimer," she said. "Nicholas and I have worried about Lilah. She's so small, just a child."

"She should grow up before she has more children." Jason was tired, irritable. The girl had no business having a baby at her age. The baby could have died. She could have died.

A child having a child, and there was a good chance that in another year Lilah would give birth again. He had seen it time and time again among the poor in New York.

"Come to the house, doctor," Maria said. "Nicholas will want to thank you."

Jason's muscles relaxed at they walked toward the house. He had never seen Herkimer's home, but he had heard it described as being almost as grand as Sir William's. It was an attractive building; brick, two stories high with a gambrel roof.

The center hall ran from, front to back, with rooms on both sides. A stairway led to the second floor. The rooms were not furnished in the expensive style of Johnson Hall, but they looked comfortable, homey.

"Lilah had a boy." Maria told the dark haired man working at his desk by the window in the south east corner of the house.

He turned at the sound of her voice. "Ja? Goot." He rose, reached out to shake Jason's bloody hand, then pulled out another chair. "Sit, Sit."

Jason eased his weary bones onto the chair.

Herkimer sat down opposite him. "Maria bring the doctor a basin of water and some goot beer."

194

Maria returned with the basin, towel, and two steins. She was wearing a clean chemise, petticoat, skirt and apron. She gave a stein to Jason, the other to her husband, and turned to leave.

"Thank you, Mrs. Herkimer," Jason said. "I couldn't have saved the girl or the baby without your help. Your wife, Colonel, is a remarkable woman."

"Ja." Herkimer beckoned to Maria and took her hand. "She is the medicine of life."

Jason smiled. Wasn't that in the bible somewhere?

Maria blushed at the compliment. Without a word, she left the room.

"Drink hearty, doctor." Herkimer raised his tankard, gauged Jason over the top.

"Colonel, may I ask a question?"

"Ja. Ja."

"Why did you send for me instead of Doctor Petry?"

"Bill is too far away. Maria said Lilah could not wait for him. You are a goot physician, Ja? Johnson would not have one who was not goot. For myself I want to see."

Jason leaned toward the Dutchman; remembering Karl Heinrick's words—'Herkimer will wait. Herkimer will see.'

"And what did you see?" Jason asked.

Herkimer laughed. "You is goot."

Jason leaned back in his chair, raised his stein.

He went home with new hinges.

CHAPTER 34

May 1775

The road east to Brant's, and west to Herkimer's was good for exercising the horse Walter had given him. Jason could give the animal its head, and let him run full out.

As he raced down the road, his mind was on the drastic step he had taken. In order to get the medicines he needed, Jason had agreed to support the Continental Congress.

Jason had severed his ties with the people who meant so much to him, but to his way of thinking, agreeing to support the Continental Congress was not a matter of politics. It was strictly a matter of survival.

There had been that business in Massachusetts on the 19th of April. What was the name of that place? Concord? Lexington? Who would have believed a bunch of farmers, who called themselves Minutemen, could rout the king's trained and disciplined soldiers?

On the 10th of May, Ethan Allen, a bumpkin from the Hampshire grants, and Benedict Arnold, a Connecticut apothecary-bookseller, one time smuggler, and Colonel of the Connecticut Militia, had taken Ticonderoga. They had simply walked into the fort, and the British Commander had surrendered.

The news of the fort's capture had made some people cocky. There had been word of a couple of happenings right here in the valley.

Guy Johnson claimed the New Englanders planned to take him prisoner. His mail was being intercepted, and read, before being delivered to him. Proof, he insisted, that the Tryon and Albany Committees of Safety were afraid the Indians would be turned loose on them, and that it was necessary for the Committees to keep the Boston people informed.

To protect himself, Guy had fortified his house, put five hundred men under arms, and cut off all normal channels of communication. People traveling east or west along the King's Highway were stopped and searched when they passed Guy Park Manor.

There had been an attempt to raise a liberty pole at John Veeder's house at Caughnawaga. Three hundred people, so the story went, were waiting to raise the symbol of freedom when Sir John arrived with Guy Johnson, Dan Claus and John Butler.

Sir John said he meant it to be a show of strength. His retainers were armed with swords and pistols, but somehow things got out of hand. Guy and Jacob Sammons had shouted at one another, traded insults and scuffled with each other. Someone knocked young Sammons down with a loaded whip and he was severely beaten.

Jason was pondering all this when he spotted Susannah Freye standing beside the road.

Susannah had taken to walking to the end of the fence where the trees grew thick and tall. It was a place to be alone, to wonder what life was like in the big cities—cities she wanted to visit, to live.

Once her father had found her there. "What are you standin' here for? Ain't nothin' to see but trees."

What could she tell him? The truth? That the road could take her away from the sameness and dullness of being stuck in a wilderness with no one but her mother, brother, and a father who smothered her with his domineering ways?

The road went farther than Canajoharie Castle, with its mixture of Indian squalor and houses like Joseph Brant had, better than the place in which she lived. The road went to Albany, east to Boston, south to New York. Cities she had never seen.

Now a man, a doctor, lived a short piece up the road, and he could take her to any of those places.

Once she had gone farther down the road. She had found a hidden copse, perfect for a tryst.

She had never brought anyone there; until Jason Dayemon came along.

She knew she was no ravishing beauty, but she was well endowed, and she knew how to use what she had. At first she gave it away, but once a man paid her. After that, nothing was free. She had never told Pa, not because she was ashamed of what she did, but because he would want some of the money.

Susannah was out of sorts. In a fool's moment, she had told her father she would find out if Jason Dayemon was a doctor, but it was Josef who told her that Colonel Herkimer had known about Dayemon all along.

Susannah had been waiting a long time, but she had not seen Jason riding his fine horse.

Had he passed by before she arrived? Possibly.

Would he come later? Perhaps.

Had he ridden in the other direction? Maybe.

Had he stopped exercising his horse? Not likely.

She was considering these things when she heard the clip-clop of the horse's hooves. She stepped out into the road so he would be sure to see her.

"Hello Doctor Dayemon," she called when he was within hearing distance.

He slowed as he came nearer. A cool breeze tousled his hair.

"Your roof patch holdin'?" she asked.

"Seems to be."

"You goin' any place special?" A sudden rush of wind lifted her skirt, revealing trim ankles, and shapely calves that her woolen stockings could not disguise. It pleased her that Jason had noticed.

"Just exercising my horse."

They moved along together.

"Where you from?" Susannah asked.

"Johnstown."

"You live right there?"

"My father has a small farm close by."

She considered his answer for a moment. "You don't act like no farmer. Don't talk like one."

"I went to Sir William's free school. Mr. Wall was a hard task master."

"Ain't no school up here," she said, "but Ma teached me how to write my name. I can read a little, and do sums. Did you know Sir William?"

"Everybody knew the Baronet."

"You know the Butlers, too?" She had heard her father mention them. The older son was supposed to be good looking and a lawyer.

Jason answered with a simple, "Yes."

"You a Tory?" Her father hated the Johnsons, Butlers, their kin and their ties to the crown.

Jason shook his head.

"If you ain't no Tory, you against the King?"

Jason rode on without answering.

Susannah watched him disappear. She would be waiting tomorrow, and however long it would take. He was wasted on that scrawny wife of his.

Jason had caught a glimpse of Susannah standing alongside the road the first day he raced Lightning. He thought nothing of it. It wasn't until the fourth day that he admitted to himself that it was not chance that brought Susannah here.

It began harmlessly enough.

They exchanged pleasantries and small talk, and he rode on. He was flattered by her attention and did not encourage her.

She was waiting for him, just as he knew she would. Fool that he was, he finally gave into her and let her ride with him.

She took him to a grove, a secluded place, far off the road, where they would not be seen. The moss covered ground was as soft as a feather bed. A stream flowed through on its way to join the Mohawk River.

Sunlight dappled the ground. Lauri would say it made her think of shadows on the hills.

The noisy Jays stopped their scolding. Only the gurgling of the water flowing over the rocks broke the silence.

Susannah stopped, whirled so fast to face him, Jason had to wrap his arms around her to keep her from falling.

She smiled as her arms circled his neck. A soft sigh escaped her lips as her mouth found his.

He freed himself from her embrace. His fingers pressed into the soft flesh of her wrists.

Susannah whimpered, and tried to pull herself free.

He stepped back, away from her, but he did not release her.

"I don't know what you're up to," he said, "but I want no part of it." He let go of her and started back to the road.

Jason was in a foul mood by the time he got home. He found Lauri in high spirits.

"Mrs. Freye came by today," she said.

He took the dipper from the water bucket beside the fireplace and drank. "What did she want?"

"To be friends. I'd like to visit her sometime. She's lonesome, seems to me."

"Are you?"

"A little," Lauri admitted.

"I guess I've left you alone more than I should. Would you like to ride with me sometime?"

Lauri nodded, smiling.

Jason relaxed. Tomorrow he would take Lauri with him.

CHAPTER 35

Late May 1775

Lauri and Jason knew who it was long before the rider came in sight. Only Walter would pick a ditty that would pester them, just as he did when they were children. Now the words coming from the mature voice sounded even more ridiculous.

"It's good to hear you can finally carry a tune," Jason said when Walter stopped in front of them.

Walter smiled broadly and slid from the saddle. His feet had barely touched the ground when Lauri threw herself into his arms.

He checked his first impulse; to kiss her the way his heart and body demanded. He gave her a brotherly peck on the cheek, and grinned at Jason as he slid his arm around her waist.

Jason gripped Walter's hand. "Put your horse in with mine."

Lauri slipped from Walter's embrace. "I'll get us some cider."

Walter followed Jason into the small enclosure near the cabin.

"Took you long enough to pay us a visit," Jason said.

"Been busy with the Indian Department."

"I thought you didn't want any part of that." Jason eyeballed Walter's leggings and moccasins, the long, fringed hunting shirt, hanging halfway down his thighs.

"Guy's called a council at John Thompson's at Cosby's Manor."

"What about Guy Park? We heard Guy was going to hold a council there."

"He did, but the good Reverend Samuel Kirkland is preaching more than religion to the Oneidas. The Mohawks were the only ones who came. Only Indians, that is."

Walter removed the saddle, blanket and bridle. "A delegation from Albany and Tryon showed up. They're worried. They're trying to get the Confederacy to come over to their side. I don't think they'll succeed. Brant will keep the Mohawks loyal. I'm sure of that.

"I don't know about the Oneidas. I hope they'll stay out of it, but if Kirkland has his way, they'll side with the rebels.

"As far as the rest—the Onondaga, Cayuga, Seneca, Tuscarora—" He shrugged. "They'll probably wait and see who's willing to offer the most."

"You're not saying the British will turn the Indians loose."

"They'll do what has to be done to put down this rebellion. They've used Indians before. They've always been our eyes and ears."

"And if it comes to fighting?"

Walter ran his hand through his thick dark hair. "No one wants an Indian war. Me, least of all. I hope I never have to take to the field with them."

Jason was stunned. "You think it will come to that.?"

"If the radicals think they can lure the Indians to their side, they'll do it, and the devil be damned. It would be different if Sir William was alive. He probably could keep the Indians in line. He should have recommended Dan Claus for Superintendent. He knows Indians.

"Blood is thicker than water, I guess. Guy isn't the man to be Superintendent of Indian Affairs. He's more interested in advancing himself than taking care of the Indians. Mark my words, before this mess is over, somebody else will be doing what Guy should have done."

Lauri waited in the cabin doorway.

Walter swallowed the lump in his throat. "You don't know how much I miss the two of you."

Lauri stepped between them, slipped her arms around them and drew them close to her. She felt Jason's arm slide around her and then Walter did the same. She knew, without looking, that their hands had touched and clasped. She was safe in their embrace.

They clung together until Lauri stretched on tiptoes and kissed each of them. "Come inside and see what we've done."

It was easy to see that this was no longer a trapper's cabin, plain and lacking in comfort. Lauri had somehow managed to make it into a home. The place was spotless, just as the little house in Johnstown had been. The makings of a rag rug lay on the floor by the fireplace. A snowy white coverlet was spread neatly on the bed. Jason's medicines and instruments were put away in the proper order and place.

Jason took Walter back outside to show him the roof that he had repaired, the things they had planted.

"Any word of Geoff.?" Jason said.

"He's in Canada."

"You're sure?"

"I've had people looking for him."

"Why?"

"Elder cut Geoff out of his will," Walter said. "Belle's afraid he'll cause trouble when he finds out."

"You're Belle's lawyer?"

Walter shook his head. "A friend of mine is. He asked for my help. Joseph told me one of his scouts saw Geoff in Montreal."

"We blamed the wrong man." Jason said. "It wasn't Elder who…"

"But Mrs. Wemple said she saw him trying to get into Lauri's house. She heard him threaten her."

"He was there earlier," Jason said. "He tried to get Lauri to go away with him. He thought Lauri was her mother."

"Her mother's been dead for years."

"Phantasmagoria," Jason said. "Elder had lost his sensibilities." He paused. "It was Geoff."—a longer pause. "Lauri lost the baby."

Walter's hands formed a fist. "Is she all right?"

"She doesn't talk about it."

They spent the rest of the afternoon catching up on the doings of their friends and families until it was time for Walter to leave.

"Come down to Brant's tomorrow. Gil and my father are anxious to see you."

He kissed Lauri goodbye and went out with Jason to saddle his horse.

He laid a hand on Jason's shoulder. "I know it's none of my business, but…Lauri's loved you since she was a child. There's never been anyone but you. I mean… Can she? Did Geoff? Damn. You know what I'm asking?"

"It's like having three people in bed. God knows I love her…but sometimes."

Walter's grip tightened. "I passed a young woman, not far from here, pretty, in a cheeky sort of a way."

"Susannah Freye," Jason said.

"When I asked how to get to your place she told me she was waiting for you. She made it plain she knew you. I didn't need a broadside to know what she meant." Walter's fingers dug into Jason's shoulder, hard enough to make him wince. "Don't ever do anything to hurt Lauri. If you do, so help me, you'll answer to me."

The news spread up and down the valley that Guy Johnson had tucked his tail between his legs, scared the Boston people, as he called them, were going to make him a prisoner. He was fleeing, taking his family, and over one hundred other people with him. He had armed guards for protection.

Good riddance some folks said, but when he holed up at Joe Brant's place, good feelings turned to concern. It was bandied about that he had brought members of the Indian Department: Dan Claus, who also had his family with him, Gil Tice, John Butler and even young Walter Butler.

It had been years since such a large number of people had come this far up the valley. Farmers stopped working in their fields, housewives walked down to the King's Highway to wave.

Excited children raced along the road, laughing and pointing at the men dressed in a knee length, skirt like, piece of clothing made out of tartan wool.

"Hey, mister," one shouted, "why you wearing your little sister's clothes?"

The men were a fearsome looking lot and the broadsword they carried was a dangerous, awesome looking weapon. They thundered at the children with strange sounding words that sent some of the children into peals of laughter, but terrified the younger ones so much they scooted into the fields or hid behind trees or bushes, peering wide eyed at the passing crowd.

Some of the men marched beside a coach and four. Another carriage full of children followed behind. Worried childish faces watched the crowds through the carriage windows.

A toil worn woman leaned on the wattle fence beside her life-wearied husband. She waved half heartedly, scowled as the coach passed by.

"Did you see them two women? Never so much as looked at us; like we was nothin'." She left him and walked back up the hill to their cabin.

He drew deeply on his clay pipe, laid a gnarled hand on his cane and hobbled down to the water's edge to watch the slow moving batteaux make their way up the river.

People who heard that the Johnsons were staying with Joseph Brant came to his village to gawk at Sir William's family.

Jason and Lauri came to see old friends.

Brant was too busy to pay much attention to them. Molly offered a cool greeting, then went to attend Nancy Claus and Polly Johnson, Sir William's daughters.

Her rude attitude did not surprise Jason. He was, in her mind, disloyal to Sir William, but it angered him to think she would turn her back on Lauri.

John Butler and Gil Tice, on the other hand, were happy to see them. Both men grasped Jason's hand warmly and slapped him on the back.

John wrapped his arms around Lauri in a fatherly hug.

"Catherine sends her love," he said. "Deborah would have sneaked into my haversack to see you if she could have."

Gil kissed Lauri on the cheek. "Christina misses you and Mrs. Wemple worries about her little lamb."

"Christina is well, I trust?"

Gil nodded.

"And Mrs. Wemple?"

"Bossy as ever," Gil said. "Mrs. Wemple's, a hard worker; but Christina wishes you were there."

The place was abuzz with the sounds of Irish, German, German-Dutch, Scottish, and English, all mixed in with Mohawk for good measure.

Bleating sheep, lowing cattle, grunting pigs, and crated fowl added to the din.

The village was a mishmash of buildings; log cabins, a few log houses, and dwellings made of animal skins stretched over wood frames. Others were made of bark. The largest was the Long House, where ceremonies and council matters of importance were held.

There were frame houses, too, but none as grand as Brant's. His place, built upon a foundation, was the largest, finest frame house in the village. He needed a big place. Joseph, his wife and their three children, shared the house with his mother, as well as Molly, and her eight Johnson children.

A woman, big with child, stood in the doorway of Brant's house. The woman was Guy Johnson's wife, Polly. She watched for a while, then turned and went into the house.

Jason judged her to be about two months away from giving birth. He turned to Walter. "What is Guy thinking of? A trip like this is too much for a woman her age and condition."

"Guy's sure the Boston people are set on seizing him or holding his family hostage if they fail to take him."

"Sir John isn't here. Lady Mary is expecting and he saw fit to keep her home."

"This is Indian Department business," Walter said. "Sir John had no reason to come."

Jason, Lauri and Walter strolled down to the river to see the batteaux waiting to portage around the little falls west of Herkimer's place.

Some of the boats, Walter told them, were carrying the personal possessions of Guy Johnson and Dan Claus, others had the gifts Guy would give to the Indians at the council.

"What kind of gifts?" Lauri asked.

"Cooking pots. Tobacco, chocolate," Walter said. "Stroud cloth to make a match coat. They use it for everything; as a coat, a chair—they wrap themselves in it when they sit—a blanket for sleeping. The more colorful, the better. They like purple.

"What else?"

"Baubles, beads. shirts of India cotton. They like the bright prints. They like earrings, too, and ear wheels, bracelets, hair plates and arm bands. They're vain, you know. One time I saw one wearing a breechcloth with gold lace."

"I don't believe you."

"On my honor."

"Walter Butler," Lauri chided, "you're going straight to hell for the lies you tell."

Walter chuckled.

"Guy must be taking some valuable things with him," Jason said. "Those Highlanders won't let anybody near the batteaux."

The Captain of the Highlanders had been watching them for a long time. Guy had given him strict orders to guard certain batteaux with his life—boats that carried tomahawks, knives, hatchets, guns and powder.

Walter, Jason, and Lauri moved on. They had not gone far when Susannah Freye joined them.

She had come to Brant's with her family, but had wandered off by herself. She spotted Lauri, Jason and their friend—what was his name? Oh, yes. Walter Butler, the well to do lawyer from Johnstown.

"Hello, Doctor Dayemon." She fell in step beside Jason; so close they were almost touching.

"Ain't never seen men wearing women's clothes before," she said, pointing toward the Highlanders. "Ain't much for fightin', be they?"

"They're fierce warriors," Walter said.

"The enemy must die of laughin'." She leaned forward as they walked, her wheat colored hair falling over her full bosom. She fixed a bewitching smile on Walter. "Guess you fathomed what I meant the other day, Mr. Butler, when you asked about Doctor Dayemon."

Walter scowled, and a lock of dark hair tumbled over his forehead. He brushed it back into place but it was stubborn and refused to stay. "I understood completely."

A besotted battman stumbled toward Lauri, swaying on his feet. "You want to sign up little lady? We can use another hand. You ain't particular strong lookin' but you sure are prettier than anythin' else I seen on this trip."

He reached for her to keep from toppling into a boat.

"Don't touch her." Walter grabbed the battman by the arm, spun him around with such force the fellow nearly fell into the river.

"Ain't no call to get rough." The battman twisted free from Walter's grip.

He spotted Susannah who had slipped away. "Susie, darlin'," he called, "what say you and me go somewhere and have a good time." He staggered off after her.

She had already disappeared into the woods with a handsome young Highlander.

Nicholas Herkimer walked away from the group of men he and his overlooker were trying to hire to move the crates and barrels from the batteaux and haul them to the top of the carry around the falls. He had caught sight of Jason, Lauri and Walter. He came over to them, his hand extended in greeting.

"You're in the Indian Department now, Walter," Herkimer said.

"Briefly, Mr. Herkimer. I'm going to the council as an interpreter."

"Guy will keep the Indians peaceful, Ja?"

"That's what we all want."

Herkimer shifted his attention to Jason and the trembling woman wrapped in Jason's arms.

"Doctor," Herkimer said. "I hope everything is all right."

"One of the men from the batteau frightened my wife." Jason pulled Lauri closer.

Herkimer bowed slightly. "You're safe protected, Mrs. Dayemon. Neither Mr. Butler or your husband will let anything happen to you."

He turned to Jason. "I need wagons to get the boats around the falls. I need men with goot strong horses. I pay two shillings a day."

"I'll think it over." Jason said.

"Ja," Herkimer said. "Do that."

He bowed to Lauri again, and went back to the men who were still discussing his proposition.

When Herkimer was out of hearing, Walter burst out laughing. "That sly old fox. He's charging Guy six shillings, paying you two, and still ends up with his usual four."

CHAPTER 36

They finished their morning meal, and Lauri cleared the table. Jason opened the cabin door, thought better of it, and closed it.

"I signed the paper," he said.

"What paper?" Lauri put the dirty dishes in the water she had warmed, and began to wash them.

"The paper that says I support what the Continental Congress is doing."

"What are they doing?" Lauri asked.

"Trying to make the crown understand that we're Americans, not British, that we know what's best for us, that we should make our own laws."

"You always said you didn't want to get mixed up in things like that."

"Desperate men do desperate things. The Committee of Safety is letting their power go to their head. They won't let anyone trade with a person who hasn't signed. I couldn't get my medicines or shot or powder. Herkimer couldn't hire me to help at the portage. I'd have no way to get money. I couldn't doctor."

"Does Walter know?"

"He must. Herkimer's a member of the Committee. He wouldn't have spoken to me about the portage if I hadn't signed. I might be gone for a couple of days. Depends on how long it takes to get the batteaux around the falls. Hannah Freye says you can stay with her. Get some things together. I'll take you down when you're finished here."

"I won't go. I won't stay in the same house with Susannah."

"There's no cause for foolish talk like that."

"You think I don't see how she looks at you? How close she gets to you? Rubs against you like a cat in heat?"

"You're jealous."

"Don't mock me. I won't go."

They continued to argue until Jason convinced Lauri that she would be safer with Hannah. Later that day, he took Lauri to Hannah. He was glad Lauri did not hear Hannah tell him Susannah had gone with Josef.

The Little Falls Portage

The batteaux, capable of carrying a ton and a half of cargo, were tied up on both sides of the river. The strongest of Herkimer's male slaves were bulling the two thousand pound boats onto the long bed of the four wheeled wagons. It was grunt work.

Teams of oxen strained to haul the heavy boats to the top. It was a long, slow trip up the portage road. What was an aggravation to the batteaux men was good business for Herkimer and the Petries, his relatives on the other side of the river.

By the time Jason reached the portage, much of the cargo had been moved to wagons waiting to haul the goods through the gorge.

A man who presented himself as Herkimer's overlooker eyed Jason's horse.

"He's big enough," he said, "but he ain't gonna drag but a load or two afore he's tuckered hisself out."

He pointed to a group of men. "Take a place over there and help load your wagon."

When his wagon was ready, Jason pulled up behind Josef Freye for the steep climb up the portage road.

The overlooker stopped beside Josef's wagon.

Josef snickered. "He here to help his Tory friends leave?"

"Don't go makin' no trouble," the overlooker said. "Gonna be hard enough work without you should be causin'a fuss."

"You standin' up for a Tory?"

"I don't care if he's Tory or he ain't. There's work needs doin'. I aim to see it's done. Get movin' and see nothin' gets broke. It'll come out of your pay if anthin' ain't whole when you reach the top."

Josef started up the portage road.

Before Jason could follow, Walter drew rein beside him.

"I stopped at the cabin to say goodbye. Lauri's not there."

"She's with Hannah and Dolf Freye. She's safe."

"When she wasn't there… If anything had happened to her… I'll stop on my way back." He nudged his horse closer, grasped Jason's hand, turned and rode away.

One of the batteau men plunked himself onto the seat beside Jason. Jason had seen him handling the long steering oar that kept the boat on course against the current, guiding it toward the bank, holding it steady until it was made fast.

"I don't like bein' around them savages. Guy Johnson says they won't do nothin' so long's their Superintendent ain't pestered. I don't trust 'em. I want to keep my hair."

Jason slapped the reins against the horse's rump and they began to move. He let the horse set the pace. He could hear the voices of the men ahead as the teams of oxen and horses labored up the portage road.

Boulders choked the chasm. Trees that had fallen from the craggy cliffs lay crisscrossed like sticks tossed by some giant's hand.

It was slow going. Jason and the batteau man were bathed with the cold spring mist from the falls. They could hear the splash of the water plunging forty feet over the jagged rocks to the bottom of the gorge.

"The settlers up on the German Flatts figured that rock over there would make a good boundary marker, seein' it's so big nobody could miss it," the batteau man said. "Up river there's a place called Stone Ridge. Ever been there?"

"Never have."

"They got burned out during the French trouble, what ones didn't get killed. Them Germans. They're like weeds. Think you're rid of them, and they just come back. Couple hundred of them livin' up there now.

"They need a fort. They got Herkimer Church on this side but them folks to the north ain't got no place to go if the British show their colors."

"What makes you think the British will come to the valley?"

The batteau man shook his head at Jason's seeming lack of insight. "I took you for a sensible man, or maybe you just don't hear much up here. Folks down Albany way are scared out of their skin. Worried the Boston trouble will spill over on them."

When they reached the top, Jason helped reload the batteau. He wished the batteaux men good luck, and turned back down the portage road.

He made one more trip. By the time he had helped unload the batteau, put the cargo in the wagon, made the second tedious climb to the top of the falls, reloaded the batteau, and returned to the bottom, the afternoon shadows were darkening the gorge. He decided to spend the night, get an early start in the morning and have Lauri back at the cabin before Josef Freye returned with Susannah.

Small clusters of men were gathered around the fires, eating and warming themselves. The night air was chilly, but he did not notice.

He did not build a fire. He sat apart from the others, brooding. Walter's stricken face, when he came pounding up the trail to tell him that Lauri was not at the cabin, troubled him. He never realized the depth of Walter's feelings for Lauri.

Walter had no right to be in love with her.

Jason's anger roiled inside him. There was no denying the intensity of his feelings. He was jealous.

He did not notice Susannah until she sat down beside him. She wore a hooded dark blue woolen cape and an emerald green woolen dress. She smelled of wood smoke.

"Eat." She thrust a crock of food at him. "Ain't much left, and them two legged pigs are already back for more. You leavin' tomorrow?"

"As early as I can. I don't like leaving Lauri alone."

"She ain't alone. She's with Ma and Dolf. Pa don't know it, but I do. I'm going with you tomorrow," she said, "and I don't want Pa to see me leave. I'll sleep here tonight."

"Sleep under the wagon then."

"You sleep there." She climbed into the wagon. "There's no blanket."

He didn't answer.

"I'll freeze."

"You won't freeze." He found a blanket and tossed it to her.

"It smells," she complained.

"Then sleep without it."

He took another blanket and the bear skin from under the seat, wrapped himself in them, and crawled under the wagon. He lay awake for a long time, listening to the horse chomp the grass where he was tethered, and wondering what he would tell Lauri when he showed up with Susannah.

He woke at first light, bone tired.

"Best get away quiet as you can," a voice said. "Freye don't take kindly to a man who cozies his gal."

"Nobody cozied," Jason snapped.

"So you say." The voice walked away.

Lauri felt her heart quicken when Dolf said, "Jason's here." She opened the cabin door. Susannah sat beside Jason, her arm linked through his. Her head rested against his shoulder.

She watched, crushed, as Susannah wrapped her arms around Jason's neck and kissed him long and passionately.

Lauri squeezed her eyes shut to keep the tears from spilling from under her lashes. She did not see Jason tear himself from Susannah's embrace, and climb down over the wagon wheel. Susannah followed him, pouting.

Lauri wiped her tears with the edge of her apron, squared her shoulders, and walked out into the yard. As she passed Jason and Susannah, she heard Susannah coo, "Thanks for sharing your blanket."

Lauri seated herself on the wagon and reached for the reins. Jason climbed up beside her, grasped the lines, slapped the horse's rump sharply, turned the wagon around and bolted out of the Freye's yard.

He raced down the road.

He nearly upset the wagon when he swung into their yard. Lauri climbed down before Jason had a chance to help her, and ran for the door. He sprinted after her, caught her by the shoulders and spun her around to face him.

"Don't touch me. Don't ever touch me again." She turned and fumbled with the latch.

Jason reached past her and opened the door.

She ducked inside.

Hurt and angry, he followed her.

She began to gather her few possessions.

"What do you think you're doing?"

She ignored him.

"Answer me or by all that's holy I'll take a switch to you. Look at me."

She faced him, frightened. Her voice quivered. "I'm going back to Johnstown."

"How are you going to get there?"

"I'll think of something. Walk."

"All the way to Johnstown? Where will you eat? Where will you sleep?"

"Not with another woman's husband."

The barb found its mark.

"There's nothing going on between me and Susannah. Nothing happened last night. I slept under the wagon. I did not touch her." He stepped toward her.

She backed against the bed, tumbled onto it, scrambled into the corner and curled into a ball.

He towered over her, reached for her.

She pulled herself into a smaller ball.

He dropped to his knees, picturing a night not so many weeks ago. How must he look to her? Like Geoff?

"Susannah wants to come between us. Don't let her. That thing about the blanket... It was Goliath's."

She relaxed, unrolled herself, and moved toward him.

He scooped her into his arms.

Lauri giggled. "She did smell like a horse." She let him hold her, turned her face to his and welcomed his kiss.

CHAPTER 37

Early June 1775

Nicholas Herkimer from the Canajoharie district of the Tryon County Committee of Safety, and Edward Wall from the western most district, German Flatts—Kingsland,—former Johnstown school master, presently a Burnetsfield trader—husband of John's Butler's niece Deborah Butler,—rode side by side on their way to meet with Guy Johnson at John Thompson's place at Cosby's Manor.

"I wish they hadn't sent me." Wall told Herkimer. "There's bad blood between me and John Butler."

Deborah Butler Wall had gone to stay with her aunt. Catherine, and her uncle John Butler. She supported the king, and Wall had sided with the rebels

Wall was hurt and angry. "It's no business of John's. What goes on between a man and his wife should be between him and her."

Herkimer let Wall talk. He knew well enough what it was like to have family side with the Tories. His own brother had done as much.

He also knew some of the Committee members doubted his and Wall's loyalty, and that they were being tested.

He supposed it was also a test for Adam Fonda, one of the three men riding behind them. Adam was from the Mohawk district, the one nearest the Johnsons. He had never attended a Committee meeting until the second of June. The power of the Johnsons had been too intimidating.

The meeting at Werner Tygets's house, where it was decided to send five men to talk to Guy, was the first time all the districts had been represented.

With Guy on the run, there was a chink in the Johnson armor. It remained to be seen how long Sir John could stand alone against the Committee.

Herkimer had no doubt Adam would be watched. He didn't like to think that the other two men, Peter Waggoner of the Palatine district and Frederick Fox from German Flatts—Kingsland had been sent to keep an eye on him, as well as Wall and Fonda. The idea nagged him.

Thompson's—Cosby's Manor

Guy Johnson sat at John Thompson's desk, a quill pen poised over the parchment. Before putting pen to paper he picked up the letter he had angrily tossed aside. It was supposedly written by Joseph Brant to the Oneidas and lost on the road.

> WRITTEN AT GUY JOHNSON'S MAY, 1775
> THIS IS YOUR LETTER, YOU GREAT ONES OR SACHEMS. GUY JOHNSON SAYS HE WILL BE GLAD IF YOU GET THIS INTELLIGENCE, YOU ONEIDAS, HOW IT GOES WITH HIM NOW; AND HE IS NOW MORE CERTAIN CONCERNING THE INTENTION OF THE BOSTON PEOPLE. GUY JOHNSON IS IN GREAT FEAR OF BEING TAKEN PRISONER BY THE BOSTONIANS. WE MOHAWKS ARE OBLIGED TO WATCH HIM CONSTANTLY. THEREFORE WE SEND YOU THIS INTELLIGENCE THAT YOU SHALL KNOW IT, AND GUY JOHNSON ASSURES HIMSELF AND DEPENDS UPON YOU COMING TO HIS ASSISTANCE, AND THAT YOU WILL WITHOUT FAIL BE OF THAT OPINION.
> HE BELIEVES NOT THAT YOU WILL ASSENT TO LET

HIM SUFFER. WE THEREFORE EXPECT YOU IN A COUPLE OF DAYS TIME. SO MUCH AT PRESENT. WE SEND, BUT SO FAR AS TO YOU ONEIDAS, BUT AFTERWARD PERHAPS TO ALL THE OTHER NATIONS. WE CONCLUDE, AND EXPECT THAT YOU WILL HAVE CONCERN ABOUT OUR RULER, GUY JOHNSON, BECAUSE WE ARE ALL UNITED.

It was signed by Joseph Brant and four others. Guy studied it carefully. He decided not to hold a council at Thompsons. The curs were dogging his heels.

He read the other letter Herkimer and his four jackals had brought from the Tryon County Committee of Safety Chairman, Christopher Yates. The Committee was being troublesome, meddling in the king's affairs.

Guy dipped the quill pen into to ink pot. His pen began to scratch:

THOMPSON'S, COSBY'S MANOR, JUNE 5th, 1775

Gentlemen,

I have received the paper signed Chris. P. Yates, Chairman, on behalf of the districts therein mentioned, which I am now to answer, and shall do it briefly, in the order you have stated matters.

When he finished, he had rehashed the things he had told them many times.

He claimed he had not seen the letter to the Oneidas until Herkimer showed it to him.

Their fears were 'propagated by malicious persons for a bad purpose.'

The present dispute was viewed differently according to a person's education and principals.

He was sure his Majesty would take care of the American grievances.

He was troubled that anyone thought him capable of setting the Indians on the inhabitants.

His office was for the benefit and protection of all. That was the reason he held meetings with the Indians.

He had received a confirming letter from one of the Committees in Philadelphia. A large party of men planned to take him prisoner; therefore, he had to fortify his house.

He closed his letter by saying they had nothing to apprehend from his endeavors.

He signed the letter, gave it to Edward Wall, and promptly made arrangements to go to Fort Stanwix.

He would be closer to the Onondagas and the Oneidas. Once he secured their allegiance to the king, he would move on to Oswego. There he would be out of the reach of the rebels, and it would be easier for the Cayugas, Senecas and the more western tribes to meet with him.

Fort Stanwix

Guy continued the journey by batteau. The road west, from abandoned Fort Schuyler to Fort Stanwix, was thickly wooded and not much more than a bad path.

It was a long, tedious trip up the Mohawk River, requiring frequent stops while fallen trees were hacked out of the way or the batteau was manhandled through the shallow water. More than once a strong Highlander carried Polly when it was necessary to lighten the batteau's load.

Fort Stanwix lay in ruins. What wood that had not been scavenged was rotting. Some of the buildings were still standing, but were in such a state of disrepair Guy ordered his marquee to be set up outside the fort. The sooner the travel cot was set up, the sooner Polly could lie down for some much needed rest.

"The tent will soon be ready, my dear," Guy told Polly. "The rest will do you good and you'll soon be your own hearty self."

Polly sat on a camp stool, her face drained of color, her eyes dull. Her sister, Ann Claus, called Nancy by the family, sat beside her, keeping an uneasy watch.

Polly was thirty one years old, almost past prime child bearing age. Death had already taken their two young daughters, and Guy was anxious about what would happen to Polly if she lost this child she was carrying.

Every now and then Polly would look westward to the woodlands beyond the fort. She, as well as Nancy and Dan Claus, knew they would go on to Oswego and then sail to Canada.

Guy had received a coded communication to take as many Indians to Canada as he could. There he was to join with General Carleton for an assault on New England.

Guy had no choice.

He had cautioned Polly that the Highlanders, those in the Indian Department, and the Mohawks, had not been told. They thought once the councils were held with the tribes they would all go back to the valley.

No need to worry, she had assured him. She had learned to keep secrets from the time she was a child. Her father had taught her well.

It was exhausting for Polly. She was already showing the strain of the trip.

It was several days before a delegation of Oneidas arrived. Their message was disappointing. The trouble, they told Guy, was between two brothers and, since they regarded both, they could not take sides against either. They would remain neutral.

He hid his displeasure. He told them that he was unable to give them some of the provisions he had promised because the rebels had seized them. They were angry, he knew, but they remained stoic, and accepted his explanation without comment. The next day they went home with what presents he gave them. They were gifts, he reminded them, from their generous father, King George.

He had given them less than half their share of trinkets and gewgaws. That was more than they deserved.

He would give the tomahawks and knives to those who would support the crown.

The next day the batteaux were hauled over the Carry to Wood Creek. As soon as they had arrived at Fort Stanwix, he had sent some of the Highlanders to clear away as many obstacles in the creek as they could. He set others to repairing sluices. When all was ready, the water in the troughs would be released, allowing the boats to float to Oneida Lake.

If good fortune smiled on them, a gentle wind would allow the sails to be raised, speeding their trip to the west shore. Shallow, saucer bottomed, the lake was a treacherous body of water. If a strong wind should kick up dangerous waves, they could be swamped.

An equally difficult part of the trip lay ahead. There was a falls on the Oswego River that must be by-passed.

…Guy worried.

Polly was beginning to feel better, and the few days of rest had brought color back to her face. The difficult trip down Wood Creek, across Oneida Lake, down the Oswego River and around the falls lay ahead.

…Guy worried.

The days wore on, and travel became more difficult.

Polly tired, spoke little, withdrew from everyone; the children, her sister, even Guy.

He tried to comfort himself with the thought that the fort at Oswego was at the end. There Polly could rest again, while he held a council with the Indians.

Then they would sail across Lake Ontario to Canada. Her journey would be over.

Still…

…Guy worried.

Oswego

There were Indians, mostly men, women and children from the Six Nations, waiting at the fort when Guy arrived. He addressed them, and asked for patience while they waited for the representatives from the western tribes.

He was also stalling for time. He was hard pressed. The provisions he needed had been intercepted and he had to send to Canada for supplies.

At long last two Shawnee deputies, some Caughnawagas from Canada and a few Huron chiefs from Detroit showed up. They listened to what Guy had to say, agreed to take his message back to their villages, then headed home.

Some of the Mohawks from the lower castle were among those who left. They were closest to the white settlers in the Mohawk Valley. Many had good frame houses, plenty of cattle. Several of them owned farms or plots of land in their own name. They had the most to lose.

Guy knew from experience, most of the 1500 Indians at the council had come for the presents. He accepted the fact that when he set out for Montreal, he would take fewer than 300 persons, including whites and Indians, with him.

He was leaving behind the most important person in his life.

Polly died in childbirth, July 11, 1775—one year to the day of Sir William's passing.

…Guy wept.

CHAPTER 38

August 1775

During the day, the clouds spattered the tops of the trees with uneven splotches; Shadows on the Hills. Now, in the early evening, Jason and Lauri sat outside the cabin enjoying the last of the summer warmth. Soon the days would become shorter and the evenings would turn cooler.

Lauri stared at Jason, not quite believing what he had had just told her—he had joined the militia.

"I didn't have much choice. Join the militia or follow Walter to Canada. I don't want to leave here. This is our home.

"I'll have to go to muster once a month. I could be fined 10 shillings if I don't go. On Muster Day, I'll take you to Hannah. She likes having you there."

The Tryon County Committee of Safety, he went on to say, had held several meetings during the summer. Few valley people knew what went on in the closed sessions, but they were aware that scouts had been out most of July, especially toward the little falls.

He did not mention the rumors that were racing through the valley. Guy Johnson, it was said, was going to fall upon the settlements. Joseph Brant and Walter Butler were going to lead a raiding party of 800 to 900 Indians, and lay waste to the land.

The people did not know that Herkimer had written to Albany for help; that *they might not be slaughtered like innocent and defenseless sheep before ravaging wolves.'*

The Tryon County Committee feared there would be panic in the valley, and quite likely the fainthearted would flee or go over to the British side.

To prevent this from happening, on the 13th of July, the Albany Committee of Safety sent 150 pounds of powder and Schenectady sent 300 pounds of lead.

If he had been able to tell her all these things, Lauri would never have believed it.

"Stuff and nonsense," she would say. "Walter would never do that to his friends and neighbors."

Jason would remind her that many people here did not think of themselves as Walter's friends and neighbors. They resented the Johnsons, and the Butlers.

The humid days and sultry nights of August slipped into the capricious days, and unpredictable nights of September…and Lauri was with child.

Jason was in high spirits. He had waited anxiously for her to tell him; feigning surprise when she did.

Lauri was fearful.

"I couldn't bear it if I lost this baby, too. I want to be the mother of your children. I wanted the other one. Not at first. Then I thought, it's part of me. How could I blame it for what Geoff did?"

Jason held her, whispering, "It's going to be all right."

Although he never let Lauri know, Geoff was also on his mind. He questioned every passing traveler he could. Geoff, they said, had not been seen in Johnstown, nor anywhere else in the valley.

Sometimes those passing through brought letters for Lauri from Christina Tice and Mrs. Wemple. Mostly they were filled with news of happenings in and around Johnstown:

Belle Baxter is having a hard time of it one letter said. *She can't manage The Meadows alone, with Elder dead and Geoff off, who knows where. She's hired a man to take care of the running of it. a most dislikable fellow.*

He's bought two more slaves. Treats them terrible.

Belle was against buying them but, he rides roughshod over her objections. Even Felicity has to work.

Patience has run off.

He says Belle's going to marry him. Heaven knows why.'

There was a letter from Jason's brother. *Pa*, he wrote, *ain't come to terms on you being in the militia. He ain't spoke your name since he heard you done it. Ma sends her love.*

Once Walter was able to slip a message to Jason. Geoff was still in Canada. Jason was not able to reply. The Committee had spies everywhere.

Walter's letter made Jason feel it was safe to leave Lauri when he was called to set a farmer's broken arm or treat a child's Sore Throat Distemper, Tussis Epidemica or Catarrh.

Lauri had Jason's pistol and he had taught her how to use it. When he went to help with a difficult delivery, one a midwife could not handle, and he knew he would be gone for hours, he took Lauri to stay with Hannah Freye.

He continued Lightning's daily exercise. Susannah no longer waited beside the road.

He was riding past the Freye's place when he saw Dolf working a field alone. He drew rein beside the fence.

"Hard work," Jason shouted.

Dolf looked up, nodded, and tramped over to the rail. He wiped the sweat from his brow with the sleeve of his shirt.

"Looks like a two man job," Jason said.

"I get more done when Pa ain't here."

"Where is Josef? I haven't seen him lately."

"Off on some secret job for the Committee, least ways so he says. Ask me, he's in some ale house. Smells like it when he comes home."

Dolf's young face took on a worried look. "Somethin' happen up at the falls when he was up there? He acts like somethin's gallin' him."

"Can't say," Jason answered.

Why tell Dolf that Herkimer's overlooker had lit into Josef. To be put down like that in front of the other men must have been a more bitter pill than Jason had ever given his patients.

"How's Susannah?"

"Queer actin'," Dolf said. "Don't say much. Seems like somethin' powerful's botherin' her. Been helpin' Ma a lot. Ain't like her. When Pa's here, which ain't much, they ain't social like they used to be."

August 21, 1775, Johnson Hall

Sir John was physically weary. He had spent the night pacing the floor, waiting for Polly to deliver their second child—the namesake Sir William would never see. Polly's travail was an emotional strain on him, as was the news of his sister dying in Oswego.

Since Dan and Anne Claus had left the valley, Sit John had made sure that Dan's cattle, except for those needed to feed Dan's tenants, had been moved to Dan's farm in the northern part of the Mohawk District. They were out of reach of the rebels who seemed to think Johnson property was for the taking. He had also supervised the planting of wheat by Dan's tenants. God willing, Dan and Anne would be back in the valley by harvest time.

Leaving her home, her brother, and concern for the welfare of her sister-in-law, had been difficult enough for Anne, but the death of her sister must have been almost too much to bear.

Anne was in need of some good news.

Sir John sat down at his desk, picked up the quill pen, dipped it in the ink pot, and began to write:

I cou'd not think of letting this Opportunity pass without informing You of the situation of affairs at home & of the relation you have this day been favored with by the Power which giveth & taketh away. About Nine this morning my Good Woman was delivered of a very fine, Stout Boy, both are well & likely to Remain so.

The good feeling that spread throughout Sir John's holdings was not shared by others in the valley. July had been a particularly bad month. The quarrel between the Tryon Committee and Sheriff Alexander White, a friend and supporter of Sir John, had worsened.

White had arrested and jailed a man named John Fonda. 50 men, led by Sampson Sammons, went to the gaol at night and, by force, freed Fonda.

From, there they marched to Tice's Tavern, planning to take White prisoner. White shot at them and they returned fire, and would have taken White if Sir John had not rallied his retainers and Scotch supporters to arms. The odds, 500 or more to 50, seemed too unbalanced, and Sammons and his band wisely withdrew.

The Tryon Committee removed White from office, but he was re-commissioned by Governor Tryon. The Committee did not recognize the appointment and elected John Frey to the office.

Puffed up by their actions, they tried again to arrest White. He fled to Johnson Hall, where Sir John helped him escape. White was pursued, captured and imprisoned. When he was released on his parole, he fled again.

Christopher Yates, of the Tryon Committee of Safety, wrote to the Albany Committee, explaining the situation and requested the loan of the field piece at Schenectady, which they could use against Johnson Hall.

The Albany Committee refused, although they wrote to the Committee that they admired their "Spirit of Freedom wherewith those Inhabitants animated, yet it was at least Impudent in them to force Mr. Fonda from Gaol as the same laws under Colour whereof he was confined will give him his remedy for unlawful imprisonment."

The letter continued: *Let our enemies never have Cause to upbraid us with an infringement of the Laws and Constitution which we are studiously endeavoring to preserve against Parliamentary encroachment."*

Despite the censure of the Albany Committee, the Tryon Committee continued to arrest suspicious people, try them, fine them, imprison them, and in some cases, execute them.

CHAPTER 39

January 1776

Hardly anyone remembered such a cold January. When Colonel Nicholas Herkimer sent out word to the Tryon County Militia that they were to march to Caughnawaga to meet General Philip Schuyler's troops, the men put on their warmest clothes. They pulled on their woolen socks, wrapped their heavy mufflers over their ears and face, leaving only their eyes and nose exposed. They stuffed their hands into the mittens their women had knitted for them, and started the long march down the frozen Mohawk River.

The snow crunched under their feet.

"What's that fool Schuyler calling us out in weather like this for?" Josef Freye leaned into the bitter wind.

"GENERAL Schuyler. Show respect. Ja?" Herkimer sat his big horse, his back rigid, his lips compressed. Freye, he thought, would be the first to run at the first sign of trouble.

"General Schuyler needs some real soldiers to show them how things is done. Ja, Honikol?" Someone said.

"COLONEL Herkimer," Freye muttered. "Show respect."

The man beside Freye elbowed him. "Shut your mouth. You'll have us all in trouble."

"We ain't real soldiers," a third man said. "We ain't even got good guns. All I got is my muzzle loader, and Karl here ain't got nothin' but his pa's old musket."

Herkimer let them grumble. It gave them something to do. He was in a sour mood himself.

It had taken long enough. If the Albany Committee had listened when he and the other members of the Tryon Committee of Safety had first warned them of the danger that Sir John Johnson presented, he and the militia would have taken care of all this during the warm weather instead of freezing their butts off in January.

He and the Tryon Committee had all but begged them to do something about Sir John. Finally, the Congress, and even Washington himself, had taken notice and ordered General Schuyler to disarm Johnson and his Scottish Highlanders.

The Tryon militia came around a bend to find a tent city on the river between the high hills on the north and south.

Men were everywhere; attending cooking pots, drilling, practicing loading their firearms.

"German George's boys ain't gonna wait on you afore they take a shot at your dumb hide." The raspy voice fit the burly body. "You ain't got but 12 to 15 seconds to load and shoot or you'll be bug meat."

Sweating and fumbling, the militia struggled to load their guns. Some were still trying when he gave the command:

"FIRE!

The roar of the guns echoed off the hills.

One of the Tryon men said, "Mebbe the British is comin'. I ain't stayin'. Them Red Coats will bring Indians. My family's alone. Ain't nobody there but my son to protect them, and he ain't but ten years old." He turned to walk away.

Jason reached out to stop him.

"It ain't the British," Josef said. "Schuyler's puttin' the screws to Johnny Johnson. He had Johnson holed up for hours down at Guy Park, laid the law down to him."

"How come you know so much, Freye? You spyin' on Schuyler?"

Josef shrugged. "Pays to know what's goin' on. I ain't sheep like you. I ain't gonna be led around by my nose."

One of the men grumbled, "Schuyler's got all them Albany men. Why're we here?"

"He don't trust Johnson," Josef said. "We're gonna make sure Johnny hands over all them guns and powder he's got, them skirt wearers, too. They gotta give up them big swords."

Josef glanced at Jason. "How do you think Johnson will feel when he sees you, the pick of the litter, with the likes of us?" The corner of Josef's upper lip moved slightly. "You gonna enjoy his undoin' as much as us?"

"I don't get any pleasure out of seeing any man humiliated; not even that day at the little falls portage."

The barb hurt. Josef's hands formed into fists. His body stiffened. He flexed his fingers, forced himself to relax.

Johnson Hall

"John do stop your pacing," Lady Mary said.

"If that arrogant cousin of yours has his way, I'll be pacing in a prison."

"The crown would never allow such a thing." Lady Mary smiled at her husband. "Philip can be overbearing at times."

"Overbearing? He was all but gloating when he gave me his ultimatum."

Lady Mary put her finger to her lip. "Hush John, you'll wake the children. Philip's jealous of you, John." She patted the seat of the chair next to her, and Sir John lowered his large frame on to it. She took his hands in hers. "My brothers delighted in baiting him when he came with Aunt Schuyler to visit my grandmother. They're sisters, you know."

Sir John nodded.

"My father felt obliged to invite them to stay with us. My mother dreaded those visits. I was little then, and I sometimes thought the boys were mean to him, but as I grew older I didn't like him either."

Sir John got up and began to pace again. He had sent his reply to Schuyler by messenger several hours ago. By now Schuyler must know that a Johnson would never comply with all the demands of any Committee or Continental Congress.

In his answer to Schuyler, Sir John had accepted two, a part of one, rejected four, and denied one of the terms.

He had agreed to surrender all but his personal arms, which he considered his own property. The Highlanders would do the same.

He did not expect to be confined to any county, but to be at liberty to go where and when he pleased.'

He claimed he did not have any military stores belonging to the Crown. He also denied having blankets, strouds or other presents for the Indians.

As to the demands for six hostages, he declared neither he nor the Scottish leaders had the power to deliver hostages since no one was in command of the other.

He cursed silently when he read that the General, *in behalf of the Continental Congress, doth promise and engage that neither Sir John nor any of these people shall be molested by any of the inhabitants of the Thirteen Colonies, that, on the contrary, they will be protected in the quiet and peaceful enjoyment of their property.*

Sir John got malicious satisfaction when he distorted the truth by telling Schuyler that he and his people would rely on "the general's assurance of protection."

He knew the rabble in the valley too well. No one, not even the pompous Schuyler, could control them once they made up their mind to harass or even attack anyone loyal to the king.

He would find a way to defend himself, his family, and those faithful to him.

Caughnawaga

Herkimer sat at the small camp table opposite Schuyler. A blast of frigid air blew in through the front flap of the General's tent. A letter of sorts was lifted from the table top and fluttered to the frozen ground.

Schuyler made no effort to retrieve it. Herkimer leaned down, picked it up, and put it back on the table. The paper was of a cheap quality; a slap in the face of the man who had received it.

Herkimer recognized the clear, firm signature: JOHN JOHNSON, BART.

"That's Johnson's answer to my demands." Schuyler flushed with indignation. "I've given him until noon tomorrow to call the Scots in, and surrender their arms. Johnson, too, arrogant son of a…"

Schuyler looked up to see Herkimer grinning.

"We have right on our side, Honikol," he said. "We'll bring him to his knees."

Johnstown

The Militia—men from Schenectady and Albany, and Tryon County— had paraded on the frozen Mohawk before they marched to Johnstown.

Many were apprehensive. They had been on edge since arriving at Caughnawaga. They were storekeepers, merchants, farmers. Soon they would come face to face with Sir John's Scottish Highlanders, who were known to be fierce fighters. The Militia had no doubt where the Highlander's allegiance lay.

The Mohawks and the other Indians might not remain neutral. Their loyalty, many of the militia believed, would be on the side of Sir William's son.

Schuyler had sent the interpreter, Bleecker, to the Lower Mohawk Castle with a message:

Their Albany brothers were sending their warriors to find out the truth of the report that men were being enlisted to *cut our throats, and stop up the road of communication to the Westward.*

The militia also knew that Schuyler had not waited for a reply, a breach of good manners, as far as the Indians were concerned.

Sir John came first, riding down the road from Johnson Hall on his magnificent black stallion. The horse pranced rather than walked, his head held high, his superior attitude matching that of the rider.

Following at a respectful distance were the six McDonells and the six men representing the English, Dutch and German inhabitants. The twelve men were hostages who would be sent to Pennsylvania to defuse the threat of attack against the people of the Mohawk Valley.

Sir John had argued strongly against their decision to turn themselves over to the rebels, but they were determined to protect their own.

They had asked that their families be allowed to go with them but their request had been denied. They would be allowed a reasonable time to get their affairs in order.

Behind them, the Scottish bagpipers played, not a dirge, as might be expected, but music that lifted the spirits of every Highlander.

The hostages smiled, knowing the music annoyed the militia and their officers.

The creaking of the wagons carrying the military stores that Sir John had agreed to give up sounded more mournful than the bagpipes.

Next came the Highland men armed with their deadly broadswords. They had refused to put them with the rest of the weapons that Sir John was turning over to the rebels. They would do that themselves. They marched with a purpose, looking neither left nor right, their faces set with an intensity that sent shivers up the spines of the militia. One swipe with their sword and a man's head, arm or leg could be lopped off.

The sobbing and wailing of the families of the men who were being humiliated could be heard in the distance.

Josef Freye glanced at Jason as Sir John passed. Neither man acknowledged the other.

Sir John stopped in front of Philip Schuyler, Nicholas Herkimer and their officers. He did not dismount.

A few words were exchanged between Schuyler and Johnson, and Sir John moved to one side.

One after the other, the Highlanders gave up their broadswords. Their dirks were concealed on their person; a fact that was missed by the rebels.

Johnson Hall

Sir John was still smarting from the degrading events of the day before. He, Sir William's son, had allowed himself to agree to the demands of the valley riffraff, had entered into a bond of 1600 pounds sterling. Now he was standing in the doorway of Johnson Hall being confronted by a Militia Captain ten years his junior.

Several men were removing the snow from the mound in the middle of the duck pond. As soon as a spot was bare, others began to dig.

"What is the meaning of this?" Sir John demanded.

The young officer sat his horse, glaring at Sir John with angry gray eyes. He thrust a folded paper at the baronet.

"I have orders from General Schuyler to search your house and property. We're here to find the two thousand arms you have hidden." He nudged his horse closer to the Hall steps. "Move aside."

Sir John held his ground,

"Sergeant." The Captain motioned toward Sir John and a beefy man tried to shove Johnson out of the way. Sir John resisted.

"You sir," the Captain said, "are a scoundrel. I thought you would have had more honor. You are a disgrace to your father's memory."

The young officer dismounted, waved his men forward, "I can't be responsible for what they might do."

They stormed into the Hall, knocking Sir John aside.

Pale and trembling, Lady Mary hustled down the hall and helped her husband to his feet. "John," she whispered, "they're going through your desk. They took money from it."

"I had 360 guineas in there," he said.

They could hear drawers dropping on the floor, chairs being overturned. Someone was pounding on the children's bedroom door. Inside the children were screaming in terror.

"Break it down," the beefy sergeant ordered.

Lady Mary dashed down the hall.

The militia captain was close on her heels. "Sergeant," he barked, "stop those men."

"Madam," the captain said to Lady Mary's back, "who's in there?"

She spun around in such a fury, they nearly collided.

"My children. Are you deaf as well as cruel? Do you always make war on children?"

"I assure you, Madam, we do not. Do you have a key?"

Lady Mary fished in her pocket.

"I suggest, Madam, you unlock the door so they can see you are unharmed and they are safe."

"I suggest, Captain, you dismiss your barbarians. I do not want my children to see who it was that frightened them."

"Sergeant, get those men out of here." He did not wait for Lady Mary to unlock the children's door. He hurried down the hall, the sergeant close on his heels. He could hear an officer bellowing orders.

He rushed out into the bitter cold. He heard peacocks complaining and then, to his chagrin, some of his men staggered around the corner of the house, dancing and singing YANKEE DOODLE, while they tried to stick peacock feathers in their hats. They had not only found a source of feathers with which they could decorate themselves, they had discovered an ample supply of Sir John's most potent spirits.

"Form up!" The sergeant stomped down the Hall steps, snarling mad. "Anything you want to say to these S 0 B's, Captain?"

Before he could answer, the Captain was distracted by the sound of pounding hooves.

The rider reined his horse inches from where his officer stood. "Sir," the rider said, "I must speak to you privately."

The Captain and messenger moved out of hearing.

"Sir, you have to come to the village, NOW. The men have gone crazy. They've gone into people's houses, robbed them. They broke into St. John's church. They destroyed the organ. They're out of control!"

CHAPTER 40

January 1776—George Dayemon's Cabin— Butlersbury

Jason was about to rap when the door opened.

George Dayemon's face registered surprise, then anger at seeing his oldest son standing there. His first impulse was to slam the door in Jason's face, but he turned to see Martha getting up from her chair, her arms outstretched, reaching to embrace her boy. George stepped aside, took his heavy coat from the wall peg, and motioned Jason in.

"One hour. For your mother's sake. Be gone when I get back. I want no traitors in my house." He shouldered Jason aside and stomped out into cold.

Martha wrapped her arms around her son.

Jason bent to kiss her cheek and tasted the salt of her tears.

"I've news to make you happy," he said. "You'll be a grandmother come next June."

Jason's three brothers were seated at the trestle table. They stared at him, mouths agape.

"Make room for your brother," Martha said.

Her second son, Jacob, stood up. "You here with the rest of the scum to shame Sir John?"

"I'm here with the militia," Jason said.

Jacob's eyes narrowed in contempt. "After all Sir William done for you."

"This isn't about Sir William."

"Jacob sit down," Martha ordered. "Be glad your brother is here. Be happy for him. You're going to be an uncle."

"No, Ma. Pa's right. Jason at nothin' but a traitor," He turned to his brothers. "You comin?"

They shook their heads.

"You ain't no better." Jacob grabbed his coat from the wall peg and stormed out, slamming the door behind him.

"You really goin' to be a Pa?" Jed asked.

"Appears so," Jason said.

"Hear that, Jer? We're uncles."

"I heard. I ain't deaf," Jeremy said.

Jason smiled. Not everything had changed. The twins were still the same; high spirited Jed, reserved Jeremy.

"I wish I could be with Lauri when her time comes," Martha said.

"I'll be there."

Martha humphed. "Ain't the same. Men are no good at a time like that. A woman needs a woman; knows what she's goin' through."

"We have a neighbor. Hannah will help."

"You'll bring the young one around to see us soon's you can."

Jason laid his hand on top of hers. "Soon as we can, Ma."

Jason and Lauri's Cabin

Jason and Lauri were bundled together in the Jack bed.

"Herkimer gave me leave to go see my family," Jason said. "My mother wishes she could be with you when the baby comes."

He was quiet for a long time. "I went to see Catherine Butler," he said at last. "Walter's in England. He's hoping to get a commission."

Lauri shifted around to face him. "You took a chance going there."

"At least she didn't turn me away. Pa wants no part of me." He turned away from her. "I wish I hadn't gone with Herkimer."

"You had to."

He rolled back to look at her. "They humiliated Sir John; made him come into Johnstown…made him give up his weapons. The Highlanders, too. They even took twelve men hostage."

They lay quiet for a long time. She traced the line of his jaw with the tips of her fingers, brushed them lightly across his lips. "Kiss me like a loving husband who has missed his wife."

Jason grinned and did as he was told.

Johnson Hall—Mid May 1776

Sir John's harassment had begun in March when he had been called to Albany to appear before General Schuyler, and answer charges that he had said the Indians would attack the Mohawk and Upper Hudson Valleys.

"Where," Sir John demanded, "is my accuser?"

Schuyler brushed the question aside. "Is it true? Have you said that?"

"I," Sir John said, "have repeated what is common knowledge."

From March until May he was repeatedly called to Albany. More often than not, his accuser failed to appear and he was sent home without explanation.

The humiliation he had been forced to endure in January, the frequent 40 mile trips and the fact that Polly was expecting their third child, did nothing to help his disposition.

The hardest blow came in a letter from his friend, Daniel Campbell, telling him that a large detachment of men were east of Schenectady, marching for Johnstown. Campbell had added a strong warning:

Do not, he wrote, *let mere bravado, anger or regret at leaving your family delay your departure for I make no doubt, if found, you will be taken. Let me remind you that you can accomplish nothing confined within prison walls.*

Leaving Polly in the care of her sister, Margaret, Sir John and 170 of his followers headed for Canada.

The large detachment of men, led by Colonel Elias Dayton, arrived too late. The fishing expedition had failed. The big catch had slipped away before the net had been cast.

Johnson Hall—May 20, 1776

Captain Joseph Bloomfield, Third Regiment of the New Jersey Continental Line, was nervous. His orders were to discover, as best he could, any evidence of malicious intentions Sir John had against the people.

Bloomfield was not good at subterfuge, but since he was acquainted with the Watts family, his commanding officer, Colonel Elias Dayton, had sent him to Johnson Hall on the pretext of visiting Margaret Watts, Lady Mary's sister.

The hand of guilt rested heavily on Bloomfield's shoulders.

"Captain Bloomfield." Polly's greeting interrupted his thoughts.

He felt foolish and awkward, but protocol required him to acknowledge her title. "Lady Mary," he said with a slight bow.

Polly eyed his uniform, and struggled to fight the resentment that threatened to overwhelm her. "I shall overlook the fact you are an officer in the army that wants to take my husband prisoner. Joseph, let us set formalities aside."

CHAPTER 41

June 1776

When Lauri and Jason heard the Continental drums they walked down to the river to watch the Third Regiment of New Jersey march by on the north side. Rumors that a fort was to be built at Stone Ridge had traveled up and down the valley for weeks.

"Do you think they're on their way to build the fort?" Lauri asked.

"It's possible, I suppose," Jason said.

"Hannah says Josef is going up there. They need men to haul timber. Will you go?"

"We could use the money."

It was not the lack of money that troubled Lauri. Susannah was going with her father; she to cook, so she said, he to work on the fort.

Hannah Freye chuckled as she approached the cabin. She could hear words she never expected would come from Lauri's mouth. Lauri was in labor.

"Hush now, Lauri," Hannah said. "You've work to do. It's time to get this baby born. Think what a wonderful thing it will be when you hold your child in your arms."

Hannah glanced at Jason, and smiled. Birthing was almost as hard for the father as it was for the mother. Jason was as apprehensive as any first time father.

"You may be a good doctor, and a fair midwife for someone else," Hannah told him, "but you'll just be in my way. This is woman's work. Scat."

He stepped away from the bed, just as Lauri let loose a torrent of abusive words directed at him.

William James Dayemon announced his entrance into the world with a lusty howl and a ravenous appetite. When Hannah placed him in Lauri's arms, he latched onto Lauri's nipple and sucked greedily.

Hannah called Jason.

He came to stand beside the bed. He gently touched his son's hand, and William's small fingers wrapped around his father's thumb.

Lauri reached for Jason's hand, brushed it with her lips. "He's perfect. Just like his father."

Stone Ridge—June 1776

Captain Joseph Bloomfield was not yet 23 years old, but he had been ordered to build a fort to protect the people of the Mohawk Valley.

Except for Fort Herkimer Church, and a few blockhouses left over from the war with France, there was no place where the people could find refuge from an attack. Fort Stanwix, at the Oneida carrying place, 30 or more miles to the west, and Schenectady to the east were too far away.

The site, land confiscated from the Loyalists who had fled to Canada, was on a rise far from the Mohawk River on the south, and Canada Creek on the east. Flooding would not be a problem.

There was an abundance of timber on the north hill. With luck and good weather, Bloomfield hoped to have the fort completed by August.

Bloomfield and his sergeant spotted the cloud of dust hanging over the King's Highway before the line of men and animals came in sight.

The farmers turned up the road that led north through the town. They prodded their oxen and horses up the road through the settlement, a cluster of some 30 houses and a population of about 200.

"Well, Captain," Bloomfield's sergeant said, "here they come. Glum looking lot, ain't they Sir? What do you suppose makes them men so long-faced?"

"They're Palatines, Sergeant."

"That reason for them to look so dour?"

"They're like people without a country. They've been driven off their lands; time and again. Glum or not, Sergeant, I'm glad to see them. If we work the troops any harder they won't wait for darkness to desert."

"That flogging you ordered should make 'em think twice."

Bloomfield let out a long breath. "Davis is a good man. I can't fault him for trying to desert not after losing his wife and child. Hated to do that to him. He probably would rather I had ordered that he be shot. What's he got to go home to?"

"He know his wife was raped before she was killed?"

"That's something I'm not about to tell him. Bad enough to know she's dead."

"Wonder what kind of punishment that Britisher got for what he did."

"Nothing compared to what Davis will do if he ever finds him."

Bloomfield stroked his chin. Work would go faster now. The Palatines were not afraid of hard labor. "Put them to work where they'll be the most use. No favoritism, Sergeant. We don't want any trouble between them and our men. I hope your German's good. I doubt if many of them speak much English. Tell them we're glad for their help. Remember, it's their wheat that feeds the army."

Captain Bloomfield went to his quarters to finish his reports to Colonel Dayton and General Schuyler, wondering if they would receive more than a cursory review. Both men had more pressing concerns.

General Schuyler was dealing with a court-martial.

Colonel Dayton was faced with the problem of the vandalism and looting of Johnson Hall. There had been strict orders not to destroy or take anything that belonged to Sir John; arms being the only exception.

Rumor had it that the door to a locked room was broken down with an ax, drawers rifled, money stolen. Furniture was destroyed. Sir John's papers were read, and those of no consequence were tossed to the wind. His books, many of which were from Sir William's library, were either stolen or discarded.

Bloomfield had heard that Colonel Dayton had taken several volumes for his own library.

Clothing, slaves, livestock and carriages were taken.

The railing and baluster of the mahogany staircase were damaged. Some said a belt ax was used. Others claimed the troops battered the railing with the butt end of their guns

He was glad he had not witnessed the ransacking of Johnson Hall. It had been difficult enough to watch Lady Mary's humiliation when he had escorted her, as a hostage, to Albany.

Stone Ridge

It was well into the second week when Susannah finally sought out Jason. He was sitting against a tree, eating.

She stood before him, smug, hands on her hips. The hem of her skirt brushed Jason's hand, unnerved him.

Susannah found his discomfort amusing. "You're afraid of me, ain't you? Afraid of what you want and what I can give you."

"You're wrong, Susannah."

Her smile said she disagreed. "You're just like every other man. It's just the price that's different, and you're afraid to pay the price."

She was full of herself. "I told you once that I wanted away from here—asked you to take me. You were too good for me, then. Well, I'm married now. I don't need you, and I wouldn't have you even if you paid me. When this foolish war is over, I'll be gone."

"Hannah hasn't said anything about you being married."

"You think I'd tell her? What does she care about me? She's got that mousey wife of yours to fuss over." A swish of her skirt, and she walked away.

"Doctor Dayemon, sir?" Jason looked up and grinned. "Adam?"

"Yes, sir."

The boy had grown taller. His shoulders had broadened. He was on the verge of becoming a man, and if he saw battle, he surely would become one. No, Jason's mind corrected. The boy had metamorphosed before he left Johnstown.

"Join me." Jason patted the ground.

"I'll stand, sir, if you don't mind."

"You made it to your uncle in New Jersey?"

"That we did, sir. Me, Jossie and my brothers and sisters. My aunt and uncle took to her right off. We're married, sir, Jossie and me."

"You're the second one to tell me that today," Jason said. "Do you know a man named Hotchkiss?"

"Blowhard. Cantankerous. Best be leery of him, sir."

"Susannah Freye, says she's married to him."

"Can't be," Adam stated. "Hotchkiss has a wife and a family in Jersey."

"She says they were married by Reverend Mister Blake."

"He ain't no more a reverend than me. Won't do no good to take 'em to task. They'll just say it was a mock wedding."

"Why'd you join the army? Men get killed in the army."

"Widows get pensions," Adam answered.

"See you don't get killed, Adam," Jason said. "Jossie would rather have you than all the money in the world."

CHAPTER 42

July 1776

On the 14th of July, Captain Bloomfield received a packet of mail from his father. With the letter was a copy of a Declaration of the Continental Congress.

He read and re-read the opening sentence; not totally unexpected, but nonetheless, sobering:

'WHEN IN THE COURSE OF HUMAN EVENTS, IT BECOMES NECESSARY FOR ONE PEOPLE TO DISSOLVE THE POLITICAL BANDS WHICH HAVE CONNECTED THEM WITH ANOTHER,....'

His hands began to tremble. His mouth went dry. His heart—he would have vowed—skipped a beat.

These men, members of the Continental Congress, were declaring:

'THAT THESE UNITED COLONIES ARE, AND OF RIGHT OUGHT TO BE FREE AND INDEPENDENT STATES; THAT THEY ARE ABSOLVED FROM ALL ALLEGIANCE TO THE BRITISH CROWN, AND THAT ALL POLITICAL CONNECTION BETWEEN THEM AND THE STATE OF GREAT BRITAIN IS AND OUGHT TO BE TOTALLY DISSOLVED...'

It was a lengthy document, written in fine script, signed by men from the 13 colonies, and ended with these words:

'AND FOR THE SUPPORT OF THIS DECLARATION, WITH A FIRM RELIANCE ON THE PROTECTION OF DIVINE PROVIDENCE, WE MUTUALLY PLEDGE TO EACH OTHER OUR LIVES, OUR FORTUNES, AND OUR SACRED HONOR...'

The next day, after the troops had drilled for two hours, Captain Bloomfield kept the men assembled while he read the Declaration of Independence to them.

Huzza! Huzza! Huzza! echoed over the valley.

Later that same day, Bloomfield read it again for the people of Stone Ridge. They listened in somber silence.

SEPARATION!

INDEPENDENCE!

It would be folly to think the King would allow his troublesome children to go unpunished.

The fort would be needed more than ever. Fighting was sure to spill over from New England, New Jersey and other neighboring colonies.

The fat was in the fire now.

War in the valley was a certainty.

Jason was among the many who listened. His thoughts were a jumble. It would surely tear his family apart.

What would this do to his friendship with Walter?

How would the valley folks look on him? One of them? A dog of the Butlers? A man not to be trusted because of his association with the Johnsons?

Although the council with the great general Philip Schuyler, was not until August, a band of Indians had arrived a few days before the men in the fort learned of the drastic step taken by the Continental Congress.

Bloomfield had been forewarned. There was little he could do, but parcel out some of the provisions supplied by the Continental Congress.

Whole families camped on the flat lands below the fort. Some of the women came with their babies strapped to the cradle board their mother carried on her back.

One, in particular, caught Jason's eye. The child could not have been more than a week old, but the mother went out with the other women to chop wood.

When he questioned one of the Indian men, Jason was told that it was good for the woman. It put the bones back in place.

While the troops and the locals worked at building the fort, more members of the Six Nations of the Iroquois League continued to show up. 230 Cayugas and Senecas arrived on August 5, swelling the numbers of Indians camped on the flats to 1700, plus.

At the council, Schuyler asked who would remain neutral, who would ally themselves with the Americans, and who would *Take up the Hatchett*. Their honesty, he told them, would be appreciated if they planned to side with the British. If they decided in favor of the king, they would have to take the consequences.

Some of the nations were wavering. The Americans held Montreal and controlled the St. Lawrence River. The Indians worried about their future if the British were bested by the Americans.

In their answer, given on Saturday, August 10, the Mohawk Chief, Abraham, implied that their allegiance to the Johnsons and the king was firm.

The Onondags and Senecas, as well as the Cayugas, said they could not be responsible for their young men if they warred against the Patriots.

Once more the Oneidas and Tuscaroras would remain neutral, and would not be a part of what they called a *Family Quarrel*. They would not fight their brothers, white or red.

The meeting did not produce the results General Schuyler had hoped for, but each side knew where the other side stood.

The next day, Sunday, August 11, Schuyler distributed the tobacco, linen, knives, blankets and other gifts to the Indians. The warriors and chiefs were given $12,000, which was divided equally among all the Indians, as were the presents the Continental Congress had sent.

Work on the fort proceeded at a more rapid pace. By August 15 it was nearing completion. The troops built bark huts for themselves. The officers moved into the blockhouse. The carpenters labored to finish the main gate.

Scaffolding for the sentries was put up on August 22, and on August 25, the Paymaster arrived, and left the next day for Fort Stanwix, called Fort Schuyler by the Continentals.

By the end of August, most of the regiment were ordered to Fort Stanwix.

"What're you doin'."

Startled, Susannah turned at the sound of her husband's voice.

"Gathering my things. To go to Fort Stanwix with you. A wife belongs with her husband."

"Wife?" Archer Hochkiss snorted. "You ain't my wife."

"Of course I am. Reverend Mr. Blake married us." She pawed through the bag she had been packing until she found what she was looking for.

She drew out a parchment. "Here," she pointed to the name on the paper. "See where he signed it? We're lawful wedded."

"He ain't no Reverend," Hochkiss snickered. "It weren't no real wedding. I got a woman and a parcel of young'uns in Jersey." He looked around to see if anyone was near enough to hear. "I aim to see 'em... Real soon."

The drums beat assembly. He hurried to join the ranks.

The fifes joined the drums. The troops moved out, faded into the distance.

Susannah stepped through the doorway into the bright sunshine, watched the troops head west to the big fort at the carry. She had not told him that he was going to be a father, and she was too hurt and angry to cry. He had promised to take her to New York when his enlistment was up.

Fort Dayton would be her home until another man came along to take her to some big city. A tear slipped down her cheek. She desperately wanted that man to be Doctor Jason Dayemon.

Josef returned home, not in the least interested in the needs of his farm or family. He left the worrying to Hannah; the work to Dolf. As before, he was frequently away, claiming he was on secret Committee and Militia business.

Jason went back to Lauri and Will, amazed at how she, with a small baby to care for, had, with Hannah's and Dolf's help, managed to grow enough to tide them over the winter to come.

Smiling as he turned into Freye's yard, he wondered if all that hard work had put Lauri's bones back in place.

The Tryon County Militia continued to muster, and on September 5, Colonel Nicholas Herkimer was promoted to Brigadier General.

In October, Captain Allen sent a letter from Fort Dayton to General

Schuyler. The fort had 123 men, four swivel guns, but not over twelve barrels of powder, some cartridges, and no ammunition for the cannon, and an enemy force of 700 Indians and whites were coming from Oswego.

Walter Butler, it was said, commanded them.

CHAPTER 43

Late May 1777

Jason had finished repairing the wattle fence. It wasn't strong enough to stop Goliath or Lightning from breaking through, but it did discourage them. Lightning liked to race, and despite Jason's efforts, he would break out.

Jason did not realize a horse and rider had stopped until he heard a voice that brought back memories of New York.

"You spent two years in my cabinet shop and the best you can do is build a fence? Not much of a fence at that."

Jason glanced up to see a lanky man with a prominent nose, and a jutting chin. The man was a Continental Officer, a Lieutenant Colonel.

"Marinus…" Jason saluted. "Colonel… Sir…"

"Let's forget the military protocol." Marinus Willett reached down and grasped Jason's hand.

"Been in the valley long?" Jason asked.

"Passing through. I'm on my way to Fort Stanwix…" He corrected himself, "Schuyler. Can't seem to remember to use the new name."

He shifted in the saddle. "I spent some time at Stanwix in '58. Ate some half cooked meat. Laid me up for a couple of months. Had to be carried like a baby to the batteau when I was well enough to leave. Shameful way to treat a dashing young man like me."

"You needed a good doctor."

"Maybe I'll take you along this time."

"You'll stay long enough to meet Lauri?"

Willett nodded.

"There's an empty stall in the lean-to. You can put your horse in there."

Willett dismounted, followed Jason to a bark shed.

Lightning snorted his displeasure, swished his tail a few times, and kicked the side of the stall.

Willett's horse ignored Lightning's adolescent behavior.

"I paid a courtesy call on General Herkimer." Willett stroked his horse's muzzle. "He speaks highly of you."

"He's a good man," Jason said.

"He told me you're in the militia. I wondered which side you'd take."

"It's not political with me," Jason said. "I've a wife and child to think of. This is my home. That's what I'd fight for. Not some king half way 'round the world."

"What about your friend? Butler, isn't it.?"

"He's loyal. Always will be," Jason said. "Not even the threat of the gallows would change his allegiance."

Lieutenant Colonel Marinus Willett continued his trip to Fort Stanwix. On orders, he had left 49 of his men at Fort Dayton to relieve the garrison.

He traveled west on the King's Highway, and forded the Mohawk River near the ruins of old Fort Schuyler. He passed through the Oneida Indian village of Oriska, dipped into the ravine a few miles beyond.

Farther on, the road opened up. He stopped at the edge of the clearing. What he saw troubled him.

Men were placing pickets, not in the ditch as they were originally, but in the covert way. Others were struggling to raise long, crossed braced poles in front of the embrasures.

When in place, they blocked the cannon. Men were sawing, hacking and chopping the upper part of the poles which were seven feet too long.

A barracks had been built outside the fort.

Why would Colonel Gansevoort put up with such stupidity?

Willett found out soon enough.

General Philip Schuyler had sent the French engineer, de la Marquisie, to repair the fort, and Peter Gansevoort would not countermand General Schuyler's orders.

Infuriated, impetuous, Willett dared being charged with insubordination, and wrote a letter to General Schuyler.

de la Marquisie was ordered back to Albany.

June 30, 1777—Fort Stanwix

Thomas Spencer, the Oneida Indian blacksmith, waited impassively in the quarters of Colonel Peter Gansevoort. He had come all the way from an Indian Council at Oswego to alert Gansevoort of an imminent attack.

A British officer, Brigadier General Barry St. Leger, was leading a combined force of over 1000 men; Indians, Tories, Hessians, Indian Department Rangers, and seasoned British soldiers. Their intent—capture Fort Stanwix.

Colonel Peter Gansevoort's fingers beat a tattoo on the scarred table. Even if the hoped for reinforcements arrived before the enemy did, Gansevoort would be outnumbered.

The fort he commanded sat in the middle of nowhere. It had been built in 1758 to protect the Oneida Carrying Place, a three mile portage between the Mohawk Fiver and Wood Creek. It replaced the three smaller forts the French had burned during the French and Indian War.

Congress authorized, and General Washington ordered, Fort Stanwix be repaired. At the end of August, 1776, Elias Dayton brought most of his 3rd New Jersey regiment from Fort Dayton to ready Stanwix to withstand a possible assault.

He was succeeded by Colonel Samuel Elmore, and his Connecticut regiment. Their enlistments were up on April 15, and as General Schuyler's letter to Washington stated: *not a man of them will remain even one day.'*

However, when the 3rd New York arrived, several men were persuaded to join the 3rd New York, serving under Major Robert Cochran, who held that rank in Elmore's battalion.

Seven days later, after Gansevoort's arrival on May 3, Elmore's regiment departed, glad to be away from that God forsaken fort in the wilderness.

To the west, Wood Creek was the connecting waterway to Lake Oneida, Oswego on Lake Ontario, and Fort Niagara, a major stronghold of the British. Gansevoort expected this would be the most likely route St. Leger would use.

The Mohawk River flowed east toward Albany, through the broad valley that was the granary for the American troops. If the British succeeded in destroying the crops, driving the farmers from their land, the American army would be in serious trouble.

At all costs, Fort Stanwix must not fall.

Lieutenant Colonel Marinus Willett, nine years Gansevoort's senior, was second-in-command. He paced back and forth, from one side of the room to the other. "How much time do we have?"

Spencer shrugged. "St. Leger not get here soon. I see many men chop, many trees fall in Wood Creek."

Gansevoort chuckled. "That will slow the British."

Willett glanced at Spencer. "Who are the Tory leaders?"

"Claus. Butler. Johnson," Spencer answered. "Claus tell Indians, 'When I come toward that fort and the commanding officer there shall see me, he shall not fire one shot, and render the fort to me.'"

Gansevoort pounded the table. "Claus better not stand in the open, then, when he comes to this fort, or he'll find out what one shot does to a man."

"Brant with them?" Willett asked.

Spencer nodded.

"What about cannon?"

"Two big, four little."

Gansevoort stood, dismissing Spencer. "Thank you, Thomas. We have a fresh horse ready for you. Get word to General Herkimer to send the militia. We'll see that your wife gets the rations she needs. I wish all the scouts were as dependable as you."

Spencer nodded solemnly. He did not think of himself as a scout. He was a spy, and he wondered how many more times he could mingle with his Iroquois brothers before he would be caught.

He had informed on them. He had stolen one of their horses. It was now out of sight, with the regiment's mounts.

A soldier was waiting outside the sally port with a fresh Continental horse.

Spencer galloped across the clearing and plunged into the forest that surrounded Stanwix. He would feel safer once he distanced himself from the garrison. Butler, Brant and Claus would have sent out scouts. If he were seen leaving Fort Stanwix it would go bad for him, and also his wife and family.

The road dipped into the ravine. At the bottom, a stream flowed north before the trail started upward. The trees were dense, the bushes and grass thick, the best place for an ambush. Butler and Brant would make good use of it.

The horse splashed through the brook, and picked his way up the other side. Horse and rider raced toward Oriska.

Tomorrow he would go down the valley, tell Herkimer about St. Leger and warn the General of a possible ambush.

Tonight he would be with his wife.

CHAPTER 44

August 1, 1777—Fort Dayton

Fort Dayton and the small settlement of Stone Ridge spilled over with people.

They were there because Brigadier General Nicholas Herkimer issued a Proclamation on July 17 calling all able bodied men from 16 to 60 to arms.

It was a wordy piece of business.

No matter. There were those who could only read German, many who could not read at all. His message was spread by word of mouth. The British were on the way with 2000 men.

The Tryon County Militia came in groups: men of the four battalions. They came as families—trades people, woodsmen, and farmers.

The men did not look like soldiers, although some wore a regimental coat from prior military service. The woodsmen wore hunting shirts, fringed frocks of linen or deerskin.

They arrived with their British .75 caliber Brown Bess musket or an American copy, Dutch, German, and trade muskets, fowlers; all of varied calibers. Their hunting bags held their horn for their priming powder, lead balls and extra flints. Cartridges were carried in a tin canister or a cartridge box at their waist.

They had a wooden or a tin canteen to quench their thirst. Knapsacks or haversacks slung over their shoulders held their food, clothing and blanket.

Before they were sent to join the others, their weapons were inspected; gun, sword, bayonet, knife or tomahawk.

Jason had insisted Lauri and Will stay at the fort where they would be safe. He had also encouraged Hannah Freye to take refuge there. Dolf was now old enough to go with the militia, and Josef claimed he was too busy with committee and militia business to worry about his wife and son.

Susannah was still at the fort. She had given birth to a boy on a bitter March morning. She was attended by a midwife, even though she demanded Jason be sent to deliver her. Her pregnancy had been difficult, and she hated the changes in her body that made men avoid her.

Most of the women who sought safety inside the fort busied themselves setting up a place for the family to wait, fighting the gnawing fear their men might never return.

Lauri stood outside the stall watching Hannah settle in. She wanted to help.

Hannah was unbending. "You'll have plenty to do, soon enough."

This was the time Lauri hated. She was big with child, ungainly. Hannah would not let her cook because she might get burned. She must rest, save her strength for the baby's birth.

Lauri did not see the woman stop beside her.

She was a big woman, full breasted, broad of hip. Her bosom sagged almost to the ragged belt she had tied around her soiled dress. She looked like she had nursed too many children too long.

"What's your name, dearie? I'm Hortense Greene," she said. "Ain't Hortense fancy for the likes of me? My ma was one for takin' to fancy things. Reckon she didn't think far when I was born. Should of know'ed from the size of me when I come out I weren't no Hortense. Well, maybe I am. Hortense means gardener, and heaven knows I've growed a lot of children.

Folks call me Tense. Just plain Tense. What's your name, dearie?"

"Lauri Dayemon."

"You married to the doctor?"

"Yes." Lauri hugged Will close to her swollen breast, his feet rested on her bulging front.

"Well, ain't you the lucky one. Your man's a handsome one, all right. I seen lots of single girls eyein' him. Married ones, too, like that one." Hortense pointed to a woman showing a baby to Jason.

Susannah.

Lauri felt her baby kick. A jealous reaction from seeing Susannah lick her lips as she stroked Jason's arm, pressing him to hold the child?

Tense was saying, "Ain't none of the married women like her. The men, now, that's different. Look at her. She ain't no tame cat. She'd like to get her claws in that fella. Baby's name's Jason, so I hear."

Tense gasped, and her gaping mouth showed yellow, uneven teeth. "Say, ain't that the doctor she's makin' up to? Ain't his name...?" She covered her mouth with a stubby hand and dirty nails.

"Didn't mean no harm, dearie," Tense said, when she recovered from her blunder, "but it's best not let him get you in the family way too often. A man starts to wander if his woman ain't to hand cause she's got a loaf in the oven. Even my Tobias would have liked to stray, but ain't no woman 'cept me would have him."

She prattled on. "I've got boys, and I'd rather a married woman be near us. I just ain't hankerin' to have no single girls gawkin' at my boys.

"Ain't none of my boys old enough to go with old Honikol, but I've had a devil of a time keepin' an eye on 'em. For sure, they'll sneak off with the militia if they get the chance."

A dirty faced, bare foot boy tugged on her skirt. "Ma, I gotta pee."

"Looks to me like you already did."

Tense glanced at Lauri. "Land-a-goshen, dearie, you look peaked." She took Will from Lauri and settled him on her hip.

Will studied her with worried eyes for a moment, then he smiled and never let out a peep of protest.

The Greene's stall was next to Lauri's and Hannah's. Children romped in the straw, grabbing fistfuls to heave at one another, scattering it hither and yon.

"Ain't I told you younguns we gotta save that straw else we ain't gonna have nothin' to sleep on? Look at you. Dirty as pigs, the whole bunch of you. Ain't you ashamed?"

The middle sized boy peered at Will. "Ma, you get yourself another baby while you was gone?"

Will gave him an impish smile. The boy reached for Will but Lauri snatched him from Tense's arms before the lad could lay his dirty hands on her son.

"We've company," Tense told the others. "Come here and meet the nice lady."

They let the straw trickle through their fingers as they came to stare at the stranger.

A young girl, only two or three years younger than Lauri, stepped out of the shadows. Her face was sweat stained, but unlike the others, her worn clothes were clean. She carried a make-shift broom and there was straw tangled in her hair.

"Ain't she the sweet one? Always workin'. Where's the boys?" Tense asked.

"The old sergeant come by and took 'em," the girl said. "They's got to stand guard in case the injuns and Tories come by."

"My, my. Imagine my boys standin' guard, watchin' for them heathens and Johnson people so's we won't all be killed in our sleep."

She glanced toward Lauri. "Here I am forgettin1 my manners. This here's Lauri Dayemon, the doctor's wife. Tobyann was sure took by your husband's good looks."

Tobyann reddened to the roots of her hair.

"Don't pay her no mind," Tense said. "She's took by any good lookin' man." She nodded toward two little girls. "This here's Faith and Hope, Never did have no Charity." She guffawed as if it were a great joke.

She eased her bulk onto an old milking stool. "My old legs don't hold me up so good no more," she told Lauri. "Sorry I ain't got somethin' for you to rest yourself on, but one stool's all I got."

Lauri asked, "Will the men be able to spend the night with their family?"

"If Honikol don't want to be left high and dry, they will. He might better walk into a hornet's nest than have a bunch of spitting mad women on his back."

CHAPTER 45

Fort Stanwix—(Schuyler)

They came out of the western edge of the forest—more than a thousand men—British Regulars, Hanau German Jaegers, Kings Royal Regiment of New York, Canadian Militia, and hundreds of Indians.

The British and Germans quickly formed ranks and marched in disciplined precision to the skirling bag pipes. The King's Royal Regiment of New York, and the Canadian Militia followed—not always in step.

In the middle of the third line of Captain Stephen Watts' Company of Light Infantry, King's Royal Regiment of New York, Private Geoff Baxter tried to focus his watery eyes, keep his puffy, rummy face solemn, and stay in step with the men around him.

If Captain Watts knew that it was he who had deflowered that wench Watts had fallen in love with, Watts would have had him flogged until his back was shredded and the ground ran red with his blood.

No matter. When this harebrained siege was over, he was going to desert, head for Johnstown or wherever Lauri was, and finish what he started.

Walter Butler had made his life hell ever since Butler learned he was in Watts' Company. Maybe he would get Butler, too. For sure, he would get Jason Dayemon.

Nights when he could not sleep, he conjured up the things he would do to Lauri while Dayemon, shackled, watched.

They had come on to the open land around the fort. Land that had been cleared of trees. Trees that had been cut down for pickets, leaving stumps. Stumps that could shield an Indian when he sneaked his way toward the fort. The fort that was protected by the garrison's guns. Guns of the troops who were in place on all sides of the fort.

Guns that could kill.

Whooping and howling, the Indians burst out of the woods: Mohawks, Onondagas, Cayugas, Senecas. Mississaugas, Schoharies, Squakies, Wyandots, Ottawas, Chippeways, Potawatomies. These were fighting men from the Six Nations of the Iroquois, the Seven Nations of Canada, the Lakes' Nations and the Ohio Nations.

They paid no attention to the commands of the British Indian Department officers. They scattered in all directions, brandishing their tomahawks and scalping knives.

One Indian dashed toward the fort, shaking two hoops. A scalp was stretched on each one.

A young Continental of the 3rd New York, steadied his gun, sighted along the barrel and fired.

The bullet struck the Indian squarely in the chest. He fell, still holding the hoops. The scalps had been ripped from two young girls who had been killed a week earlier, while berry picking outside the fort.

The unseasoned soldier sank to his knees, sobbing.

Colonel Gansevoort, Lieutenant Colonel Willett, and the other officers were clustered together watching the spectacle taking place outside the fort.

"You've seen the enemy," Gansevoort told his junior officers. "Don't underestimate them. They mean to have this fort. We are determined they won't."

He and Willett turned away, walked over the hard packed parade ground, past the adjutant's daughter—the whipping post—used too many times, as far as the rank and file were concerned. Dried blood covered the ground around it. Willett ducked as his lanky frame followed the colonel's sturdy form through the door of Gansevoort's quarters.

"Divine Providence," Willett said.

"What?" Gansevoort asked.

"Divine Providence," Willett repeated. "What else can it be? A few weeks ago you hardly had enough men to defend the fort. 450 or so, and 50 militia. Then Major Ezra Badlam came with]50 men, and yesterday, before St. Leger's toadys got here, Lieutenant Colonel James Mellon brought 100 more.

"That's 750 by my calculations, and don't forget the four batteaux of supplies, enough to last six weeks if we're careful. And we got it all in by the skin of our teeth.

"We have 11 cannon. Better than St. Leger's," Willett added. "Enough to keep him at bay, I'll wager."

Willett's light hearted chatter helped to lift Gansevoort's spirits. The responsibility of holding the fort, and the safety of the people in it, weighed heavily on his 28 year old shoulders.

Following the killing of the berry picking girls, he had sent as many women and children, as were willing to go, down the valley to safety.

He went to a cabinet, pulled out a bottle of wine, and two glasses, filled both, handed one to Willett, and raised his glass, "To Brigadier General St. Leger."

"May he have a swift trip back to Canada." Willett set his empty glass on the scarred table, and headed for the door.

The noisy yipping and yapping of the Indians spilled through the open windows.

"Don't those savages ever stop?" Gansevoort asked.

"It's when they don't make noise that worries me," Willett said. He stepped out into the August heat.

The din continued most of the day while St. Leger's troops set up camp on all sides of the fort. Sir John Johnson led his King's Royal Regiment of New York southeast to the carry, killing any hope of assistance reaching the fort.

At three of the clock, the sentry near the front gate called to the officers on the parade. "Unarmed man carrying a flag approaching."

"Challenge him," Willett ordered.

"Aye, Colonel."

"State your name and business," the sentry shouted.

"Captain Gilbert Tice, Six Nations Indian Department, Niagara. I have a message for Colonel Peter Gansevoort from Brigadier General Barry St Leger, Commander of His Majesty's Crown Forces."

The sentry could hear the officers conferring below him. One hurried away toward Colonel Gansevoort's quarters. He returned shortly, following in Gansevoort's foot steps.

"Bring him in," Gansevoort ordered.

"Aye, Colonel. Stay where you are, Captain. We'll send out an escort. No foolishness, now, or we'll shoot you where you stand."

Six men from the 3rd New York stepped forward, their guns resting against their shoulders.

Tice, blindfolded, was escorted by the six men, two in front, two behind and one on each side gripping his arms so he would not trip and fall.

"Watch your step Captain. We're going through a doorway."

Tice felt a slight pressure on his arm as he was led into what he guessed to be a large room. He could smell the wax and felt the warmth of burning candles. His blindfold was removed and as his eyes adjusted to the dimly lit room he saw that the shutters were tightly closed and the door secured, not only keeping out the sunlight but denying him any chance of seeing how prepared the garrison was against the British.

He was surprised to see officers from Massachusetts, as well as New York. He recognized several of the New York staff. They had served together in the French and Indian War, or as the British referred to it, the Seven Years War.

The Commanding Officer, a full Colonel of the 3rd New York Continental Line, was younger than Tice expected. Not quite thirty, he was a little more than six feet tall, with deep set gray eyes, and a ruddy complexion.

The man standing next to him, wearing the uniform of a Lieutenant Colonel, 3rd New York Continental Line, was a lanky fellow with a long angular face, prominent narrow nose and jutting chin.

"Please be seated Captain." Gansevoort pointed to a chair to his left as he seated himself at the head of the table. He introduced his second-in-command, Lieutenant Colonel Marinus Willett, who sat down opposite Tice. Gansevoort presented the other officers who had seated themselves around the table according to rank.

Cheese and wine had been set out on the table.

"You have a message for me from General St. Leger, I believe, Captain."

"I have, Colonel." Tice took a folded parchment from his pocket and handed it to Colonel Gansevoort.

Gansevoort scanned the paper, then leaned back in his chair. Methodical and exact, as was his nature, he read St. Leger's proclamation more slowly, digesting every word, sentence and paragraph:

It was long and bombastic.

It introduced Barry St. Leger, Esq., as commander-in-chief of a chosen body or troops from the grand army, as well as an extensive corps of Indian allies from all the nations.

Phrases like 'restore the constitution, relieve the suffering, free those being persecuted by tyranny,' jumped out at Gansevoort.

Those who agreed to overthrow the rebel government would be paid in solid coin. Those who rejected his offer of protection would suffer.

Gansevoort noted the manifesto was signed: *By the order of the Commander-in-chief Will OSB. Hamilton, Secretary.*

When Gansevoort was finished, he handed the paper to Lieutenant Colonel Willett.

Each officer read it, passed it to the next, until it had gone around the table and back to Colonel Gansevoort.

"Well, Gentlemen," Colonel Gansevoort said, "you have read General St. Leger's Proclamation. How say you?"

In one voice they chorused, "NAY!"

"There Captain," Gansevoort said to Tice, "you have your answer. You can tell General St. Leger his offer is rejected with disdain.

Smiling, Gansevoort asked, "Captain, will you join us in drinking some wine, and refresh yourself with some Mohawk Valley cheese?"

Tice fought to control his Irish temper. "I reject your offer with disdain."

He was blindfolded once more and escorted out of the fort. After he stepped through the small door in the larger, heavier main gate, his blindfold was removed. He could hear the cheers and laughter of the fort's defenders.

"Let's pray," Colonel Gansevoort said to Lieutenant Colonel Willett, "that Thomas Spencer got word to Nicholas Herkimer."

CHAPTER 46

August 3, 1777—Fort Dayton

It was crowded in the stall that was to be home for Lauri and Will. Will was asleep in his makeshift bed. Jason held Lauri in his arms. He could feel her warmth, her love for him, their need for each other; and all the while, Susannah came between them.

He could not get her out of his mind. She had come to him that afternoon, carrying a boy child in her arms.

"I must talk to you," she said.

"So talk." He glanced over his shoulder. Lauri was watching.

"Not here. What I have to say is between you and me."

She led him to a place at the far end of the fort. The baby whimpered. She pulled the blanket away from his face, kissed his cheek and whispered softly in his ear.

"I named him Jason," she said.

"For heaven's sake Susannah. Why?"

"Because I'm in love with you. You should have been his father."

"I've never given you any reason…"

"I could make you happy."

"Lauri makes me happy."

"Not always. You think I don't know you ain't the only man who loves her? I seen the way Walter Butler looks at her, and I know all about how Stephen Watts squired her when you was workin' day and night puttin' small pox in Sir William's people."

Jason started to walk away.

She grabbed his arm to stop him. "Jason's father was a liar and a cheat. I thought we was married right and proper. We said the words. I got the signed paper says we was married. Don't mean nothin.

"One night, on the way to Stanwix, he run away. He got caught. He got what was comin' to him."

"Why are you telling me? It's none of my affair."

"Because I ain't gonna be here when you come back."

"Where will you be?"

"Boston. New York maybe. There's a wagoneer will take me to Albany. You ain't to tell Dolf or Ma."

"You'll break Hannah's heart."

"Like you broke mine."

August 4, 1777—Fort Dayton

800 men had answered Brigadier General Herkimer's Hue and Cry. The militia was ordered to march. The 40 mile trek to Fort Stanwix began.

Excited youngsters ran along side, cheering the men, until worried mothers called them back.

Lauri stood outside the open gate—the gate through which Jason had gone—perhaps never to return. Her ears strained to hear the sound of the shrill fifes and the rat-a-tat tat of the small militia drums.

Will squirmed in her arms. He had been delighted with the troops, but with no more commotion to amuse him, he was restless.

She felt a hand on her shoulder.

"He'll come back." Susannah's voice broke in a sob. "God willing, he'll come back."

10 miles west of Fort Dayton, the militia made camp at Staring's Creek. Stanwix lay another 30 miles beyond, another grueling march. Even the young men grasped the fact that this was no frolic.

August 5, 1777

The brutal August sun bore down on the militia. They kept to the north road until they came to the turn south leading to old Fort Schuyler. They forded the Mohawk River, headed west and tramped on. The road became little more than a trail. The trees closed in on them.

Herkimer cursed in German. Several days earlier, he had sent 200 militiamen to clear the road between German Flatts and Fort Stanwix. They had been stopped by a committeeman, ordered to return to Fort Dayton—all because of petty jealousy between civil and military authority.

The militia made camp at Oriska, the Oneida Indian village. Being around so many Indians made some of the men nervous. These were Oneidas, friendly to the cause, they were told, but the words did little to ease the militiamen's minds. What difference did it make who scalped you? Mohawk Seneca, or Oneida.

August 6, 1777—Oriska

The sun was rising, turning the sky blood red. Some of the men said it was a sign of what lay ahead. They were hooted down, but they claimed their gut feeling never lied.

Word spread that Herkimer and his officers were holding a council. Men rushed from their cook fires to listen.

Dolf prodded Jason with the toe of his boot. "Wake up. Cox is arguing with the General."

Groggy, Jason sat up, knuckled the sleep from his eyes. Every bone in his body complained, but he got to his feet.

"Hurry." Dolf was already running toward Herkimer's tent.

Herkimer sat on his faded blanket, smoking his clay pipe, facing west. His eyes were half closed, his head cocked, listening.

Colonel Ebenezer Cox, commanding the Canajoharie regiment, glared at Herkimer. "When do we move?"

"I sent Adam Helmer, Hon Yost Folts, and Mark Demooth to Gansevoort to tell him to keep St. Leger busy, to fire the cannon three times to let us know he got the word we're on the way. When we hear the cannon, we go."

Cox cursed. "You old fool. We should be on the move. NOW."

"Molly Brant sent a runner to her brother. He knows we're here." Herkimer took a long draw on his pipe. "Tom Spencer and old Skenandoa say Brant and Butler are bringing the Indians down."

Cox was not to be put off. "You put too much stock in what Spencer says, and Skenandoa don't know truth from lies."

A fly buzzed around Cox's head. He brushed it away. "Them three men didn't go to Gansevoort. You got somethin' cooked up with that Tory brother of yours, ain't you? You ain't just a coward. You're a traitor!"

Cox turned to the men behind him "If Herkimer won't go, I will. Who's with me?"

Herkimer's face flushed scarlet. "You want to fight Indians? By damn, I take you to fight Indians."

Colonel Ebenezer Cox rushed back to his regiment. He felt good, really good. He had bested Herkimer, a man known to be cautious, sometimes overly cautious; one who weighed the effect of every action, good or bad, right or wrong.

To allow him to be goaded into making such a hasty decision must be the most galling thing Herkimer ever did.

For years, Ebenezer had brooded over what he felt was an injustice. There had been bad blood between the two families since the time Ebenezer's father had been arrested for non-payment of a debt the Herkimers claimed was owed them.

Cox gloated. If a ball with Herkimer's name on it found its mark, he was ready to come forward and lead the militia to victory.

Herkimer ordered the men to ready their weapons, and mounted his old white horse.

"Vorwaert!"

Even the men who did not speak German knew what that meant.

Officers mounted and galloped back to their men. Josef Freye and others raced to relay the order to the weary men spread out along a three mile stretch of rutted road.

"March!"

General Herkimer's old horse sloshed through the cold waters of Oriskany Creek, up the western bank, and disappeared into the forest. Ahead of him, the dense ground cover had forced the flankers out of the woods and on to the road.

The road dipped into a ravine. Herkimer's horse labored up the far side. Jays scolded from the towering beech, maple, birch and hemlocks. Squirrels scurried from limb to limb.

Cox's mount crossed the corduroy bridge that spanned the stream. The Canajoharie regiment followed.

Laughing and shouting, they rushed down the eastern slope, threw themselves on the ground, scooped the water, drank, and let it dribble down their chins.

The oncoming wave of men pushed on. "Out of the way," they shouted. "Save some for the rest of us."

In their rush to quench their thirst, they shoved Dolf aside. Jason grasped Dolf's arm to keep him from falling, from being trampled.

The men splashed water on their face, drank deeply. When they looked up, they found their friends had moved on. They grabbed their guns laying on the ground beside them, got up and crashed through the underbrush to catch up.

Jason scanned both sides of the road. He could not see the hidden bronzed bodies lying belly down, dark eyes peering out of painted faces, but he knew they were there.

CHAPTER 47

The Battle

The shrill sound of a whistle was followed by a volley. The screams of wounded men filled the air.

Jason saw the flashes, heard the roar of the guns, saw Colonel Cox slip from the saddle, and the colonel's horse plunge headlong into the woods.

Herkimer raced up and down the road, shouting encouragement to the militia. A ball tore through his horse, and into the general's leg. He freed himself from the dead steed, moved away crab like, and grabbed his leg above the knee.

Jason reached into his haversack for his medical kit, and sprinted to Herkimer's side.

Dolf followed close on Jason's heels.

"Doctor Dayemon, Ja?" Herkimer said when Jason knelt beside him.

"That's right, General," Jason had just begun to examine Herkimer's wound, when Doctor Petry crouched next to him.

"I'll defer to you, Doctor." Jason said, and moved aside.

"Such a lucky man I am," Herkimer muttered. "My old friend, Bill Petry, und Sir William's own physician."

"Can't probe for the ball here, Honikol," Petry said. "Got to get you to a safer place."

The horse's hair, bone, muscle, and blood, as well as parts of Herkimer's clothing had gone into the general's wound. Corruption and mortification could follow.

Herkimer's brother-in-law, Colonel Peter Bellinger, Commander of the 4th German Flatts and Kingsland Regiment, had come up as soon as he heard Herkimer had been hurt.

Doctor Petry turned to Bellinger. "Help us get him away from here."

Herkimer pointed to a Beech tree higher up the hill. "I can watch the boys better from there."

"Ja, Honikol," Bellinger said, "if that's what you want."

Jason slipped his arms under Herkimer's armpits.

Petry gently lifted the generals's injured leg. Blood soaked through Herkimer's clothes.

Bellinger's hands shook as he took hold of Herkimer's other leg.

"Bring my saddle." Herkimer bit down on the pipe he had found in the pocket of his regimental coat. Color drained from his face.

Dolf took the saddle off the dead horse, hoisted it to his shoulders and slowly followed the group up the slope.

"Put it there, sohn." Herkimer pointed to the base of the tree.

Dolf set the saddle down, and the men carefully lowered the general to the ground.

Herkimer clutched his shattered leg, and leaned against the saddle for support. "Ja, dat is goot."

On the road below them, a militia officer turned and raced toward the rear. He was shouting something. Other men began to follow him.

"My God, Honikol," Bellinger said. "They're running away."

The men were fleeing back toward Oriska. "Damn cowards." Herkimer muttered.

A horse came pounding up the road, and an officer charged into the panic stricken militia, yelling and hitting the men with the broad side of his sword.

Bellinger said, "He's turning them."

The rout slowed. The frightened men turned back, and joined the fight

The Storm

When they entered the ravine, the militia thought they heard thunder. They didn't. They heard the roar of the guns that were firing down on them from the north, south and west sides of the road.

Now they thought they were hearing cannon fire. They weren't. It was thunder from a fast moving storm from the southwest.

The black clouds above the towering trees were split by streaks of lightning, creating a ghostly aura as bone chilling as a graveyard at midnight.

For the militia, it was all too real. They were fighting blood and bone demons, not phantoms conjured up by a disordered mind.

The sluice gates of heaven opened. The militia took shelter in the downed trees and tangled brush that were thick enough to conceal them. For an hour, until the storm played itself out and the sky cleared, the rain drenched men struggled to keep their powder dry.

The Battle

The storm moved off to the north. The men crawled from the deadfall, scrambled to their feet.

Young warriors poured out of the woods, shrieking, howling. They charged down the road toward the militia.

The valley men clubbed the Indians with the butt of their guns, hacked them with their hatchets, and slashed them with their knives.

General Herkimer watched the fighting from his vantage point on the hill. He reached up and touched Dolf's arm.

"Sohn, find your way down there und tell the officers to order their men to take to the trees by twos. Shoot one gun while the other man loads. Den they have the other gun ready when the savages rush them."

Captain Stephen Watts' Light Infantry Company of the King's Royal Regiment of New York advanced with drawn bayonets.

As the columns of men drew closer Jason recognized many of them— Mohawk Valley Loyalists. He saw Geoff Baxter step out of line, raise his gun to his shoulder, aim…Jason felt Dolf slam into him. He found himself spread eagle on the ground, Dolf atop him.

He heard the ball strike the tree that had protected him moments before. Dolf rolled off and helped Jason sit up.

An Indian Department Officer stepped out of the woods, raised him pistol and fired. Baxter slammed face down onto the ferns growing along the roadside.

Walter Butler grinned at Jason, saluted and disappeared into the forest.

What was Walter doing in the Indian Department? He was an Ensign in the 8th Regiment of Foot. Maybe the rumors Jason had heard were true. John Butler had managed to get Walter temporarily transferred to the Indian Department, where he would be more useful.

Without so much as a glance at the dead soldier lying beside the road, the Light Infantry Company marched on.

Captain Watts' Company had turned their coats inside out. From a distance they looked like they were wearing the linen frocks favored by many of the Continentals. The ruse almost worked. They came so close to breaking through the militia's defensive perimeter, one of Captain Jacob Gardinier's men rushed forward to greet an old neighbor. Tory hands reached out and seized the surprised militiaman.

Far to the west, a cannon boomed three times. Helmer, Demooth and Folts had gotten through. Gansevoort knew the militia was on the way. He was sure to send reinforcements. The idea that help would arrive lifted the spirits of the exhausted militiamen.

The cussedness of the militia, and the failure of the crown's forces to wear down the rebels, weakened the Indians will to fight.

The Senecas had suffered staggering loses in a fight that was not theirs. More than half of their fighting men had been killed. Too late, they realized they had been gulled by that sly old fox, Dan Claus. He had won them over with his boast: *Go with us and watch us whip the rebels. Sit down and smoke your pipes and see what a grand show we will provide. We shall not need your help.*

ONAH! ONAH! Alone, and in small groups, the warriors slipped away into the woods.

Cannon fire coming from the fort signaled something was afoot.

If Gansevoort was sending men to help the militia, the Royal Yorkers would be trapped. It would be better to meet the Continentals head-on, to pick the place to fight. The Yorkers, Indian Department men and remaining Indians withdrew.

The heavy fighting slowed. Only occasional gun fire could be heard. The quiet was almost worse than the din of battle.

Herkimer stared at the carnage.

Loyalists, Indians, Militiamen lay in grotesque positions where they fell. The dead were everywhere...shot, tomahawked, scalped.

"We whipped "em!" Dolf crowed. "We whipped 'em!"

Herkimer wiped his eyes with the back of his hand. He could not tell Dolf the truth. He had been ordered to reach Fort Stanwix and raise the siege, and he had not done it.

He had failed.

If something had not pulled the Tories and Indians from the battle, most of what was left of the militia would be dead or captured. Water was almost gone. They were running out of ammunition. There was no place to go, no one to help them.

HE HAD FAILED HIS MEN! THAT WAS THE WORST OF ALL!

CHAPTER 48

The Aftermath

After the hurried retreat of the king's soldiers, the militia officers rushed to carry out Herkimer's orders to take a count of the able bodied, wounded, and as much as possible, of the dead.

Some said it was the living that mattered; that there were too many dead for the too few living to bury the dead. They were left where they lay.

Men were sent out to gather up the wounded. Those who could not walk were carried on litters made from blankets. Men with one good arm assisted the men who could hobble on one leg.

They headed back to Oriska. There, the most seriously wounded would wait for batteaux to be sent up to take them back down the valley. For the others, the long journey home began.

Dolf was one of the searchers. "I got to find Pa," he told Jason. "Ma'll be asking after him. I ain't seen him since the fightin' began. I got to tell her what become of Pa."

Jason nodded. The responsibility for treating the wounded had fallen on him. Brigadier Surgeon Moses Younglove had been wounded and taken captive. Doctor William Petry helped as much as he could, but he also knew the pain of the enemy's weapon.

The injured man winced when Jason tightened the bandage on his arm. "What's the boy's pa called?"

"Josef Freye," Jason said. "He carried messages to the officers."

"Rode a white and brown horse?"

"That's him."

"The boy ain't gonna find his pa. Freye took off when that fool officer come tearin' down the road shoutin' for us to run, we was all gonna git killed. Freye was ridin' hard and fast. Must be half way to Canada by now, unless some Indian shot him or knocked him in the head."

He stood up, shook Jason's hand. "Thanks, Doc. Guess I'll have a look see. Mebbe I can help some other poor fool who went and got hisself hurt."

The wounded continued to pass by, helped by men who were not much better off.

Dolf stumbled out of the line of men, his head bowed. His slumped shoulders shook, his dirt caked face was streaked with tears. "He ran away," Dolf choked on the words. "What can I tell Ma?"

"He's missing. That's all she needs to know. Sooner or later she'll learn the truth. Later she'll be better able to deal with it. Come on. Let's make tracks."

"Not yet," Dolf said. "I come across a Tory officer. One of Johnson's Royal Yorkers. Captain maybe. Bad leg wound. Says he knows you. Wants to see you."

Jason shook his head. "Let Johnson take care of him."

"He sounded like he needed to talk to you. Kinda nice fella. Asked me for water. I gave him a drink out of my canteen, then filled his and mine. I got a feeling you ought to go."

The wounded officer leaning against a maple tree was an unwelcome trespasser who often intruded on Jason's thoughts.

"You wanted to talk to me, Watts?"

"I wondered if you'd come." Captain Stephen Watts held his hand on a piece of a torn white shirt that bound his bloody leg. He was wracked by a spasm of searing pain. His eyes glazed in his ashen face. He drew a labored breath, grimaced. He closed his eyes and waited for the pain to pass.

Jason squatted beside him. "I don't have anything to help you."

"I'm not going to die on you, if that's what you want. I'll just wait for John to send someone to find me. We take care of our own."

"You won't last long if you don't stay still."

"So you want me to live?"

"It makes no difference to me one way or the other."

"John told me you married Lauri. You're a lucky man, Doctor Dayemon." Watts reached for the crumpled green coat on the ground beside him, and pulled a gold watch from a pocket. He placed it in Jason's hand. "Give this to Lauri."

Jason opened the case. A lock of light brown hair was carefully spiraled inside—Lauri's hair.

"I resented you for a long time," Jason said.

Watts forced a smile. "I never stood a chance."

"I hope they find you soon." Jason snapped the lid closed, stood up, handed Watts his canteen. "You'll need this."

The searing pain returned. "I still love her." Watts bit down on the stick he held in his hand.

Fort Stanwix (Schuyler)—August 8, 1777

At one of the clock in the morning, Lieutenant Colonel Marinus Willett and Lieutenant Levi Stockwell, slipped quietly out of the fort's sally port.

If Stanwix was to hold on, they had to get to Albany, convince General Philip Schuyler to send troops, supplies and ammunition, even though General John Burgoyne might be knocking on Albany's door.

St. Leger's troops were digging trenches toward the fort, getting ready to move cannon closer. Food was getting in short supply and desertions were becoming too common.

Willett was relying on Stockwell's woodsman's skills to get them there safely. They crossed the river east of the fort by crawling along a log. A barking dog warned them they were near the Indian camp. Death by torture awaited them if they were caught.

To keep from getting lost, they spent what was left of the darkness huddled together against a tree, waiting for early light.

As soon as it was safe, Willett and Stockwell continued their trip to Fort Dayton, keeping to the north side of the river, at times sloshing through the Mohawk's cold water, often stepping on rocks beside the river, leaving no foot prints.

August 10, 1777—Herkimer's Home

Lieutenant Colonel Willett stood in the doorway, appraising the man who had led his poorly trained farmer soldiers into a hard fought battle against insurmountable odds.

In the short time he and Jason had talked at Fort Dayton, Willett had learned about the gruesome battle, the appalling loss of life, the terrible number of wounded and captured.

Despite the bad leg wound, Herkimer had refused to move to a safer place. "I will face the enemy." he had told his officers.

"Hello General," Willett said.

Nicholas Herkimer sat propped up against his pillow, dozing, a now cold clay pipe clamped between his teeth, an open bible on his lap.

Herkimer opened his eyes. His face brightened. "Ah, Colonel Willett. Come sit mit me. Maria, fetch some stout German beer for the Colonel and me."

It wasn't until Herkimer spoke that Willett realized that a young woman, twenty years Herkimer's junior, sat quietly in the corner, closely watching every breath that the General took. She appeared haggard and near exhaustion.

She rose, acknowledged Willett with a nod and left the room.

"Maria worries," Herkimer said. "She cries when she thinks I'm not watching. She never sleeps. 'Maria, I tell her, you must sleep to stay strong.'" The long monolog tired the General.

Willett found a chair and set it beside Herkimer's bed.

They sat together without speaking until Herkimer asked, "How is tings at the fort?"

"We're holding on," Willett replied. "We're running low, but we'll never surrender. Demooth, Helmer and Folts got through. We knew you were on the way."

Herkimer turned his head toward the wall. When he looked at Willett again, the Colonel saw tears in the General's eyes.

"All those men," Herkimer said. "Dead because of mein pride. Cox would not giff up. Called me a traitor and a Tory." He swallowed hard. "I led them right into the ambush Joe Brant had set up."

"Nicholas, you must stop blaming yourself. It is not good for you." Maria Herkimer had returned with two steins of beer. She gave one to Willett, set the other on a table next to Herkimer's bed, fluffed his pillow to make him more comfortable, handed him the other stein, and went to sit in her chair by the window.

To perk up Herkimer's sagging spirits, Colonel Willett told him about the sortie that he and 250 volunteer troops, half Massachusetts men, half Gansevoort's New Yorkers, had conducted against the camps of Sir John Johnson, and the Indians.

"We brought back blankets, brass kettles, powder and ball, even a bundle of letters. One of them was addressed to me. We saw one man take to the river; Sir John, maybe."

He paused to take a swig of beer.

"We took some flags. Ran them up under our country's new flag. Makes your eyes water and your heart pound just to look at it."

"Where did you get the makings?" Herkimer wanted to know.

"The blue canton," Willett said, "is from a British Officer's camlet cloak. He tossed it aside when we chased him out of Peekskill. Captain Swartout of my regiment claimed it.

"Swartout wouldn't give it up until Colonel Gansevoort assured him Congress would buy him another."

That brought a belly laugh out of Herkimer. "Swartout will be an old man before he sees any money coming from that Congress."

"We made the white stripes out of ammunition shirts, and the red stripes are from a petticoat one of the women gave us. She said she was giving it away for her country, but," Willett added with a smile, "the gossips claim that isn't the only thing she's ever given away."

"Did you have any cannon when you attacked Sir John's camp?" Herkimer asked.

"A field piece—an iron three pounder," Willett said. "St Leger sent a party to head us off, but Captain Savage gave them a taste of grapeshot. That stopped them

"Our men carried as much as they could on their backs, and headed for the fort. They were the bravest men I've ever seen. Brave. No other word can describe them. Brave. Just like your men, General."

"How many men did you lose, Colonel?"

Willett's answer stuck in his throat.

"None."

CHAPTER 49

Shoemaker's Tavern—August 15, 1777

The crowd was churlish, belligerent. Walter was not surprised. Most of them were Palatines; sons and grandsons of the men who had settled this part of the valley.

Guttural babble filled Rudy Shoemaker's taproom; tongues loosened by the beer Walter had ordered and liberally served by Shoemaker.

St Leger had rejected Sir John's argument that fear and confusion would bring the inhabitants back to the fold, and now was the time to send troops into the valley.

"Strike while the iron is hot," Sir John had advised. "Show them the error of their ways. We have many loyal people who will support us. Make examples of those fools who do not."

St Leger refused; claiming he could not spare that many men. The capture of Fort Stanwix was more important.

He would consider the idea if someone offered to go on a fool's errand, knowing full well there would be no one sent to rescue him if he were taken prisoner.

Walter was that fool. He had volunteered to come into this hostile country to recruit men still loyal to the king. St Leger had let him take 14 white soldiers and 14 Indians with him.

It was stifling with the taproom's doors and windows closed, and the August heat that did not lessen at night.

Walter wished he could take off his King's 8th Regiment coat, but he was an officer on the king's business; granted, he was only an Ensign. He would wear his coat.

He stood on the platform hastily thrown together by Rudy Shoemaker's sons, and gauged the crowd. He probably would not sign up many of these men; not if they had been in the battle a few days earlier. It would be hard to convince them of the superiority of the crown's forces if they had witnessed the hasty retreat of the king's men.

Walter nodded and Peter Ten Broeck moved to Walter's side. A part of an old Albany Dutch family, Peter spoke German, the reason Butler had picked him for this mission.

"Some of you know me—Walter Butler," he began in his practiced lawyer voice. "I've represented some of you in court." He saw a few heads bob. "I didn't always win." Some chuckles, mostly grumbles.

He paused, waited for Peter to put his words into German.

Walter continued. "I'm here to invite you to join us in throwing off the yoke of tyranny thrust upon you by a few zealous, misguided despots."

Peter translated.

"Lieutenant-General John Burgoyne is near Albany, may even be there now," Walter said. "Brigadier General Barry St Leger will soon sweep down the valley to join General Burgoyne. Join us and set the country free!"

Caught up in the intensity in Walter's voice, Peter almost forgot to speak in German.

Walter pressed on. "Most of you know my father, John Butler. Listen to his words and those of Sir John Johnson, and Daniel Claus." He reached inside his coat and removed a folded paper.

It was not an overly long letter.

The writers said they wanted to bring peace to the valley. They would forgive all past wrongs, but the Indians, because of their loses—would, *put every soul to death, without regard to age, sex, or friends if the troops at Fort Stanwix did not surrender.*

However, the valley folks would be protected if they convinced the men in the fort to give up.

Surely, the letter went on to say, *you can not hesitate a moment to accept the terms proposed to you by friends and well wishers to the country.*

It was signed by: John Johnson, D. W. Claus, John Butler, Superintendents.

Well, there it was; down to earth common sense. The responsibility for the lives of the valley people was dumped right in their laps.

He folded the paper carefully and put it in his coat pocket.

Before Peter finished translating, men were on their feet, raising their fists, snarling in English and German, surging toward Walter.

"Go to hell, Butler, you and your Tory father, and take them fine gentlemen, Johnson and Claus, with you."

Shouting and the sound of pounding feet outside drowned out Walter's attempt to quiet the angry men.

The taproom door burst open. The bulk of a Continental Officer filled the doorway. He moved purposely toward Walter, shouldering the milling farmers out of his way.

"Walter Butler, in the name of the Continental Congress, I'm placing you under arrest for attempting to seduce the inhabitants of this colony into the service of that killer of women and children, King George the Third."

The thumping of Walter's heart was loud in his ears, but he did not budge. He glanced quickly around the room. Peter was still beside him.

The Indians were gone. They had slipped away at the first sign of trouble.

Some of the soldiers were also missing. The thought of the young Britishers trying to make their way back to Niagara stung him. Some of them were nothing more than boys. They did not know how to survive in the wilderness. They would be fair game for two and four legged animals.

Off to the side, Hon Yost Schuyler, who liked to say, "When God called 'brains', I forgot to run." stood grinning his silly grin.

He was smart enough, Walter suspected, to volunteer so he could come down the valley and sneak off to see his family.

Hon got along fine with the Indians because of his lack of smarts. Walter had called on him more than once when the Indians began to get out of hand.

Rough hands pulled Walter off the platform.

"Make tracks, Butler," the officer ordered, "we have a nice spot in the guard house for you."

Walter and Peter were shoved toward the door. Hon Yost followed behind.

CHAPTER 50

August 17, 1777

"Colonel's orders. Ain't nobody allowed to see the prisoners." He was young, a farm boy, not yet twenty years of age; uneasy with the responsibility of guarding the butchers who had slaughtered the brave men of the Tryon County Militia.

Jason waved a folded paper in front of the lad's face. "It's my pass to see the prisoner, signed by Colonel Wesson. You know I'm a doctor. You want to get in trouble if Butler and the others are sick, and it spreads to the rest of us?"

The young man made no effort to take the paper.

A smile tugged at the corners of Jason's mouth. The lad was unschooled, unable to read the forged pass.

The young soldier considered the situation. "I ain't suppose to do this." He turned the key in the lock, and opened the guardhouse door.

Jason quickly stepped inside, heard the door close behind him.

Walter got up from his bed of straw, grasped Jason's hand. "It's good to know I have one friend."

"I'm not a friend," Jason said. "I'm a physician appraising your sickness."

"What sickness?" Walter nodded toward the other two men in the small cell with him; Captain Peter Ten Broeck, and a blonde haired youth, Hon Yost Schuyler. "We aren't ill."

"Maybe you'll wish you were. Word's going 'round Arnold's planning a court-martial for you."

Walter grinned. "I've met your pompous General. I'm going to make him an important man in your army." He started to pace. "Maybe I was crazy to think I could get men to come over to our side, but what I've done, I've done of my own accord."

"How could you think you could come into the valley and recruit?" Jason asked. "There's hardly a family who hasn't lost a son, brother, father or husband."

"That's what happens in war," Walter said.

"That wasn't war. That was a bloodbath."

Walter stopped in front of Jason. "No matter what happens, I want you to stay out of it. Lauri needs you. Your children need a father."

"You saved my life. Lauri's too," Jason laid his hand on Walter's shoulder. "We don't have to worry about Geoff anymore."

Ten Broeck and Schuyler had hoped for some good news, instead they were subjected to maudlin reminiscing. They drifted off to continue their game of Five and Forty. Ten Broeck was near to scoring his 45 points. Schuyler liked to play, but he was too slowwitted for the card game. He never won.

A commotion—anguished voices, sobbing women, crying men, sent Jason to the cell door. He called for the guard.

"What happened?" he asked when the lad's face appeared at the grill in the door.

Tears ran down the boy's cheeks. "General Herkimer died last night. They cut his leg off and they couldn't stop the bleeding."

August 20, 1777

Walter, his hands and legs shackled, was taken from his cell to go to his court-martial.

Major General Benedict Arnold had come earlier in the day to deliver the news. "We will give you a fair trial, Butler, find you guilty, and hang you. It's what we do to spies."

A surly crowd had gathered behind the Continental troops.

Lauri, big with child, stood on the fringe, crying. She held a small boy in her arms.

Walter felt a twinge. If things had been different, it would be his child she was going to birth.

The shackles on his ankles were removed and he was boosted up onto a plow horse; his wedding gift to Jason and Lauri. Goliath protested, and it took several soldiers to calm him. Walter gripped the pommel to keep from being thrown.

Someone threw a stone. It missed Walter, struck Goliath.

"Arrest that man." Arnold ordered. The crowd shouted protests.

A mob had already gathered at Peter Doxtater's place where Walter's trial was being held.

Walter scanned the throng looking for a familiar face. It occurred to him that this must have been the way Sir William's monkey felt—on display, laughed at, an oddity for the curious.

Walter was hauled from Goliath's back by a burly sergeant, and hustled inside. Every available inch of space in the room was occupied.

He spotted Jason. Their eyes met, but neither acknowledged the other. Jason, Walter reasoned, was suspect because of their long friendship.

Thirteen officers, including Jason's friend, Marinus Willett, were seated at a table.

Walter recognized one of the officers—Lieutenant Colonel John Brooks, the man who had arrested him at Shoemakers; a Massachusetts man, judging from his uniform.

Willett, serving as Judge Advocate, and the other members of the court were sworn in and the trail began.

Walter was charged with being a traitor and spy under the pretense of being a flag. He was accused of trying to persuade the people to give up their allegiance to the fledgling country.

Walter pleaded, "Not Guilty."

He was asked if he had contacted the Commanding Officer.

He answered, "No." He told them he knew of no Commanding Officer except Rudolf Shoemaker, who was a Justice of Peace. His business, he said, was with the inhabitants.

One after the other, those who testified against him, said they understood Butler was encouraging the people of the valley to lay down their arms and join the British.

The most damaging evidence against him was the letter signed by his father, Dan Claus and Sir John Johnson.

The only bright spot was Shoemaker's testimony. *Spies* Shoemaker said, *did not wear a uniform.*

After several others testified against him, the court retired to reach a verdict.

As Walter expected, he was found guilty, sentenced to suffer the pain and penalty of death; to be hanged.

Fort Dayton

To Major General Benedict Arnold's way of thinking, trials and quick convictions, followed by severe sentences, including hanging or flogging, would help strengthen the resolve of the valley people and bolster their morale.

However, he had received orders to send the flag prisoners to Albany.

Hon Yost Schuyler had pleaded guilty to being a deserter from the American army, and was sentenced to receive 100 lashes on his bare back.

Now, Schuyler's mother and brother were pleading for leniency.

It was Lieutenant Colonel John Brooks who came up with a plan—send Schuyler back to Fort Stanwix with the story that Arnold was on his way with an army—numerous as the leaves on the trees.

Schuyler was dim-witted. The Indians held him in awe. They would believe him. To back up his story, send some Oneidas, a few at a time, telling the same lie. If enough of St Leger's Indians believed Schuyler, and left, St. Leger would be forced to withdraw.

If Brooks' ruse worked, it would be a feather in Arnold's cap. He would chance it.

August 1777—On the Road to Albany

As Butler, Ten Broeck and their guards made their way down the King's Highway toward Albany, people turned out by ones, twos, threes, and in larger and larger numbers. Some came to jeer, to raise their fists, throw stones, and. in one case, a ball of mud and manure, splattering Walter's uniform.

When they neared the city, the mobs of angry people increased, surging toward Butler and Ten Broeck, forcing the soldiers to fire a warning shot over the heads of the raging crowds.

When Walter and his guards crested the hill above Albany, memories came flooding back; of the days he spent studying law, nights of parties and dances. Girls—some shy and sedate, others flirtatious and frank, all of them pretty.

They started down the slope. Part way down, they turned onto the road to Fort Frederick. It was a formidable four sided stone structure, with a bastion and cannons on each corner. A flag similar to the one he had seen at Stanwix—red and white stripes, 13 stars on a blue canton flew on the south west bastion.

If this was to be his prison, it would be difficult to escape, but he was determined to be free.

CHAPTER 51

Early April 1778

Jason closed the cabin door, and shut out the waning winter cold. He held a paper in his hand; orders to report to the doctor in charge of the hospital in Albany. General Washington had ordered that the Continental troops were to be inoculated against smallpox.

Jason considered himself a soldier. He could not disobey a direct order.

He was also a doctor. He would do anything he could to keep the men from getting the dreadful disease.

"There's been an outbreak of smallpox down the Hudson," Jason said. "I've been ordered to go to Albany to help with the inoculations. Start getting things together. We'll have to leave as soon as we can."

He did not want to take Lauri and the children to Albany, but he had no other choice. Will was almost two, inquisitive, always getting into trouble, a handful, even for his father. Seven month old Alva Martha had taken to clinging to Lauri, often rejecting Jason, crying when Lauri was out of her sight.

He ruled out leaving them with his folks. His mother would be happy to have her grandchildren, but even if his father agreed, he could be unpleasant.

Nothing had been heard of Josef Freye or Susannah. Dolf was an express rider, carrying communications up and down the valley, Hannah had gone to Schenectady to live with her sister.

The only hope left was to find a half-way decent place to stay in Albany.

They were on the road early the next morning. Lauri had dressed the children in their warmest clothes and wrapped them in blankets. Both protested being bundled up, and Will had a knack for escaping his confinement. Alva simply wailed.

They spent the first night at Nellis Tavern. Jason was surprised that Christian Nellis remembered them.

"A family you're growin', Ja?" Nellis said.

Mrs. Nellis welcomed Will and Alva with a friendly pat on the head. Will responded with outstretched arms, and let Mrs. Nellis hold him and fuss over him. Alva buried her face on Lauri's shoulder.

The Road to Johnstown

Jason turned off the King's Highway, and started up the road to Butlersbury and Johnstown.

The Butler's house was empty. No one was about, and from the looks of the untended land, there had not been anyone there for a long time.

Catherine, the children, John Butler's niece, Deborah Wall, and others had been sent to Albany where they could be more easily watched.

Jason snapped the reins across Goliath's rump and they moved on. He had made up his mind. He would see his mother, and his father would not stop him. Seeing what had happened to Butlersbury, he was more determined than ever to go to his old home.

No smoke drifted from the Dayemon's chimney. There were footprints around the cabin, but no sign of life. He stopped short, jumped to the ground and began to look around. The door was ajar. He eased it open, found no one inside, but several things were missing. There was a rickety hand cart was near the door, partly filled with some of Martha's pots and pans.

He heard someone shuffling down the side of the house.

A stooped, withered old man came around the corner.

"Hiram, what are you doing here?"

Hiram Helpelwaite dropped an arm full of George Dayemon's tools. "Land-a-goshen, that you, Jason?"

"What are you doing with my folks things?"

"Just takin' 'em for safe keepin' so's nobody steals 'em. I was goin' give em back when your ma and pa come back."

"Come back from where? Why aren't they here?"

Hiram leaned against the cart, waiting for his racing heart to slow down.

"Where are my brothers?" Jason demanded.

"You ain't heard? Sir John's been sendin' men down to take anybody wants to go to Canada. Your ma and pa have been gone for sometime."

"What about Jacob and the twins?"

Hiram wiped his brow with a dirty rag. "Jacob took off with Sir John when he flew the coop. Just in time, too."

"And the twins?" Jason asked.

"Them two?" Hiram shook his head. "Had a big set to. Darn near killed one another. Jed was all for going north. Jeremy, well he's of a different stripe. He up and joined the Continentals. Neared to broke your pa's heart."

"Keep my folk's things in a safe place, Hiram. If I hear of you selling anything of theirs, I'll be back. I'll take it out of your hide." Jason turned and climbed up beside Lauri.

Hiram limped over to the wagon. "This must be your woman." He doffed a soiled liberty cap. "How do, mam. I remember you when you was a little girl. Lived with the Baxters as I recollect. Worked at Gil Tice's."

"This is Hiram Helpelwaite," Jason said. ""He's the town crier. Knows everything that's going on."

"Please, Mister Hellpelwaite," Lauri said. "Do you know anything about Christina Tice or Mrs. Wemple.?"

"Mrs. Tice was rounded up same time as Catherine Butler. I don't know nothin' about Mrs. Wemple."

"Remember what I told you, Hiram," Jason clucked, and Goliath pulled the wagon around to face down the road. "Hold on to my family's things."

Schenectady

When they neared Schenectady, Jason was all for pushing on to Albany, but Lauri persuaded him to stop and see Hannah.

The directions to Hannah's sister's house proved to be right. Hannah came running, her arms outstretched to welcome them in a warm embrace. Nothing would do, but they must stay the night.

Albany

The Dayemons were on the road early. It warmed enough for Lauri to hold Alva on her lap. Will fidgeted on the seat between his mother and father.

They reached Albany, and started down the hill, the city spread out before them.

Lauri gripped the edge of the seat. Color drained from her face. Scenes of her mother and father sliding over the rail of the ship flashed before her eyes. "I remember…when I was small…down there…by the river. That's where they took me after Ma and Pa died."

"To the Wilkins?" Jason said.

Tears welled in Lauri's eyes. She nodded, unable to speak.

They moved into the city, stopping at tavern after tavern. It was always the same answer: they were full, no rooms available. A few told them outright they would not take the children.

A wooden sign squeaked on metal hinges. The OX HEAD was their last hope.

CHAPTER 52

Ox Head Tavern—Albany

Tom, the barkeep, was a young man about Jason's age. He listened without comment while Jason explained why he needed a place for Lauri and the children to stay.

When Jason finished, Tom went into the room behind the bar.

Lauri and Jason could hear Tom's and two women's voices.

The discussion ended, and three people came into the public room.

Both women were angular and homely—. "Felicity and. Patience."

Felicity addressed Jason. "So, you're here to save the army from something worse than death. Keep them healthy enough to fight in a battle and get killed.

"I suppose you plan on seeing Walter Butler. Well, he's not far from here…just a few blocks, at Cartwright's tavern. We can help you. Can't we, Tom?"

Before Tom had a chance to answer, he was called away.

"It'll cost you," Felicity said. "Tom's brother is one of the men guarding Butler and Ten Broeck. His price is dear.

"How much?"

Her cackle garbled her answer.

Jason repeated his question.

This time, there was no mistaking the amount.

"Good coin," Felicity told him. "None of those paper Continentals that ain't worth nothin'."

"I don't have that kind of money."

"But you know somebody who does. Catherine Butler will pay anything we ask just to get word about her son. I'll take you to where Catherine Butler is staying."

Felicity cackled again. "We ain't greedy, but it's chancy business, sneaking somebody in to see Butler. It could go hard on Tom's brother. Hard on us, and you too, so don't go runin' to the army. We'll tell them you put us up to it. That you planned on helping Butler escape."

Felicity turned to Patience. "Take Lauri and the children to the room we keep for special visitors. If Tom asks, tell him I may be gone for a while."

The Ox Head was beginning to fill with regulars who were there for the noon meal. They called out to Felicity. She ignored them.

"I'll take you by Cartwright's tavern," she told Jason. "Then we'll go see Catherine Butler. Remember what I told you. You'll need money if you want to see Butler."

Jason let her take him up one street, down another. If she thought she could confuse him enough to get lost, she was mistaken. When they were boys, he and Walter had spent hours pretending they were scouts, plunging deep into the forest, until, on more than one occasion, they really did get lost.

When they worked their way out, they found their fathers waiting for them. Not only were their fathers waiting, so were the chores that had not been done, plus the ones their fathers had heaped on them.

Jason was surprised to find Butler was not too far from the Ox Head. He and Felicity passed by Cartwright's, continued on, turning one way then another, until Felicity stopped and pointed to a house on the opposite side of the street.

"That's where Catherine Butler's staying," Felicity said. "Get the money."

She waited until Jason crossed the street, climbed the stoop, rapped on the door, and went inside.

At the Ox Head, the people in the common room were demanding service.

Patience paid no attention. She told Lauri to follow her.

At the first landing, Patience looked to see if anyone was within hearing. "Leave here as soon as you can find another place," she told Lauri. "Felicity will make your life hell when Jason isn't around. She'll pretend she likes the little ones, but she doesn't like children. I'm afraid of what she might do to them. You, too, she's hated you from the day you came to The Meadows."

Patience started up the next flight of stairs that led to the attic.

"What are you doing in Albany? Where's Belle?" Lauri asked.

Patience stopped again. "After Papa died," she said, "Mama tried to keep things going, but she didn't know one fur from another, how to order goods, how to price. When she learned she was being cheated, she raised the roof, nearly drove away the people who were trying to help.

"Mama hired a man to run things. Hector Smith is his name. At first it was good, but he talked Mama into marrying him. He sold off the slaves, kept the money.

"Felicity and me had to do their work. I run off with a boy—Bob's his name—Mr. Smith brought with him. Bob's an orphan like you. I remembered how bad it was for you, and I wanted to make up for all the mean things I did to you. I couldn't leave Felicity with that horrible man, so all three of us took off.

"Guess Mr. Smith didn't care. He never came after us."

"What about Belle?" Lauri asked. "She must be worrying herself sick, wondering where you are."

"Mama passed over. Her heart wasn't strong. Mr. Smith couldn't wait to get her buried. I wish I knew where Geoff is. He'd take care of Mr. Smith."

"There was a battle at Oriskany," Lauri said. "Geoff was killed."

"Guess Mr. Smith didn't think that mattered. He never told us."

They had reached the top of the stairs.

Before she opened the narrow door in front of her, Patience took a deep breath. "I'm sorry I tried to take your doll, Lauri. I really was going to put it back. I only wanted to look at it."

She pushed, and the door swung in on rusty hinges.

The room under the roof smelled of dust and mold. There was only one small window, nailed shut. An iron bed, with a lumpy straw filled mattress, was the only real piece of furniture in the room. There was no chair on which a person could sit.

Tom came pounding up the stairs.

"Patience," he bellowed, "what the hell are you doing? Why aren't you getting the food ready? Are you and that witch of a sister trying to drive me out of business?"

"Felicity told me to put Lauri and Jason in this room."

"Without heat or fresh air. My pa used to lock me in there when he punished me for something I didn't even do. Put them in my room. Felicity can move in with you. Bob and I will sleep in the tack room until somebody moves out of one of the tavern rooms."

"Felicity's not going to like that," Patience said.

"I run this place. Not Felicity. Do as I tell you."

CHAPTER 53

Two days later Jason received a note. The package was ready for him. The note was signed C. B.

Jason took Lauri and the children with him when he went to see Catherine Butler. He made sure they were together at all times. He did not question whether or not Felicity was capable of harming his family.

Catherine Butler welcomed Lauri and the children with open arms, took them to a small room off the long entrance hall, closed and locked the door.

Jason set Will down on the floor. Will took off as fast as his little legs could carry him. There were all kinds of nooks and crannies to explore.

Catherine chuckled when Jason made a move to go after him. "There's nothing here he can get into. Your mother and I thought you and Walter would be the death of us, and look how well you both turned out."

She unlocked a cabinet, removed two bags.

"Just as you wanted them," she said. "The new coins are on top, the old worthless ones are on the bottom.

"I've tried so hard to see Walter. I've asked the Committee to allow me a visit. They told me to try General Schuyler. He says it is a Committee problem.

"I've even written General Washington. No one wants to accept the responsibility for his imprisonment."

Alva reached out to Walter's mother.

Catherine took her from Lauri, and cuddled the child.

Alva touched Catherine's cheek and made cooing sounds. Will stopped his exploring, and hurried over to be picked up. She kissed the top of his head.

"Deborah, the boys and I go by Cartwright's every day," Catherine said. "The boys insist they saw him wave. If only I could see him, hold him in my arms, and tell him how much we love him…"

Ox Head Tavern

Felicity was in a snit. She and Tom had been arguing.

"Well?" she asked when Jason came into the tavern. "Did you get it?"

"I did."

"Let me see."

"Don't be greedy, Felicity. You'll get yours."

"Don't be a fool, Felicity," Tom cautioned. "You know what will happen to you and Archie if you're caught."

"This ain't none of your affair, Tom. Come on Jason. Archie's waitin'." She stormed out of the room.

Cartwright's

Archie opened the door when he saw them, and ushered Jason, Lauri and the children in.

Felicity started to follow them.

"You know you can't come in. I'll see you later." He closed the door.

"That the money?" A powerfully built fellow, a bully who knew how to fight dirty, Archie tried to grab the bag Jason was holding.

"Not until I see Butler."

"Suppose I just take that away from you."

"Suppose I make a mistake and put too much pox serum in your arm…" Jason said.

Archie blanched. "Guess it don't make no difference if I just wait a little longer, long's you got the money."

Peter Ten Broeck sat quietly at the far end of the room. He was unfettered.

Walter was sitting on a hard chair, shaking with Ague. His hands and feet were shackled. There were sores on his wrists and ankles.

Lauri muffled a gasp and stepped toward Walter.

"Stay away from the prisoner," Archie snarled. "He ain't allowed no contact."

"She was only…" Jason protested.

"…gonna slip him a knife," Archie snarled.

"I resent that remark," Jason said.

"Now ain't that too bad. Play by my rules or get the hell out of here." Archie moved toward Jason. "First, give me the bag."

Jason handed it to him.

Archie hefted it. "It ain't all here."

"Felicity has the rest," Jason lied. "You'll get it when I'm satisfied Butler's all right. Take those irons off."

"I ain't takin' no orders from you."

Jason's heart was pounding. So much depended on his bluffing. "Maybe you'd rather explain to General Schuyler how we got to see the prisoner."

Archie cursed, freed Butler, pulled out his pistol. He went to stand by the door. "One wrong move and Butler will never see that sweet mother of his."

Walter began to shake. His breathing was labored.

Jason started toward him.

"Stand back," Archie snarled. "I've been waiting for a chance to send him to his reward. You touch him, and you're both dead."

"He's sick. Don't you have any decency in you? I'm a doctor. Let me have a look at him."

"Maybe you're a doctor. Maybe you ain't. You keep away from him."

"When was the last time a doctor saw him?"

Archie pointed his pistol at Jason. "Doctors don't got no time for the likes of him. They got enough to do to take care of our own. He don't get no special treatment."

A knock on the door interrupted any further talk. Archie held the pistol in his right hand, opened the door with his left.

A man, a doctor by appearances, stepped into the room, saw the gun. "What's going on, Sergeant?" He didn't wait for Archie's answer.

"Jason? What are you doing here?" He didn't wait for a reply to that question either.

He turned to Archie. "Put that gun away. Do you want to kill one of our best doctors? We can't spare him. We don't have enough good ones to go around as it is."

He shook Jason's hand, and thumped him on the back.

"I never expected to see you in a Continental uniform, Bart," Jason said.

"I got drunk one night, and before I knew it, I was in the army." Bart looked from Jason to Walter. "How'd you get to see the prisoner? Visitors aren't allowed."

"You of all people should know there are ways around rules."

Bart smiled. "Butler's been ill for a long time. I don't have to care for him, but what kind of a doctor would I be if I didn't try to help a sick man?" He walked over to Walter. "How are you feeling today, Butler?"

"Still have the shakes."

"I'd give you some Peruvian Bark if I had any." Bart said. "But…"

"Use Willow, Bart," Jason advised. "I've used it in cases of low continued fever. Peruvian Bark's better, but you can't let a man suffer because you don't have any."

"You eating anything, Butler?" Bart asked.

"Fussy as an old maid," Archie said. "Says he doesn't like rebel slop."

"Got to keep up your strength, Walter," Jason said. "You don't know when you'll need it."

Bart poked and prodded, considered bleeding Walter, decided against it.

"Lauri," Jason said. "This is Bartel Granvil."

Bart reached for Lauri's hand and brushed it lightly with his lips.

Jason grinned. "Ever the Gallant. You haven't changed."

"You done, Doc?" Archie asked. "You and me's gonna be in a heap of trouble if we don't get these Tory lovers out of here."

"Careful who you're calling a Tory lover, Sergeant," Bart said. "Come on Jason. Let's find some willow bark. I want to try that."

"Where's Will?" Jason asked, panic in his voice.

Lauri lifted the hem of her skirt.

Will was clinging to her leg, his eyes closed. He had hidden under there when he saw Archie pull out his gun.

Jason squatted down to Will's eye level and spread his arms. "It's all right, son. No one's going to hurt you."

Will opened his eyes and reached for his father.

"Where are you staying?" Bart asked.

"The Ox Head," Jason answered.

"A tavern's no place for children," Bart said. "Come with me. I'm staying with a widow. Her husband, the captain, crew, and the ship were lost in a storm.

"Officers are being billeted in private homes. She wants no part of that. Let's talk to her."

"What about her children?" Lauri asked.

"She never had any. She'd have made a good mother, too. I've been told she once took in a young girl whose parents died. The girl was taken away by a family friend. She's still mourning the child."

Bart led them down streets that took them closer to the Hudson River. The river smells became stronger, and when they turned the corner on to a side street, Jason heard Lauri gasp. She began to tremble.

Jason handed Will to Bart, lifted Alva out of Lauri's arms. He slipped his arm around Lauri's waist, and drew her close. Her face was drained of color.

Half way down the block, Bart climbed the stairs to a house that once was attractive, but now needed repairs. He unlocked the door, waved the others inside.

A woman met them in the entrance hall. Her coal black hair was graying, but her dark blue eyes had not lost their luster.

"Oh Bart," she said when she saw Lauri, "you brought my child back to me."

Ox Head Tavern

It didn't take long for the news to spread. One of Walter Butler's guards had taken a bribe.

Just before Archie was taken into custody, Felicity, Patience and Bob slipped away in the dark of night.

Tom was forced to hire a new stable boy and barmaid. The barmaid was well liked by the men.

Susannah.

A couple of weeks later, alarming news swept through the city.

WALTER BUTLER HAD ESCAPED!

CHAPTER 54

Adam Helmer's Run

Adam was out scouting when he came upon some of Joseph Brant's Indians. He was almost caught like some bumbling boy on his own for the first time. Adam spun around and high-tailed it back toward the German Flatts.

The best runner in the valley, he outdistanced the three Indians who had taken off after him. He reached the bottom of the hill, and saw the first runner come over the crest. The other two were holding back, ready to move up when the lead man tired. It was an old trick, running the prey into the ground.

Adam had no one to spell him, but he was determined to keep his hair. That thought gave him his second wind, and whatever more it would take to reach Fort Herkimer Church, and sound the alarm.

The three Indians chased him for 24 miles, almost to the fort's gates.

Fort Herkimer Church

The roar of the cannon in the church belfry signaled the settlers to seek safety at the fort.

Joseph Brant arrived too late to attack. Adam Helmer had spoiled that for him. Brant had to content himself with burning nearby houses, barns, hay and wheat, while the farmers watched their summer's work go up in smoke, and the Indians danced and shrieked, beyond the reach of the fort's cannon.

After that failure, Brant carried the war into the south and east, attacking and burning settlements and isolated farms along the Delaware River on the southern border of New York. He returned from a raid to find Unadilla, Tioga, and Chemung, his home bases, destroyed by the rebels, and Walter Butler waiting for him.

November 1778

An eternity ago, Walter Butler had left Niagara with 5 companies of Rangers, several hundred Indians, a score or so of the 8th Regiment, and 50 British Regulars who had refused to leave their cumbersome equipment behind.

He had set his sights on Fort Alden at Cherry Valley. He hoped to capture the fort, make it a supply depot, a jumping off place for harassing the rebels, and push the frontier back to Schenectady.

This was the time to strike. No one would expect an assault this late in the year. They might never get another chance. He had planned on marching to Cherry Valley days ago; instead, he was squabbling with his officers, and Joseph Brant.

Who, Joseph wanted to know, was going to lead this force?

Walter was taken aback. He was!

Joseph argued that Butler had no experience. He had never led men on such a campaign: in bitter weather, snow, ice. He knew nothing about the difficulty of moving such a large force through a snow storm.

His men, Joseph added, had been gone all summer. They wanted to see their families. They needed to hunt, to provide food.

Some of Joseph's white men refused to go with Butler. They would serve under Brant, but not Butler. They were Tories from the valley who had suffered abuse; had their properties confiscated. Brant's white followers simply up and left.

Many of the Ranger Officers also objected. Their men, too, were tired; some were ill. They needed boots, and moccasins. They only had a week's supply of food.

"We won't take all the Rangers," Walter said. "Those who are sick can make moccasins, and we'll all have foot wear for the return trip to Niagara.

"The men can trade boots, clothing. We'll hunt for deer and bear to last until we reach Fort Alden. We'll bring back enough supplies to use on the way back to Niagara."

The older officers shook their heads. Butler could not see the forest for the trees; but they were good soldiers. They would follow him to the ends of the earth.

On to Cherry Valley

The weather turned nasty. Rain changed to sleet. Butler ordered the men to protect their flintlocks.

Roads that had been muddy ruts became ankle twisting gutters. The cold seeped through their clothing, chilling them to the bone. They moved like automatons, shoulders hunched, heads thrust forward.

They made camp 20 miles from Cherry Valley in a blinding snow storm. The fires at night did little to ease their misery,

November 10, 1778

Walter kept the scouts out longer, sent them farther, demanding detailed reports when they returned.

"Captain, they've brought in prisoners," Lieutenant John Hare said. "They found them sleeping not far from us, huddled around a big fire. Their guns were stacked against a tree."

Walter shook his head in disbelief. Any fool would know enough to keep his weapon near him. "Are they from Alden?"

"Yes sir," Hare answered.

"Good. Let's see how willingly they'll answer a few questions."

The snow continued to fall, coating Butler's and Hare's shoulders. The soldiers grouped around the prisoners looked like military snow-men.

"I'm Captain Walter Butler, Commander of this Company of Butler's Rangers. Are you all from Fort Alden?"

They glared at Walter; did not answer.

"Their tongues are frozen in their mouths, Lieutenant." Walter said. His smile, empty of all warm-heartedness sent shivers up the backs, not only of the captives, but Walter's own men. "Maybe our Indian friends will enjoy loosening them for us."

"Yes, we're from Alden," the sergeant said. "You'll get a warm welcome there."

"Don't make the damned misbegot mad, Sergeant," One of the Continentals said. "Can't you see them redskins are aching to get at us?"

The captives began to blabber.

Yes—Colonel Gansevoort had advised Colonel Alden of an attack.

No—Colonel Alden did not take the warning seriously. It was too late in the season. There were too many hardships to face. Indians did not like to fight in the winter.

Yes—Colonel Alden and the officers continued to live in the villager's houses.

Butler called a council with his men.

As he and Lieutenant Hare walked toward the gathering officers, Hare voiced his fears: something was brewing in the Indian camp. The Indian Department Officers were aware of it. The Indians whispered and laughed among themselves, quieting and sobering when a white man was within hearing.

"I'll speak with Brant," Walter said.

"All due respects, Captain. Can you be sure Captain Brant is not in on it?"

"I prefer to think not; but I've never been able to fathom how his mind works. We'd best keep an eye on him."

"Colonel Alden's been informed that we're on our way. He refuses to believe it." Walter told the men who gathered around him. "Little Beard, and officers and men from the Indian Department will secure the town. One party will surround the house where the officers stay…"

There was a murmur of disbelief. Officers who had been warned of an attack were not in the fort with their men?

CHAPTER 55

Cherry Valley—November 11, 1778

If Walter was of a superstitious nature he would have said the fates were against him. He had planned an early start, but his forces were slow moving.

He could not fault the men. He had pushed them for days. They were cold, hungry, and now that they were so close to completing their mission, they did not have the energy to do it.

It was nearly eleven of the clock before he could attack the fort.

He considered his plan to be a good one. The Rangers, the British detachment, and most of the Indians were to head for the fort. Rangers would make a direct frontal attack on the main gate while Brant and his Indians circled around, and tried to scale the back walls.

They came over a hill in time to see a man running toward the fort. Indians and Rangers raced after the fleeing man. One of the Indians fired a shot, missed, and destroyed all hopes of surprise.

Butler and the Rangers rushed the fort. They came within 70 yards of the gate just in time to see it close.

They felt the smart fire of the Continental guns.

In the village, two Continental officers rushed out of a house and made a mad dash toward the fort.

Colonel Alden and Lieutenant Colonel Stacy, Walter reasoned. Scouts had told him the two men lodged with a family named Wells. Neither officer made it. Colonel Alden was tomahawked and scalped. Lieutenant Colonel Stacy was taken prisoner.

They heard gun fire in the village. Once more, Lieutenant Hare called Walter's attention to the Indians.

An Indian Department man came running from the direction of the village, shouting—"The Indians have gone crazy. They're killing…

There was a flash and a roar. A ball missed him by inches. He threw himself on the ground and crawled to Walter's side. "Brant can't control them. They're killing everybody…men, women, even the children. Burning…"

He turned his head toward the village. Most of the nearby Rangers did the same. House after house was going up in flames.

"John," Butler said to Hare, "take as many Rangers as you need. Try to gather up as many villagers as you can. Give them whatever protection you can. Take care. God be with you."

The troops in the fort, and the Rangers shivering on the frigid ground sniped at each other for three hours. A cannon ball struck a tree, showering the prone men with snow.

The killing and sacking of Cherry Valley tapered off.

John Hare returned with 40 prisoners. "I hope I never see anything like that again," he told Butler.

They withdrew about a mile to the south to wait for the expected onslaught from the fort. None came.

As soon as he could, Walter sent all the women and children, except Mrs. Campbell, Mrs. Moore and their offspring, back to the fort.

He was in the process of returning others when Brant warned him that the temper of the Indians was such, they might turn against all of them. One scalp looked like any other, and the British were paying eight dollars for scalps.

Walter thanked him, but resolved to keep Mrs. Moore and Mrs. Campbell to exchange for his mother, siblings, and relatives.

The weather continued to plague them. They turned west, and the long journey back to Niagara began.

CHAPTER 56

Dayemon's Cabin

Winter was knocking at the door.

Lauri came in carrying an armful of fire wood. She would need Will and Alva's help. They were old enough now.

She was surprised to see them kneeling beside Jason's trunk. The lid was open.

They had been playing "hide the acorn", a game they often played with their father. One person hid the acorn, and the others searched for it. Whoever found it earned the right to be the next one to hide it.

Lauri was tempted to scold them, but curiosity got the better of her.

"Look, Ma. Look what we found." Alva held up a doll for Lauri to see.

The doll was dressed in a fur trimmed cape and hood. Small hands were hidden inside a white rabbit skin muff. She was wearing a pair of shiny black shoes.

An involuntary gasp escaped, and the wood slipped from Lauri's arms.

"We found these watches," Will added. "How come your picture is in this one?"

Lauri's hands were shaking as she took the two watches from her son.

"That isn't me Will. It's a painting of your grandmother." She looked closer at the second watch, a gold timepiece. The letters S W were engraved on the cover…Stephen Watts.

"Where did you get the doll, Ma?" Alva asked.

Lauri beckoned Will and Alva to sit with her on the settle. It was crowded, but when Will tried to move away, she wrapped her arm around him.

"Do you remember when Pa had to go to Albany to make sure the soldiers didn't get smallpox?"

"I don't remember," Alva said.

Disgusted, Will told her, "You were just a baby,"

"Do you remember the lady we stayed with?" Lauri asked.

"Yes," Will said.

"When I was a little girl—older than you, Will—my Ma and Pa died."

Alva looked like she was going to cry. "Are you gonna die, Ma?"

Lauri hugged her. "No, Alva. I'm not going to die, but my Ma and Pa did, and I went to live with Catherine Wilkins for a little while. Ma and Pa had a friend named Elder Baxter. He came to Albany, and took me to his house to live with his family.

"Do you remember the two women who worked at the tavern where we almost stayed when we first got to Albany?"

Will nodded, although he wasn't sure if he did or not.

"Patience and Felicity were Elder's daughters, like you're mine, Alva.

"Catherine gave me that doll the day I left her to go away with Mr. Baxter. I thought I'd lost it."

"What about the watches?" Will wanted to know.

"The one with your grandmother's picture belonged to Mr. Baxter. The other belonged to a friend. I don't know how they got in Pa's trunk. Where did you find the key? Pa's told you many times never to open his trunk."

Will was shamefaced. "We're sorry. When I found where Alva had hidden the acorn, I saw the key and I took it. You won't tell Pa, will you?"

Lauri gave them each a hug and a kiss. "It'll be our secret. Now let's put them back before Pa gets home from General Herkimer's place. Let's pick up this wood and get some more so Pa won't have to do it. He'll be tired."

They heard a horse stop in front of the cabin. Dolf called for Jason.

Lauri went to the door.

"Tell him the militia's called out," Dolf shouted. "He's got to report to Fort Dayton as soon as he can. You better get there, too."

Fort Dayton—Late October 1781

Some where north of the valley, there was a British and Tory force of over 600 men; British Regulars, Royal Yorkers, Indians, Butler's Rangers

Colonel Marinus Willett had fought a battle at Johnstown, with Major John Ross, backed up by Butler's Rangers, commanded by Captain Walter Butler. They had slipped away before daylight, and now they were on the run.

Scouts had brought the news that Ross was not returning to the boats he had left at Lake Oneida. He was taking a north-west route through the wilderness toward Carleton Island.

Willett had pushed himself and his horse to reach Fort Dayton. Snow was in the air, the wind biting.

"I've got men dogging his heels," Willett told Colonel Bellinger. "I need good scouts and men. We've killed some of Ross's men, and taken a few prisoners. I want to get ahead of him and hit him from the front."

"Ja, you want to hit him where Mount's Road and Jerseyfield Road come together." Bellinger offered. "His men are tired. I'll you get fresh troops. There are Oneida here that are good trackers. Militia are goot, too."

The Jerseyfield Road

At one point, Willett. had been as close as two miles, but Ross had picked up the Jerseyfield Road before Willlett and the militia got there.

Ross's men were exhausted. In spite of the frigid weather, they had thrown away blankets, provisions, even their guns, to lighten their load. It was their need to escape that drove them on.

West Canada Creek

Willett was sorry he had let Jason come. If there was a skirmish, and he was sure there would be, Butler would be in the midst of it. He had seen how Butler's court martial had affected Jason. He was afraid of what would happen to Jason if Butler was killed. It was too late now.

The snow began to fall harder. It was difficult to see farther than an arm's length.

Willett pushed his men. They came over a hill just as there was a break in the storm. On the other side of the rushing waters of West Canada Creek, Willett saw the last of Ross's men disappear in to the woods.

Butler's Rangers were ready to protect their fleeing comrades.

A volley scattered Willett's men. They sought the protection of the trees, returned fire, and Willett saw Butler fall, his face covered with blood.

Before he could stop them, the militia swarmed across the frigid waters of the West Canada. Some never bothered to look at Butler, others let out a victory halloo, and raced after Ross and his men.

One of the Indians asked the Colonel for permission to scalp Butler.

Jason did not hear Willett reply, but he saw the scalping knife do its work.

Jason forded the rushing waters of West Canada Creek and fell to his knees beside the stiffening body of his best friend. Dolf stood a pace away, not knowing what to say or do.

"I've got to bury him," Jason sobbed. "I can't leave him to the wolves."

"We don't have anything to dig with," Dolf said.

"Find a hole. We'll cover Walter with rocks and heavy brush and limbs."

Dolf found a downed tree where a bear had made a den underneath. It didn't look like it had been used in a long time. Not much chance of a bear coming back, he decided.

Together, he and Jason managed to drag Butler's body over to the hole.

When they had finished piling the rocks and covered them with brush, Jason stood and bowed his head.

"Almighty Father, we commend the soul of your servant, Captain Walter Butler, to your loving care. You, who knows all things, knows that the hateful things that are said about him are not true. He was a faithful friend, a loving son, and a good brother. He will always have a place in our hearts. Amen."

They walked away, leaving Walter alone in a snow covered wilderness.

CHAPTER 57

Fort Dayton

When the first of the militia had come back to the fort, Lauri had grabbed her cloak, ordered the children to stay put, and rushed outside. Jason and Dolf were not with them.

It was a day later before she saw Jason and Dolf coming down the road.

It was Oriskany all over again, only this time, something terrible had happened to Jason. He moved like a walking dead man. If it weren't for Dolf's strong arms supporting him, Jason would have fallen.

Lauri helped Dolf bring him into the barrack that Colonel Bellinger had turned over to the families of the militiamen.

They sat Jason on a stool close to the fireplace. She gently touched his face. He did not respond. She took his hands in hers and began to rub them.

Other women brought blankets to wrap around Jason. They built up the fire, warmed broth for him to sip.

Will and Alva huddled together, anxious eyes focused on their father.

When the other children pressed close, their mothers shooed them away.

Alva slowly approached. "Hello Pa." Tears welled in her eyes when he did not answer.

Torn between fear for her husband, and concern for her daughter, Lauri beckoned Alva with open arms.

314

Sobbing, Alva threw herself at her mother. "Don't Pa love me anymore?"

"He's just too tire to talk," Lauri said.

"Mrs. Dayemon," Colonel Bellinger was framed by the doorway. "I've turned another barrack over for some wounded come down from West Canada. Doctor Petry's there now. Some hearty men outside will take Doctor Dayemon over there."

Lauri hesitated. She couldn't leave Will and Alva alone, but Jason couldn't stay with the families. "The children..." she began.

Hortense Greene, almost a permanent fixture at Fort Dayton, pushed her way past Bellinger. She had stayed on at Dayton when Tobias was killed in a skirmish with some Indians. "I'll watch them, dearie. Heaven knows I've growed enough of my own to know how."

Marinus Willett elbowed his way into the room. "He'll get good care there. Doctor Petry will see to it." He leaned down and whispered in Lauri's ear. "Jason's 'bout froze to death. I've been told he lagged behind to bury Captain Butler. It hit him pretty hard—seeing Butler killed."

Walter killed. Lauri's ears heard the words, but her heart refused to believe. Not Walter. Not the boy who had taught her to read and write. Not the man who had loved her enough to step aside because he knew how much she loved Jason.

Lauri's head was spinning.

Walter's mother and the children, who were so dear to him, had finally been exchanged for some women who had been taken captive at Cherry Valley. Did he have much time to spend with them?

Colonel Bellinger spotted Dolf standing apart from the rest. He glanced at Laurie, and motioned to Dolf to follow him outside. "You up to riding?"

"Yes Sir."

"Goot," Bellinger said. "The word we must get out. Butler's dead."

It was a week before Doctor Petry would allow Jason to leave. Petry had bled him several times, against Lauri's wishes. Jason never bled his patients unless it was absolutely necessary. Jason got weaker.

"Please, Doctor Petry," Lauri begged, "Let me take him home. I can care for him."

Petry finally agreed. "I've done all I can. Take him, and good luck, Mrs. Dayemon."

The Cabin

There were times when Lauri despaired.

Jason sat staring, seeing nothing. Or was he seeing Walter shot, falling into the snow? She had learned enough to know that Walter had been shot in the head. Most likely, he had died instantly. She prayed it was true.

Will seemed to grow up overnight. He was at his mother's side whenever there was work to be done. He attacked chores without complaint, even those that were beyond him.

He often sounded like, acted like his father. Once he took Lauri to task, just as Jason did. Lauri started to reprimand him, but she stopped short, and burst out laughing.

Alva, on the other hand, withdrew, spoke little, became listless.

"Help Ma," Will chided, "She can't do everything."

Lauri was at her wits end. Her nerves were raw. One day when Will went at Alva again, she shrieked, "Leave your sister alone. She's only a child."

Lauri burst into tears. Alva was not the only child. In spite of Will's efforts to be a man, he was a child, too.

The days dragged on until Jason surprised them all.

"Come give Pa a kiss," he said to Alva.

She ran to him, climbed up on his lap, wrapped her arms around his neck, and covered his face with kisses.

Jason managed to untangle himself, and motioned to Will. "I've been watching you, Will. You aren't a little boy anymore. Let's shake."

Will wasn't able to hide his disappointment. "Don't I get a kiss?"

"Men don't usually do that," Jason said, "but I've never seen a rule says we can't"

Alva slipped off Jason's lap to make room for her brother.

He felt awkward, but Will allowed his father to plant a quick kiss on his cheek.

"Don't I get a kiss, too?" Lauri asked.

Jason stood, wrapped Lauri in a warm embrace, and kissed her so deeply they were both gasping for breath.

Will made a mouth puckering face, a rude sound, and announced. "I ain't never gonna kiss a girl."

EPILOGUE

November 1781—The Cabin

For Lauri and Jason, the news was bitter sweet.

Eleven days before Walter was killed, a British Officer few valley people had even heard of, Lord Cornwallis by name, surrendered to General George Washington at a place called Yorktown, in faraway Virginia.

Express riders carried the news.

Church bells rang in cities, towns and distant settlements.

THE FIGHTING WAS OVER

The Destructives would no longer appear out of nowhere, burn the cabin, barn, destroy the crops, steal or slaughter the animals, kill the men, women and children, then move on.

NO FLINTLOCKS NOR FLAMES.

It was cold. The sky was gray. The trees were bare. Snow had fallen on the northern hills. The children were asleep in the loft.

Jason and Lauri made love like a young couple on their wedding night. Jason snuggled Lauri in his arms, kissed her again and again, like he couldn't get enough of her.

"Jason?" she whispered.

"Uh-huh?"

"If we have a boy, let's name him Walter."